CARRYING THE
SINGLE DAD'S BABY

KATE HARDY

THE FAMILY
THEY'VE
LONGED FOR

ROBIN GIANNA

MILLS & BOON

CLACKMANNANSHIRE COUNCIL	
31513400365495	
Bertrams	15/08/2018
CAR	£5.99
ADU	AF

First Published in Great Britain 2018
by Mills & Boon, an imprint of HarperCollins*Publishers*
1 London Bridge Street, London, SE1 9GF

Carrying the Single Dad's Baby © 2018 by Pamela Brooks

The Family They've Longed For © 2018 by Robin Gianakopoulos

ISBN: 978-0-263-93370-3

MIX
Paper from
responsible sources
FSC™ C007454

Printed and bound in Spain
by CPI, Barcelona

CARRYING THE SINGLE DAD'S BABY

KATE HARDY

MILLS & BOON

To my editors, Sheila and Megan,
with love and thanks for being so patient with me!

CHAPTER ONE

The letters stood out, white on a blue background. Just the same as they had in the last hospital where Beatrice had worked.

Except at Muswell Hill Memorial Hospital she would be getting a fresh start. This was a new place, where nobody knew about her past, so nobody could pity her. Not for her divorce, not for the baby, not for the way her life had totally imploded four years ago.

They'd all see her for who she was now. Beatrice Lindford, the new emergency consultant. Beatrice who was cool, calm and perfectly controlled. Who led her team from the front. And who'd baked brownies the night before to say hello to her new department.

She took a deep breath, pushed open the swing doors with her free hand, and walked into the reception area.

Michael Harcourt, the head of the department, was waiting for her.

'Beatrice, lovely that you made it. Come and meet the team.' He looked quizzically at her. 'What's in the boxes?'

'Home-made brownies. Just my way of saying hello to everyone.'

'You didn't have to bring anything,' he said with a smile, 'but they'll go down very well in the staff kitchen. Now, let me find someone to show you round... Ah, Josh.' He called over one of the younger doctors. 'Josh, I think you're rostered in Resus with Beatrice, our new consultant, this morning. I'd like you to show her round before it all gets hectic.'

Was it her imagination, or was Josh looking at her slightly oddly?

'Beatrice, this is Josh, one of our juniors. He's a good lad, but don't ever let him drive you anywhere—unless you don't mind risking ending up with a tension pneumothorax, eh, Josh?' Chuckling, Michael walked away.

Josh groaned. 'Please don't take too much notice of what the boss just said. My pneumothorax was months ago, and it was only because I wasn't used to go-karting on ice and I took the corner too fast.'

'Go-karting on *ice*?' Beatrice raised an eyebrow. That sounded like the definition of insanity, to her.

'Sam—he's one of the registrars and you'll meet him shortly—thought it would be a good team-building exercise,' Josh explained. 'And it was. It was great fun. Except I, um, crashed. And nobody's ever going to let me forget it. Ever.' He groaned again. 'Even in the Christmas secret Santa last year, I got a modified model motorcycle.'

She smiled. 'Oh, dear. So Sam's a bit of a daredevil?'

Josh smiled back. 'He used to be. He's changed a bit, now he's a dad.'

Babies.

Of course people in the department would have babies and small children. The same as they would anywhere she worked.

She wasn't going to let it throw her. This was about her job, not her personal life.

'Can we start with the staff kitchen so I can drop these off?' She indicated the plastic boxes she was carrying.

'Sure.' He looked interested. 'What's in them?'

'Brownies.' The recipe they used at Beresford Castle that had actually got a write-up in one of the Sunday supplements, and made all the tourists come back for more. 'I hope I made enough for everyone working in the department today.'

'You made them yourself?'

'Last night.' With a bit of help from her niece and nephews.

'That's a lot of work. And it's really nice of you.'

'Just my way of saying hello to my new team,' she said with a smile. 'And I was planning on buying everyone a drink tonight after my shift, if you can maybe recommend somewhere. I've only just moved here, so I don't really know the area yet.'

'The Red Lion, just round the corner, is fairly popular,' he said.

'The Red Lion it is, then,' she said.

Once they'd dropped the boxes of brownies in the staff kitchen, with a note she'd written earlier propped against them inviting the team to help themselves, Josh showed her round the department and introduced her to the team.

Everyone seemed friendly enough, but when a doctor strode out of cubicles, clearly ready to see his next patient, Josh suddenly looked awkward. 'Um, and this is Daniel Capaldi, one of the registrars. Daniel, this is Beatrice Lindford, our new...' His voice trailed off.

Why was Josh suddenly acting like a cat on a hot tin roof? Beatrice wondered. What was it about Daniel Capaldi that had made the junior doctor so nervous?

Quite apart from the fact that Daniel looked as if he could've graced the pages of a high-end glossy fashion magazine; she didn't think she'd ever met anyone so good-looking in her entire life. He was tall enough for her to have to look up to him, with dark hair brushed back from his forehead—the type of hair that would curl when it was wet—dark eyes, the longest eyelashes she'd ever seen on a man, and a mouth with an incredibly sensual curve.

He was breathtakingly beautiful.

Maybe he was the type who knew just how good-looking he was, and was used to women falling at his feet. Well, she didn't care what her colleagues looked like. She just wanted them to be good at their jobs, communicate properly and work with her as a team to give their patients the best care possible. She wasn't interested in anything else. Not any more.

'Beatrice Lindford, the newest member of the team,' she said coolly, and held out her hand to shake his.

What she hadn't expected was the tingle all the way down her spine when Daniel took her hand and shook it firmly. She couldn't even remember the last time she'd reacted so strongly to anyone.

Not good.

Really not good.

Because she didn't want to get involved with anyone. Ever again.

Beatrice Lindford. The new consultant. The one who'd just been appointed to the job everyone had thought

had Daniel's name on it. A job that part of Daniel had
wanted; but part of him hadn't, because he knew he
couldn't give the department what it needed from him
in that role at the same time as being a good single parent to Iain.

If things had been different with Jenny, he wouldn't
have hesitated to apply for the job.

But it was pointless dwelling on might-have-beens.
The situation was as it was. Jenny was remarried now—
to someone else. He had custody of Iain. And his son
would always, always come first.

Beatrice wasn't what Daniel had expected. She was
tall, maybe four inches shorter than his own six foot
two. Almost white-blonde hair that she wore tied back
with a scarf at the nape of her neck. The bluest eyes he'd
ever seen—the colour of the sky on a late summer evening. And an incredibly posh accent, which made her
his polar opposite: clearly she came from a privileged
background, whereas Daniel was the son of a teenage
mum who'd been brought up mainly by his grandparents
until his mother was able to cope with being a parent.
They were worlds apart.

But the bit that really threw him was when he shook
her hand. That handshake was meant to be businesslike,
maybe even slightly on the cool side. Instead, it felt as if
every single nerve ending in his body had just woken up.
He'd never been so physically aware of anyone before.

Absolutely not.

Even if Beatrice Lindford was single, and even if she
was interested in him, he wasn't in the market for a relationship. Iain was his world, and that was the way it
was going to stay.

And he wanted a bit of distance between himself and

Beatrice until he could get himself perfectly back under control and treat her just like any other member of the department, instead of behaving like a teenager who'd just felt the heady pull of sexual attraction for the first time in his life.

'Welcome to the department, Ms Lindford,' he said, giving her a cool nod. 'Josh, shouldn't you be in Resus?'

'As should I,' Beatrice said, narrowing her eyes slightly at him. 'Michael Harcourt asked Josh to show me round and introduce me to everyone, and he's been kind enough to do just that.'

He liked the fact that she'd stood up for the junior doctor. But he didn't want to like Beatrice Lindford. He wanted to keep his distance from her, at least until he could get this unwanted attraction under control. 'Indeed,' he said.

'There are brownies in the staff kitchen,' she said. 'Do help yourself.'

There was a touch of haughtiness to her voice. She sounded for all the world as if she'd just taken over their department. Which, he supposed, she sort of had, being their new consultant. 'Thank you,' he said.

'And I'm buying drinks at the Red Lion after my shift,' she said.

Drinks he definitely wouldn't be going to. 'Noted.'

'I guess Josh and I had better get back to Resus.'

Daniel knew he hadn't been particularly friendly to his new colleague, and he felt slightly guilty about that. But his response to her had flustered him, and right now there was no room in his life for anything other than his son. 'Uh-huh,' he said, and turned away.

Daniel hadn't been openly hostile, but there had definitely been something there. Beatrice couldn't understand what the problem was. They'd never met each other before or even knew of each other by reputation. Or was Daniel just offhand like that with everyone, and that was why Josh had looked so awkward before he'd introduced them?

Not that she wanted to put the younger doctor in a difficult position by asking him outright. It wouldn't be fair. Instead, she encouraged him to chatter on their way back to Resus. And then she didn't have time to think about Daniel Capaldi when the paramedics brought in a patient. Dev, the lead paramedic, did the handover.

'Mrs Jane Burroughes, aged sixty-seven, otherwise healthy until today when she slipped in the garden and banged her head on the rockery. She remembers blacking out but she was conscious when we arrived. We put a neck brace on and we think she's fractured her cheekbone and her arm. I'm not happy about her eye, either,' Dev said.

From the amount of blood on Jane Burroughes's cheek, it was entirely possible she'd damaged her eye and they'd need to bring in a specialist.

'Pain relief?' Beatrice asked.

'She refused it,' Dev said. 'I haven't put a line in.'

'Thank you,' she said.

She introduced herself and Josh to Mrs Burroughes. 'We'd like to make you a bit more comfortable while we check you over. I know you refused pain relief in the ambulance, but can I give you some pain relief now?'

'I don't like the way it makes me feel, woozy and sick,' Mrs Burroughes said. 'When I had my wisdom teeth out and they put stuff in my arm, I felt drunk for two days afterwards.'

'I could give you some paracetamol?' Beatrice suggested. 'That won't make you feel woozy, and it'll take the edge off the pain. It won't be as effective as a stronger painkiller, but you'll feel a little bit more comfortable.'

Finally Mrs Burroughes agreed to have paracetamol.

'We'll need to do a CT scan of her neck,' Beatrice said to Josh, 'and call the ophthalmology team for their view on Mrs Burroughes's eye.'

Thankfully the CT scan showed no problems with Mrs Burroughes's neck, so they were able to remove the neck brace; the ophthalmology team was able to confirm that the laceration was fixable and Mrs Burroughes wasn't going to lose her sight. Finally the X-ray showed that the break in Mrs Burroughes's arm was clean and could be treated with a cast rather than surgery.

Beatrice had just finished treating her patient and arranged a handover to the ward when Sam Price came in.

'Beatrice, it's lunchtime,' he said, 'and Hayley—my wife, who's coming back to work here part time next month—suggested meeting us in the canteen. Josh, are you coming with us?'

The younger doctor blushed. 'I...um...'

Sam raised an eyebrow. 'Got a date?'

Josh nodded, and Sam patted his shoulder. 'Just be yourself and don't worry. She'll adore you.'

Sam took Beatrice to the canteen. 'So how was your first morning?' he asked.

'Fine.' Apart from Daniel Capaldi. Not that she was going to let herself think about him. 'Josh is a sweetie.'

'He's a nice lad. Though I feel a bit guilty because— well, I assume you must've heard about the staff day out I organised?' Sam asked.

'Go-karting on ice, you mean?'

'It's great fun,' he said with a grin. 'But I'm a reformed character now. No bungee-jumping, no go-karting on ice and no abseiling—well, unless it's for work.'

'Abseiling at work?' Beatrice couldn't help laughing. 'I'm not sure that's part of the average Emergency Department's duties.'

He laughed back. 'It can be, if it's a MERIT team job, but don't tell Haze because she worries.'

'Got you.'

Hayley Price was waiting for them at the entrance to the canteen. Sam greeted her with a kiss. 'Beatrice, this is Hayley; Hayley, Beatrice.' He smiled. 'And this gorgeous little bundle is Darcie.' He scooped the baby out of the lightweight pram, and the baby cooed at him and pulled his hair.

'Lovely to meet you, Beatrice, and welcome to Muswell Hill Memorial Hospital,' Hayley said. 'So how has your first day in the department been?'

'Great. Everyone's been lovely.' Almost everyone. She wasn't going to make a fuss.

'They're a good bunch,' Hayley said.

'She's a good one, too,' Sam said. 'Our kitchen's full of the best brownies I've ever tasted. Did you spend all last night baking them, Beatrice?'

She smiled. 'No, and I had a bit of help. Make sure you grab one for Hayley.'

By the time they'd bought their lunch and settled at a table, still chatting, Beatrice was feeling very much part of the team.

'So you're coming back part time next month?' she asked Hayley.

Hayley nodded. 'Much as I love my daughter, I miss work. Part time seemed like a good compromise.'

'I agree,' Beatrice said.

'If you'd like a cuddle with Darcie, better get it in now because the whole department will swoop on her when we walk in,' Sam said.

A cuddle with the baby.

Beatrice thought of her own baby, the stillborn daughter she'd held for a few brief minutes. What if that car hadn't crashed into her? What if she hadn't had the abruption, and Taylor had been born around her due date, alive?

But now wasn't the time or place to think about it. None of that was Sam's or Hayley's fault. She forced herself to smile brightly and scooped the baby from Sam's arms. 'She's gorgeous.'

'You're good with babies,' Hayley said when Darcie promptly yawned and fell asleep.

Again, Beatrice shut the door in her head. 'It comes from having three nephews and a niece. The youngest one's four now.' And how hard it had been to hold him. 'But I'm an old hand at getting them to go to sleep.'

'I'll remember that and get you to teach me some tricks when Madam here starts teething,' Hayley said. 'Right. So, tell us all about you. Where did you train, where were you before here, do you have a partner and children…?'

'Haze, give the poor woman a chance to breathe!' Sam admonished, though he was smiling and looked as if he wanted to know the answers, too.

'It's fine. I trained at the Hampstead Free and I worked there until I came here,' Beatrice said with a smile. The next bit was more tricky. Telling the whole truth would mean that her new colleagues would pity her as much as they had at the Hampstead Free, and she really didn't want that. Better to keep it simple and stick to the bare bones. The facts, and no explanations. 'No partner, no children.' To make sure nobody would try any well-meaning matchmaking, she added, 'And I'm concentrating very happily on my career.' And now it was time to change the subject. 'Can I ask you something confidential? I know I probably could've asked Josh, but I didn't want to put him in an awkward position.'

'Sure. Ask away,' Hayley said.

'It's about Daniel Capaldi,' Beatrice said.

Sam and Hayley exchanged a glance, looking slightly uneasy.

'I knew there was something. What am I missing?' Beatrice asked.

'Daniel's a nice guy,' Sam said carefully.

What he wasn't saying was obvious. Beatrice wasn't afraid to put it into words. 'But?'

Hayley blew out a breath. 'There isn't a tactful way to say it, but I get the impression you're a straight-talker so I know you won't take this the wrong way. Everyone thought his name was on the consultant's job.'

'So I've got his job and he resents me for it.'

'Not *necessarily*,' Sam said.

'But probably. Anyone would feel that way, in his shoes.' Beatrice bit her lip. 'OK. Thanks for the warning. I'll be careful what I say to him. I don't want to rub it in and make him feel bad.'

'At the end of the day, the management team chose you,' Hayley said. 'He'll get over it.'

At least now Beatrice understood why Daniel had been a little snippy with her and less welcoming than other members of the team. She'd be careful with him—not patronising, but not throwing her weight around, either.

After Hayley scooped the sleeping baby out of Beatrice's arms and transferred her to the pram, Beatrice enjoyed having lunch with them. Muswell Hill was a good place. She had the strongest feeling that she was going to be happy here.

'It's not just about work, though,' Hayley said. 'There's the regular pub quiz between us, Maternity and Paediatrics. How's your general knowledge?'

Beatrice thought of her brothers. 'A bit obscure.'

'Good. You're on the team,' Sam said. 'There's a team ten-pin bowling night in a couple of weeks—everything's on the noticeboard in the staff kitchen, if you want to sign up. Oh, and we're having a football morning in the park on Saturday. It's not a serious thing, really just the chance for everyone to kick a ball around, but we do a pot-luck picnic thing afterwards. And, after trying your brownies this morning…'

Beatrice smiled. 'Hint taken. OK. I don't mind kicking a ball about. And I'll make some more brownies.'

'Excellent. I think you're going to fit right in,' Sam said with a smile.

'Josh said the Red Lion's the place to go, so I'm buying drinks after my shift today,' Beatrice said. 'If you can both make it, it'd be lovely to see you.'

'That's nice of you,' Hayley said. 'Thanks. We'll be there.'

Back in the staff kitchen, as Sam had predicted, everyone wanted to cuddle baby Darcie. And people Beatrice hadn't yet met patted her on the shoulder, welcomed her to the department, and thanked her for the brownies.

Daniel Capaldi was conspicuously absent; and Beatrice noticed that he didn't come to the Red Lion with the rest of the team after their shift. She could understand that. If you were really disappointed at not getting a promotion everyone thought you'd earned, it would be hard to celebrate someone else getting the post instead.

But there was a strong chance she and Daniel would have to work together in the future, and she needed to be sure that they could do that and put the needs of their patients before any professional rivalry. As the more senior of them, it was up to her to sort it out.

There were two ways she could deal with this. She could either pretend it wasn't happening and wait for Daniel to stop resenting her; or she could tackle the problem head on and come to some kind of understanding with him. She'd grown up with their family motto, *tenacitas per aspera*—strength through adversity—so the second option was the one the rest of the Lindfords would choose.

Tackling him head on it was.

The next day, she was in Cubicles and Daniel was in Resus. Just as Sam had done, the previous day, she slipped into Resus at lunchtime. Daniel was on his own, to her relief, and it looked as if he was writing up notes. 'Dr Capaldi. Just the man I wanted to see,' she said.

He gave her a cool look. 'Something I can help you with, Ms Lindford?'

'Yes. I'm buying you lunch.'

'Thank you, but that's not necessary.'

He was trying to fob her off? Well, she wasn't put off that easily. 'I rather think it is. You and I need a chat.'

'Hardly.'

'Definitely,' she said. 'I'm not pulling rank, but I

think there's a problem and we need to sort it out rather than let it grow out of proportion.'

'There isn't a problem,' he said.

'Then have lunch with me.'

He looked reluctant.

'Don't worry, I'm not going to put arsenic in your coffee,' she said. 'Apart from anything else, I don't have the licence to get hold of that grade of poison.'

He didn't even crack a smile.

Taking him by the shoulders and shaking him until his teeth rattled wouldn't achieve anything other than a temporary relief from frustration. She folded her arms to help her resist the temptation. 'I could offer you a pair of boxing gloves, if that would make you feel better. Though I should probably make you aware that I could take you in the gym.'

He blinked. 'You box?'

'I box,' she confirmed. Her personal trainer had suggested it, and boxing had been one of the things that had got her on the slow road back from rock bottom. 'I might be a galumphing five foot ten, but I'm very light on my feet. I can do the whole Muhammed Ali thing. So. Your choice. Boxing gloves or lunch?'

'Lunch. Because I'd never hit a woman.'

'I wouldn't have any qualms about hitting *you* in the ring,' she said.

Was that a fleeting and grudging glimpse of respect she saw in his face?

'But I think coffee night be more civilised,' she said.

He didn't make polite conversation on the way to the canteen, but neither did she. And although Daniel protested when she insisted on paying for his sandwiches, Beatrice gave him the look she reserved for patients who were drunk and obnoxious on a Saturday night and he backed off.

'Thank you for lunch,' he muttered when they sat down.

At least he had manners. Even if he wouldn't look her in the eye. And that was going to change, too. She'd make him smile at her if it killed her.

'Let's put our cards on the table. I understand why you don't like me. I got the job that everyone thought had your name written all over it. Of course you resent me.'

'Not true,' he said.

She scoffed. 'You were the only person who didn't take a brownie yesterday.'

'Because I don't like chocolate.'

That hadn't occurred to her. But she hadn't finished with her evidence. 'And you didn't come to my welcome drink after your shift.'

'And you think that was because I'm sulking?'

'Isn't it?'

'No,' he said. 'Everyone else thought my name was on that job. That's the only bit you got right.'

She frowned. 'So what's your take on it?'

'Not that it's anybody's business, but I didn't actually apply for the job.'

She stared at him. 'You didn't?'

'I didn't,' he confirmed. 'Because I can't give the department what it needs, right now. I'm a single dad, and my son's needs come before the job. Always.'

She blew out a breath. 'Fair enough. I didn't know that.'

'Well, you do now.'

'Then I apologise for jumping to conclusions.'

* * *

Daniel hadn't expected her to react quite like that. He'd expected her to go haughty on him, as she had the previous day.

And he hadn't exactly been fair to her. He could've told her that he wasn't going to her welcome drinks, and why. Instead, he'd chickened out and just avoided her.

He needed to put that right. 'And I'm sorry for letting you think I resent you for taking my job.'

'OK. So we're saying now that the problem between us isn't a problem.'

Oh, there was a problem, all right. His libido was practically sitting up and begging. But he was just going to have to ignore it. 'There isn't a problem,' he lied. 'Welcome to Muswell Hill.'

'Thank you.'

'And you didn't have to buy me lunch.'

'Call it in lieu of the drink you didn't have last night,' she said.

He inclined his head. 'Then thank you.' Polite, he could do.

'So how old is your son?' she asked.

'Four.' Was it his imagination, or did she just flinch?

Imagination, maybe, because then she smiled. 'It's a lovely age. My youngest nephew is four.'

She had a killer smile. If Daniel hadn't known it was anatomically impossible, he would've said that his heart had just done a backflip. But, for Iain's sake, he couldn't act on the attraction he felt towards Beatrice Lindford. It wouldn't be fair to bring someone else into the little boy's life—someone who might not stick around. Someone who was, to all intents and purposes, his boss. It would be too complicated. Inappropriate. 'Uh-huh,' he said, not sure quite what to say to her. How to stop this from tipping over into personal stuff he didn't want to share. Such as why he was a single dad.

'Stating the obvious, but from your accent it sounds as if you're from Scotland.'

'Glasgow,' he confirmed.

'With an Italian surname?'

'My great-grandparents were Italian.' He paused. 'And you're posh.'

'Yes. But I'm a girl and I'm the youngest, so I got to choose what I wanted to do.'

Meaning that her brother—or brothers—had been expected to go into the family business? But asking her would be too personal; and it would also mean she could ask him personal stuff that he didn't want to answer. He backed off. 'So you trained as a doctor.'

'Here in London. What about you? Glasgow or here?'

'Here,' he said. And please don't let her ask about his son.

'So what made you pick emergency medicine?' she asked.

Relief flooded through him. He could talk about work and why he did what he did. It wasn't quite so personal, so it was easier to deal with. 'I like the fact that we make a real difference, that we can save people.' He paused. 'You?'

'Pretty much the same. Though we can't save everyone.'

Again, there was an odd look on her face—as if she was talking about something personal. But he wasn't going to ask. It was none of his business. Instead, he said, 'We do our best. That's all any of us can do. Strive to do our best.'

'True.'

He finished his coffee. 'Thank you for lunch. And for the chat.'

'So we're good?'

'It won't be a problem working together, if that's what you mean.' He'd already heard Josh singing her praises, saying that Beatrice was good with patients and she listened to the rest of the team. That was good. He hated it when senior colleagues went all arrogant. It was never good for the patients.

'I'm glad. We don't have to be friends,' she said. 'As long as we agree that our patients come first.'

'That works for me,' he said. 'We'd better get back to the ward.'

'OK.' She swallowed the last of her own coffee. 'Let's go.'

CHAPTER TWO

THE REST OF the week went smoothly; Beatrice still wasn't rostered in the same part of the department as Daniel during their shifts, but at least he was civil to her if they happened to be in the staff kitchen at the same time.

On Saturday morning, she headed to the park for the team's football day out. As Sam had requested, she made some brownies. Remembering that Daniel didn't like chocolate, she also made flapjacks, as a kind of peace offering. Then again, Daniel might not be there.

She'd just added her offerings to the picnic table when Daniel turned up with a small boy in tow. Even if she hadn't known that he had a four-year-old son, she would've known that the little boy was Daniel's because they looked so alike. And she was faintly amused to discover that the little boy had a Glaswegian accent almost as strong as his father's.

But what she hadn't expected was that Daniel would look so gorgeous in a football kit. The tight-fitting T-shirt showed that he had good abs, and his legs were strong and muscular. He looked more like a model than a doctor, and she wasn't surprised to see how many admiring glances were headed his way.

'I didn't think you'd be here today,' Daniel said. 'Or are you a football fan as well as a boxing fan?'

She pushed away the thought of getting hot and sweaty in a boxing ring with him. That really wasn't appropriate. 'Hayley and Sam said everyone turns up and has a huge picnic afterwards. I thought it might be a nice way to get to know the team outside work,' she said.

Daniel shrugged. 'Fair enough.'

'Do you work with my daddy?' the little boy asked.

'I do,' Beatrice confirmed.

He looked at her. 'You're *really* tall for a girl.'

'Iain, don't be rude,' Daniel began.

'It's fine, and he's right—I *am* tall.' She smiled, and crouched down so she was nearer to the little boy's height. 'Is that better?'

'Yes,' he said. 'Hello. I'm Iain.'

'I'm Beatrice.' She held out her hand for him to shake.

He shook her hand, but frowned. 'That's a strange name.'

'You can call me Bea, for short.'

He wrinkled his nose. 'Like a buzzy bee?'

She couldn't resist Iain's charm and chutzpah. 'Just like that,' she said.

'Hello, Bee. Are you going to play football?'

'No, I'm just going to watch,' she said.

'I play football. Just like my dad,' Iain told her proudly, puffing out his chest.

'Then I'll make sure I cheer really loudly when you score a goal,' she said.

Although football really wasn't her thing, she enjoyed chatting to Hayley on the sidelines, and dutifully clapped and cheered every time a goal was scored.

Iain was running past her, clearly intent on getting

to the ball, when he tripped and fell over. Instinctively, she looked up to see where Daniel was: on the far side of the field.

Iain was on his knees, crying and shielding his arm.

What could she do but go over to him until his dad arrived and see if she could sort out the problem?

'You're lucky we're all in the emergency department so we know just how to deal with things when people fall over,' she said. 'Where does it hurt, Iain?'

'Here.' He pointed to his elbow.

It was very obvious to her that he'd twisted his arm when he fell, so the ligament holding the radial bone in place had slipped, letting the bone dislocate. Given that he was so young, it would be easy to manipulate the bone back into place—but she also knew that it would hurt like mad, very briefly.

'I need you to be super-brave for me, Iain,' she said. 'Do you like chocolate?'

'Aye.'

'OK. I can fix what's wrong, but it means I have to touch your poorly arm and it'll hurt for about three seconds. After that, it'll stop hurting,' she said. 'I made some really special chocolate brownies you might like, so you can have one afterwards. I just need you to be brave for three seconds, that's all. Can you do that for me?'

Iain sobbed, 'I want my dad.'

'And he's running across the field towards you right now. He'll be here really soon. But I really need to slip that bone back into place for you,' she said. 'Close your eyes and sing me a song, Iain.'

'I don't know any songs,' he wailed, clearly too scared to be able to think.

'I bet you know "The Wheels on the Bus",' she said. 'I'll help you sing it. And I want you to sing it really, really loudly. Can you do that?'

He nodded, his face wet with tears.

She started singing, and the little boy closed his eyes and began to sing along with her, very loudly and very out of tune. The perfect distraction, she hoped. One quick movement and she'd manipulated his arm to put the bone back into place.

Iain was halfway through yelling when he clearly realised that his arm had stopped hurting.

'Oh. It doesn't hurt any more,' he said. 'You fixed me!'

'I did,' she said with a smile.

Daniel arrived just as Iain flung his arms around Beatrice and hugged her. 'Thank you, Bee!'

'What happened?' he asked.

'He fell over and dislocated his elbow. I've just manipulated it back, but we need to check his pulses and his range of movement.' Just in case there was a problem and Iain needed an X-ray, Daniel knew.

His own heart was racing madly with fear for his child, but she'd been calm and sorted out the problem without any fuss. He'd do the same. It was what he'd trained all these years for: to be calm when there was an accident or an emergency.

'Iain, can you move your arms for me and copy what I do?' he asked.

'Aye, Dad.'

He checked Iain's pulses, which were fine, then talked Iain through a range of movements. The little boy copied every movement without flinching or stopping as if he was in pain. Everything seemed completely normal.

'I hardly need to tell you what happens next,' Beatrice said.

'Pain relief if he needs it, put him in a sling for the rest of today to support his elbow, and if he stiffens up and doesn't use his arm tomorrow take him in for an X-ray.'

She spread her hands. 'Textbook perfect, Dr Capaldi.'

'Thank you for looking after him,' he said.

'That's what I'm here for. That,' she said, 'and chocolate brownies. I haven't forgotten what I promised you, Iain.'

'My dad doesn't like chocolate. We never have chocolate brownies,' Iain said.

'Then your dad can go and finish playing football while you sit and eat brownies with me,' she said.

'I...' Daniel looked at her, wanting to be with his son but not wanting to let the rest of the team down, either.

Beatrice shooed him back to the field. 'He'll be fine with me.' And then she gave him the sassiest smile he'd ever seen, one that made him want to grab her and kiss her. Not good.

'Trust me—I'm a doctor,' she said.

It was the cheesiest line in the book. But he'd seen her at work and he'd heard others praising her, saying that she always put the patient first. And Iain seemed to like her. He gave her a speaking look, but headed back to the field. He played for another ten minutes, and then to his relief he was substituted by one of the nurses.

When he went back over to where the spectators were, Iain was chatting animatedly to Beatrice. And Beatrice had used the scarf from her hair to fashion into a sling.

'Dad! You're back!'

'That's my playing over for today,' he said. 'Thank you for looking after Iain. I'll take over now.'

'My pleasure. We've had a nice time, haven't we, Iain?' she asked.

'She made me a special sling,' Iain said. 'Look.'

'Very nice,' Daniel said. 'I'll wash it when we get home and get it back to you on Monday at work. And now we must let Ms Lindford get on, Iain.'

The little boy frowned. 'But I like talking to Bee.'

'She's busy.'

Out of Iain's view, she shook her head.

She wasn't undermining him as a parent—he appreciated the fact she'd disagreed with him without actually saying so in front of his son—but the idea of spending time with her was dangerous. Right now Beatrice's hair was loose, she was wearing denims cut off at the knee, a strappy top and canvas shoes; and she looked more approachable than she did at work in tailored trousers and a white coat. The way she looked right now, he could just imagine walking hand in hand with her in the sunshine and kissing her under a tree.

He didn't want to walk hand in hand with anyone in the sunshine or kiss them under a tree, and that included Beatrice Lindford, he told himself sharply.

'Five more minutes, Dad?' Iain pleaded. 'Please.'

Again, out of Iain's view, she nodded.

Iain's brown eyes were huge and pleading. How could he resist? 'All right. Five more minutes.'

'Bee makes the best chocolate brownies in the world,' Iain said. 'Even you would like them, Dad.'

'I made flapjacks as well.' She gave him a cheeky

grin. 'And don't tell me that you don't like oats. You're a Scot.'

'Aye, he is.' Iain was all puffed up with pride. 'And so am I.'

'Peas in a pod, you two.'

But Daniel could see she was laughing with them, not at them.

'Can I have some flapjacks, too, Bee?' Iain asked.

'That's your dad's call, not mine,' she said, lifting her hands in a gesture of surrender.

'Yes,' Daniel said. 'Though there's a word missing, Iain Capaldi.'

'Please,' Iain said.

Daniel ended up trying a flapjack himself, and it surprised him. 'That's actually better than my grandmother's—and don't you dare tell your great-gran I said that, Iain,' he added swiftly.

'My great-granny makes the best ice cream in the world,' Iain said. 'Do you like ice cream, Bee?'

'I do,' Beatrice said with a smile, completely charmed by the way he pronounced his Rs.

'You should come to Glasgow and try my great-granny's special ice cream. It's fab.'

'Maybe sometime,' Beatrice said.

Iain chattered away to her, and Daniel couldn't help watching them. Iain was usually shy with strangers, so it was unusual for him to be so talkative. Maybe it was because Beatrice had reduced his dislocated elbow and stopped him being in such pain. Or maybe he was responding to her gentleness.

Against his better judgement, he was starting to like Beatrice Lindford. Too much for his own peace of mind.

She was the first woman since Jenny he'd even thought about holding hands with, let alone anything else. Which made her dangerous.

Iain didn't stop talking about her all the way home, either.

'She looks like a princess,' he said. 'She's got real golden hair.'

Hair that Daniel couldn't get out of his head, now he'd seen it loose.

'And it's long.'

Yeah. Daniel had noticed.

'Like the princess in the story Miss Shields told us in class. The one in the tower. Her hair was so long she could make it into a ladder. Ra...' He paused, his forehead wrinkled in a frown as he tried to remember the princess's name.

'Rapunzel,' Daniel supplied.

'Aye. And she talks like the Queen, all posh.'

'Yes.'

'I like her. Do you like her, Dad?'

Awkward question. 'I work with her,' Daniel prevaricated.

'She's nice. Can she come for tea tonight?'

'No, Iain. She's busy.'

But his son wasn't to be put off. 'Next week, then?'

'She might be busy.'

'Ask her,' Iain said. 'Go on, Dad. Ask her. Please.'

'Do you want to go and get pizza?' Daniel asked, hoping to distract his son with a treat.

It worked. Until bedtime, when Iain started on about princesses again. 'Do you think Bee's married to a prince?'

Daniel had no idea, but maybe if Iain thought Beatrice was married he'd drop the subject. 'Probably.'

'Then why didn't the prince come to play football today?'

Daniel loved his son dearly, but the constant questions could be exhausting. 'Maybe he can't play football.'

'Oh.' Iain paused. 'If she's a princess, do you think she knows the Queen?'

'I don't know, Iain.'

'Mum likes Prince Harry.'

Daniel tamped down his irritation. 'I know.'

'Do you think Bee knows Prince Harry?'

'I think,' Daniel said gently, 'it's time for one more story and then sleep.'

He just hoped his son wouldn't say anything about Beatrice next weekend, when Iain was due to stay with his mother. The last thing he wanted was Jenny quizzing him about whether he was dating again. He knew she still felt guilty about what had happened between them, and that if he started seeing someone it would make her feel better, but he really didn't want to date anyone. He wanted to concentrate on bringing Iain up and being the best dad he could be.

On Sunday, Iain seemed to have forgotten about his new friend. But then on Monday Daniel picked up his son from nursery, and Iain handed him a picture: a drawing of a woman with long golden hair and a crown, a man playing football and a small boy with red lines coming out of his elbow.

'It's Bee making me better on Saturday,' he announced, although Daniel had already worked that out for himself. 'I drawed it for her. Can you give it to her tomorrow?'

'All right.'

Iain beamed. 'I know she'll like it.'

'I'm sure she will.' If she didn't, he'd fib and tell Iain that she loved it. No way was he going to let his little boy be disappointed.

Beatrice was in the staff kitchen when he walked in, the next day. 'Are you busy at lunchtime?' he asked.

She looked surprised, then answered carefully. 'It depends what it's like in Resus.'

'OK. If you're not busy, I need to talk to you—and lunch is on me.'

She shook her head. 'There's no need.'

'I want to say thank you for rescuing Iain on Saturday. His arm's fine, by the way.'

'Good, but really there's no need to buy me lunch. I just did what anyone else would've done because I was the nearest one to him when it happened. Though thank you for the offer.'

'Can I just talk to you, then?' He really didn't want to give her the picture in front of everyone.

She nodded. 'We'll go halves on lunch.'

'Good.'

Daniel switched into work mode, and managed to concentrate on his patients for the morning: two fractures, a badly sprained ankle and an elderly woman who'd had a TIA and whom he admitted for further testing. He had no idea how busy Resus had been, but at lunchtime Beatrice appeared. 'Are you OK to go, or do you need a bit of time to finish writing up notes?'

'I'm OK to go,' he said.

He waited until they were sitting in the canteen before handing her the envelope.

'What's this?' she asked.

'Iain asked me to give you this,' he said.

She opened the envelope, looked at the picture and smiled. Her blue eyes were full of warmth when she looked at him. 'That's lovely—me, him and you at the team football day on Saturday, I'm guessing?'

He nodded.

'Tell him thank you, I love it, and I'm going to put it on my fridge, right next to the picture Persephone drew me of her horse at the weekend.'

'Persephone?' Daniel asked.

'My niece.'

He blinked. 'So your family goes in for unusual names.'

She nodded. 'My generation's all from Shakespeare— Orlando's the oldest, then Lysander, then me.' She spread her hands. 'It could've been worse. My mother could've called me Desdemona or Goneril. And, actually, Beatrice is Shakespeare's best female character, so I'm quite happy to be named after her.'

Her accent alone marked her out as posh. The names of her brothers and her niece marked her out as seriously posh. And had she just said that her niece had a horse? Posh *and* rich, then.

Then he realised what he'd said. 'I didn't mean to be rude about your name. We just have...simpler names in my family.'

'Then you'd approve of Sandy's choices—George and Henry.'

'Sandy?'

'Lysander.' She smiled. 'Mummy's the only one who's

allowed to call him that. Anyone else gets his evil glare and never dares do it again.'

'So Persephone is your oldest brother's daughter, then?'

She nodded. 'We call her Seffy, for short. And her older brother is Odysseus.'

'Odysseus.' Who wouldn't have lasted three seconds in the playground at Daniel's school. Why on earth would you call a child Odysseus?

As if the question was written all over his face, Beatrice explained, 'Orlando studied classics. So did his wife. They wanted to use names from Greek mythology for their children—and their dogs.' She grinned. 'They have a black Lab called Cerberus—although he only has one head, he barks enough for three and it drives Mummy crackers.'

She called her mother 'Mummy'? Posher still. Beatrice Lindford was way, way out of his league.

Not that he was thinking of asking her out.

The attraction he felt towards her needed to be stifled. The sooner, the better.

She looked at the drawing again. 'Why am I wearing a crown?'

'Iain says you talk like the Queen and you've got hair like a princess, so he's decided you must be a princess and therefore you also know the Queen and Prince Harry.'

She laughed. 'That's cute.'

'I tried to tell him you're not a princess.'

'Absolutely not.'

'Are you sure? Because... Well...'

'Because I have a posh accent and most of my family have unusual names? That's a bit of a sweeping generalisation. It'd be like me saying you're from Glasgow so everything you eat must be fried.'

'True, and I didn't mean to be rude.'

Beatrice definitely wasn't going to tell Daniel that she had grown up in a castle. Or that actually her father was a viscount, making her family minor royalty. He didn't need to know any of that. All he needed to know about her was that she was a doctor, and she was good at her job.

'Apology accepted. And I love Iain's drawing.' She smiled at him. 'He's a nice boy.'

'And he hasn't stopped talking about you, or asking when you can come to tea. I've told him you're busy and you're probably married to a prince.' Daniel rolled his eyes. 'That's what started all the Prince Harry stuff. His mum likes Prince Harry.'

So Daniel had clearly split up from his partner rather than being a widower. It was unusual for a dad to have custody of the child, but asking him about the situation felt like prying. 'Prince Harry is gorgeous,' she said. 'Your wife has good—' She stopped dead. Uh-oh. *Good taste.* That was tantamount to saying that she fancied Daniel.

Which she didn't.

Well, a little bit.

Well, quite a lot.

But things were complicated. She had the job he claimed he hadn't applied for but which everyone thought had had his name on it. He had a son who was clearly the focus of his life, and dating would be tricky for him. Plus she didn't want to tell him about her past and see the pity in his face.

Better to keep this professional.

'Good taste in princes,' she finished.

'I'll tell her that. Because Iain's going to tell her all about you when he sees her this weekend.' He sighed. 'You wouldn't believe how much a four-year-old boy can talk.'

Or girl. She thought of Taylor and her heart squeezed. Would her little girl have been a chatterbox?

Not here. Not now.

'Oh, I would. George could talk the hind leg off a donkey. He's four,' she said. A month younger than Taylor would've been. And how hard it had been to walk into her sister-in-law's hospital room and hold that baby in her arms for the first time. She'd had to force herself to smile and hold back the tears. 'George is the youngest of my nephews, and his big thing is dinosaurs. You wouldn't believe how many complicated names he can pronounce. Give him a bucket of wooden bricks and he'll build you a stegosaurus in two minutes flat.'

'Iain loves dinosaurs, too. And rockets. My mum painted a mural in his bedroom of dinosaurs in a rocket heading for the moon, and he loves it.'

'I bet.' She glanced at her watch, knowing that she was being a coward and cutting this short. But she couldn't afford to get emotionally involved with Daniel Capaldi and his son. 'Better get back to the ward. Please thank Iain for his drawing. It's lovely.'

'I will.' He looked relieved, as if she'd let him off the hook.

So did that mean he felt this ridiculous attraction, too?

Well, even if he did, they weren't going to act on it. They were going to be professional. Keep things strictly business between them. And that was that.

CHAPTER THREE

OVER THE NEXT couple of days, Daniel's determination to keep things strictly professional was sorely tested, particularly when he and Beatrice were rostered on together in Resus.

Their first patient of the day was Maureen Bishop, an elderly woman who'd slipped and fallen backwards off the patio, and was badly injured, enough for the air ambulance to bring her in.

'Thankfully her neighbour had arranged to pop round for a cup of tea, couldn't get an answer and went round the back of the house and found her,' the paramedic from the air ambulance explained. 'She was unconscious, so the neighbour called the ambulance—who called us to bring her in. She's come round now, but she's got a nasty gash in the back of her head from falling against a pot, plus fractured ribs, and we're a bit worried she might have a crack in her skull or a bleed in her brain.'

'Have you given her any pain relief?' Beatrice asked.

The paramedic nodded and gave her full details. 'We've put her on a spinal board with a neck brace.'

'Great. Has anyone managed to get in touch with her family?'

'Yes. Her daughter's on the way in.'

'That's good.' She went over to the trolley with Daniel. 'Hello, Mrs Bishop, I'm Beatrice and this is Daniel,' she said. 'We're looking after you today. May we call you Maureen?'

'Yes, love,' Maureen said.

'Can you remember what happened?'

The elderly woman grimaced. 'I slipped and fell.'

'Can you remember blacking out, or do you have any idea how long you were unconscious?' Beatrice asked.

'No,' Maureen whispered. 'I'm sorry.'

Beatrice squeezed her hand. 'No need to apologise. You've had a nasty fall. I'm going to send you for a scan because we need to check out that bump to your head, and also for X-rays so we can have a better look at your ribs, because we think you might have broken a few. Your daughter's on her way.'

'I didn't want to worry her. I told them not to call her at work,' Maureen said.

'If you were my mum,' Beatrice said gently, 'then I'd want to know you'd been taken to hospital. I'd be more upset if they didn't call me. And I'm betting it's just the same for your daughter.'

The CT scan showed a bleed to the brain; by the time Beatrice had liaised with the neurology team and persuaded them to admit Maureen, her daughter Jennifer had arrived.

'What happened?' Jennifer asked.

'Your mum slipped off the patio and banged her head against a pot. We know she was unconscious for a while, but not for how long. Fortunately her neighbour found her and called the ambulance,' Daniel explained.

'We sent your mum for a scan and X-rays,' Beatrice said. 'I'm pleased to say there's no evidence of any bones broken in her neck, so we can take the spinal collar off now, but she has fractured a couple of ribs, and when she hit her head it caused a bleed in her brain. She seems fine at the moment, but a bleed is a bit like a stroke in that sometimes it takes a few days for us to see what's happened. We're going to admit her to the neurology ward, so she's going to be monitored for the next day or so.'

'But she's going to be all right? She's not going to die?'

'She's holding her own at the moment,' Beatrice said, taking Jennifer's hand and squeezing it, 'but we want to keep an eye on her in case that bang on the head causes a problem. She'll be in good hands and we can treat her straight away if anything happens.' She smiled at Jennifer. 'Your mum was a bit worried about the paramedics calling you at work.'

'I got someone to cover my class,' Jennifer said. 'I'd be more upset if they hadn't called me.'

'That's exactly what I told her,' Beatrice said. 'I'll take you through now. It's going to look a bit scary because your mum's on a spinal board with a neck collar on, but that's absolutely standard when someone's had a fall and we think there might be any damage to the back or the neck. I'll let you say hello to her, and then we'll take off the collar and make her a bit more comfortable before she goes up to the ward.'

It was the first time Daniel had worked with Beatrice, and he could see for himself why Josh had sung her praises. Beatrice was very clear when she was managing Resus; everyone knew what they needed to do, and she was completely approachable. Josh had said that one of the nurses hadn't quite understood her instructions, the other day, and Beatrice had taken the time afterwards to go through the case, explaining exactly why she'd made certain decisions. And he really liked the way she was calm and kind to their patients.

The more Daniel worked with her, the more he liked her.

And, worse still, the more attracted he was to her. He couldn't seem to get a grip and push the unwanted feelings aside. Instead, he found himself wondering how soft her hair would be against his skin, and how her arms would feel around him. How her mouth would feel against his own.

For pity's sake. He was thirty-four, not seventeen. He had responsibilities. He didn't have time for this. He couldn't keep wondering what it would be like to date Beatrice.

If he didn't manage to sort his head out, he thought grimly, he'd need to have a word with whoever was doing the roster next month, to make sure he and Beatrice weren't working together.

Late on Thursday afternoon, Beatrice had to steel herself slightly when the paramedics brought in a woman who'd taken an overdose.

'I brought her in for the same thing, a month ago,' Dev, the lead paramedic, told Beatrice quietly. 'And another team brought her in a fortnight ago.'

'Three times in a month.' Beatrice frowned. 'I'll check her notes to see if anyone's referred her for counselling, but if they haven't then I definitely want to bring the psych team in. She needs help with the root cause. We can't just patch her up and send her home so she takes another overdose and comes back in again. That isn't fair to anyone.'

Dev spread his hands. 'Mental health. You know the situation there as well as I do.'

'Overstretched. I know.' Beatrice sighed. 'But I'll push as much as I can for her. Thanks for your help, Dev.'

She went over to the bed. 'I'm Beatrice, and I'm part of the team looking after you today,' she said to her patient. 'May I call you Sally?'

The young woman nodded.

'The paramedics tell me you took an overdose of paracetamol.'

Sally hunched her shoulders, and Beatrice sat down and took her hand. 'I'm not here to judge you, Sally, I'm here to help you. But I do need to know how many tablets you took, when, and over how long a period, so I know the best way to look after you.'

'A dozen tablets,' Sally whispered. 'An hour ago.'

'What did you take them with?' Beatrice asked, really hoping that alcohol wasn't involved.

'Water.'

That was one good thing; she didn't have to worry about complications from alcohol. 'OK. Normally paracetamol's safe to take as a painkiller, but if you take too much you can risk damaging your liver and your kidneys. I need to take some blood tests, and the results will tell me what the best treatment is for you. Is that OK?'

Sally nodded, and Beatrice took the bloods. 'Can I get you a cup of tea or something while we're waiting for the results?'

Sally shook her head. 'I'm all right.'

'I'll need to see some other patients while I'm waiting for the results, but I'll be back very soon to see you,' Beatrice said. 'If you're worried about anything, just press this buzzer to call one of us and we'll come in to see you, OK?'

Sally didn't ask for help while Beatrice called the psych team and asked for an urgent referral, or while Beatrice checked a set of X-rays for Josh and dealt with a nasty gash on an elderly man's arm where he'd slipped and knocked against a gatepost. But finally the blood test results came back, and Beatrice went into the cubicle where Sally was waiting quietly. The poor woman looked as if a huge weight was about to drop on her.

'I've got the test results back,' Beatrice said. 'We do need to treat you, to stop any damage happening to your liver, so I'm going to give you a drug through a drip— that's a line that goes straight into your vein. It means you'll need to stay with us another day while we give you the drug. Is that OK with you?'

Sally looked worried again. 'I felt so bad, last time. I was sick everywhere.'

'This is a different drug from the one you had last time. It's a special trial, but I used it in my last hospital and it's really good,' Beatrice said. 'It means you're less likely to have side effects, like being sick or itching. Tomorrow we'll do another blood test to see how you're doing, and we'll be able to let you go home if we're happy that there's no damage to your liver.'

Sally bit her lip. 'I'm so sorry.'

Beatrice squeezed her hand. 'You really don't have to apologise. You're not well and it's my job to make you better.'

'I know you're all busy here and you should be saving lives that matter, not bothering with me.'

'We are saving a life—*yours*,' Beatrice said gently. 'You're important, too.'

'I know I shouldn't have done it.'

'We all make mistakes.' And Beatrice had made this particular one herself. She could still remember how low she'd felt when she'd opened the box of paracetamol and popped the tablets out of their foil packaging. How hopeless.

'It seemed like the only way out.'

Just as it had for Beatrice. 'There's always another way,' she said, squeezing Sally's hand again. 'Though sometimes you need someone else to help you see it. Is there anyone we can call for you to let them know you're here? Your family, a friend?'

'Nobody.'

Beatrice remembered that feeling, too. Once she was out of Resus and in cubicles, she hadn't wanted the emergency staff to call her husband or her family, because she knew they'd blame themselves for not picking up on the signs. And she hadn't wanted to burden any of her friends with how low she was feeling. She'd just been grateful that she hadn't been treated in her own department so she hadn't had the sheer embarrassment of having to face them all afterwards.

'I just don't want to be here,' Sally said, her voice shaking.

'I know, sweetheart, but I really can't let you go until you're better,' Beatrice said, still holding her hand. 'I need to be sure you're not going to collapse with liver damage.'

'It's wrong to be here.' Sally dragged in a breath. 'I just wish I was dead.'

Beatrice had once been in Sally's shoes, wanting to

be with her lost baby instead of stuck here in this world. 'I promise, there's light at the end of the tunnel. We'll help you find it,' she said gently.

The psych team had sent a message to say that nobody was going to be available for another hour. Maybe there was something she could do for Sally until they got here, Beatrice thought. The same thing that the psych team at a different hospital had done for her, all those years ago: a grounding exercise she still used from time to time, when things got on top of her.

'I want you to do something for me, Sally,' she said. 'It might sound a bit weird, but humour me.'

'What's that?' Sally asked.

'I want you to tell me five things you can see.'

Sally blinked and frowned. 'Um—you, the curtain, the bed, I don't know the name of the machine over there, and a cup of water.' She ticked the items off on her fingers.

'That's great. Now four things you can hear. It doesn't have to be here or right now in the hospital, just four sounds.'

'Waves on a beach, a machine beeping...' Sally paused. 'A bird singing, a child laughing.'

'That's great.' Especially because she'd named something positive. 'Now I want you to name three things you can touch—and touch them.'

'The sheet, a cup, the bed frame.' Sally touched them as she named them.

'That's really good. Two things you like the smell of?'

'Coffee and fresh bread.' Sally sounded more confident now.

'Brilliant. And now I want you to take one slow, deep breath. In for three—and now out for three.'

Sally did the deep breath while Beatrice counted, then looked at her. 'I don't know what you just did, but I don't feel as panicky as I did.'

'It's a grounding technique,' Beatrice explained. 'You can do it yourself any time you feel bad. It makes you focus on something external instead of your thoughts and feelings, and it stops the spiral of misery getting tighter. Five things you can see, four things you can hear, three things you can touch, two things you can smell, and one slow, deep breath.'

'What if I can't remember the order?' Sally asked.

'It doesn't matter. Just think of the five senses, pick one and start with that,' Beatrice said. 'Count down each time, and just remember that one breath at the end.'

Sally's eyes filled with tears. 'Thank you.'

'That's what I'm here for. To help,' Beatrice reassured her.

Although it was time for Beatrice's break, no way was she leaving her patient. She remembered what it was like to feel that you had nobody to understand or rely on. She sat with Sally until one of the nurses came in to say that the psych team had arrived, then headed out of the cubicle briefly to have a word with her colleague first.

'Keith Bradley from the psych team,' he said, introducing himself. 'Apparently you wanted a quick word?'

'Beatrice Lindford.' She shook his hand. 'It's my patient, Sally. I'm treating her for her third overdose in a month. I know resources are stretched,' she said, 'but this is just a revolving door and we're not helping her. We're just providing a sticking plaster and that's not good enough. We need to find the root cause of why she keeps taking an overdose and help her sort that out. Can you get her referred to emergency counselling?'

'It's like you said—resources are stretched—but I'll do what I can,' Keith said.

She rested her hand on his shoulder. 'Thanks. I appreciate it. I've done a grounding exercise with her, which has helped a bit, but she definitely needs you right now.'

She went back in to the cubicle and introduced Keith to Sally. 'I'm going to leave you with Keith now, but I'll be back to see you later today and see how you're getting on.'

Sally was pale but still determined not to call anyone when Beatrice dropped in to see her at the end of her shift.

'Keith was nice. And I did that thing you taught me when I felt bad after he'd gone, and it helped,' Sally said. 'Thank you.'

'I'm glad it helped. Are you sure I can't call anyone for you?'

'I'm sure. Right now I just can't face anyone,' Sally said.

But a good night's sleep had clearly made her feel differently, because in the morning when Beatrice came in with the blood test results Sally agreed to let the team call her mother.

'I'm happy to let you go home,' Beatrice said, 'but if you get a stomach ache or a really bad headache, you feel sick or drowsy, the whites of your eyes go yellow or you can't have a wee within the next eight hours, I want you to come back. I know that's a lot to remember, so I have a leaflet with all the information on that you can take home with you.'

'Thank you,' Sally said.

When Sally's mother came into the department, Beatrice had a quiet word with her in one of the cubicles.

'Keep an eye on her for the next twenty-four hours,'

she said. 'I've given her a leaflet with symptoms to watch out for, following the treatment we gave her, and I can let you have a copy of that as well. We've got her referred to a counsellor, too, which should help.'

Sally's mother folded her arms; her mouth was set in a thin line. 'I can't believe Sally's done this yet again. This is the *third* time in a month. She's so selfish—she doesn't think about how it feels to get that call from the police or the hospital, or how hard it is to get time off work at the last minute to pick her up from here and look after her because she can't be left on her own.'

'I understand that it's hard for you, and it's worrying, too, but it's really not her fault,' Beatrice said. 'She's depressed to the point where she can't think clearly. She isn't doing it to cause problems for anyone else.' Her own family's stiff upper lip and refusal to talk about things had been tough enough to deal with, but overt hostility and anger like this… Poor Sally. Beatrice just hoped she had some good friends who would support her.

'I suppose so.' Sally's mother rolled her eyes. 'I'd better get her home. And let's hope she doesn't do it all over again next week.'

Daniel was in the cubicle next door and couldn't help overhearing the conversation.

Although he agreed with every word Beatrice had said, something about it felt personal. He was even more convinced during his break, when he'd boiled the kettle to make coffee and Beatrice walked into the kitchen, filled only half her mug with boiling water and then topped up her coffee with cold water so she could drink it straight down.

'Are you OK?' he asked.

She didn't meet his eyes and her voice was a little bit too bright when she replied, 'Yes, thanks, I'm fine.'

'I couldn't help overhearing you with the mum of your patient who'd taken an overdose. That sounded rough.'

Beatrice shrugged. 'I just hope she listened to me and realised that it's the illness at fault, not her daughter. Mental health's tricky to handle, and I know it's hard for the family to deal with.'

Mental health was very tricky; he knew that one first hand from Jenny's postnatal depression. Beatrice's words sounded personal, too. Had someone in her family or one of her friends suffered from depression? he wondered. Not that it was any of his business, and he wasn't going to pry. 'We do what we can,' he said.

'Yes.' She changed the subject. 'Are you going to the team ten-pin bowling thing tonight?'

'No. I'm looking after Iain,' he said. 'Are you going?'

'Yes. I'm rubbish at bowling, but it's fun—and it's good to get to know people outside work.'

'Well, if I don't see you before the end of your shift, have fun,' he said lightly.

'Thanks. You have a good evening, too.'

Though Daniel had forgotten that he'd mentioned the team night out to his mother, who'd picked up Iain from school and given him his tea.

'I really think you should go on that team thing. It's Friday night. When did you last go out on a Friday night?' Susan asked.

Daniel couldn't actually remember, though he had a nasty feeling that his mother did.

'You're still young, Dan. You're thirty-four,' Susan said.

'And my focus is on bringing up my son.'

'Which is fine, but I'm not doing anything tonight so I can babysit for you. A night out with the team will do you good.'

'I don't need a night out, Mum, I'm fine.'

'It'll do you good,' Susan repeated. 'And Iain will be fine with me.'

'I know he will, but I can't ask you to give up your evening for me.'

'I've already told you I'm not busy, and you're not asking, I'm offering. And if you're worried about packing his stuff to go to Jenny's for the weekend, I can do that as well. It's no problem.' She rolled her eyes. 'Dan, I made enough mistakes when you were young. I let you down then. I want to be here for you now.'

'You have been there for me, Mum, when I needed you,' he reminded her. 'When it all went wrong with Jenny, I couldn't have coped without you. And I feel bad enough that you've relocated from Glasgow to London because of me and Iain.'

'You're my son. I love you dearly. Of course I was going to move to be with you and support you. But right now I want to shake you,' she added, folding her arms. 'Are you still in love with Jenny?'

'No.'

'Good, because she's married to someone else and she's not in love with you any more.'

He winced. 'Tell it to me straight, Mum, why don't you?'

'That's the only way to tell it,' she said. 'What you need is to move on and start dating someone.'

He thought of Beatrice, and quickly shoved the thought away. 'I don't need to date anyone.'

'Yes, you do, before you turn into a crabbit old man

before your time.' She paused. 'What about Iain's Princess Bee?'

He shook his head. 'She's my colleague. Technically she might even be my boss. We can't date.'

Susan pounced. 'So you *have* thought about it, then.'

Several times. 'No,' he fibbed.

'Call her. Ask her if she's busy. Or maybe she'll be at the team thing tonight and you can see her there.'

Which was another reason why he shouldn't go. Spending time with her outside work could be dangerous for his peace of mind. 'Mum, I'm not looking for another relationship.'

'Iain's not going to be little for ever and ever. And I don't want you to be lonely when you're older.'

'You always tell me you're not lonely,' he pointed out.

'I'm not. I like my life. I go out with friends, I have a good time, and I enjoy working with my students.' She narrowed her eyes at him. 'You're going out tonight, Daniel Capaldi, whether you like it or not. And you're going to have a good time. Don't argue with your mother, because she knows much better than you do.'

He gave it one last shot. 'They had to book the places. They'll be full up.'

'There'll be room for you, even if you have to take turns bowling with someone.' She pursed her lips. 'It's a shame it's not tomorrow night, or you wouldn't have any excuses in the first place. But your excuses won't wash with me. You're going.'

And so he found himself going to the ten-pin bowling alley after he'd put Iain to bed and read him three stories.

'Daniel! So glad you're here—Kundini couldn't make it at the last minute and we were going to be one short,' Josh said. 'You're on Bea's team.'

Oh, help. She was the last person whose team he needed to be on. How was he possibly supposed to keep his distance?

It was made worse when he saw her; wearing jeans and a T-shirt, with her hair pulled back and tied by a scarf at the nape of her neck, she looked young and approachable—just as he imagined her to have looked in her student days. And right at that moment he wanted to walk up to her, wrap his arms round her and kiss her.

Which was the last thing he should do.

Instead, he walked up to her and said, 'I believe I'm your team's new substitute.'

The warmth of her smile almost knocked him sideways.

'Well, hello, there. Is Iain with you?' she asked.

'No, my mum's babysitting,' he explained. 'And my mum's not the kind of person you argue with, once she gets an idea into her head.' He rolled his eyes. 'She thinks a night out will do me good.'

'Maybe she's right,' Beatrice said. 'It's obvious to me how much you love your son, but parenting is hard—and being a single parent is even harder. Sometimes you need to make time to do something for you.'

'Maybe,' he said.

'Welcome to the team. I really hope you're good at this,' she said, 'because you need to make up for me.'

He'd wondered if she was really as hopeless as she claimed; but then her first ball went straight down the gutter. So did the second.

'Sorry, guys. I'm a bit better at emergency medicine than I am at this,' she said with a rueful smile.

He wanted to give her a hug, but settled for putting up the bumper bars for her. She zig-zagged her way to a half-strike, everyone on their team cheered, and it encouraged her enough that she managed a full strike on her next turn.

'Has anyone actually taught you how to bowl before?' he asked.

'Um, no,' she admitted. 'It's not the kind of thing I normally do.'

'Would you let me help you?'

She looked worried. 'Are you sure that's OK? The other team aren't going to say you're cheating?'

He grinned. ''Course it's OK. Let's start with the ball. You might be better off using a lighter one than the one you picked—which isn't me patronising you,' he said quickly.

'No, it's you explaining properly,' she said. 'Which is an important skill at work, and I wouldn't expect anything less from you.'

He inclined his head in acknowledgement of the compliment; but it warmed him all the way through that she thought that highly of him. 'You stand behind the line, bring your arm back behind you, then bring it forward and let the ball go—try and aim for the middle of the pins. The ball will follow the line of where you let it go,' he said, 'which is why you're zig-zagging. You're leaving it just that little bit too late to let it go.'

She tried a couple of practice bowls, which went horribly wrong. 'Maybe I'd better stick to medicine,' she said.

'No, you can do this. Do you mind if I help guide your arm?' he asked, knowing even as he said it that he really shouldn't let himself get that physically close to her.

'OK.'

Keep this professional. You're helping her bowl a ball,

not holding her as if she's your date, he reminded himself silently. He stood behind her, and helped her bring her arm back to the right position, then helped her move forward. 'And now let go.'

'That's amazing! It didn't zig-zag,' she said, her tone full of wonder and delight as the ball went straight down the middle of the lane. 'Thank you.'

And then she turned round and hugged him.

He hugged her back before he realised what he was doing.

Oh, help. This was bad. Really bad. Because Beatrice Lindford fitted perfectly in his arms. And he liked the feel of her arms round him, too.

But he wasn't in a position to start anything with her. Even if she wasn't sort of his boss, there was Iain to consider. How could he get involved with her? If things went wrong between them, and Iain had got close to her, it would devastate the little boy. And, even though she'd been good with his son at the football day, there was a huge difference between helping out at a team event and having a small child as part of your life. Who was to say she even wanted children?

As if she sensed the sudden tension in him, she blushed and let him go. 'Sorry. I got a bit carried away with actually bowling properly for the first time ever.'

'No problem,' he fibbed.

He managed to keep a little bit of physical distance between them for the rest of the evening, even when they stopped midway through the game for tortilla chips, chicken wings and hot dogs. But then his fingers accidentally brushed against hers when they each dipped a tortilla chip into the guacamole, and his heart actually skipped a beat.

He couldn't help looking at her. Her eyes had widened, her pupils were huge and her lips were slightly parted. So did she feel it, too, this weird pull of attraction?

Well, they weren't going to act on it.

He concentrated on the bowling, and the evening went incredibly quickly.

But, at the end of the evening, his mouth decided it had had enough of playing by his brain's rules, and he found himself asking, 'Can I walk you home?'

She looked at him. 'Am I on your way?'

This was his get-out. 'Where are you?'

She told him her address.

'No,' he admitted. But then his mouth took over from his common sense again. 'Though I'd like to walk you home.'

Her smile was slow, sweet, and felt as if it had pole-axed him. 'I'd like that. Thank you.'

On the way back to her place, his hand brushed against hers. He wasn't quite sure how it happened but, the next thing he knew, his fingers were twining round hers and they were holding hands properly.

She didn't say a word, but it wasn't an awkward silence.

How long had it been since he'd last held hands with someone? He thought back. It must've been with Jenny, before Iain was born. When they were still expectant parents, still in love, still thinking that the future was rosy and bright. Before her postnatal depression ripped their new little family apart.

She stopped outside a gate. 'This is my flat,' she said.

It was in one of the beautiful Edwardian townhouses that overlooked the park.

'Very nice,' he said.

'You could come in for a coffee, if you like,' she said.

It was tempting. So very tempting.

But it wouldn't be fair to her to start something that he knew he couldn't finish.

'Thanks, but…'

'But no thanks,' she finished. 'I understand.'

But there had been a flash of hurt in her eyes. It made him want to make her feel better. And all his common sense went out of the window, because he wrapped his arms round her. Lowered his mouth to hers. Brushed his lips against hers once, twice…

Her hands were in his hair and she was kissing him back when he came to his senses again and broke the kiss.

'I'm sorry. That wasn't fair of me,' he said. 'I'm not in a position to date anyone. I have Iain to think of.'

'I know. And I'm not looking to date anyone. I'm concentrating on my career.'

Why was someone as lovely as Beatrice Lindford single in the first place? Daniel had the feeling that someone had hurt her—as much as Jenny had hurt him—but he didn't have the right to ask.

'If my situation was different,' he said, 'I'd ask you out properly.'

'And I'd turn you down, because I'd still be concentrating on my career.'

Whoever had hurt her had *really* hurt her, he thought.

And she'd just been really kind to him. Taken away the guilt.

'Message understood,' he said. 'Goodnight, Beatrice.'

'Goodnight, Daniel. I'll see you at work. And thank you for walking me home.'

'Pleasure,' he said. 'See you at work.'

And he turned away before he did something stupid. Like asking her to change both their minds.

CHAPTER FOUR

SOMEHOW DANIEL WAS going to have to scrub that kiss out of his head.

He couldn't get involved with Beatrice. The sensible side of him knew that. She was his senior at work, so it could be awkward. Their backgrounds were poles apart—she was from a posh family, and he couldn't see them being happy to accept him as Beatrice's partner, not when he was a single dad, and also the illegitimate son of a teenage mum who'd gone massively off the rails. He'd been brought up by his grandparents until he was ten and his mother had settled down again. He didn't have a problem with his past; he was proud of the way Susan had turned her life around. But he also knew that not everyone would share his views.

And most importantly there was Iain.

What if he let Beatrice get close to Iain and things didn't work out? It would devastate his son. It was hard enough for Iain, dividing himself between his parents. The little boy didn't need any extra calls on his heart from someone who might not stick around.

So it was obvious that Daniel needed to keep things strictly business between himself and Beatrice. For all their sakes.

Dropping Iain over at Jenny's for their usual alternate weekend together occupied part of Saturday morning, but the rest of the day dragged. Cleaning the bathroom, catching up with the laundry, doing the grocery shopping: none of it kept his mind off Beatrice or how it had felt to kiss her. How his lips had tingled. How he'd wanted to draw her closer. How he'd actually forgotten that they were in the street, in full view of any passers-by, because his head had been full of starbursts.

Saturday evening was worse. Why on earth hadn't he made sure he was working both days while Iain was at his mother's for the weekend? Several times Daniel picked up his phone—which was totally pointless as he didn't actually know Beatrice's number, and besides which she'd told him that she was focusing on her career and wasn't interested in a relationship with anyone.

What was wrong with him?

For four years now he'd focused on his son. He'd turned down offers of dates. Women hadn't appeared on his radar other than as friends, colleagues or patients. He hadn't wanted to get involved with anyone.

Why had Beatrice Lindford got him in such a spin? What was so different about her? Why couldn't he get her out of his head? The questions went round and round his head, and he just couldn't find an answer.

Somehow Beatrice was going to have to scrub that kiss out of her head.

She couldn't get involved with Daniel. Iain was almost the same age that Taylor would've been; he was a gorgeous little boy, but every time she saw him she'd remember her lost little girl, and the pain would rip another layer off her scar tissue. She wasn't sure she was ready for a relationship with anyone, let alone with someone who had a small child. Plus, if she told Daniel about her past, would he assume that she only wanted to get involved with him so she'd have a ready-made family to help fill the hole in her life?

This couldn't work. Not in a month of Sundays.

And what was it about Daniel that drew her so much? Yes, he was physically attractive, but she'd met plenty of attractive men since she'd split up with Oliver. She just hadn't really noticed any of them. Hadn't dated any of them. Hadn't wanted to get involved with any of them.

But Daniel Capaldi was different.

She'd felt that weird awareness right from the start, even when he'd been slightly frosty towards her. As he'd started to thaw out towards her, she'd found herself thinking of him more and more often.

Then he'd kissed her on Friday night, and every nerve ending in her body had reacted.

And it had scared the hell out of her. She couldn't remember the last time she'd reacted like that to anyone—even to Oliver, because her emotions had just shut down after Taylor's death.

She was pretty sure it was the same for Daniel, because he'd looked dazed when he'd broken the kiss. And he'd used his son as an excuse why they couldn't see each other. She'd come straight out with the excuse that she wasn't dating, she was concentrating on her career.

The whole thing was like a house of cards. Fragile. So easy to fall apart.

She didn't want to risk getting involved again. Getting hurt again. Losing her heart again.

So she needed to keep things strictly business between herself and Daniel.

* * *

It wasn't working.

Even though Sunday had been busy at work—and thankfully Beatrice had been off duty—and the evening had been taken up with Iain chattering about what he'd done at the weekend with his mum and Jordan, Daniel just couldn't get that kiss out of his head.

Worse still, every time he caught Beatrice's eye at work on Monday, there was a fleeting expression on her face that made him pretty sure she was remembering that kiss. That she, too, was in this weird state where her head was telling her this was a bad idea but she still wanted to repeat it anyway.

What was he going to do?

After another night spent fitfully waking from dreams of Beatrice—dreams where they were dancing together, holding each other, kissing—Daniel came to a decision in the shower.

He needed help.

Ironically, he thought the best person to help him would be the same person who'd caused him a problem in the first place: Beatrice herself. Maybe if he told her about his past, explained about what had happened with Jenny when Iain was tiny, then she'd help him to be sensible and keep things platonic between them.

They were both rostered on Minors that day, so he was pretty sure they'd be able to take their lunch break together.

'Can we have a chat over lunch?' he asked when he saw her in the staff kitchen during their break.

She looked slightly wary. 'A chat?'

'Somewhere quiet. Maybe a sandwich in the park, as it's a nice day?' he suggested.

She still looked wary. 'A chat.'

'To clear the air,' he said.

'All right,' she said eventually.

'Meet you at twelve-thirty, here?' he asked.

'OK. Twelve-thirty,' she said, 'depending on our patients' needs.'

'Of course,' he said.

He made it through the morning; and then he headed for the staff kitchen to meet Beatrice. She was already there. 'Still OK for a sandwich and some fresh air?' he asked.

'Sure,' she said.

They bought sandwiches from the hospital canteen, then went out to the park in a slightly uneasy silence.

'I owe you an explanation,' he said when they found a quiet bench and sat down.

She shook her head. 'You don't owe me anything.'

'I think I do. And the best way I can do that is to explain about my situation,' he said. 'About Iain.'

Did that mean he wanted her to explain her situation, too? Beatrice wondered. Because she wasn't prepared for that. She didn't want to talk about losing her baby, or the way her marriage had collapsed, and she definitely didn't want to talk about what she'd done. But she'd listen to what he had to say.

'Obviously I'll keep anything you say in confidence,' she said.

'I've worked at Muswell Hill Memorial Hospital for long enough that pretty much everyone knows what happened,' Daniel said dryly. 'But thank you.'

Not quite knowing what to say next, she waited.

'Jenny—my ex-wife—had serious postnatal depression after Iain was born,' he said. 'I let her down. I should've picked up on it a lot sooner than I did.'

'You're not being fair to yourself. You work in emergency medicine, not obstetrics or general practice,' she reminded him.

He shrugged. 'Even so, I should've noticed that it was more than just the baby blues that you hear people talking about. That she wasn't sleeping well and she was really tired, and it wasn't just because she was getting up at night to feed the baby. That she was feeling low, and it was more than just the usual worries a new parent has about whether you're going to be good enough. That she worried and worried about whether Iain was all right. That she checked him in his cot a bit too often, to make sure he was still breathing.'

Would she have been like that if Taylor had lived? Beatrice wondered. Worrying constantly, checking on the baby?

She forced the thoughts away and tried to concentrate on what Daniel was telling her.

He blew out a breath. 'I was busy at work, so I didn't pay Jenny enough attention. I didn't notice that she was gradually withdrawing from everyone. I didn't ask her enough about her day or notice that she made excuses not to meet up with the other mums from our antenatal group. I didn't see that she wasn't coping.'

'You can't put all the blame on yourself,' she said. 'As you said, you were working, so you weren't with her all the time. Even if you weren't getting up to do any of the night feeds, when Iain woke and screamed it probably woke you, so you weren't getting enough sleep either. You were tired and trying to do your best. Plus you weren't the only one to see Jenny. What about her family, her friends, her health visitor? Didn't they say anything?'

'Her best friend did,' Daniel said. 'She noticed Jenny didn't wash her hair as much as she used to, and she didn't dress the way she used to before Iain arrived. I'd noticed, too, but I assumed it was just because she was adjusting to a new routine with the baby and I wasn't going to pressure her to look super-glamorous every second of the day.'

Beatrice liked the fact Daniel was so sensitive. After Taylor's funeral, Oliver had expected her to dress up and keep going to his office functions. She'd forced herself to do it, not wanting to let him down any further than she already had. Inside, she'd been falling apart; outside, she'd kept the stiff upper lip expected from her by everyone. In the end, it hadn't made a difference. Going along with the same routine, smiling at people and pretending that everything was all right simply hadn't made everything all right. It had just made her bottle everything up until she finally broke down.

'She'd lost her sense of humour,' Daniel continued, 'and I just put it down to the stresses of being a new mum. I didn't pay enough attention.'

'It's harder to spot when you see someone every day and when it's a gradual change,' Beatrice pointed out.

'I still should have noticed,' Daniel insisted. And she could see the guilt racking him, reflected in his dark eyes. 'And then one day, when Iain was about two months old, I got home from work and she wasn't there. Iain was lying in his cot, screaming his head off. I changed his nappy and fed him—thankfully we'd got a bottle and some cartons of baby milk in case of emergency—and I called her, but her phone was switched off. I tried her mum, her sister, her friends from work, just about everyone in our phone book, but nobody had heard from her or seen her that day.'

Beatrice sucked in a breath. She'd done the same thing, two months after the accident. Waited until she had a day when she thought she wouldn't be disturbed. Except her intentions had been a lot more final. If Victoria, her sister-in-law, hadn't knocked on her door and refused to take silence for an answer...

She pulled herself together, this wasn't about her. It was about Daniel and Iain and Jenny. 'That must've been really hard for you,' she said.

He nodded. 'If she'd taken Iain with her, I wouldn't have been quite so worried. I would've thought maybe she was having coffee with a friend and had forgotten the time. But the fact that she'd left Iain on his own—I didn't think she'd just popped out to get a pint of milk or something while he was asleep. She would've taken him with her. I thought she might have...' He tailed off, his expression full of pain.

He didn't have to finish the sentence. Beatrice knew exactly what he meant. He'd thought that Jenny might have done exactly what Beatrice herself had done.

'I reported her to the police as missing, and I put stuff all over social media in case someone saw her, begging them to let me know—I just needed to know she was safe. Obviously I called work and said I needed emergency parental leave until Jenny was home. And my mum flew down from Glasgow the next morning to help out with Iain while I pestered everyone I knew and tried to find Jenny.'

His family had rallied round, Beatrice thought. Hers—even her sisters-in-law—had panicked and refused to talk about what she'd done. Pretending it hadn't happened meant they didn't have to face the fear that she might do it again.

'What happened?' she asked.

'I was tearing my hair out. But three days later someone at a hotel recognised her from a photograph I'd put on social media and called the police, who brought her home. I was just so relieved she hadn't...'

'Yes,' Beatrice said softly. She'd put her family through just as much worry as Jenny had, and it still made her feel guilty.

'Anyway, I got her an appointment with our family doctor and Mum looked after Iain while I went with her to support her.' He grimaced. 'I asked her why she'd left him—I wasn't going to judge her, because I knew it was so out of character. I just wanted to understand, so I could help her. And I was so shocked when she said she'd thought she was going to do something to hurt him because he wouldn't stop crying and she didn't know what to do—she left to keep him safe.'

'I can understand that,' Beatrice said. 'If you're already low with postnatal depression and you're panicking that everything's going wrong, a crying baby would send you over the edge.' In her case, though, it had been the opposite. She would've given anything to hear her baby cry. It was the lack of crying, the lack of anything, the sheer *emptiness* that had tipped her over the edge. 'And I'm guessing she knew you'd be back relatively soon and would be there for him.'

He nodded. 'She thought he'd probably cry himself to sleep. Maybe he did; and maybe he woke up again just before I got back. I don't know.'

'And the doctor helped?'

'He gave her antidepressants as well as referring her for CBT. Jenny's parents live miles away in the Cotswolds, so Mum moved down from Glasgow permanently to help support us.' He blew out a breath. 'She got better over the next few months, but things between us were terrible. I felt guilty for not supporting her better; I felt angry with her for leaving him alone when he couldn't look after himself and something could've happened to him; and I felt guilty for being angry because I knew it wasn't her fault that she was ill and her judgement wasn't what it normally was. But no matter how much I tried I couldn't get past it; it was like a vicious circle that spiralled tighter and tighter. We couldn't seem to find our way back to how things were before Iain was born. It was as if all the love we'd shared just drained away and there was nothing left.'

Beatrice knew exactly how that felt.

'In the end we split up and she agreed I could have custody of Iain.'

'Does she see him at all?'

'Yes, he stays with her every other weekend. He stayed with her this weekend. But that's why I don't want to get involved with anyone—Iain's already had a rough start, and it's up to me to give him stability.'

'Is Jenny involved with anyone?'

He nodded. 'She remarried a year ago. We talked about the custody situation with Iain and, even though he's older now and it's fine between them, she doesn't trust herself not to let him down again. I'm never going to withhold access or anything spiteful like that, because she's his mum and I want him to know her and love her as much as she loves him—but I'm the one who looks after him, with support from my mum, and that's the way it's going to stay.'

Beatrice had been in that same dark place—except she'd never see Taylor grow up, the way Jenny would see Iain change from a child to a young man. She and Oliver had been in the same vicious circle as Daniel and Jenny except, unlike Daniel, Oliver hadn't tried to understand why his wife had tried to get out of the situation. And, instead of talking about it, or getting her to talk, he'd taken the stiff upper lip approach; in his view, if they didn't discuss it, it hadn't happened.

The cracks had grown wider and wider; and finally Beatrice had had the strength to leave him and let him find happiness with someone else.

Maybe she should tell Daniel. Given his own experiences, she was pretty sure he would understand. But she also thought he'd see her differently, once he knew what she'd done. She didn't want him to pity her or avoid her—not now, when they were starting to gel as a team at work.

'I'm sorry you've all been through so much,' she said.

'We're good now,' Daniel said, 'but I don't want to risk ever being in that position again.'

Which made her the last person he'd ever want to get involved with. Her own depression wasn't quite the same as Jenny's, but it had similar roots. She'd been on Jenny's side of the illness. And what if they did get together and her depression returned? She'd be letting him down—and she'd be letting his son down, too. Daniel hadn't been able to forgive Jenny, so it was pretty clear that he wouldn't be able to forgive Beatrice, either.

It was better to stick to being colleagues. 'Thank you for telling me. As I said, I won't be gossiping about you.'

'I appreciate that.'

A little voice inside her head said, *Tell him.*

But she just couldn't.

Instead, she said brightly, 'I guess we'd better be getting back to the department. The waiting room's probably filled while we've been at lunch.'

'Agreed,' Daniel said.

And if she kept reminding herself that this thing between her and Daniel couldn't even start, she'd come to believe it.

CHAPTER FIVE

FOR THE REST of the week, Daniel managed to keep everything between himself and Beatrice completely professional.

But then, on Friday lunchtime, he was just grabbing a coffee from the staff kitchen when his phone beeped.

The message was from his childminder.

Daniel, please ring me urgently.

He frowned. Diane rarely texted him. Something was obviously wrong.

His heart skipped a beat. *Iain.*

No, it couldn't be. Iain was at school. They would've called Daniel straight away, not Diane—wouldn't they?

He called her immediately. 'Diane, it's Daniel. What's happened?'

'It's my mum,' Diane said.

And how horrible was he that relief flooded through him? Not Iain. His precious son was all right.

'She collapsed and she's being taken to hospital.'

'Here? I'll keep an eye out for her and ask to make sure she sees me.'

'No, she lives in Essex.' Her voice shook. 'They don't

know what's wrong. It might be a stroke. I need to be with her, so I won't be able to pick Iain up from school today.'

Which left him with a huge problem. But Diane had enough to worry about, with her mum's health, so he wasn't going to make things worse for her. 'Of course you need to be with your mum. Don't worry. I'll sort something out for Iain. Let me know if there's anything I can do to help or if you want the medics there to talk to me.'

'Oh, Daniel.' She sounded close to tears. 'Thank you for being so nice about it.'

'No problem,' he fibbed. There wasn't exactly anything else he could be other than nice. 'Take care, and I hope your mum is okay. Let me know how she's getting on.'

He frowned as he ended the call. What was he going to do now? Normally he would have called on his mother, but Susan was away in Birmingham, running a three-day course, and she wouldn't be back until tomorrow. Jenny was leaving work early because she was going away for the weekend, so he couldn't ask her to help, either. And if he asked for unpaid leave it would mean the department was short-staffed, which wasn't fair on the team.

There had to be someone he could ask. Someone who knew Iain. Maybe he could ask the mum of one of Iain's friends to take him home for a few hours, until he'd finished his shift?

At that moment, the kitchen door opened and Beatrice walked in.

'Are you all right?' she asked.

'Yes—well, no,' he admitted. There wasn't any point

in lying. 'My childminder's mother just collapsed so she can't pick Iain up from school. Mum's running a course in Birmingham and Jenny's away.' He raked a hand through his hair. 'I'm just going to have to call round the mums of Iain's friends and see if any of them can help me out.'

Beatrice knew that this was her cue to wish Daniel luck, make herself a coffee and let him get on with it. But he looked worried sick. How could she just turn her back on him, when he clearly needed help?

There was an obvious solution. Part of her thought it was a bad idea, tantamount to getting involved with him. And having a four-year-old child in her flat—a child the age her daughter would've been—was that really a good idea? Wouldn't it just rip the top of her scars?

Then again, what was the difference between George, her four-year-old nephew, and Iain? Plus she'd met Iain and they'd got on just fine.

It would be the best solution for both Iain and Daniel. And, as Daniel's senior, she needed to support him. Right?

Before she could talk herself out of it, she said, 'I'm off duty at three. I could pick him up for you.'

He blinked. 'You? But...'

'I'd do the same for any colleague who was a bit stuck and needed help,' she said. 'Iain knows me. I don't think he'll mind me looking after him for the afternoon. And I can take him back to my place—I've got a box of toys and books for my niece and nephews, so I'm sure we can find something he'll enjoy in there.'

'That's very kind of you, but I'm on a late. I can't swap shifts.'

'It's not a problem. Iain can have dinner with me,' she said. 'Any allergies I need to know about?'

Daniel raked a hand through his hair again, and the dishevelment made him look absolutely scrumptious. *Colleagues*, she reminded herself sharply. They were colleagues. With her past, she was the very last woman that he needed to get involved with.

'No allergies,' he said. 'Are you quite sure it's not going to cause you any hassle? You might already have plans for tonight.'

'I don't have any plans,' she said. Not because she wanted him to know that her social life was pared down—or why—but because she didn't want him feeling guilty. 'It's fine. I guess you'll need to contact his school to let them know I'm picking Iain up with your permission. If you want to send them a photo of my work ID card, that's fine. And I'll need the school's address and your mobile number, and you'll obviously need my details.'

'Thank you,' he said. 'I owe you.'

She shook her head. 'From what I've seen so far of the department here, it's like my old one at the Hampstead Free. Everyone mucks in and helps each other. It all evens out in the end.'

'It'd be a huge weight off my mind,' he admitted.

'Well, then. Let's get it sorted out.'

It didn't take long for Daniel to arrange things with the school and send them a copy of Beatrice's work ID, and to synchronise information with Beatrice.

And so, at the end of her shift, Beatrice found herself heading for the local infant school.

School.

Taylor, like Iain, would have been in her first year

at school. A summer-born child, about to turn five: one of the younger members of the class. If life had gone to plan, Beatrice would have been working part time so she could take her daughter to school and pick her up.

But it hadn't worked out that way.

And she couldn't afford to let herself think about what she'd lost. What she'd never have now.

Besides, it wouldn't be the first time she'd picked up a child from school. She'd met all her nephews and her niece from school, on more than one occasion. She could do this.

She hung back in the playground as the children filed out of the class to join their parents or carers, feeling out of place, but finally Iain appeared at the doorway, holding his teacher's hand.

'Bee!' he called, waving his free hand. 'Miss Fisher said you'd be here!'

She was pleased to note that Miss Fisher kept him by her side, rather than letting the little boy run over to her. She went over and showed her ID. 'I'm Beatrice Lindford and I work with Daniel,' she said.

'He told us to expect you, Dr Lindford.' Miss Fisher looked at Iain. 'Are you happy to go home with Dr Lindford?' she checked.

The little boy nodded. 'She's the one I told you about, the one who fixed my arm when I fell over at football. She's nice. I drawed that picture of her.'

'Which has pride of place on the outside of my fridge right now,' Beatrice said. 'Let's go, and you can tell me what your favourite food is so I can make it for tea.'

'Pasta!' Daniel said happily.

'Pasta it shall be,' she said.

It didn't take long to walk back to her place. Iain was

thrilled to see his drawing on her fridge. 'Who drawed the other pictures? Do you have a little boy or girl?'

A little girl. *Born asleep.*

She pushed the wave of misery back. This wasn't something to dump on a small child. 'That one was drawn by my niece, Seffy,' she said, pointing to a picture of a horse.

'Seffy? That's a funny name,' Iain commented.

'It's short for Persephone.'

'Pu-sef...' He stumbled over the name.

'Persephone,' Beatrice said. 'And that's her pony.'

His eyes went wide. 'She has a pony?'

'Because she lives in the country,' Beatrice hastened to add. The last thing she wanted was to cause Daniel problems, if Iain turned out to be as pony-mad as Seffy was. 'And this train was drawn by my nephew George. He's four, just like you.'

'It's a good train,' Iain said politely. 'I like trains.'

'So do I,' Beatrice said. 'And I have a train set. And dinosaurs,' she added, remembering what Daniel had told her. 'Let's get you a glass of milk and some fruit to keep you going until teatime, and then we can play with the trains and the dinosaurs, if you like.'

'Yes!' Iain said. And then he looked horrified. 'Please,' he added.

'Excellent,' Beatrice said with a smile, and busied herself slicing up an apple. While Iain was drinking his milk, she prepared a tomato sauce and left it to simmer on the hob.

She thoroughly enjoyed making a train track with him through a world of dinosaurs, and took a picture of him on her phone to send to Daniel as reassurance that the little boy was settled and not fretting.

Iain loved the pasta and sauce, to her relief. And then she looked at him. 'I haven't got anything for pudding. Shall we make some cake?'

'Chocolate cake?' he asked hopefully. 'Like the ones you made for football?'

'The brownies? We can do that,' she said with a smile. 'You can be chief mixer.'

'Yay!' he said, looking thrilled.

She set him up with a tea towel as a makeshift apron to keep his clothes clean, then helped him weigh out the dry ingredients into a bowl and the wet ingredients into a jug. 'And now you just mix them together with a spoon until it's all gloopy.'

She loved baking with her niece and nephews at Beresford, and she enjoyed her cooking session with Iain just as much.

Fortified with a warm brownie and another glass of milk, Iain cuddled up to her on the sofa and fell asleep while she read him one of George's favourite stories.

She put the book down but didn't move, not wanting to wake him; luckily it was a warm evening so she didn't need to get a blanket for him. Was this what it would have been like with Taylor—curled up together on the sofa on a Friday night, waiting for Oliver to come home from work?

But it was pointless, wishing. Oliver's love for her hadn't survived the loss of the baby, just as her love for him had leaked away. They both had a new life now. Oliver was happy with his new wife—and with their new baby son. And Beatrice was doing just fine.

When her phone pinged, the message was from Daniel.

On way to pick him up. Be with you in ten minutes.

She woke Iain gently. 'Your dad's on his way to pick you up.'

He cuddled into her. 'I had a nice time today. Thank you for looking after me.'

'My pleasure,' she said, and she meant it. Even though having a child around had brought back her old regrets about what might have been, she'd enjoyed his company.

Daniel rang her doorbell ten minutes later.

'He's fine, he's been a total sweetheart, and you really don't have to worry,' she said.

'You got me out of a real hole. Thank you—I really appreciate it,' he said, and handed her a bunch of flowers. 'Sorry they're only supermarket ones, but it was all I could get at this time of night.'

He'd actually taken time out to get these for her? Her heart melted. 'They're lovely, though you really didn't need to,' she said. 'Have you eaten?'

'I'm fine,' he said.

Meaning he hadn't. Was he fudging the issue because he didn't want to impose on her any further, or did he not want to spend any more time here than he had to?

'I've got spare pasta and sauce from earlier,' she said. 'It'll take a couple of minutes in the microwave. Take it with you if you'd rather not eat right now.'

Oh, help.

When she looked at him with those big blue eyes… It would be so easy to say yes. To lose his head.

'We had pasta for tea and it was yummy,' Iain said, running over to him and hugging him.

Take it home, she mouthed out of Iain's eyeline.

Thank you, he mouthed back, and wrapped his arms round his son. 'I need to get you home to bed, young man.'

'We made brownies, Dad. The best chocolate brownies in the world.'

The kind of cake Daniel really didn't like. He hated the cloying sweetness. And if there was oily buttercream in the middle...

'We saved you some,' Iain said.

There was absolutely no way he could get out of this. Not without disappointing his son and making Iain feel pushed away and he'd never do that. So he'd just have to smile and choke it down.

'I'll cut you a small piece,' Beatrice said, as if she guessed what he was thinking. Or, more likely, it was written all over his face but Iain was that bit too young to decipher his expression.

'Thank you,' he said.

But, to Daniel's surprise, the cake wasn't sticky and oversweet and vile. It was light and dense at the same time, chocolatey without being too sugary. 'This is fantastic,' he said.

'Take some more home. I'm not going to be able to eat the rest over the weekend.'

'My granny's coming home tomorrow. Can I take some for her?' Iain asked, adding a belated, 'Please?'

'Sure you can,' she said, and wrapped up several pieces in greaseproof paper. She put the pasta and sauce into a plastic lidded box. 'Put it in the microwave for three minutes on full power, stir, and then give it another minute,' she said to Daniel.

'I... I don't know what to say,' he said.

'I'd do the same for any of my colleagues,' she said, 'as I'm sure you would, too.'

True. Except he still couldn't get himself to think of Beatrice as strictly his colleague. He still remembered what it had felt like to kiss her. How sweet her mouth had been. How good it had felt to walk along the street holding hands with her.

He needed to leave. Now. Before he did or said something stupid.

'Thank you for having me,' Iain said, and hugged her.

'My pleasure. I enjoyed having you here to play trains with me,' Beatrice said.

'Next time, can George come, too?' Iain asked.

George? She had a son?

Daniel shook himself mentally. Of course she didn't. She'd told him about her nephew. The one who had a less unusual name.

Before he could correct Iain and explain that it was rude to invite yourself to someone's house, Beatrice said, 'I'll see what I can do.'

Iain hugged her again.

'Let's get your things,' she said, and helped him on with his shoes.

Seeing her with him like that made Daniel ache; it made him realise how much Jenny's postnatal depression had taken away from all of them. And it brought out his own doubts: was he enough for Iain? Should he be trying to find someone who would be a mum to Iain when he wasn't at Jenny's? Daniel had vowed he wouldn't get involved with anyone again, but was he being selfish? Surely he should put his son's needs first?

'I'll see you at work on Monday,' Beatrice said with a smile, as if completely oblivious to what was whirling round in his head. Or maybe she was too kind to broach the subject.

'Yes. Thanks again for having Iain.'

'Any time.'

Was she just being polite or did she mean it? He had no idea.

Iain, now he was awake, chattered about how wonderful Beatrice was—all the way home, all the way through two bedtime stories, and he would have kept going all night if Daniel hadn't said to him, 'It's time to sleep or you'll be too tired to go to the park tomorrow.'

'Football?' Iain asked hopefully.

'Football,' Daniel promised.

When he finally sat down, Daniel was almost too tired to eat. He was grateful for the fact that Beatrice had saved him some pasta. And the sauce was definitely home-made rather than just heated through from a jar.

Beatrice Lindford was a puzzle.

She'd been adamant that she wasn't looking for a relationship and she was concentrating on her career. And yet the way she'd been with Iain—picking him up from school without a fuss, cooking him his favourite dinner, playing with him and reading with him—those were the actions of a woman who was used to being part of a family. OK, so she'd hinted that she was close to her brothers and their children; but what had happened to Beatrice to make her so determined not to date and have a family of her own?

Asking her felt too intrusive, especially when she'd just done him such a huge favour. It was none of his business. Besides, they were supposed to be keeping their distance from each other, not getting closer. He needed to back off.

* * *

The next morning, Iain was still talking about Beatrice.

He didn't change the topic of conversation when his grandmother came home, either. 'Granny, Granny, me and Bee maked you some cake!'

'Bee?' Susan looked mystified.

'You know, Princess Bee, who fixed my arm when I fell over.'

'Why were you making cake with her?'

'Diane couldn't pick me up from school and Dad was working, so Bee gave me my tea and played trains with me. And we maked cake.'

Susan gave Daniel a look that meant they were going to have a talk, later. One that was going to make him squirm.

'They're chocolate brownies. Dad liked them. I brought some home for you.'

'Let's give Granny her cake,' Daniel said, hoping that it might distract his mother but knowing that it probably wouldn't.

'You're right, this is excellent chocolate cake,' Susan said after her first taste. 'I hope you remembered to say thank you to Bea, Daniel.'

'I did. And Dad gave her flowers.'

Daniel had hoped that Iain had been too tired or too excited to notice. But not only did Iain have eyes like a hawk, he was intent on telling every detail to everyone who would listen.

'Flowers? That's nice.' Susan gave him an arch look. 'But, Iain, if someone invites us for dinner, we have to be polite and invite them back for dinner.'

Oh, no. Daniel could see exactly where this was

going. 'Mum, she works in my department and she's my senior. She won't have time.'

'You don't know unless you ask her.'

Which wasn't the worst thing she could have said, in Daniel's view. He knew that Iain wouldn't budge from the subject until he gave in; which meant Bea would be put on the spot. Unless Daniel texted her to warn her, and suggested that she tell Iain she was working…

Before he had the chance—and no doubt his mother had already guessed what he was thinking and was pre-empting him—Susan said, 'I think you should ask her to tea, Iain. Tomorrow. Her number's in your dad's phone, isn't it?'

Iain squeaked with excitement and grabbed Daniel's phone.

'She might be w—' Daniel began.

But Iain was too excited by the idea to listen and thrust the phone at him. 'Call her now, Dad, and I'll ask her.'

What could Daniel do, other than hope that her phone went through to voicemail? He unlocked his phone, set up the call, and handed the phone to Iain.

'Hello, Bea. Will you come to tea tomorrow?'

Say no, Daniel thought. Say no.

'Yes, it's Iain. How did you know? Your phone told you it was my dad? Oh. Will you come to tea?'

Iain paused, clearly waiting for an answer, then frowned. 'I don't know. What time, Granny?'

'Six,' Susan said.

'Six,' Iain repeated.

'Ask her if she likes Scottish roast beef,' Susan prompted.

'Granny says, do you like Scottish roast beef?' Iain

asked. Then he smiled. 'She does, Granny. And she says she'll bring some apple crumble to go with it.'

'Tell her thank you,' Susan said.

'Thank you,' Iain said. 'See you tomorrow.'

'I think you need to go and tidy your toys,' Susan said when Iain handed the phone back to Daniel.

'I will, Granny,' Iain said, and rushed off.

'Don't go getting any ideas, Mum,' Daniel warned. 'Beatrice is my colleague, as good as my boss. I was in a jam and she helped me out—just as she would have helped out anyone else in the department.'

'Hmm,' Susan said.

'We're *colleagues*,' Daniel insisted.

Beatrice texted him half an hour later.

Just checking. Is tomorrow OK or would you rather I make an excuse?

He could have kissed her. The perfect let-out. She could make an excuse…

But then Iain would be so disappointed. And also, if his mother met Beatrice and saw for herself that they really were just colleagues, then maybe she could help persuade Iain to back off a little bit.

It's fine. See you tomorrow, he texted back. Better give you the address.

Iain was almost beyond excited, the next day, when Beatrice arrived, and greeted her with a squeal and a hug.

'It's lovely to meet you, Bea. I'm Susan, Daniel's mother,' Susan said.

'Thank you for asking me over. It's kind of you to

cook for me, especially as I'm sure you must be tired after your course,' Beatrice said.

'Daniel told you about me?'

'Not much. Just that you were an artist. Y chromosomes,' Beatrice added in a stage whisper, and Susan laughed and patted her arm.

Uh-oh. That looked as if two people from his immediate family had bonded with her almost instantly, Daniel thought.

'Come and sit down,' Susan said, ushering her to the kitchen.

Daniel gave in to the inevitable and followed them. 'I'll make some coffee,' he said.

'I hope you like apple crumble, Iain,' Beatrice said. 'I made this with our own apples.' She put the dish on the table.

'Our?' Susan asked. 'You have an orchard?'

'My parents do. I went to see my family yesterday,' she explained, 'and I raided the stores.'

'Bee's family lives in the country and her niece has got a pony,' Iain informed them.

Daniel could see the intrigued expression in his mother's eyes and headed her off by talking about her course.

'So what sort of thing do you paint, Susan?' Beatrice asked.

'Granny's done loads of paintings. Come and see,' Iain said, and tugged at Beatrice's hand. 'Granny lets me paint with her, sometimes.'

'Don't grill her,' Daniel begged his mother softly when Beatrice left the kitchen.

'As if I would,' Susan said, with an arch look.

Yeah. He was in trouble.

Beatrice duly admired the paintings, and then it was time for dinner.

'This is fabulous. Thank you so much for inviting me,' Beatrice said.

'You can come every Sunday,' Iain said. 'Oh, but not next week because I'm at my mum's.'

'That's kind of you, but it would be greedy of me to eat here every Sunday,' Beatrice said.

'We can take turns. So we can come to you, next time,' Iain answered, his eyes sparkling.

How had this happened? Daniel wondered. Iain hardly knew Beatrice. Shouldn't he be shy and hardly saying a word, instead of chattering away as if he'd known her for ever? This was just what he wanted to avoid: his son getting close to someone who probably wasn't going to stick around.

As if it was written all over his face, and Beatrice had noticed, she said gently, 'That would be nice, because we're friends, your dad and me. Just like he's friends with Josh and Sam and Hayley at the hospital, because we all work together.'

'Oh,' Iain said, but he seemed to accept it.

But, as Beatrice talked to Susan about art and Iain about school, she sparkled, and Daniel found himself spellbound by her.

'The crumble's excellent,' Susan said. 'So were your brownies—thank you for sending me one via Iain. So your parents have a café as well as an orchard?'

'Sort of,' Beatrice said.

He already knew that her family was posh. He had a feeling there was more to it than a café, and he could she was sidestepping the issue.

'My parents had a café in Glasgow,' Susan said. 'An

ice cream café. My great-grandparents came to Glasgow from Italy, between the wars, and started the business. My grandparents and then my parents took over.'

'So you have a brother or sister who runs it now?'

'Cousin,' Susan said. 'I'm an only one—like Daniel. But I always wanted to do art. And there's Daniel with medicine. And who knows what Iain will do?'

'I'm going to be a footballer, Granny,' Iain said, rolling his eyes. 'And I'll play for Scotland *and* England. And then I'm going to be an astronaut and go to the moon in a rocket.'

She ruffled his hair. 'You can do anything you put your mind to. I know you have a niece with a pony, Bea, so you're not an only child.'

'I'm the youngest of three,' Beatrice said.

'And your siblings, they're involved in the café?'

Susan steadfastly refused to meet Daniel's gaze, so she completely ignored his mouthed, '*Stop grilling her.*'

'They're involved in the family business,' Beatrice said with a smile. 'We just get the odd scientist in a generation—I'm the one in ours. I take after our great-great-uncle. I was tiny when he died, and I always wish I'd had a chance to get to know him because he's the one who built the telescope in the cupola.'

Iain's eyes went wide. 'You've got a telescope?'

'At my parents'.' She nodded. 'I used to spend hours watching the stars. If I hadn't been a doctor, I might've been an astronaut.'

'That's what *I* want to be, after I've been a footballer,' he said. 'Can I show you my rocket Granny painted on my wall?'

'Later,' Daniel said.

'Can I come and see your telescope?' Iain asked.

'I'll see what I can do,' Beatrice told him.

'A telescope in a cupola,' Susan said thoughtfully.

Yes. Daniel had picked that up, too. An architectural feature that, on a family home, marked that family out as more than just ordinarily posh. He had a nasty feeling that his son's original assessment of Beatrice Lindford might be right.

'What's a cupola?' Iain asked.

'It's a dome on a roof,' Beatrice said.

'Like the big one on St Paul's, the place where we whispered to each other from opposite sides and could hear each other?' Daniel said.

'Do your parents live in a church?' Iain asked.

Beatrice smiled. 'No, sweetheart, they don't.'

'Well, it must be a really big house if it's got a dome,' Iain said. 'Is it a castle? Because you talk like a princess and you've got long golden hair like the princess in the story.'

Beatrice blew out a breath. 'Yes, it's a castle, but I'm not a princess.'

Her family lived in a castle. So the chances were she had a title of some sort. Which put her even more out of his reach, Daniel thought. So much for the orchard and a café: they were clearly part of an estate. A café that perhaps meant her family home was a stately home open to the public?

'Do you know the Queen? And Prince Harry?'

'No.'

Iain looked disappointed. 'My mum likes Prince Harry.'

'Everyone likes Prince Harry,' Beatrice said with a smile. 'Now, once we've had our tea and I've done my share of the washing up, can we play with your train set?'

'Yay!' Iain said.

Daniel was still trying to process it when he helped them build the train track. She was a senior doctor. A woman who had a title. And yet here she was, playing trains on the floor with his son, looking as if she belonged. She'd made friends with his mother almost immediately. She'd wielded a dishcloth in his kitchen.

He and Beatrice were worlds apart. They couldn't possibly have a future.

Or could they?

After Beatrice had left and he'd put Iain to bed, Susan made them both a cup of tea.

'I like her,' she said. 'A lot.'

'Don't get ideas, Mum. We've been through this already. We're colleagues. You heard her say it yourself.'

'You don't look at each other like colleagues.'

'Our backgrounds are too diff—' He stopped and grimaced. 'That came out wrong. I wasn't having a pop at you, Mum.'

'I know. And you have a point. Her family home is a castle. She might not be a princess, but she can probably trace her ancestors all the way back to William the Conqueror—whereas you don't even have your father's name on your birth certificate and you come from working-class stock. But that doesn't matter. I'm proud to be a Capaldi.'

'So am I, Mum.'

'And if that sort of thing does matter to her, then she doesn't deserve you. Though I don't think that sort of thing matters to her.'

'We're not dating, Mum,' he reminded her.

'Maybe you should. Jenny found happiness again. There's no reason why you can't, too.'

Panic flooded through him. But what if it went wrong? 'There's Iain. He's had enough disruption in his life. I'm not prepared to let anyone into his world, only for them to leave him high and dry.'

'Iain adores Bea. And I like her, too. She might be from a posh family, but she's down to earth. She'll get on the floor and play trains with Iain, she'll do baking with him and not mind about the mess, and she's not a haughty mare who won't even pick up a dishcloth— I think you're troubling trouble before it troubles you, and that's never a good thing.' She folded her arms. 'You like her.'

He sighed. 'Yes, I like her.'

'Then do something about it. If you want to protect Iain—not that I think he needs protecting from Bea— then I'll babysit and we don't need to tell Iain where you're going. See how things go.'

Daniel shook his head. 'It's not as easy as that. She doesn't want to get involved either. She's focusing on her career.'

'The way I've seen her with Iain today, she's all about family. I think someone's hurt her—as badly as you got hurt with Jenny.' She put both hands up in a stop gesture. 'I'm not blaming Jenny for anything. I know she was ill. But both of you came out of that marriage with scars. All credit to the pair of you that you never let Iain be aware of them.'

'Yeah.' Daniel sighed. 'I think Beatrice and I will just be colleagues. Maybe friends.'

'Hmm,' Susan said.

'Really, Mum. I can't take that risk. For Iain's sake.'

'I think,' Susan said, 'you're scared and you're hiding behind your son.'

He couldn't argue with her, because he knew she was right. 'I'm not ready,' he said.

She reached over and squeezed his hand. 'I don't think she'll hurt you. There's something about her. An inner strength.'

'Maybe.' But he was pretty sure that Beatrice had been hurt, too. And he hadn't been a good enough support to Jenny. He'd let her down. What was to say he wouldn't let Beatrice down, too, if things went wrong?

CHAPTER SIX

'I'M SORRY ABOUT the grilling,' Daniel said when he saw Beatrice in the staff kitchen the next morning.

'No problem.' She smiled at him. 'I liked your mum.'

'Thanks. She liked you, too.'

The fact that both Daniel's son and Daniel's mum liked her was a really positive thing; but she couldn't let herself think that this thing between her and Daniel could have a future. He, Jenny and Iain had had a rough time with Jenny's postnatal depression; Daniel didn't need to risk a repeat of all that with another woman who'd suffered badly with depression. So she needed to get her head back in the right place and not let herself dream of what might have been. It wasn't going to happen. The only thing they could offer each other was friendship—and that would have to be enough.

'Iain hasn't stopped talking about your telescope.'

'I'll sort something out so he can come and see it.' Which was being kind to a small child; it had nothing to do with arranging to spend more time with Daniel.

'Won't your family…?' He looked awkward.

'Mind? No. It's fine. Anyway, I guess we need to get on. Patients to see,' she said brightly.

She knew she was being a coward and avoiding him.

But she managed to get herself back under enough control during the morning so that for the rest of the week she treated him exactly the same way she treated Josh and Sam and the rest of the team. As a colleague who was becoming a friend, now she'd settled in to her new job. Repeating silently to herself that he was her colleague and nothing but her colleague seemed to be working.

Until Thursday afternoon, when they were both rostered to Resus and she answered a call from the paramedics.

'Hello, Resus. Beatrice speaking.'

'Beatrice, it's Dev Kapoor. We're at an RTC.'

Road traffic collision. That covered a whole range of cases; but, given that he was calling in, it clearly was a more serious one. 'OK. What have you got for us?'

'A guy who may or may not have whiplash and a bump to the head. We're getting another crew out to him, because I'm less worried about him than the other patient: a pregnant woman who's bruised and panicking.'

Beatrice went still. She'd been here before. Nearly five years ago. Except she'd been the one needing the ambulance, not the one on the team treating the patient. With an effort, she got herself back under control and managed to keep her voice steady as she asked, 'How far along is her pregnancy?'

'Twenty-eight weeks,' Dev said.

Oh, God. Twenty-eight weeks. The same as her own had been. But she couldn't afford to think about that now. She needed to compartmentalise it and put her patient's needs first. 'Have you examined her?'

'Yes. Her uterus is woody, and I can't feel the baby.

I'm thinking possible abruption. I've put a line in and put her on oxygen.'

'Good call. I'll talk to the maternity unit and get them on standby. Thanks, Dev. See you when you get here.'

'ETA about ten minutes,' he said.

Everything he'd described sounded like the classic symptoms of placental abruption. A tear in the placenta that pulled it away from the uterine wall. Such a little, little thing.

And it had ripped her life apart.

She took a deep breath. Not now. She needed to get the right specialist support. Support that would hopefully mean this poor woman wouldn't have to go through the same nightmare that Beatrice had struggled through, nearly five years ago.

She called up to the maternity unit. 'Hi, it's Beatrice Lindford from the Emergency Department. Are any of the consultants available? I've got a mum coming in with a suspected abruption.'

'I think I saw Alex Morgan go past a few seconds ago—hang on and I'll try and find him for you,' the midwife who'd answered the phone said.

It felt like for ever, but finally the phone was picked up again.

'Alex Morgan speaking. How can I help?'

'Alex, it's Beatrice from the Emergency Department. I've got a mum coming in with a suspected abruption. She's twenty-eight weeks. Her uterus is woody and the paramedics can't feel the baby. They're bringing her in now; she'll be here in the next ten minutes. I don't know how big the abruption is—whether we'll need to just admit her for monitoring, or whether we'll need to deliver the baby early and get the neonatal special care team involved.'

'I'll call the neonatal team and get them on standby, and I'll come down,' Alex said.

'Thanks. I appreciate it.' She turned to Daniel and filled him in on the situation.

'I'll get the portable scanner,' Daniel said.

'And a Doppler, please,' Beatrice added.

A few minutes later, Dev came in with their patient on a trolley. 'Jessica Rutherford, aged thirty,' he said, and talked them both through the treatment he'd given Jessica on the way.

Jessica was white-faced and clearly panicking.

Beatrice knew how that felt, but strove to push it behind her. Jessica needed help, and her own emotions just weren't necessary right now. The Lindfords had always managed to keep a stiff upper lip; she was going to follow the family line rather than following her counsellor's advice to talk it through. There was a time and a place.

'Hello, Jessica. I'm Beatrice Lindford and this is Daniel Capaldi, and we're going to be looking after you this afternoon. I've got someone from the maternity team coming down to see you, too. Can you tell us what happened?' she asked.

Jessica took the oxygen mask off so she could talk. 'There was a guy on a motorcycle driving behind me, weaving from side to side and getting a bit too close to me.' Her voice was shaking. 'When he finally overtook me, he was still weaving from side to side—I don't think he was drunk, more like he was young and showing off. I kept my distance, because I had a funny feeling about it, but then he tried to overtake the car in front, misjudged it and had to brake suddenly. I managed to brake and stop before I hit him, but the car behind me didn't stop in time.'

Beatrice knew what that felt like, the shock of a car crashing into you when you were stationary. Again, she pushed the thought away. Not now. 'I'm sorry you've been through something so scary. Can you tell us how you're feeling, Jessica—any pain anywhere, anything that doesn't feel quite right?'

'My back hurts, but I don't care about that. It's the baby,' Jessica said, the pitch of her voice rising with anxiety. 'I haven't felt him move properly but I don't know if it's because I'm panicking because the guy in the ambulance said he couldn't feel it, or if, if...' She choked on the words.

If her baby hadn't made it.

Beatrice squeezed her hand. 'You're here and we're going to help. Anything else?'

'My bump. It feels tender, like—like a bruise, I guess.'

Beatrice could also see tell-tale bleeding on Jessica's jeans: another likely symptom of an abruption. Jessica didn't appear to be going into shock, so hopefully it was a small abruption rather than a very serious one. Especially as Alex still hadn't arrived from the maternity department. Something had clearly held him up; she really hoped he'd manage to deal with it and get here in the next couple of minutes, or send someone else in his place. 'Daniel, can you get someone to chase Alex up?' she asked.

'Sure,' he said.

'Jessica, I'd like to examine your bump and give you a scan to see what's going on with the baby, if that's all right?'

Jessica's brown eyes were wide with worry. 'Is my baby going to be OK? The paramedics couldn't feel him and he's not moving.'

'You're in pain and your uterus will feel hard in this sort of situation, so it's difficult for them to feel the baby, and as you said you're worried sick so you're thinking the worst,' Beatrice reassured her. 'Let me put the Doppler on—it's a machine that uses sound to pick up your baby's heartbeat and it doesn't hurt. Would you mind pushing your top up for me and pushing the top of your jeans down so I can check the baby's heartbeat? And then I'd like you to put the oxygen mask back on for me.'

Jessica did as she asked, and Beatrice checked for the heartbeat. *Please let it be there. Please don't let this be like what happened to me.*

She only realised that she was holding her breath when they heard a nice, steady clop-clop: the baby's heartbeat.

'That's sounding good—a nice, steady heartbeat,' she said, smiling at Jessica. 'Did the paramedics call anyone for you?'

Jessica pulled her oxygen mask to one side again. 'Yes. My husband's coming in.'

'Good. I can see there's some blood on your jeans,' Beatrice said, 'but that could be for several reasons, so don't assume the worst. I'm going to do a scan first, and then we'll be able to see if we need to do an internal exam. The scan is identical to the one you had for your dating scan and your twenty-week scan, so you know what to expect. I'm afraid our gel tends to be a bit cold because we don't have all those huge scanners in the room to warm everything up, but it's not going to hurt. If anything does hurt, I want you to tell me straight away, OK?'

'OK,' Jessica said, still looking worried, but the high-pitched edge of panic in her voice had gone.

Daniel came back over. 'Alex has been held up, but someone from the unit will be with us as soon as they can.'

'Thanks,' she said. 'Can you do the gel for me?'

Daniel nodded and squeezed gel onto Jessica's stomach.

Beatrice swept the head of the transponder over Jessica's abdomen; on the screen, she could see the baby clearly and also signs of the abruption. Right at this point, she didn't think the tear was bad enough to warrant an emergency Caesarean section, but she definitely wanted to keep Jessica in overnight for observation in case the situation changed.

She took Jessica's hand. 'OK. I can see everything clearly and I can see what's happened. The baby's looking OK. The reason why your tummy feels as if it's bruised is because there's a little tear in your placenta and part of it has come away from your womb. It's called a placental abruption.'

Jessica looked too shocked and scared to say anything.

'It sounds a lot scarier than it is,' Beatrice said. 'It's actually quite common; around one in a hundred women have a tear in their placenta.'

'Sometimes it happens after an accident, like the one you just had, and sometimes it just happens and nobody knows why,' Daniel added.

'The good news is that I don't think we need to rush you into Theatre and give you a Caesarean section,' Beatrice reassured her, 'but I do want to admit you to the ward so they can keep an eye on you and the baby, in case the situation changes overnight.'

'And then they'll have to rush me into Theatre and give me a Caesarean?' Jessica dragged in a breath. 'But I'm only twenty-eight weeks. It's too soon for the baby to born. He can't possibly survive.'

'Twenty-eight weeks is early, yes,' Daniel said, 'but if we do have to deliver the baby then he's got a good chance of survival. Neonatal intensive care is really good nowadays.'

Beatrice thought of Taylor, and it was as if someone had punched her hard and taken her breath away. But this situation was different. Taylor hadn't been breathing at all and had no heartbeat; she hadn't stood a chance. This baby had a strong heartbeat and he was fighting.

'Is there something you're not telling me?' Jessica asked, her voice shrill with fear.

'No, not at all,' Beatrice said.

'But, just then, the look on your face...'

Memories. Jessica really didn't need to hear that particular horror story. She needed reassurance. Beatrice squeezed her hand. 'I promise you, there's nothing I'm not telling you. Let me show you so you can see for yourself and relax a bit.' She turned the monitor round so Jessica could see it and swept the scanner head over her abdomen again. 'See? One beating heart, four waving limbs, one baby who's holding his own very nicely right now and is completely oblivious as to how worried his mum is.'

A tear trickled down Jessica's face. 'Thank you,' she whispered. 'I was just so scared that—' her breath hitched '—that the baby would die.'

Beatrice had been there. Except in her case her baby *had* died. 'I know,' she said gently. 'Everything's going to be OK. It's easy for me to say, but try not to worry. We'll keep a really close eye on you both.'

And then, thankfully, Alex came rushing in, full of apologies. Once she'd introduced him to Jessica and filled Alex in on their findings, Alex took over Jessica's care, and Beatrice was able to concentrate on clearing up and checking everything was stocked ready for the next emergency, and doing the routine tasks helped her push the old memories back into place.

Something was wrong, Daniel thought. He'd seen that look on Beatrice's face, when he'd said that twenty-eight weeks was early but the baby had a good chance of survival. Misery and pain and worry had blurred together. It had been brief, but long enough for their patient to notice, too, and panic that Beatrice was trying to work out how to tell her some bad news.

Right now Beatrice was all brisk and smiling and sorting everything out. But he couldn't shake the feeling that something was wrong. She was a little bit too bright, as if by forcing herself to smile she could lift her mood.

He'd been there himself, when Jenny's postnatal depression had been at its worst. Trying to keep everything together, being bright and brisk and smiling.

The one thing that had helped was talking. And maybe he could do that for Beatrice. Listen to her, as she'd listened to him when he'd explained about Jenny. Dating her, much as he wanted to, wasn't an option— but he could be her friend.

Before they saw their next patient, he called his mother. 'Mum, can you do me a massive favour and pick Iain up from Diane's today?' Thankfully Diane's mother was on the mend from a mini-stroke, so Diane was back in her usual routine of picking Iain up after school.

'Yes, of course,' Susan said. 'Is everything all right?'

'Just busy,' he fibbed, not wanting to share his suspicions about Beatrice even with his mother.

'Leave it to me, love. I'll take him back to yours and give him his tea.'

'Thanks, Mum. I owe you.'

'That's what I'm here for. To support you,' Susan reminded him. 'I didn't do it when you were young, so it's payback.'

'That's all in the past and you've done way more than your fair share, these past five years,' Daniel said. 'And I hope you know you're the best mum and gran in the world.'

'Och, away with you,' Susan said, but the thickening of her accent told Daniel she was pleased.

He caught Beatrice at the end of her shift. 'You and I,' he said, 'are going for a cup of tea.'

She blinked. 'Are we? Why?'

'Resus, this afternoon.'

She spread her hands. 'What about it?'

He recognised the brittleness in her eyes. He'd seen it in Jenny's. 'When our patient said there was something you weren't telling her, I saw it in your face, too.'

Just as he could see the moment of horror in her face now, quickly masked.

'We're friends, Bea,' he said gently.

'Friends,' she echoed.

'I think you need someone to listen to you.'

She shook her head. 'I'm absolutely fine.'

'I've been there,' he said, 'so I don't think you are.'
When she said nothing, he added softly, 'Whatever you
say to me isn't going to be passed on to anyone else.'

'I...' Her eyes filled with tears, and she blinked them
away and wrapped her arms round herself.

'Tea,' he said. 'Not in the hospital canteen. Mum's
picking Iain up from Diane, so I have all the time in
the world.'

'Let's go to my place,' she said, and there was the ti-
niest wobble in her voice.

'OK.' He didn't push her to talk on the way, guessing
that she needed to get her head together. She let them in,
and he followed her into the kitchen.

All the colour had leached from her face, and she
looked bereft. 'Sit down,' he said, gesturing to the table
in her kitchen. 'Tell me where you keep your tea and
I'll make it.'

'The teabags are in the cupboard above the kettle,'
she said.

He filled the kettle with water and switched it on,
then opened a couple of cupboard doors and retrieved
two mugs. Somehow it didn't surprise him that her tea
was a fine and delicate Earl Grey. Well, she didn't need
fine and delicate right now. She needed strong tea with
sugar—even though he knew she usually didn't take
sugar. He busied himself making two mugs of tea, added
milk to both and sugar to hers.

'Here go you.' He put one of the mugs in front of her,
and pulled out the chair opposite hers.

'Thank you.' She took a sip and grimaced. 'Sugar.'

'Simply because you need it right now.'

She didn't protest again, just took another sip and
stared into the mug, as if bracing herself. Then she took

a deep breath. 'What you told me about Jenny—I've kind of been there.'

Postnatal depression? But as far as he knew she didn't have children.

Kind of. Perhaps not PND, then.

He said nothing, just reached across the table and took her hand. No pressure, no demands: just letting her know that he was here. He didn't push her to talk; from working with his patients, he knew that sometimes you needed space and time until you felt comfortable enough to talk.

And eventually the words came out.

'It was our patient, this afternoon. The one with the abruption.'

He guessed then that it had brought back memories for her. A past patient, or someone close to her?

'That happened to me, nearly five years ago,' she whispered.

An abruption? He went cold as he realised what she was about to tell him. His own personal nightmare was if anything should ever happen to Iain, and no doubt it had been the same for her.

'What happened?' he asked softly, still holding her hand.

'I was in a queue of stationary traffic. I'd had an antenatal appointment that morning and I was driving over to my parents' for lunch.' She blew out a breath. 'It was just an ordinary day. The sun was shining and I was singing along to the radio.'

Just an ordinary day. One, he guessed, that had turned into a nightmare.

'The couple in the car behind me were having a fight.

They didn't notice that the traffic had stopped, they crashed into me and pushed my car into the one in front.'

A concertina crash.

The way she was talking about it, it was if she'd detached herself from the situation and was describing it happening to someone else. An impersonal statement of facts. Because sometimes things went so deep, hurt so much, that it was the only way you could deal with them, he thought.

'The airbag didn't go off because I was stationary.' She shrugged. 'Oliver asked about it, but apparently if an airbag goes off when the car isn't moving it can cause more problems than it solves.'

He knew neither of her brothers was called Oliver; presumably Oliver had been her partner, and because she'd told him she was single it was a pretty fair chance the relationship hadn't survived the fallout from the accident.

'I don't remember the steering wheel hitting my abdomen. I think I blacked out for a minute or so. But I knew immediately that something was wrong. I had pain in my back, my abdomen was tender and felt as if I was having contractions. You shouldn't feel even Braxton-Hicks at twenty-eight weeks, let alone real ones.'

Twenty-eight weeks. The same as their patient today. It had taken an incredible amount of courage for Beatrice to deal with the case.

'The ambulance came and the paramedics took me in, but I knew even before I got to the Emergency Department that it was all wrong. It felt wet and sticky between my thighs and I knew it was blood. And I couldn't feel the baby kicking.'

Again, the same as their patient today.

'I was trying not to panic—I knew if the crash had caused an abruption and my uterus was woody, I wouldn't feel any movement, but there'd still be a chance that the baby would make it. A tiny one. That I'd be whipped in for an emergency section and the baby would be in intensive care for weeks, but she'd make it.' She swallowed hard. 'But the doctors couldn't find the baby's heartbeat with the Doppler. They gave me a scan and that's when they said I'd had a severe placental abruption and the baby hadn't survived.'

'I'm so sorry,' he said. 'That's such a hard thing to go through.'

She gave him a grim smile. 'That was the start of it. They had to induce me. I gave birth to a stillborn girl, Taylor.'

He really didn't know what to say, so he just held her hand and let her speak.

'I didn't cope very well. I didn't want to go to work and face everyone's pity, and I really didn't want to be in our house and see the nursery we'd put together for Taylor—even though Oliver's sister was really kind and packed up the nursery for us so we wouldn't have to do it. I went to stay with my parents, because I still couldn't face the house. I knew they wouldn't push me to talk about it, because my family's really not good with talking. They always have a stiff upper lip and pretend everything's fine—even my sisters-in-law are the same.' She lifted one shoulder in a shrug.

'When I saw my doctor, I said everything was fine. But it wasn't. It was like a black hole sucking me in. Nothing felt right and I was totally disconnected from everyone. I suppose the only place I coped was work, because I was too busy to think about what had happened to me. That, and the gym, where I pushed myself harder and harder, doing the kind of training where you count repetitions so you don't have any space in your head to think of anything else. I didn't want to think. I didn't want to remember.'

No wonder she'd understood about Jenny, Daniel thought. She'd been through something very similar herself.

'I kept my lunchbreaks short and I avoided seeing my friends. I avoided Oliver, too. I just didn't want to be with anyone. I got through the days, but that was about all.' She blew out a breath. 'My sister-in-law was due to have George, the same week as Taylor was due. It was so hard to walk into the hospital where I'd lost my baby and visit her, the day George arrived. I couldn't look at Oliver. I felt as if I was drowning, but I couldn't say anything because I didn't want to make them feel bad.'

'Didn't they guess how you were feeling?'

'Probably. But, as I said, my family always pretends everything's just fine and keeps a stiff upper lip. So we never discussed it. And I held that baby and I smiled and said how gorgeous he was, even while my heart was being shredded.' She looked away. 'I love George. But every time I see him, a little bit of me wonders what Taylor would've been doing now.'

Nearly five years ago. A child who would've been four years old. Late summer-born, just like Iain. Was it the same when she saw his son? Daniel wondered. Did she see Iain and think of her lost little girl? She'd been kind and helped him out last week when he'd desperately needed a babysitter. How much had that hurt her? How much had that cost her in unshed tears and pain?

He wanted to hold her and tell her everything was

going to be all right, except he knew it wasn't. How did you even begin to come to terms with a loss like that?

'About a month later, I'd got some leave and I was spending it at the castle. And in the middle of that week I just woke up and realised I didn't want to be here any more. I didn't want to be anywhere.' And this time she met his eyes. 'So I took an overdose. Vicky found me—she'd knocked on my door, planning to ask me to go and help feed the ducks with Henry, and when I didn't answer she had a funny feeling and opened my door and saw me lying there with the empty packet of paracetamol beside me.'

An overdose of paracetamol. She'd had to deal with a patient who'd done that, too, very recently. He remembered how the girl's mother had been raging at her selfishness and Beatrice had stuck up for her and explained it was an illness, not done on purpose.

'She called the emergency services, and they patched me up—thankfully not in my own emergency department, because I think that would've been so much worse, facing everyone's pity.' She grimaced. 'When I went back to work, everyone was sympathetic and kind. It just made me feel worse. And then my boss called me into her office. She'd called in a favour from a friend and got me some counselling sessions—and she made me go to them. She took me to the sessions herself; she never asked me anything and never judged me. She just greeted me with a hug when I came out, and took me for coffee and a sandwich, to make sure I ate something healthy.'

'That's really nice,' Daniel said. And it sounded like something Beatrice herself would do, paying it forward.

'The counsellor did a lot for me. She taught me how

to talk—something I couldn't do before, and I'm probably talking too much now.'

'You're doing just fine,' he said.

'And she taught me a good grounding exercise.'

'Would it help you to do that now?' he asked.

She nodded. 'You name five things you can see, four things you can hear, three things you can touch, two things you can smell or like the smell of, and take one slow, deep breath. I sometimes do that with my patients if I think it'll help.'

He'd remember that one. 'OK,' he said. 'Tell me five things you can see.'

'The picture Iain drew me from the park. My kitchen table. Two mugs of coffee. The kettle.' She paused and looked him straight in the eye. 'You.'

For a second, he couldn't quite breathe. All he was aware of was Beatrice. 'Four things you can hear,' he prompted, hoping that she wouldn't hear the slight creak in his voice—or, if she did, that she hadn't guessed what had caused it. Now was really *not* the time to have inappropriate thought about her.

'A dog barking. A guitar being played. Waves swishing against a beach. A fairground ride.'

'Three things you can touch.'

'And you touch them. The table. My mug of coffee.' She looked down at their joined hands. 'Your hand.'

Did he let her hand go? Or did he keep holding her hand? He had no idea. All he could do was be guided by Beatrice's actions, and she didn't pull away, so he left his fingers linked with hers.

'Two things you can smell.'

'Coffee,' she said. 'And stocks.'

'Stocks?'

She gestured towards the kitchen windowsill with her free hand. 'My big vice. I love fresh flowers. Especially ones that smell as gorgeous as those stocks.'

A sweet yet spicy fragrance. He could understand why she liked it so much.

'And one deep, slow breath.'

She marked off the seconds with her fingers as she took a slow, deep breath in and out. 'Thank you.'

'It helped?'

'It helped,' she confirmed. 'And thank you for listening.'

'What you've said goes no further than me,' he said. 'And I'm sorry you went through such a terrible experience. Which isn't me pitying you—it's empathy.'

'Because you were in Oliver's shoes. You've been there from the other side. Nothing you can do makes it better, and you feel so helpless and useless. And the wall goes up between you, and you can't talk about it, and all the love just leaks away.'

His fingers tightened around hers. 'And you hate yourself for it, but you can't stop it happening.'

'Are you friends with Jenny now?'

He nodded. 'And I never, ever say anything negative about her in front of Iain. She was good enough to let me have custody. She's remarried and she's happy.'

'Same with Oliver. Well, obviously without the custody issues. But he's remarried and they have a son. I see them occasionally at events.'

Posh events, he guessed, where you smiled and smiled and pretended everything was just fine, no matter how you were feeling.

'It's probably inappropriate,' he said, 'but what helps

me most is a hug. Usually Iain, sometimes my mum. Would a hug help you now?'

Her eyes filled with tears, and she blinked them away. 'You're a kind man.'

'I'm not pitying you,' he said.

She loosened her hand from his hold and stood up. 'A hug would be great.'

He walked round to her side of the table and wrapped his arms round her. She wrapped her arms round him and they stood there together, just holding each other.

She'd been through hell and back. He could understand why she didn't want to get involved with anyone and wanted to concentrate on her career. To lose your child in such an awful way, to lose your marriage... It would be hard to get past the fear that it wouldn't happen all over again. Yes, he and Jenny had had a rough time and their marriage hadn't survived, but they still had Iain and they'd managed to get to the point where they were friends and he was genuinely pleased to see her. For Beatrice, it must be so much harder, seeing her ex with the child they should've had.

He had no idea how long they stood there, just taking comfort from each other's closeness. He dropped a kiss against her hair, wanting to make her feel better. The next thing he knew, they were looking at each other. Her pupils were huge, so her blue eyes looked almost black. Wide and full of longing.

A longing that pulled at him, too.

A shared longing that temporarily took away his sanity, because then he dipped his head and brushed his mouth against hers. Once. Twice. Every nerve-ending in his lips felt as if it had suddenly woken up after years of being asleep.

And then they were really kissing. Hungrily. Desperately. Clinging to each other as if they were drowning in a sea of emotion.

He couldn't remember the last time he'd wanted someone so much. And he was at the point of picking her up and carrying her to her bed when his phone beeped.

The unexpected sound shocked him back to his senses and he pulled back.

'Beatrice. I'm so sorry.'

She looked just as horrified as he did.

'I wasn't hitting on you.' That wasn't strictly true. But he had forgotten himself. Acted on his feelings instead of putting her needs first.

'I know. I...' She shook her head, as if the words just wouldn't come.

He knew how that felt. He was in exactly the same place. He didn't have a clue what to say. 'It was meant to be comfort,' he said. 'Just a hug. Except...' He blew out a breath. Maybe honesty was the best thing he could hope for. 'I haven't felt anything like this about anyone since before Iain was born. I don't actually know what to do right now. Or say.'

'Me, too,' she whispered.

'It was meant to be comfort.'

And it had turned into white-hot desire.

She laid her palm against his cheek. 'I know. And I wasn't...' She grimaced. 'I'm thirty-four years old and I feel like a teenager.'

'So do I.'

'We can't do this.'

'I know.' But it didn't stop him twisting his head so he could press a kiss into her palm. 'In another place and another time, maybe it would be different.'

'We're colleagues.'

'Friends,' he corrected. 'Though I'll try to head Iain off so we don't bother you in future.'

'You don't bother me. He's a sweetheart.'

'You said seeing your nephew brings it back. And Iain's the same age. Surely it's the same situation for you?'

She nodded. 'But you can't have a perfect world. And I'm coming to realise it's better to have a little sadness at the same time as having the pleasure of children around than to avoid them and pretend you're OK.'

'Friends, then,' he said.

'Friends. But I'm not going to kiss your cheek,' she said, 'because it won't stop there. And you need to check your phone. It might be important.'

Reluctantly, he let her go and took the phone from his pocket. 'Mum.' He checked the message. 'She's put Iain to bed.'

'You need to go.'

What she wasn't saying practically echoed between them: *but you could stay...*

Right now, she was vulnerable, and he didn't want to take advantage of her. He was going to follow his head rather than his heart and do the correct thing. Leave, rather than sweep her up in his arms and carry her to her bed. 'I'll see you tomorrow,' he said.

She nodded. 'Thank you for listening.'

'Any time. And that's not me being polite. I'm a Scot. I tell it like it is.'

'Aye, you do,' she said.

He laughed, and retorted with his best attempt at a cut-glass accent, 'That's the worst Glaswegian accent I've ever heard.'

'And the worst posh accent I've ever heard,' she said. 'Thank you, Daniel. For noticing that I was having a wobble, and for making me feel stable again.'

'That's what friends do. Like when you helped me out with Iain.' And how much that must have cost her, he realised now. 'If you can't sleep tonight, call me.'

'I will,' she said, though he knew she wouldn't. 'See you tomorrow.'

CHAPTER SEVEN

BEATRICE HIT THE gym early the next morning, so early that only half a dozen people were there and the punch-bag was free.

She'd made such an idiot of herself last night. Spilling her heart out to Daniel, telling him all about the accident and Taylor and her overdose.

He must think she was a basket case.

One good thing might come out of it, though. Last night he would have had time to think about it and realise just how unsuitable she was. That getting involved with her would be risking a repeat of what he had already been through with Jenny—and the most important thing was to keep life stable for Iain. Which meant not getting involved with her.

As for that kiss…

Well, he'd said it last night. In another place and time, it would have been different; they could have acted on the attraction they'd both admitted to. Taken that kiss further. Much further.

She concentrated on the bag, punching out her frustration.

It wasn't going to happen. They could be colleagues—perhaps friends—and nothing more.

By the time she'd finished her workout, showered and walked into the emergency department, she'd got her mask firmly in place. Beatrice Lindford, Emergency consultant, cool and calm and capable and kind.

That was who she was. Not needy or broken, not the woman who'd let a patient's situation bring back memories, not the woman who'd let her emotions out and felt like a teenager when Daniel Capaldi kissed her.

There wasn't going to be any more kissing.

No more holding each other or holding hands or touching.

Professional. That was the way forward.

Her resolution almost deserted her when she walked into the staff kitchen and saw Daniel there, leaning against the worktop and drinking coffee.

'Hi.'

She was not going to let a pair of dark eyes knock her off course. No matter how sensual they were and no matter how sexy she found Daniel's Scottish accent. The way he rolled his Rs, the way he pronounced world as 'wuruld'—she wasn't going to let it throw her.

And how annoying was it that she could feel the colour rush into her face? Just as well that nobody else was in the kitchen just yet to notice her reaction and join the dots together.

'Hi,' she said.

'Did you sleep OK?' he asked.

No. She'd lain awake until the small hours, thinking of the way her life had imploded and how hard she'd had to work to get it back on track. Thinking of that kiss. Thinking of the way Daniel made her feel. Thinking about how she had to be sensible. 'Yes,' she fibbed.

'Good.' Though his eyes said he didn't quite believe

her. 'Tomorrow,' he said, 'Iain is at his mum's. I'm on a late shift. I was thinking, if you're not busy, maybe we could go for a drink or something to eat.'

This was her cue to tell him that, sorry, she was busy—that she was spending the weekend with her family or something like that. But her mouth wasn't with the programme and she found herself saying, 'I'd like that.'

'Great. I'll pick you up after work,' he said.

Had she just agreed to a date, or was this his idea of being friends? Not that she could ask without feeling like a gauche teenager. 'OK,' she said.

'Good.' And his smile made the whole room feel as if it was filled with sunshine.

That feeling stayed with Beatrice all day, despite her being rostered in Resus and having to face the scene of the case that had affected her so badly yesterday. At the end of her shift, she went up to the maternity unit to see how Jessica Rutherford was doing.

'They're going to let me home tomorrow,' Jessica said, 'on strict condition that I rest.'

So the baby was going to be fine. Relief flooded through her. 'That's so good to hear.'

'And they've been looking after me so well,' Jessica said. 'Thank you—you were all so wonderful yesterday when I was terrified that I'd lose my baby.'

'It's what we're there for,' Beatrice said with a smile. 'I'm glad it's all worked out for you.'

Asking Beatrice out for a drink. When she'd told him all about her past and he knew exactly why she didn't want to get involved with anyone. How stupid was he?

Daniel half expected Beatrice to call it off.

But she didn't. And when she answered the door to

him, she was dressed casually, in jeans and a T-shirt, and her glorious blonde curls were loose rather than being tied back, the way she wore her hair at work.

He felt as if his tongue had just stuck to the roof of his mouth and all the words had disappeared out of his head. This behaving like a teenager thing seemed to be becoming a habit when he was around Beatrice Lindford. 'Um, hi.'

'Hi.' She actually blushed. So was it the same for her? And if her marriage had fallen apart at roughly the same time as his own, then like him she probably hadn't dated in years and she'd be just as clueless as he was. And, weirdly, instead of making him feel more awkward, that realisation made him relax.

'So how's your day been?' he asked.

'Very domestic. Cleaning, laundry and grocery shopping. How was yours?'

'Saturday. People coming in, needing to be patched up after a Friday night out when they were so drunk they'd not realised they'd fallen over and hurt themselves until they tried to get out of bed this morning.'

'Ouch.' She grimaced. 'And half of them still had breath that could strip paint, I assume?'

He nodded. 'Plus the gardeners who overdid it and ricked their backs, a few sporting injuries, someone who jumped into a fountain to cool down, slipped over and broke his arm...'

'Usual Saturday stuff, then. Lucky you.' She raised her eyebrows. 'So where are we going?'

'I don't have a clue,' he admitted. 'It's so long since I've been out with anyone other than Iain and my mum, I'm really not there with the cool kids. The only places

I know are where the team has a night out, or those in-door play centres with ball pits and slides.'

'I'm not with the cool kids, either—and not just because I don't know the area.' She looked at him. 'We could stay in. Because I'm on the ground floor, I've got a patio leading off from my living room; and there's a table and chairs. The garden's communal and it's very pretty. We could cook something together to take outside and open a bottle of wine.'

'That,' he said, 'sounds lovely. Except I haven't brought any wine or anything with me.'

She smiled. 'That's not a problem.'

'It is,' he insisted. 'It's imposing on you, expecting you to feed me and give me wine.'

'How are you imposing on me when it was my suggestion?' she pointed out.

He didn't have an answer to that, but the strike wasn't comfortable. 'It isn't the way I was brought up. If we're doing this as friends, then we should go fair shares.' He looked at her. 'If this is a date, then I'm the one to provide everything, because I'm the one who asked you.'

She reached out and took his hand. 'So you're an old-fashioned man, Daniel Capaldi? That's nice. But I'm a very modern woman. If it's a date, I expect to pay my own way. And friends take turns. Maybe if you let me provide the wine and food tonight, you can do it next time.'

So she was already thinking about a next time? That was good. Though he still had no idea if she saw this as a date or as friendship. He wasn't sure which way he saw it, either.

'You're a puzzle, Beatrice Lindford.'

'I'm just me,' she said. 'So would you prefer to go out, or to sit on my patio?'

It had been a long, long day. He just wanted to chill out.

With her.

'The patio,' he said, 'sounds wonderful. Provided you let me help prepare dinner and the washing up is all mine.'

'Deal,' she said.

It had been so long since he'd prepared dinner with someone—apart from alternate Saturday nights with Iain, when his son helped him make the dough and add the toppings to the pizza, but that wasn't quite the same. In the last few months of his marriage, he'd done most of the cooking on his own or bought microwave meals from the supermarket, because Jenny had lost all interest in food. And he'd forgotten how much he enjoyed the domesticity: just pottering about the kitchen with someone.

They divided up the tasks; Beatrice chopped the salad and made the dressing while he grilled mini chicken fillets and warmed through some wholewheat tortillas, and then together they made some makeshift burritos.

'Perfect for summer,' she said. She put on some music while he opened a bottle of dry white wine, and together they took everything out to the patio.

'This is really nice,' he said when they'd finished eating.

'That's why I rented the flat, because it has a patio and a garden,' she said. 'I went to see Jessica Rutherford yesterday at the end of my shift.'

Their patient with an abruption, he remembered. 'How was she?'

'Fine. They're letting her home today, on strict orders to rest. And the baby's doing well.'

'That's good. And it was nice of you to go and see her. Especially as...' He let the words tail off, realising how tactless he was about to be.

'Especially as it was the same thing that happened to me?' She spread her hands. 'Or, let's be honest, the way my counsellor taught me to be. Maybe it was self-ish, because I wanted to know that she was OK. That this time there was a good outcome.'

He reached across the table and took her hand. 'Was that the first abruption case you've had to treat since it happened to you?'

'The first one after a car accident, yes.' She gave him a smile tinged with sadness. 'I hope the other driver in the accident knows she's OK.'

'Did the one who crashed into you know what happened?'

She nodded. 'He felt terrible about it. So did his wife. The police were going to prosecute him for driving without due care and attention, but taking him to court and giving him a fine and getting his licence endorsed wasn't going to bring Taylor back. There was nothing anyone could do to make it better. I just had to come to terms with the situation.'

'Have you?' he asked gently.

'Yes. I get the occasional bad day, but most of the time I'm OK.' She looked at him. 'But that's why I haven't dated anyone since I split up with Oliver. Because I don't think I can handle the risk of another abruption and los-ing a baby again. I know intellectually that the chances are I'll be perfectly fine—the abruption was caused by an accident, and thankfully I've not been in many—but emotionally I just can't do it.'

'I understand,' he said. 'It's one of the reasons I haven't dated again since Jenny and I split up. Even if I found someone who can love Iain as much as I do and will stick around, what if she wants a baby and what if she ends up with postnatal depression as severe as Jenny had?' He blew out a breath. 'Like you, intellectually I know the stats, but actually taking that risk…' He shook his head with a grimace.

'Given what I did after I lost Taylor, I'm just about the worst person you could get involved with,' she said.

'On paper, you're probably right,' he said, knowing how cruel it sounded—but this was important. Important enough that only brutal honestly had any place here.

'And on paper you're the worst person I could get involved with. A man whose child is the same age my little girl would've been. A constant reminder of what I've lost,' she said.

Equally brutal, but true.

So now they were both clear what was standing in the way.

'Except,' he said, 'you're the first person who's made me feel anything since Jenny.'

'And you're the first person who's made me feel anything since Oliver,' she said.

So it was the same for her. This crazy pull of attraction that really shouldn't work. 'Where does this leave us?' he asked. 'Do we just ignore how we feel and try to look at each other as strictly a colleague?'

She looked at their joined hands. 'Whenever I see you outside work, it makes me feel like a teenager.'

'Me, too,' he admitted. 'Thirty-four going on seventeen.'

'So we're going to have to do something.' She paused. 'Get it out of our systems, perhaps?'

He hadn't expected her to suggest that. 'A fling?'

'I don't know. Maybe I don't mean a fling, Maybe more seeing where this takes us.' She looked at him. 'Which means, as far as Iain's concerned, we're just friends who work together.'

So if it went wrong between them, Iain wouldn't be collateral damage. He wouldn't be hurt. Wouldn't feel abandoned. 'Thank you for putting him first,' Daniel said. 'I appreciate that.'

'It's how I'd feel if I were in your shoes.'

Putting himself in her shoes was much harder. 'Are you sure you can cope with seeing Iain?' he asked. If he'd lost his precious boy, it would rip him to shreds every time he came into contact with a child who would've been Iain's age.

'As I said, I have good days and bad days. And he's a total sweetheart. I enjoyed having him here.' She sucked in a breath. 'But I don't want you to think that I'm just using you to get the child I should've had.'

'No, I don't think that. I think it's going to be complicated,' he said, 'but I also think it's going to be worth it.'

'So this is a date?' she checked.

'I think it is,' he said.

'And, right now, there's something I really want to do.' Still keeping his hand linked with hers, he stood up. 'Would you dance with me?'

She'd been more honest with Daniel than she had with Oliver; her time in counselling had taught her how to open up properly and really talk about a situation, rather than burying her emotions under a smile and pretending everything was just fine. Oliver hadn't been able to cope with the depth of her pain, shying away from the emotion.

But Daniel was different. He, too, had had life implode around him. He'd been just as honest with her about his doubts as she'd been with him about her worries.

This was going to be a new start for both of them.

No promises of what the future would hold: which meant that everything was wide open. They could crash and burn, or they could find new strength and new joy in each other.

It had been a long time since she'd felt that sudden surge of possibilities.

'I'd like that.' She stood up and walked into his arms.

She couldn't remember the last time she'd danced with someone. Oliver, probably, at a wedding or something. Years ago. But it felt right to be in Daniel's arms.

'OK?' he asked.

'Very OK. Right now I feel as if I'm floating on air,' she said.

'Me, too.' He drew her close and they swayed together in the late evening sunshine, cheek to cheek.

She wasn't sure which of them moved first, but then they were kissing. The softest, sweetest kiss that started out making her feel all warm and cherished and wanted; and then it was like lighting touch paper and desire flared though her.

Daniel clearly felt it, too, because when he broke the kiss he looked dazed.

'Beatrice, I...'

'Me, too,' she said.

His eyes were full of longing. 'Right now, I'd really

like to carry you to your bed. But I don't have anything with me.'

Meaning he hadn't automatically expected her to have sex with him tonight, even though this evening had been sort of a date. She liked that. 'I don't have anything, either,' she admitted.

'We can't take risks.'

'Absolutely,' she agreed.

'Let's take a rain check,' he said. 'I'm going to do your washing up, and then I'm going home, because you tempt me beyond anything I've felt in years, and that isn't fair to either of us.'

'Rain check,' she said. 'And maybe we'll be better prepared another time.' That wasn't a maybe. It was a definite. Because she was going to buy contraceptives for the first time in years.

He stroked her face. 'Another time. A night when Iain's at his mum's, so we'll have all the time we want. No pressure, no expectations.'

She could hardly believe she was actually *planning* to have sex with Daniel Capaldi. But neither of them wanted an accidental baby, so this was being sensible. Acknowledging the attraction and the fact that they both wanted to do something about it.

'That sounds good,' she said. And her voice *would* have to croak.

'I'm going to do the washing up, then leave you in peace,' he said.

'Maybe I'll let you off washing up duties,' she said. 'On the grounds that the longer we're together, the less likely we are to be sensible.'

He stole a kiss. 'You're probably right. I'm on a late, tomorrow, how do you fancy a walk in the park? We'll be in public so we'll be sensible And I'll buy you a coffee and a bacon sandwich in the café.'

'That,' she said, 'sounds perfect.'

'Half-past nine at the boating lake,' he said. 'The views over the city are amazing.'

'Half-past nine at the boating lake,' she agreed.

The kiss goodbye he gave her at her front door made her feel as if her knees were melting.

And the kiss hello he gave her at the boating lake, the next morning, had exactly the same effect.

'Well, hello.' He stroked her face. 'I'm glad you didn't change your mind overnight.'

'I thought about it,' she admitted. 'We've both got a lot of baggage.'

'So we know to be careful with each other. No pity and no pressure,' he said. 'And maybe we both deserve a second chance.'

'Agreed.' She looked at him. 'This is scary. But, at the same time, being with you makes it feel as if someone turned the brightness up.'

'Same here,' he said, and took her hand. 'I promised you views. Let's walk up here by Alexandra Palace.'

She gasped when they stopped at the edge of the hill and looked over the railing. 'That's stunning. That's the whole of the City.'

'I hoped you'd like it.'

They headed down to the park, which seemed to be full of dog-walkers and families out playing ball, but instead of thinking about the might-have-beens, this time Beatrice focused on just enjoying the here and now. The sunshine, fresh air, gorgeous scenery—and the equally gorgeous man holding her hand.

She noticed two collies streaking across the park; then the dogs came over to her and Daniel and circled them.

'I think we're being herded,' she said with a grin.

'What?'

'Look.' She pointed to the collies. One of them was lying down, watching them closely and keeping his yellow eyes trained on them. 'If he was human, he'd be playing a character like one of Robert de Niro's, pointing his index and middle fingers at his eyes and then his index finger at us,' she said.

'Seriously?' Daniel asked.

'I dare you to move,' she said, indicating the other collie, which was standing watching them, 'because that one's waiting to round us up.'

Daniel took three steps to the side, and the collie moved towards him.

'See? He wants you to stay put.' She crouched down and extended one hand. 'Come on, boy. I think you're meant to be playing, not working.'

The collie moved towards her and sniffed her hand, just as its owner came puffing up, looking apologetic.

'I'm so sorry,' she said. 'They don't mean any harm.'

'Just their working instinct kicking in,' Beatrice said with a smile. 'We used to have sheep when I was younger, and the collies used to round up all the children in the garden whenever we had people over on a Sunday afternoon. They used to round up the cats as well.'

The woman smiled and looked slightly less embarrassed. 'Thank you for being so understanding. They can be a bit intimidating. I thought that by having two they'd be company for each other and they'd play together, but instead they just go into herding mode.'

Daniel smiled. 'Well, it's the first time I've ever been herded.'

Once the collies had trotted off with their owner, he looked at Beatrice. 'So you're a dog person?'

'Yes. We've always had dogs at Beresford. I would've liked a dog of my own, a liver and white English springer spaniel, but you know the hours junior doctors work, and Oliver worked long hours, too.' It had been part of her dreams: a baby and then a dog, taking them both out to the park and playing endless games of fetch. But her life was a different shape now. It wasn't going to happen.

'I like dogs,' Daniel said, 'but I never grew up with them. My grandparents worked really long hours so it wasn't practical. We had a ginger cat—I got to name him when I was tiny, so he was called Mr Marmalade—but you can't take a cat for a run in the park.'

'We had cats, too. And in our kitchen you'd find an orphan lamb or two every spring—we'd take turns in bottle-feeding them.' She wrinkled her nose. 'We don't have a big flock any more, though. Sandy's in charge of the farming side now and he's part way through turning it into a rare breeds farm park so he can do something about conservation. We've got Hereford cattle and those big woolly Highland cattle with the long horns, and we've got Soay sheep and Jacobs. And every single one of them has a name.'

'It sounds amazing. Iain loves that sort of thing.'

'He could come and help feed them,' she said.

'We'd both like that.' He looked at her. 'So if your

middle brother's in charge of the farming side, is your oldest brother in charge of the castle?'

'That, and learning the ropes from Daddy.'

'Are you sure your dad isn't a prince?' he asked.

His tone was light, but she could tell that he was worried about her background. 'No. He's a viscount—which isn't as grand as it sounds. In peerage terms, that's the fourth rank; it's below an earl, who in turn is below a marquess, who in turn is below a duke. And then you have the Queen.'

'So I'd call your dad Viscount Lindford?'

'Lord Lindford,' she said. 'But he'd probably tell you to call him Edward.'

'Does that mean you're Lady Lindford?'

'No, that's Mummy. My brothers and I have a courtesy title—we're all Hons—but don't worry. My brothers aren't stuffy in the slightest. You'd get on well with them.' She smiled. 'I love my family to bits, but they're hopeless at talking about wobbly stuff. As soon as conversations start to get a bit deep or awkward, they get changed to something bright and breezy. I'm the only one of us who doesn't do that—and that's only because I've learned how to discuss things from working with patients and from exercises my counsellor did with me.'

'Uh-huh,' he said.

She decided to ask him outright. 'Does my background worry you?'

'Sort of,' he said. 'Your family sounds so much grander than mine. You can probably trace your ancestors back to William the Conqueror, and I've never even met my father. His name isn't on my birth certificate.'

He really thought that would matter to her? 'Firstly,' she said, 'we don't go back as far as William the Conqueror. The first Viscount Lindford was created by Charles II, and the family story is that's because his wife was one of Charles's favourite actresses. Secondly, there's a bit of a question mark over who was the second Viscount Lindford's dad—it might have been the first viscount, or it might have been Charles, or it might have been another actor from Lizzie's troupe. So don't ever think that your background would make the slightest difference to me or to my family. It's *you* who matters.'

'Thank you. And I'm sorry for—well.' He looked awkward.

'Thinking I might be a snob?'

'Thinking it might matter.'

'It doesn't. And, at the risk of behaving like my family and avoiding wobbly stuff, I think we'd better go and get that bacon sandwich,' she said, 'or you're going to be late for your shift.'

CHAPTER EIGHT

OVER THE NEXT couple of weeks, Beatrice and Daniel snatched as much time as they could together. Not at work—neither of them wanted to be the hot topic on the hospital's gossip grapevine—but if they were both on a late shift they'd meet for breakfast in a café after Daniel had dropped Iain at school, or they'd stroll through the park and grab a bacon roll from the kiosk there, or Beatrice would make eggs Florentine or smoked salmon and cream cheese bagels and they'd eat breakfast on her patio, teamed with strong Italian coffee. And in the evenings, after Iain had gone to bed, Daniel video-called her and they talked for hours about life, death and the universe.

Beatrice was finding Daniel harder and harder to resist. At work, whenever she caught his eye and he smiled at her, it made her knees go weak. Remembering what it felt like to be in his arms—what it felt like to kiss him. And she really liked the man he was: clever, capable and kind.

And, even though part of her was wary about taking their relationship to the next stage, a greater part of her found it more and more difficult to stop at just kissing.

On Friday night, Daniel video-called her as usual.

'Iain's at Jenny's tomorrow,' he said casually.

Her heart skipped a beat. 'What shift are you on?'

'Early.' He paused. 'And I've a day off on Sunday.'

Meaning they could have the whole night and day together—because her off-duty just happened to dovetail with his.

'What did you have in mind?' she asked carefully, aware that her heart rate had just sped up a couple of notches.

'I don't have to be home early.'

'Or at all.' The words slipped out before she could stop them.

'Are you saying...?' He paused.

Crunch time. He was giving her the choice. She could back away—or she could be brave and reach out for what she wanted. She took a deep breath. 'You could,' she said, 'stay. I have a spare unused toothbrush.'

'A spare unused toothbrush,' he repeated.

'And a washing machine.' So she could put his clothes through it quickly that night and they'd be dry by morning. And he wouldn't need pyjamas.

'So we could go out somewhere. A proper date. Dinner or dancing or something. And then...'

The sensual expression in his eyes was obvious, even on a tablet screen. It sent her pulse rate even higher. 'And then,' she whispered.

'Think about where you'd like to go and text me,' he said. 'And I'll pick you up tomorrow after my shift.'

She thought about it for the rest of the evening.

Were they rushing this, making a mistake?

Or was it better to seize the chance of happiness when you found it?

The next morning, she texted Daniel.

How about an early showing at one of the cinemas in the West End, then dinner out?

He texted back.

Sounds great. You pick the film and I'll organise dinner. Somewhere near Leicester Square?

Perfect, she said.

They'd talked enough for her to know that they both liked good drama. She found a film she thought they'd enjoy and booked the tickets online, then texted him with the show times. And although she normally spent her day off catching up with laundry and domestic chores, she found it hard to concentrate.

An official date.

A movie and dinner.

And Daniel was going to stay the night.

Her breath caught. Oh, for pity's sake. Anyone would think she was seventeen, not a thirty-four-year-old senior doctor. But she was nervous and excited in equal parts, like a teenager on her first date.

Though there was one essential bit of shopping she needed. Hoping that she wasn't going to bump into anyone from work—or at least that she could hide the condoms in her basket by covering them with a large slab of chocolate—she headed to the supermarket.

When Daniel rang her doorbell later that afternoon, she was a bundle of nerves.

'Hi.' He presented her with practically an armful of sweet-scented stocks, her favourite flowers.

'They're gorgeous. Thank you.' And he looked gorgeous, too, dressed up for a night out. She was glad she'd made the effort with a pretty summer dress and strappy sandals; Daniel was tall enough for her to be able to wear high heels and not tower over him. 'I'll put them in water.'

'I brought this as well. Which doesn't have to be for tonight, and there aren't any strings attached to it.' He handed her a carrier bag.

She looked inside. 'Champagne?'

'English sparkling wine. It has good reviews.'

'It looks lovely. Thank you. I'll put that in the fridge.'

He followed her into the kitchen and kissed her lingeringly. 'You look beautiful.'

'So do you.'

'Men can be beautiful?'

'Aye, ye big, sleekit…'

'Tim'rous beastie?' He exaggerated his accent deliberately. 'I hate to tell you this, but Rabbie Burns was describing a mouse. And I might be holding back at the moment, but I'm no mouse.'

No. He was all man. Heat shot through her.

'I might even be a troglodyte,' he said, and twirled the very ends of her hair round his fingers. 'I love your hair like this.'

This was getting dangerously close to wobbly talk. She took refuge in the way her family normally did things, and changed the subject. 'Good shift?'

'Typical Saturday. Made much better for the fact that I'm seeing you tonight.' He stole another kiss. 'We have a date. Much as you tempt me to switch this to a night in, I think anticipation is going to make this all the sweeter.'

'What if I disappoint you?' The words were out before she could stop them.

'You're not going to disappoint me.' He stroked her face and smiled. 'It's not going to be perfect. We're on a learning curve until we find out what each other likes. But it's going to be fun finding out.'

And suddenly that took all her worries away so, like him, she could look forward to tonight with anticipation rather than nervousness.

It was a long, long time since she'd held hands with anyone in a cinema. Or sat with their arm round her shoulders. And she thoroughly enjoyed the film; more than that, she enjoyed dissecting the film with Daniel over dinner.

He'd picked a restaurant just off Covent Garden that she'd never been to before, but she loved the way the room was lit by strings of fairy lights threaded through the branches of bay trees dotted between the tables, and there were tea lights in glass and ironwork lanterns that turned the candlelight into shapes of stars.

'This is so romantic,' she said. 'I didn't even know this place was here. How did you find it?'

'Seriously?'

'Seriously.'

He laughed. 'I looked up "romantic restaurants near Leicester Square" on the Internet.'

She liked the fact that he'd admitted it rather than trying to feed her a line about knowing all the best places to go in the city. 'Good find.'

'The reviews all said the food was as good as it looks, so I thought it was worth a try. Luckily they'd just had a cancellation so I was able to get us a table,' he said.

And it was fabulous. A sharing platter of *meze*— baked feta cheese, bread, olives, taramasalata and stuffed vine leaves—followed by lemon chicken with rosemary potatoes, spinach and honey-roasted tomatoes, and then a selection of tiny sweet Greek pastries served with bitter coffee. He ordered a bottle of sparkling wine to go with it—the Greek answer to champagne—and everything was absolutely perfect. The food, the wine, the conversation, the company.

'I've had a wonderful time tonight,' she said when he walked her home from the tube station and they stood outside her front door.

'Me, too.' He took her hand. 'No pressure. If you want me to go home right now, that's fine.'

'Do you want to go home?' she asked.

'No. But this is all new. We don't have to do anything you're not comfortable with. I could sleep on your sofa.'

'No. I want you to stay. And not on my sofa,' she said, feeling the colour bloom in her face.

'I'm glad,' he said softly. 'But if you should change your mind at any point, that's OK.'

She took a deep breath. 'Let's be brave. Take a risk on each other—but that's the *only* risk,' she added as she unlocked the door.

He followed her inside. 'Great minds think alike. I went to the supermarket yesterday.'

'So did I,' she said. 'So let's open that fizz.'

'And as I didn't get to dance with you earlier...'

'You do the wine and I'll do the music,' she said. Teamwork. It was how they functioned at work. Home wasn't so very different.

'Deal. Where do you keep your glasses?' he asked.

'Top of the cupboard next to the kettle.'

She connected her phone to the speaker, flicked into her music app and chose a playlist of slow dances.

He handed her a glass. 'To us. And to second chances.'

'To us, and second chances,' she echoed, and took a sip of wine before placing her glass on the kitchen table.

He held out his arms and she walked over to him.

'This is perfect,' he said, 'for dancing cheek to cheek.'

She closed her eyes and swayed to the music with him. And it felt so right when he kissed the corner of her mouth. She turned her head slightly so that he could kiss her properly.

Daniel and the music and the last vestiges of the sunset spilling in through the kitchen window—this was perfect, she thought.

And when he broke the kiss and looked at her, his sensual dark eyes filled with a question, there was only one answer. 'Yes.'

His smile was sweet and slow and sexy as hell. 'Forgive me for being a troglodyte.' And then he scooped her into his arms.

'You're carrying me to my bed?' she asked.

'That's the idea. Like a chieftain carrying his lass off to his lair. Except it's your lair rather than mine,' he said with a grin.

Desire flooded through her. 'Out of the kitchen, second door on the right,' she said.

And he carried her to her bed.

The next morning, Beatrice woke feeling warm and comfortable, with Daniel's arms wrapped round her.

'Good morning,' he whispered against her hair.

'Good morning.' She twisted around to face him. Funny, she'd thought she might feel shy with him, this morning. Yet this felt real and natural and right. A slow, easy Sunday morning.

'What do you want to do today?' he asked.

'I don't mind, as long as I'm with you,' she said.

'I have to pick up Iain from Jenny's at four,' he said.

And she knew he meant on his own. Which was fine by her, because she, too, thought they needed time to be sure where this was going before they told anyone, especially someone who was so young and could be so badly hurt by the fallout if anything went wrong. 'That's fine.' She paused. 'We could go out for the day. Maybe to Notting Hill and browse in the antique shops and then have lunch in a café somewhere—I know we won't get the market stalls on Portobello Road, with it being a Sunday, but it could still be fun.'

'Notting Hill.'

She smiled. 'That's one of my favourite films, actually. I love Hugh Grant. We could go location-spotting and find the little square where he kisses Julia Roberts.'

'Kissing,' he said thoughtfully. 'You had me at kissing…'

It was a lot later by the time they finally got up. And they held hands all the way on the tube to Notting Hill, all the way down Portobello Road, and all the way to the little private gardens used in the film. 'You can't go in there because it's locked,' Beatrice said, 'but this is definitely the place.'

'So how exactly did you know where this was?' Daniel asked.

'My sisters-in-law agree with me that it's the best romcom ever. We had a girly weekend in London when I qualified as a doctor,' she said. 'A *Notting Hill* weekend. We went location-spotting—Portobello Road, the bookshop, the flat with the blue door, the restaurant and the cinema. And then we had afternoon tea at the Ritz, and we went back to my flat for pizza and bubbles and we watched *Notting Hill* twice.'

'Twice?'

'It's a girl thing,' she said with a grin. 'My brothers thought we were crackers, but we had a ball. I think I might even have a couple of the pictures still on my phone.' She flicked through. 'There you go. Us with the blue door, the bookshop, and here at the gardens.'

He looked at the photographs. Three young women, with their arms round each other and the broadest smiles.

'So you're close to your sisters-in-law?' He knew how stupid the question was as soon as it left his lips—from those smiles, they were clearly very close indeed.

But she didn't seem to mind. 'Like my brothers, they can't talk about wobbly stuff, but they'll be the first with cake and a hug and then a very awkward pat on the back.' She smiled. 'I love them dearly.'

'*Notting Hill.*' He wasn't entirely sure he'd seen the film—as far as he was concerned, a lot of the romcoms blended into each other—but she'd mentioned that this place involved kissing. 'Then I think a selfie is in order,' he said, and took out his phone to snap them standing by the entrance gate with their arms round each other. 'And a kiss.'

'I thought you'd never ask,' she said, and kissed him.

And his mouth tingled for the next ten minutes.

It was a fun, frothy and light-hearted afternoon and, even though he'd never thought of himself as the sort who'd poke about in an antique shop, he thoroughly enjoyed being with Beatrice.

'Oh, perfect,' she said softly as they browsed in one shop.

'What?'

'Vicky collects those Staffordshire mantel dogs,' she said, gesturing to a pair of stylised china dogs. 'It's her birthday next month. And that's a nice-looking pair.'

'Are you sure? They don't look like a pair. I mean, the decorations are different,' Daniel said.

'Which is one of the ways you can tell they're antique and not reproduction,' she said. She picked one up and looked at it. 'And, look, there are fine brush-stroke details of the dog's hair, the gold isn't shiny and doesn't reflect things, and there's paint on the back.' She looked at the base. 'And no casting holes—this is a press mould, not slipware.'

He coughed. 'If I hadn't seen you treat patients for myself, I'd be wondering if you were an antiques expert rather than a doctor.'

She grinned. 'This is all stuff Vicky taught me. I bought her a pair for Christmas one year and they turned out to be reproductions—and I'd paid well over the odds for them. She showed me what to look for and I've got a much better idea of value, too. She'd love these. I'm going to haggle.'

'This is a shop, not a market stall. You can't haggle!' Daniel said, scandalised.

'Yes, I can.' She went over to the cash desk, and he followed in her wake.

Beatrice was utterly, utterly charming.

And she was a hard negotiator. By the time she'd finished, she'd knocked twenty-five per cent off the price, and the man in the shop had offered them both very good coffee and expensive biscuits while he wrapped the Staffordshire dogs carefully.

'You,' Daniel said when they left the shop, 'are amazing.'

She gave him a sketchy bow. 'Thank you.'

'And this has been such fun.'

She glanced at her watch. 'But you need to go. Iain's expecting you, and if you're late he'll want to know why.' She kissed him. 'Go.'

'I should see you home.'

She shook her head. 'I'm fine. And I'm going to call Vicky and get her to meet me off the train so I can give her these. Thank you for the weekend. It's been...'

'Amazing,' he said softly, and kissed her lingeringly. 'If you're sure, then I'll see you tomorrow.'

Over the next fortnight, they managed to snatch some time together—including a Friday evening at a departmental pub quiz where Beatrice's more unusual general knowledge meant that the Emergency Department won, to the delight of the rest of the team.

But Daniel was reflective on the Monday evening— Iain had gone to a friend's after school, so he and Beatrice had grabbed the chance to spend some time together.

'Are you going to tell me what's wrong, or would you prefer me to pretend I haven't noticed that you're brooding?' she asked.

He blew out a breath. 'Sorry.'

'Don't apologise. If you want a listening ear, I'm here. If you don't, no offence taken.'

He took her hand and pressed a kiss into her palm. 'It's not the most tactful subject.'

'I'm still listening.'

He sighed. 'Jenny told me last night that she and Jordan are expecting. She's just had her twelve-week scan.'

A baby.

'Has she told Iain yet?'

'No. She said she wanted to talk it over with me, first, and work out the best way to tell him.'

She didn't think it was the baby that was worrying him. She could just pretend that everything was fine and be bright and breezy; or she could be open and honest, and let him talk about his real feelings. 'And you're worried she's going to get postnatal depression again?'

He nodded. 'You know as well as I do, statistically there's an increased risk of having postnatal depression again if you've had it before.'

'But,' she said, 'forewarned is forearmed. As long as her family doctor and her midwife know, they can monitor her and help her if they think she's showing any signs. There are support groups, too. She can get help beforehand and make sure she gets plenty of rest afterwards—and exercise, because the endorphins are really good at helping.'

'Is that what you'd do?' he asked.

Put things in place so she wouldn't end up being depressed after the baby's birth, remembering Taylor? There was just one tiny thing that would affect that plan. 'I don't intend to have any more children,' she said. 'But, hypothetically speaking, if I was in Jenny's situation that's what I'd do. I'd make sure I had counselling during the pregnancy and enough support during the pregnancy and afterwards. If she needs antidepressants, then the doctor can give them sooner rather than later, to make sure she doesn't hit the same low she had last time round.' She looked at him. 'I assume that's what you said to her?'

He grimaced. 'I might need to apologise and buy her flowers and tell her she'll have support from me, from Mum and from Iain as well as from Jordan and his family.'

'You actually told her you were worried she'd have postnatal depression again?'

'I was thinking of Iain. I should've considered her.' He sighed. 'I need to call her, don't I?'

'Do it now,' Beatrice said. 'I'll hang around in the kitchen and make us a pot of tea, and you can call her from the garden or the sitting room, whichever's more comfortable for you. Come and get your tea when you've talked to her.'

She was halfway through her own mug of tea when Daniel returned to the kitchen and wrapped his arms round her. 'You're a good woman and I don't deserve you. That's a quote from Jenny, by the way.'

'You told her about us?'

'In strictest confidence. I think I owed her honesty, when I was a bit too honest with her yesterday,' he said. 'She wanted to know what caused my sea-change in attitude.'

'I see,' she said.

'I told her we weren't ready to say anything to Iain yet, because we wanted to be sure and not let him get hurt. She understands. She said to thank you for the advice, that you're a better doctor than me, and she owes you lunch.'

'Because she wants to check me out?' Beatrice asked.

He wrinkled his nose. 'Iain's already told her about you—oh, and by the way, I explained that you don't know Prince Harry so he won't be having lunch with you both—and I said that Mum likes you. Which she says is fine, but she'd still like to have lunch with you.'

Beatrice smiled. 'It's nice that she's still looking out

for you. And you're still looking out for her—otherwise you wouldn't be so worried about her having postnatal depression again.'

'I'm still worried,' he admitted. 'And Iain's old enough now to notice what's going on. What if she does get it again, and it reminds her of the first time round, and she rejects him?'

'She's his mum. She won't reject him. I'm sure she'll talk to him about being an older brother and being able to boss his little brother or sister around. And I'm the youngest of three, so I can back her up,' Beatrice said.

Daniel hugged her. 'You're a good woman.'

She smiled. 'I try.'

Almost two weeks later, Jenny still hadn't told Iain about his little brother or sister to be, but she'd arranged to take him to the seaside for the weekend, picking him up from school on the Friday afternoon. Both Beatrice and Daniel managed to arrange getting Friday off as well as the weekend.

'I think we can go to the seaside, too,' Daniel said. 'Except obviously not the same place. I was thinking Cornwall.'

'Good choice,' Beatrice said. 'Miles of sand, *Poldark* and good fish restaurants. Cornwall would be wonderful.'

Except when she got up on Friday morning, ready to pack, she felt odd. Queasy.

She hadn't eaten anything unusual, or anything that might've made her feel that way.

And her breasts felt tender.

The last time she'd felt like this, she'd been pregnant with Taylor...

She shook herself. This was utterly ridiculous. Of course she wasn't pregnant. She couldn't be. She and Daniel had been super-careful about contraception. Neither of them wanted a baby.

But the nagging feeling wouldn't leave her, all the way through packing.

'Don't be so *feeble*, Beatrice Lindford,' she admonished herself out loud. 'You know perfectly well that you can practically set your calendar by your menstrual cycle. More regular than clockwork. Your next one's due…'

She went still.

Her next period was due in two weeks' time. Meaning that *her last period had been due two weeks ago.*

She counted it up in her head again. And then on a physical calendar, just to make sure.

Two weeks late.

She went into the bathroom and splashed her face with water. Her period was late. That didn't necessarily mean that she was pregnant. There were all kinds of reasons why your period could be late or you'd miss one. A hormonal imbalance, for starters—though she knew that wasn't likely, and she could discount thyroid issues or polycystic ovary syndrome, too. Ditto the menopause, diabetes or coeliac disease. She could cross off doing extreme exercise and suffering from an eating disorder, too, and her body weight was smack in the middle of the normal range for her height. She hadn't just started the Pill, so her body didn't need to adjust to that.

Maybe it was because she'd started her new relationship with Daniel. Even though she was happy and enjoying it, subconsciously she could be worrying and the stress had affected her cycle.

Though the fact that she was mentally going through every single medical reason—except the most likely—was telling in itself, she thought grimly. She and Daniel had been careful about contraception to the point of being paranoid, but there was only one method that was one hundred per cent guaranteed. Abstinence. A method they most definitely hadn't used.

There was only one way to settle things. And there was no way she could go to Cornwall with Daniel for a long weekend without knowing the truth. She glanced at her watch. She had an hour until he was due to pick her up. Which gave her enough time to nip out to the supermarket, buy a pregnancy test and use it.

She downed a large glass of water, then headed out. Actually going to the shop and buying the test was a blur. But then she was in her bathroom, doing the test. Peeing on the stick. Waiting for the test to work.

The last time she'd done this, she'd waited so hopefully and happily, praying that it would be positive. She'd been thrilled to see the second line on the screen, a nice clear stripe that said she was definitely pregnant. She'd cried with joy when she'd walked out of the bathroom to tell Oliver the news.

This time, she was filled with panic. She couldn't be pregnant. She and Daniel were still in the early stages of their relationship. Daniel had Iain to think about. And her pregnancy last time had ended in utter heartbreak. Yes, people said that lightning didn't strike twice, but it did. There were trees on the estate back at Beresford that been hit three times. Supposed it happened again? What if she was involved in another car accident that meant her bump hit the steering wheel and caused an abruption? What if she had a spontaneous abruption? *What if? What if?*

The panic spiralled tighter in her head.

One line. The test was working.

Please don't let there be a second. Please.

This was the only test they'd had in the nearest shop. An old-fashioned one. Why hadn't she gone somewhere else and bought a different one, the sort that actually said the word *pregnant* in clear letters so there could be no doubt about it, no possibility that the line was so faint she could kid herself it wasn't there?

She squeezed her eyes tightly shut. Please let the test be negative. *Please.*

And what if it was positive? How would Daniel react? Two weeks ago, he'd reacted badly to Jenny's news, worrying that she would have postnatal depression again and Iain would get hurt. With Beatrice's own history of mental health, there was a high chance that she would be affected by postnatal depression. Daniel's worst nightmare, repeated all over again.

He was a good man. She knew he'd try his best to support her.

But if it was a question of supporting her or protecting Iain, there was only one choice he could make. Walk away.

She wrapped her arms round herself, shivering despite the warmth of the day. Right now, she was panicking too much to think clearly. She couldn't answer any of her own questions; all she could do was worry. Wait. Rinse and repeat.

She opened her eyes and stared at the test.

Two lines.

Positive.

She was pregnant.

What the hell was she going to do?

She couldn't go to Cornwall with Daniel today, that much was clear. OK, so she knew the truth now, but she needed time to process it. To work out how she felt, what she wanted to do—and how she was going to break the news to Daniel.

She glanced at her watch.

Half an hour until he was due to pick her up.

That wasn't enough time for her to get her head together. She needed space. And there was only one place she wanted to be right now.

She was already packed for the weekend, so all she had to do was to lock her front door and sling her bag in the back of her car.

And then she sat in the driver's seat with the engine still turned off and her mobile phone in her hand.

Knowing she was being an utter coward, but unable to think clearly enough to find a better solution, panicking as the seconds ticked by faster and faster, she tapped out a text to Daniel.

Sorry. Can't make Cornwall. Will call you later.

She pressed 'send', then switched off her phone, turned the key in the ignition, and drove away.

CHAPTER NINE

'BYE, DARLING. HAVE a lovely time at the seaside with Mummy and Jordan,' Daniel said, kissing his son goodbye.

Even though he knew their son would be perfectly safe with Jenny, that Jordan treated Iain as if he were his own flesh and blood, and Daniel himself had plans for a romantic weekend away with Beatrice, it was still a wrench to say goodbye to Iain. And Daniel lingered for a last glance of his boy as Iain trotted in through his classroom door, chattering away to his friends.

He walked back to his flat to pick up his car, then drove to Beatrice's. Funny, this weekend had been a last-minute decision, but everything had worked out perfectly. And he was really looking forward to spending time with Beatrice. Walking hand in hand with her at the edge of the sea in starlight.

It felt as if they'd known each other for much longer than two months. And it was years since he'd felt this light of spirit. He liked just being with her; she made the world feel full of sunshine.

Iain adored her, too. A couple of times over half term, Beatrice had met them after an early shift and they'd gone to the park and then out for pizza. And there had been a Sunday morning where Beatrice had refused to tell them where they were going, claiming it was a surprise, and then had presented them with tickets for the children's show at the Planetarium in Greenwich. Iain had been ecstatic—he loved outer space as much as he loved football—and he'd held Beatrice's hand all the way through the show and chattered excitedly to her over lunch about the stars and the planets and the big bear in the sky. She'd been patient with him and helped him draw pictures of constellations that he'd taken into school the next day for show and tell. And when Daniel watched them together he was pretty sure that Iain's feelings towards Beatrice were very much mutual.

They'd insisted that Beatrice was just Dad's friend from work, including when Susan had joined them for pizza. But Daniel's mother had said quietly to him afterwards, 'You don't look at each other like friends.'

No. If he was honest with himself, Daniel didn't think of her as just a friend. But he wasn't ready to declare himself just yet. It was still early days. They were taking things slowly, carefully; they'd both been through a lot in the past, and there was Iain to consider. But he was really looking forward to spending the whole weekend with her.

On the way to Beatrice's, his phone pinged to signal an incoming text. Probably something last-minute from Jenny or his mother, he thought. He'd pick up the message later.

But, when he got to Beatrice's, her car wasn't parked where it usually was. And when he rang her doorbell there was no answer.

Maybe she'd nipped to the shop for something she'd forgotten. Though the woman he worked with in the

Emergency Department was incredibly organised, and he couldn't imagine her forgetting anything or running out of anything. Maybe that text was from her, then, to warn him that she'd had to go out briefly and would be back any second. He took his phone from his pocket and glanced at the screen.

The message was indeed from Beatrice, but it was the last thing he'd expected.

Sorry. Can't make Cornwall. Will call you later.

What did she mean, she couldn't make Cornwall? They'd planned the trip together. He'd found a gorgeous hotel situated right next to a beach. They were going to paddle in the sea, walk for miles on the sand, and eat way too many scones with jam and clotted cream.

The only thing he could think of was that there had been an emergency in her family. A sudden illness, perhaps, or an accident. But surely she would've called him on her way out, or at least added a couple of words of explanation of her text? Beatrice was a very clear communicator at work; in the emergency room, everyone knew exactly what their role was and what she expected of them. This text raised way more questions than it answered—and it wasn't like the woman he'd got to know over the last couple of months.

It didn't make sense.

Frowning, he called her.

'The number you are calling is not contactable. Please try later or send a text,' a recorded voice informed him, and he cut the connection.

They were in London, so it was unlikely that she was out of signal range; and, like him, if she was driving she connected her phone to the car's hands-free system. For that voicemail message to kick in, she must have switched off her phone. Given that she must've known he'd call her as soon as he picked up her text, it was looking as if she really didn't want to talk to him.

Why?

They hadn't had a fight, and he couldn't think of anything he might have done that would upset her.

Puzzled and hurt, he called her again, and this time he left a message on her voicemail. 'Beatrice, it's Daniel. Are you OK? Whatever's happened, is there anything I can do? Give me a call when you can.'

Home.

Seeing the house with its four square turrets and the copper-roofed cupola made Beatrice feel slightly less panicky. When she got to the black iron gates of the rear entrance the family used, she hopped out of the car and punched in the security number. The gate swung open without so much as a creak; she drove through, waited for them to close behind her, then drove down to the house and parked on the gravel next to her sister-in-law Vicky's four-by-four.

The house wasn't open to the public until the afternoon, so she didn't have to worry about visitors. She just let herself in through the side entrance and walked into the family kitchen.

'Bea! I didn't know you were coming this weekend or I would've made sure your bed was aired. The kettle's hot,' Vicky said. 'Sandy's out doing farm stuff and Orlando's somewhere with Pa, and Ma and Flora have gone dress-shopping.'

'And you thought you were going to have a morning of peace and quiet?' Beatrice asked.

'Considering this miscreant ate Henry's school shoes and then threw them up everywhere,' Vicky said, gesturing to the black Labrador whose nose was poking out from under the table, 'I didn't get the P and Q anyway.' Vicky gave her a hug. 'So why didn't you say you were coming? I could've got something nice in for lunch. You'll have to slum it with a cheese sandwich, or go and sweet-talk them in the café—oh, my days.' Vicky patted Beatrice's arm, seeing the fat tear rolling down her face.

'Sorry. I'll pull myself together in a second.'

'What's happened, Bea? Something at work? I'll make you that cup of tea.'

Beatrice could see the alarm on her sister-in-law's face. 'Vicky, it's all right. You're not going to knock on my door later and not get an answer. And you don't have to lock up all the paracetamol in the medicine cabinet. I'm not going to take another overdose.'

'Good.' Vicky blew out a breath of sheer relief. 'I— Look, you know we're all useless at wobbly stuff, and I don't know what to say to make anything better, but if you want to talk...' She delved in the cupboard. 'Banana bread. There's a new boy in Henry's class who's dairy intolerant, so I've been trying a few things before he comes over for supper. You can be my guinea pig.'

Cake and a cup of tea was Vicky's standard answer to any problem, Beatrice knew. 'You,' she said, 'are a total sweetie. Cake and a cup of tea sounds perfect.'

The fear went from Vicky's expression, and she bustled around, organising tea and cake.

When they were sitting at the kitchen table with mugs of tea, and Cerberus had plonked himself on Beatrice's feet to comfort her, Vicky reached across and squeezed Beatrice's hand. Beatrice knew this was her sister-in-law's way of saying she was ready to listen.

There wasn't any way she could think of to soften the news, so she came straight out with it. 'I'm pregnant.'

Vicky almost dropped her mug. 'What? But—how?'

'You've got two children, Vicky. I think you know how babies are made,' Beatrice said with a smile.

'Well, of course, What I mean is—I didn't know you were even dating.' Vicky's eyes widened. 'How far along are you? How long have you been seeing him? And have you told him?'

Beatrice sighed. 'We've been seeing each other for a few weeks, I'm two weeks late and I did the test today. And, no, I haven't told him. It's complicated.'

'Because of Taylor?'

'Partly. Plus we work together. Daniel's a single dad.'

'Ah. Does his child like you?'

'Iain?' Beatrice couldn't help smiling when she thought of him. 'Yes. He's four. He wants to be a footballer and an astronaut, he thinks I'm a princess, and he also says I make the best chocolate brownies in the world.'

'Beresford brownies?'

'Of course Beresford brownies,' Beatrice confirmed.

'So what's he like?' Vicky asked. 'Daniel, I mean.'

'He's nice. He's a good doctor, he's kind and he's thorough.'

Vicky rolled her eyes. 'I don't mean at work. I mean the man himself.'

'Tall, dark and handsome. He has the most amazing dark eyes. He's sweet and he's funny. He makes me feel like a teenager, holding hands in the back row of the cinema. We talk every night on a video call after Iain's gone to bed.' She smiled. 'And we went to Notting Hill.'

'So you'd seen him the day you brought me those gorgeous Staffordshire dogs?' Vicky asked thoughtfully.

Beatrice nodded. 'Thinking back, that might have been the weekend *this* happened.'

'You were glowing, Bea. I haven't seen you look like that since...' Vicky let the words tail off.

'Since before Taylor,' Beatrice finished. 'He makes me feel lighter of spirit.'

'Do you love him?'

Beatrice wrinkled her nose. 'We've been dating for six weeks. How can I be in love?'

'OK, let's scale back. Do you like him?'

'Yes. A lot.' But love...? She wasn't sure she was ready to say that.

'Ignore the baby for now, but imagine life without him. Would there be a hole?' Vicky asked.

Beatrice didn't even have to think about it. 'A big one,' she admitted.

'Well, then. There's your answer. Call it any name you like, but you love him.' Vicky paused. 'Does he love you?'

'We haven't discussed it.'

Vicky frowned. 'OK. Does he know about Taylor? And...?'

'The overdose? Yes.'

'Then what's the issue?' Vicky asked. 'He knows what happened to you—so you must really trust him to have told him. He's already a dad so, if he's got custody, he must be a really good dad. Is he a widower?'

'Divorced. Iain stays with his mum every other

weekend—like this one. Daniel and I were meant to be going away.'

'As you're here, clearly you called it off.'

Beatrice winced. 'By text.'

'Oh, *Bea*. You can't do that to the poor man.'

'I know.' Beatrice squirmed. 'I'm a cow. But I did the test and I panicked. I can't go away with him, knowing I'm pregnant and knowing that he has no idea.'

'Then tell him about the baby. He's a doctor, so he knows how babies are made.' Vicky threw Beatrice's words back at her.

'I don't know how he's going to react.'

'He's close to his little boy, yes?' At Beatrice's nod, Vicky continued, 'Then my guess is he'll be pleased. Shocked at first, especially as you haven't been together that long, but when he thinks about it he'll be pleased.'

Beatrice wasn't so sure. 'It's complicated,' she said again.

'It's not going to be an easy conversation, but you're better at talking than the rest of us put together,' Vicky said. 'And remember the family motto.'

The one carved into the dining room fireplace. *Tenacitas per aspera*. Strength through adversity.

'Strictly in confidence—' and Beatrice knew Vicky wouldn't say a word to anyone '—Iain's mum had postnatal depression. Badly. She left the baby and disappeared for a couple of days,' Beatrice said.

'Ah.' Vicky grimaced. 'One step down from what you did.'

Beatrice nodded. 'And she's pregnant again now. Daniel's panicking that Iain's going to get hurt. And now on top of this there's me. How can I tell him?'

'You're right. It's complicated,' Vicky said, 'but running away here—which isn't that far from what his ex did—isn't going to solve anything.'

'I know.' She was fast becoming Daniel's nightmare re-personified. 'What am I going to do, Vicky?'

'I guess we start with the tough one. Do you want the baby?'

Which, right now, was a collection of cells. Beatrice rested her hand on her abdomen. 'I lost Taylor. Pregnancy scares me stupid. The idea of something going wrong and losing another baby...' She blew out a breath. 'I don't want a termination.'

'So that's the big decision made,' Vicky said. 'If Daniel doesn't want to be involved, we'll support you.'

Beatrice felt tears pricking her eyelids. 'Oh, Vicky.'

'Of course we'd support you, Bea. I know how hard it was for you when I had George. Every time I took him to postnatal class or toddler group or anything, I kept thinking about how you and Taylor should've been there with me. It was miserable for me, so it must have been hell on earth for you.'

'I have good days and bad days,' Beatrice said.

'Call him. Talk to him,' Vicky advised. 'Dragging your feet about it won't achieve anything. I don't know him so I have no idea how he'll react. But there's only one way to find out.'

'I know. And thank you.' Beatrice stood up, walked round the table and hugged her. 'You're a lot better at wobbly stuff than you give yourself credit for.'

'Hmm. Stop wriggling out of it and call him,' Vicky said.

Beatrice took her phone from her bag and switched it on. 'Oh. There's a voicemail.' She listened to it and swallowed hard. 'Oh, God. I sent him that text saying I couldn't go to Cornwall with him and I didn't even make a feeble excuse. And he hasn't left me an angry message asking what the hell I'm playing at—he's just asked me if I'm all right and if there's anything he can do.'

'A man who didn't love you would be furious. He's putting you first,' Vicky said thoughtfully. 'That makes him a keeper. Look, I'm going to take this vile hound out to do this business—and why Orlando had to leave him with me this morning I have no idea—so you go ahead and call him.'

Daniel's phone shrilled and he looked at the screen.
Beatrice.

He answered swiftly. 'Beatrice? Are you all right?'

'Yes.' She paused. 'I'm sorry, Daniel. I haven't been fair to you. And I'll pay for the hotel.'

'It doesn't matter about the hotel,' he said. 'As long as you're all right. What's happened? Where are you?'

'At Beresford,' she said.

So he'd guessed right and it was a family emergency. 'Something's happened to your family? Is there anything I can do?'

'They're all fine,' she said. 'Daniel, we need to talk.'

His stomach swooped. Had she left because she'd realised she didn't want to be with him after all, and she'd wanted space to find the right way to tell him? Just like Jenny had walked out on him, and their marriage had fizzled out after her postnatal depression? 'OK,' he said carefully.

'Would you mind coming here? Nearly everyone's out—there's just my sister-in-law Vicky at the house, so we can have some privacy.'

She wanted him to drive all the way out to her family home so she could dump him? Hurt lashed through him. 'Just give it to me straight,' he said. 'Actually, no, I'll save you the trouble. I come with complications and you'd rather keep this thing between us strictly professional, right?'

'It's not that at all,' she said. 'We need to talk. Please, Daniel. Or I could come back to London, if you'd rather.'

If she didn't want to break up with him, what did she want to talk to him about? And if there wasn't an emergency at her family home, why had she rushed there and cancelled her weekend?

'What aren't you telling me?' he asked.

'Something I need to discuss with you face to face. I find talking hard, Daniel, and this isn't something I can do over the phone.'

Reluctantly, he said, 'OK, I'll come to you.'

She gave him the postcode for his satnav. 'Let me know when you're ten minutes away and I'll walk down to the gate and let you in.'

'Tradesmen's entrance?' he asked, knowing it was nasty but not being able to stop himself lashing out. She'd hurt him. He didn't have a clue what was going on in her head.

'Family private entrance, rather than the one we use for visitors with the public car park,' she corrected, and he felt small.

'Sorry,' he muttered.

'I'm sorry, too,' she said. 'I'll see you in a bit.'

Beresford Castle was almost an hour's drive away. As Beatrice had asked, he called her when he was ten minutes away.

'Thank you for coming, Daniel.' She sounded cool

and calm, completely in control of herself. 'I'll walk down to the gate.'

It was a ten-minute walk from the house to the gate?

Then again, she was the daughter of a viscount. The house was open to the public, so it must be enormous.

As he drove past the front entrance, he discovered that the castle was even bigger than he expected. It wasn't like a child's storybook castle: more like a mansion, with a square turret at each corner, a parapet, and a dome with a green copper roof on the top.

He was way, way out of his league.

And he didn't have a clue what Beatrice wanted to talk to him about. What was so important that it would make her cancel their weekend only minutes before they were due to leave, and she couldn't talk to him on the phone about it?

She'd implied she wasn't dumping him—but had he got it wrong?

There was only one way to find out.

CHAPTER TEN

WHEN BEATRICE MET Daniel by the unassuming wrought iron gates, she looked cool and calm and completely at home. Well, of course she would, he thought, cross with himself for being stupid. She was the viscount's daughter and she'd grown up here.

'Hi,' she said.

Her expression was carefully masked. He didn't have a clue what was going on in her head. Or what to do. Should he get out of the car, the way he wanted to, and take her in his arms? Or would she back away, preferring him to keep his distance?

Then he noticed the black Labrador by her heels.

'Yours?' he asked.

'My brother Orlando's,' she explained.

The one whose children had Greek names—and so did his dog, Daniel remembered. 'Cerberus.'

The Labrador wagged his tail politely at the sound of his name.

'Fortunately this one has only one head. He's in disgrace for chomping Henry's school shoes this morning and then being sick everywhere,' she said brightly.

'Uh-huh.' This was slightly surreal. Beatrice was talking to him—but she wasn't talking about whatever had made her flee from London to here. He might as well be a million miles away.

'Welcome to Hades,' she said.

He frowned. She'd come straight here. Why would she be here if she hated the place? 'I thought you loved your family home?'

'I do. I meant me,' she said.

She saw *herself* as Hades? But why would she be his idea of hell? He really didn't understand. 'Are you getting in?' he asked when she'd closed the gate behind them.

'Do you mind if Cerberus comes in the back of your car? For once, he's not muddy—but he might shed a few hairs.'

'I can live with dog hairs. I'm here because you wanted to talk,' he reminded her.

'We'll talk at the house.'

And her tone was so determined that he knew it was pointless arguing and trying to get her to put him out of his misery right here and right now. The quicker he drove them to the house, the quicker she'd tell him what was going on. Though he couldn't help feeling hurt. He'd driven here all the way from London, because she'd asked him to. Right now, she was all efficient and professional, the way she was in the emergency room; there was none of the warmth and sweetness of the woman he knew outside work.

She let the dog into the back of the car, where he lay down on the seat and behaved impeccably, then she got into the passenger seat.

'Where shall I park?' he asked as she directed him to the back of the house.

'Anywhere on the gravel. Next to me would be fine.'

He parked the car; she climbed out and let the dog out of the back, and Cerberus trotted over to a door and sat patiently staring at it.

'The kitchen. He's probably going to try scrounging banana bread from Vicky,' she said. 'Would you like some? It's almost lunchtime, so you must be starving.'

Daniel's stomach was rumbling, but he ignored it. He'd had enough of Beatrice's politeness. 'I'd rather know what's going on,' he said.

'Fair enough.' She opened the door, and ushered him inside. 'Oh. Vicky must've gone somewhere,' she said, sounding surprised that her sister-in-law wasn't in the kitchen. 'Cerberus, you bad hound, on your bed. You know you're not allowed in the main house until the evening.'

The Labrador gave her a mournful look, but went over to a larger wicker basket and threw himself down on the cushions with a dramatic sigh, then lay with his nose on his paws.

'This way,' she said to Daniel, and led him through to the main part of the house. The grand entrance hall had a chequered marble floor and oak panelling. There was a very fancy grandfather clock in one corner, cabinets with inlaid marquetry, and what looked like some kind of weighing machine. There were also enormous oil paintings on the wall, all with ornate gilt frames, and Venetian glass chandeliers hung from the ceiling.

It felt more like a film set than a home. One of those Jane Austen comedy of manners films that Jenny had loved, but had annoyed him because he hated all the snobbishness.

This didn't bode well.

In silence, he followed her up the wide curving staircase, through corridors lined with more of the huge oil paintings—portraits of Lindford ancestors, he guessed—up more stairs, and finally up a spiral stone staircase.

When they got to the top and she led him out of a narrow wooden door, he realised they were standing on the roof of the house. 'I wasn't expecting this.'

'The view's pretty amazing from up here.'

'It is,' he agreed.

'But that isn't why I brought you here. This is.' She gestured to the cupola. 'My Great-great-uncle Sebastian's observatory.'

She opened the door and switched on the light. 'There are two lights. The red light's for night-time when it's being used as a proper observatory, and obviously this one is for daytime.'

The walls inside were wooden-panelled; there was a shelf of what looked like books on astronomy, and the ceiling of the dome was painted like an old star map, complete with mythological creatures. In the centre of the room was a large mounted telescope. It was absolutely amazing. 'Iain would be beside himself with excitement if he saw this.'

'And I'm looking forward to showing him,' she said.

But—wasn't she trying to dump him? Why would she suggest bringing Iain here if she was going to split up with him?

'My great-great-uncle turned the cupola into an observatory when he came back here after the First World War, so he could sit up here and watch the stars. I guess it was his way of coping with shell shock,' Beatrice said.

'PTSD, as we know it now,' Daniel said.

'It's a good place to think. Just you and the sky. Especially after midnight, when the only lights here are security lights that switch on if they detect movement—otherwise it's miles and miles to the nearest street lamps, so the skies are incredible.' She pressed a lever, and a slice of the roof slid open. 'The roof of the dome rotates—there's another switch for that—so you can move it with the telescope to see whatever you want, at any time of year.'

Then he realised why she'd brought him here. This was obviously her safe place, the way it had been for her great-great-uncle. Her place to think. 'Is this where you came to sit after you lost Taylor?' he asked.

'Yes. Looking up at the stars was the only thing that made any sense, for a while. I got to understand Sebastian very, very well.' She looked at him. 'I'm sorry, Daniel. I haven't been fair to you.'

'I'm sure you had your reasons.' He held her gaze. 'Though I would appreciate an explanation. Right now I don't have a clue what's happening. And, if I'm being honest, I'm a bit hurt that you didn't even give me a reason—you just left.'

'I'm sorry,' she said again. 'I've been trying to find the right words. I'm still trying. And I just don't know how to say it.'

So was she dumping him or not? 'Keep it simple,' he said. 'That's usually the best way, even when you think it's complicated.'

'Oh, it's complicated, all right,' she said. 'I can't think of a way to soften it, so I'll try it your way. Forgive me, because this is going to be a bit of a shock.' She swallowed hard. 'I'm pregnant.'

He stared at her, not sure that he'd really heard her correctly. 'Pregnant?' he repeated.

'Pregnant,' she said again.

It felt as if someone had just dropped him from a great height into the middle of the sea. His ears were roaring and he couldn't breathe. Pregnant? But she couldn't be. They'd been careful. They hadn't taken a single risk.

OK, so there was a tiny, tiny—infinitesimally tiny—chance that a condom wouldn't prevent a pregnancy. A chance so small that he hadn't really considered it to be a risk at all. They were both over thirty, her fertility levels were dropping by the day, and all the unexpected pregnancies he'd ever heard about were due to taking risks.

But that tiny, tiny chance had resulted in a baby.

'I'm sorry.' She looked anguished.

'It's not your fault. It takes two to make a baby.'

'I don't mean that. I mean I'm sorry for giving you this news just after Jenny dropped her bombshell. I know this is your worst nightmare.'

Now he began to understand what she'd meant about 'welcome to Hades'. She'd known she was about to resurrect the past for him. Jenny, the postnatal depression, the way Jenny had walked out and left Iain. He'd been very sure that he didn't want to take that risk ever again and have another child.

But she'd also been very clear that she didn't want a child. That she couldn't face the possibility of things going wrong again and losing a baby the same way she'd lost her daughter. 'It's your worst nightmare, too.' He looked at her. 'So how pregnant are you? When did you find out?'

'My period's two weeks late,' she said. 'I guess with all that's been happening, I haven't really been thinking about my cycle. But I've been regular as clockwork for years and years. The only time I missed a period was when I was pregnant with Taylor. And this morning when I got up I felt odd—like I did the last time I was pregnant. When I counted back to my last period and I realised I was late, it was the obvious answer. I kept trying to tell myself that I was being ridiculous and I went through every single medical reason for missing a period, the vast majority of which didn't apply to me.' She grimaced. 'So I bought a test. Just to prove to myself that we'd been careful and of course I wasn't pregnant. Except the test was positive—and then I panicked.'

And she'd fled to her safe place. Here.

'I know you don't want another child,' she said.

'You said you didn't, either.' He paused, trying to work this out. 'So if you count back to your LMP, that makes you six weeks.'

'And I'm scared,' she said softly. 'Not just about whether I'm going to be able to carry a baby to term or if I'm going to have an abruption.'

'What else are you scared about?'

'Honestly? I don't know how this is going to work out. We haven't been seeing each other for very long.'

Then the penny dropped. She hadn't brought him here to dump him—she'd asked him to come here because she thought *he* was going to dump *her* when she broke the news about her pregnancy, and she wanted to be here to lick her wounds.

'Put it this way, you're the first woman I've dated since my marriage broke up,' he said. 'The first in four years. Which I think counts for something.'

'It's the same for me. You're the first man I've dated since my marriage broke up,' she echoed. 'The first in four years.'

'Which I think also counts for something,' he said.

The fact that they'd taken a risk on each other, when both of them were so wary about relationships.

'Maybe. But none of this was supposed to happen.' She spread her hands. 'We were supposed to be seeing where this took us. Taking it slowly.'

'Maybe it's just happened a little faster than we intended,' he said wryly.

'Faster? I'm pregnant,' she said. 'That's so fast it's almost supersonic. And this is your worst nightmare. You're worried enough about Jenny's new pregnancy and what effect it might have on Iain; and you know I had mental health issues after my baby died. That I took an overdose. Doesn't that make me too risky to be around Iain?'

'It happened years ago. You're in a different place now. And what you suggested about Jenny applies to you, too,' he pointed out. 'If your health professionals know about your history and they're keeping an eye on you, and if you have the right support at home...' He let the words tail off, and sighed. 'I let Jenny down. I didn't give her the right support. Who's to say I won't let you down, too?'

'For what it's worth, I know you weren't deliberately unsupportive. Everyone missed the signs.' She looked him straight in the eye. 'You're not the kind of man to let someone down.'

She had rather more faith in him than he did in himself, he thought.

'So where does this leave us?' she asked.

'Honestly? I don't have a clue. I've just found out that you're pregnant. I'm still trying to get my head round that,' he said. 'A baby.'

'Believe me, I've only had a couple more hours than you to get my head round it,' she said.

'And have you managed it?'

She grimaced. 'Yes and no. I talked to Vicky.'

'What did she say?'

'She was better than she thought at the wobbly stuff,' Beatrice said. 'Though she was a bit brutal. She asked me if I wanted a termination.'

'That's one option,' he said, striving to keep his tone non-judgemental. It was an option that didn't sit well with him; if there were medical reasons for a termination, if the mum's life was at stake, then fair enough. But to get rid of a baby just because it wasn't convenient... To him, that felt wrong.

'It's not an option for me,' she said. 'I lost a baby at twenty-eight weeks, Daniel. Yes, I know that right now our baby could be considered as little more than a collection of cells, but I just can't...' She blew out a breath. 'I told her no.'

'I'm glad,' he said. 'Because that's how I feel.'

'OK. So we're agreed that we're keeping the baby. That leads us to the next decision we have to make,' she said. 'Do we raise the child together, or will I be a single parent?'

'You and me. A family,' he said. 'We could do that.'

'There's not just us to consider,' she said.

He could have kissed her for that; it told him that she wasn't going to push Iain away.

'How would Iain feel about it? About us all living together, about the baby?'

'Iain hasn't stopped talking about you since you fixed his arm on the football field. I don't know if it's that, the fact you play trains with him, your brownies, or that

amazing day out you organised at the Planetarium—
he adores you and he's forever asking me when we can
see you next,' Daniel said. 'I think I can safely say he'd
be happy about it. But, I warn you, if you live with us
you'll have to put up with hours and hours of questions
from him.'

'He's bright.' She smiled. 'He'll come up with interesting questions. I'll enjoy that.'

'On a Friday night, when I'm tired and I can't think
of answers, it'll be nice to have someone else to come
up with suggestions.' He paused. 'So how about you? Is
that what you want?'

'All I can think about right now,' she admitted, 'is
how scared I am that everything's going to go wrong.'

'There's a fairly big part of my head doing the same
right now,' he said. 'But then I think of my little boy.
Things *did* go wrong for us, but we've muddled through
and we're doing OK.'

She swallowed hard. 'My situation didn't have an option for muddling through.'

'What happened to you,' he said softly, 'was terrible.
I'm sorry you lost the baby, and I'm sorry that you were
so low you didn't want to be in this world any more.
But there's an inner strength to you, Beatrice. You got
through it. And you know what we said about this being
our second chance?'

She said nothing, but he could see a spark of hope
in the fear in her beautiful blue eyes. And he wanted to
fan that hope into a proper flame. 'Maybe this baby is
part of that second chance. Yes, we both have fears—
even though we're doctors and we know the risks are
small, we're human so of course we're going to worry
that the past will repeat itself—that you'll have an ab-

ruption, putting the baby at risk, and that I won't spot any signs of postnatal depression and I'll let you down. But we can talk about our fears instead of shutting them away inside, and then they'll lose their power to hurt us.'

The hope in her eyes brightened and then dimmed again. 'I let you down. I knew what had happened with Jenny, and I shouldn't have just walked out on you. I should've at least told you that I'd come here.'

'You said yourself that you panicked. If I put myself in your shoes—well, maybe I would've done the same thing,' he said. 'And at least you called me a couple of hours later. You didn't let it get to the stage where I had people looking for you, worried sick that something had happened.'

'I was so looking forward to going away with you,' she said. 'I thought it was going to be a romantic weekend where we'd spend time together and get closer. Sunshine and sand and the sound of the sea.'

'That's what I wanted, too,' he said.

'We've only known each other a few weeks. The way I saw it, we'd keep dating for a while and we'd get closer, and then maybe we'd fall in love. We'd make a family with Iain when we were ready and we'd all got used to the idea. But the baby's changed all that.'

'Has it? Maybe it's just changed the timescale a bit,' he said.

'So, what—we make a family and then hope we fall in love?'

Did that mean she didn't feel the same way about him? Or was she trying to be brave and breezy and not put any pressure on him?

If she didn't love him, he had nothing to lose.

If she did love him and she was trying to be brave

because she didn't think he loved her, then he had everything to gain.

'I didn't say the order had changed, just the timescale,' he pointed out.

Her eyes went wide. 'So are you saying…?'

'I'm saying you're right, we haven't known each other for very long—but we've known each other for long enough for me to know that I love you,' he said. 'There's you at work, all kind and calm and professional. You're very easy to like. But it's not just the fact I like you. It's not just a physical thing, either, even though you're gorgeous and, as Iain says, you have hair like a princess. It's *you*. The woman who talks to me last thing at night so I go to sleep smiling. The woman who makes chocolate cake that I actually enjoy eating, and believe me I've had more than thirty years of loathing chocolate cake. The woman who dances with me in her kitchen and makes me feel as if I'm walking on air. It's you. The way you make me feel. When I'm with you I feel that I'm living, not just existing.'

'That's how I feel about you, too,' she whispered. 'That I'm living, not just existing. That there's always something to look forward to in a day, whether it's a walk in the park or talking to you on the phone before I go to sleep, or drinking Prosecco in the sunset on my patio. I like being with you.' Her eyes filled with tears. 'And I hurt you today. I was a coward. Instead of talking to you, I ran away—just like Jenny did. I hurt you.'

'Yes, you did.' It was only fair to acknowledge it, now they were being honest with each other. 'But I understand why.' He paused. 'And you could always try kissing me better.'

'I could.'

The flicker of hope in her eyes was now the blaze he'd wanted it to be. He opened his arms, and she stepped into them.

And then she kissed him.

It was slow and sweet at first, even a little shy. But then he let her deepen the kiss and he wrapped his arms tightly round her. This was where he wanted to be. With her. Holding her. Loving her. Being part of her life.

When she broke the kiss, they were both shaking.

'I love you, too, Daniel,' she said. 'And I want to be a family with you. The two of us, Iain and our baby. And the extended family—I like your mum, and I think you'll get on just fine with my lot. I'd like to be friends with Jenny, so she'll know she's always welcome in your life. And it really doesn't matter whether we get married or not, as long as we're together.' She stroked her face. 'But I think we shouldn't move in together until we're sure that Iain's happy with the situation. That he knows you're still his dad; that although I'm not his biological mum and I'd never try to push Jenny out, I'd like him to think of me as his other mum; and that he's going to have another little brother or sister to boss around.'

'Agreed,' he said.

'And,' she added, 'I'm going to try and push past all the fears. I don't want our pasts to get in the way of our future and I know you'll have my back—just as I'll have yours.'

'Always,' he said, and kissed her.

EPILOGUE

A year later

'THE PLANETARIUM?' BEATRICE ASKED. 'I love it here, darling, but I'm not sure your baby brother's quite old enough to come here.'

'But, Mum,' Iain said plaintively, 'it's my favourite place—well, except Great-great-great-uncle Sebastian's observatory on Grampa's roof, and maybe the park if we're playing football.'

'Let's do the park and play football today, and then we can come to the Planetarium another day, when one of your grandmothers or your mum can look after Rowan for us,' Beatrice suggested.

Iain shook his head. 'But he'll love it, Mum. He loves the starry sky lights I chose him.'

The light show that played constellations, the moon and the sun over the ceiling. They'd chosen it together after the twenty-week scan—which Iain had come to with them, and had been convinced that his new baby brother had waved to him, so Iain had been adamant that the starry sky light should be his 'welcome to the world' present to his baby brother.

'He might start crying in the middle of the show,'

Beatrice said gently, 'and that isn't fair to all the other people who came to see it.'

'But we *have* to go,' Iain said, hopping from foot to foot. 'Tell, her, Dad!'

'I'm with Iain. My vote's for the Planetarium today,' Daniel said with a smile.

She was all for the father-son bond, but the pair of them really hadn't thought this through properly. 'What if Rowan starts crying in the middle of the show?' Beatrice asked again.

Daniel coughed and indicated the fast asleep baby in the pram he was pushing. 'I'm pretty sure he's out for the count.'

'He might wake up.'

'*Mum*. It's our special place because we live in London and we can't always go to Great-great-great-uncle Sebastian's observatory,' Iain said. 'I know he'll love it there. Please.'

Daniel produced an envelope from his back pocket. 'We've got VIP tickets, as it's Rowan's first time at the Planetarium.'

'Oh, for goodness' sake. You've got more money than sense,' Beatrice said, rolling her eyes. 'And if your son does start crying in the middle of the show, Daniel Capaldi, you'll be the one taking him out and checking his nappy.' She put her hands on her hips and stared at Iain. 'And you'll be going with your dad, Iain Capaldi, to hold the nappy bag. And if it's a really stinky one, it'll serve you both right.' But her indignation was mostly for show. She loved Iain's enthusiasm for the stars, she loved the fact that he'd wanted to call her 'Mum' as well as Jenny—with Jenny's blessing—and she loved the fact he wanted to share everything with his new baby brother.

Life with her new family was pretty much perfect. Although she and Daniel had worried about the pregnancy and what would happen afterwards, her maternity team had kept a close eye on her throughout the pregnancy and reassured them both. She'd flinched every time she'd got behind the wheel of the car in her twenty-eighth week, but she'd made herself drive to help her put the past behind her, and Daniel had been there to reassure her that everything would be just fine. And it had been; she got to the twenty-ninth week, and finally she could put the fears behind her.

Everything had gone smoothly for the rest of her pregnancy, and Rowan had decided to make his appearance on his actual due date rather than surprising them early or making them wait longer.

After Rowan's birth, it had been Daniel's turn to be twitchy and Beatrice's turn to reassure him. As the days passed and she hadn't shown any sign of postnatal depression, he'd begun to relax. Now Rowan was three months old, happy and healthy; they'd moved from Daniel's flat to a house with a garden and the potential promise of getting a rescue dog. And the world felt full of sunshine.

The auditorium was remarkably empty, Beatrice thought as they made their way inside. 'Are we super-early for the show?' she asked Daniel as they took their seats—ones she'd chosen as near to the door as possible, so they could make a quick and quiet exit with the baby if they needed to.

'No, we're right on time,' Daniel said.

'But nobody else is here.'

'We've got VIP tickets, Mum,' Iain reminded her. 'Especially for Rowan's first show.'

Which the baby was sleeping through quite content-edly, Beatrice thought wryly. 'OK,' she said. Maybe Daniel had booked a short private viewing for the four of them—though surely he would've said that rather than telling her that they had VIP tickets?

A man she assumed was that session's astronomer took the stage. 'Today's showing is a special tour of our solar system,' he said. 'Starting with a flight through Saturn's rings.'

That was an odd choice, Beatrice thought. She would've expected him to start either with Neptune, the furthest out, and work inwards; or the sun itself and work outwards.

The lights dimmed and music began playing. As the first pictures of Saturn came into view, the astronomer left the stage.

That was odd, too, Beatrice thought. The astronomer usually stood to the side of the stage and talked every-one through what they were seeing.

Even odder was that Iain and Daniel both quietly got up and walked towards the stage.

She was about to protest and call them back to their seats when the picture changed, becoming static rather than a video of Saturn and its rings. The picture was still Saturn, but there was a message written on the planet's rings in bright pink lettering.

Beatrice Lindford, will you marry us?

The lights came up to reveal Daniel and Iain on the stage, both of them kneeling on one knee in the tradi-tional pose.

'Mum, we love you to the end of the universe and back,' Iain said.

Daniel opened his hand to reveal a velvet-covered box with a solitaire diamond ring nestling in it. 'For the last year, since you moved in with us, you've made us both so happy. And now we've got Rowan, too.'

'You're the only one in the house who isn't a Capaldi, and you *need* to be a Capaldi,' Iain added.

'So will you marry us?' Daniel asked.

Beatrice blinked away the tears, checked that Rowan was still fast asleep, then walked over to the stage to join them—the man she loved and the little boy she loved as if he was her own. 'Yes,' she said. 'Most definitely yes.'

Daniel slid the ring onto her finger and kissed her thoroughly. Iain, meanwhile, was busy using Daniel's phone. And then Daniel's phone pinged to signal an incoming text.

'I'll get it, Dad.' Iain peered at the screen.

'All OK, son?' Daniel asked.

'Yup.' Iain was grinning his head off, clearly delighted about something.

But Beatrice didn't have a chance to ask what her menfolk were plotting, because Daniel said, 'Our slot's about to finish. Let's go out this way and we'll go and get a cup of tea to celebrate.'

'And cake,' Iain said. 'It won't be as good as your cake, Mum, but almost.'

'Tea and cake it is,' Beatrice agreed. She followed them out of the door, only to be greeted with a barrage of party poppers and loud cheering.

It took her a moment or two to realise what was going on—but then she saw that all their family was there. Her parents, her brothers and sisters-in-law, her niece and nephews, Daniel's mum and his grandparents, Jenny and Jordan and their new baby girl. There was also a fair sprinkling of their friends outside work, along with everyone from their department who wasn't on duty. 'I can't believe everyone's here!'

'It's not every day you get engaged. And you can't have an engagement without a party,' Daniel said, looking very pleased with himself.

'But—how did you manage to get everyone here?' she asked.

'We asked them,' Iain said, looking even more pleased with himself than his father did.

'You both arranged this whole party on your own?' The room was decorated, there was food and drink, there was music, there were balloons… Everything was perfect.

'We had a bit of help,' Daniel admitted. 'Our mums and Vicky organised the invitations and did all the booking, so you wouldn't accidentally see an email or anything.'

'So everyone knew except me?' She was amazed that they'd managed to organise everything without her knowledge and that everyone had kept it secret—especially Iain, who was still young enough to blurt things out and frequently did so.

'It was *really* hard not telling you,' Iain said, 'and I nearly told you three times, but Dad said you'd be so happy if we surprised you that your eyes would go all shiny, like when I called you "Mum" the first time and when Rowan was born.'

'I *am* happy, darling.' Beatrice hugged him. 'You and Dad and Vicky and the grannies have done a wonderful job. Look at all those balloons. Oh, and the cake!'

'Vicky made the cake,' Iain said. 'She put Saturn on it.'

'That makes it even more special.' She hugged Iain again, then straightened up and turned to Daniel. 'And you are amazing.'

'I had help,' he said again. 'I really can't take very much credit for this. Our mums and Vicky were phenomenal.'

'We wanted to help because you're perfect together,' Catherine said, coming over arm in arm with Susan.

'Exactly,' Susan agreed. 'And when Daniel said he wanted to ask you to marry him somewhere special, Iain said it had to be here. We looked into it, and...' She spread her hands. 'Well, here we are. I knew when I first met you that you and Daniel were meant to be together. Welcome to the family, Bea.' She hugged Beatrice warmly.

'Welcome to the family, Daniel,' Edward said, handing him and Beatrice a glass of champagne. 'And, yes, Bea, before you say it, I know you're feeding Rowan, but a celebratory sip won't hurt.'

'Can I have some champagne, Grampa?' Iain asked.

'My little Scottish chieftain, I have something even more special for you. Let's go and find it,' Edward said, and swung Iain onto his shoulders.

'Congratulations.' Jenny hugged them in turn. 'I'm so happy for you both, And Iain's thrilled that you're officially going to be his other mum, Bea.'

'I'm thrilled, too,' Beatrice said, hugging her back.

Rowan was scooped up by his grandmothers, and Daniel held his hand out to Beatrice. 'Come and dance,' he said with a smile.

Once they were on the dance floor and they were

dancing cheek to cheek, he said, 'Iain and me, we love you to the end of the universe and back.'

'That's how much I love you, too,' Beatrice said. 'And this has to be the most perfect place for you to propose and for us to get engaged. I can't believe you all set this up between you. It's fantastic. All our family and friends here to celebrate with us, and you all kept it so quiet!'

'It's going to be a very short engagement,' Daniel warned, 'because I can't wait to marry you. Besides, if we leave it too long, our young wedding planner's going to start suggesting that we get married on the moon and get everyone there by rocket.'

Beatrice laughed. 'We could always hire a film set...' She kissed him. 'I love you. And I don't mind where we get married or when, just as long as we're together.'

'Together.' He kissed her. 'Always.'

* * * * *

THE FAMILY
THEY'VE
LONGED FOR

ROBIN GIANNA

MILLS & BOON

This book is dedicated to awesome cousins
George, Christie, Soula and Django.
Thanks so much for answering all my questions
and giving me great insight into your Alaskan world.
Prepare to have me come visit soon! xoxo

CHAPTER ONE

"Just follow the standard orders for her release from the hospital as I wrote them," Dr. Aurora Anderson said into her phone. "I know Dr. Jones has her chart, but he doesn't know all the nuances of her problem. Any questions, call me and I'll get back to you as soon as I can."

Overhead, the last call for her flight to Alaska was urgently announced and she huffed out an impatient breath as the intern asked a few more questions.

"Listen, I have to board my plane. I'll call when I get to Fairbanks. You need to follow my instructions. Yeah, I *get* that Dr. Jones is filling in for me while I'm gone, but I already talked to the parents about the plan. I don't want anyone deviating from that and confusing them. They know I'll be seeing their daughter as soon as I get back, and that they only need to contact Dr. Jones if something seems wrong."

Rory shoved her phone into her backpack, grabbed her carry-on bag and ran to hand her boarding pass to the airline attendant, ignoring the disapproving frown the woman gave her. Being late to board wasn't catastrophic, but messing around and changing her orders for a patient post-op absolutely might be, so she couldn't worry about being the last on the plane.

After four years of med school, five years of residency and finally getting the board exam under her belt, she'd damned well earned her title: Doctor of Pediatric Orthopedic Medicine. She knew all this second-guessing from the intern was because she wasn't yet an attending physician. But having her orders followed was supremely important—not only for the patient, but for her future on the doctors' roster. If all went well, she'd have a permanent position there in a matter of weeks, and she'd never have to think about uprooting her life again.

She wrestled her bag into the overhead compartment and apologized as she squeezed her way past the two people in her row before finally plopping into the window seat. She drew a calming breath and pulled out her phone again, calling a nurse to give her instructions about a couple of other patients before they were told to turn off all electronics for takeoff.

Why they insisted on that, she had no clue, since people used computers and phones around all kinds of electronic medical equipment and not once had it interfered with testing and diagnostics. Then again, she thought to herself, she wasn't an engineer, so she should stick with what she knew instead of offering opinions—something a few people in her past had frequently pointed out... one of whom she'd be seeing again this week whether she wanted to or not.

That painful realization had her stomach twisting like a terrifying tornado. Seeing him again, being in her hometown at all, was going to be torture; it would bring back all the horrible memories, all the guilt, all the sorrow she'd tried so hard to leave behind.

The plane lifted, propelling her toward the one place she absolutely didn't want to go. She swallowed hard, trying to control the sickly feeling in her stomach, and tipped her forehead against the window to stare down at what had been her home for the past nine years.

The dizzying concrete mass of freeways connecting the hulking city of Los Angeles and all its suburbs couldn't be more different from where she'd grown up. Where she was heading now.

With serious effort she managed to move her thoughts to the patients she'd just performed surgery on, and the others she was scheduled to see in her office the rest of the week. It wasn't going to happen now. Because a different kind of patient needed her help. The woman who'd always needed some kind of care or guidance throughout Rory's whole life.

Her sweet, wacky, childlike mother.

The plane rose higher above the clouds, leaving LA far behind. Rory dropped her head against her seatback and closed her eyes.

It would be okay. It *would*. Being with her mother for the next week would be really nice, since she'd spent so little time with her these past nine years.

Her mom loved her life in Eudemonia, Alaska, and hadn't been too interested in visiting Rory in LA. The few times her mom had come to Southern California had been a joy, and a huge source of entertainment to everyone she'd been in med school with, and later her friends in the hospital. There weren't too many people like Wendy Anderson, and her unique way of dressing was startling even in a big city like Los Angeles.

A smile touched her lips at the memories—until reality hit her like a hard fist all over again. Taking care of her mom would be the easy part. The hard part would be being back home. The worst part would be seeing Jacob Hunter again.

Yesterday, the sound of his voice on the other end of the phone had made her heart jolt hard in her chest, then hammer wildly—even after she had found out the reason he'd been calling. He'd been letting Rory know about her mother's emergency surgery for a ruptured appendix, telling her that she was fine, and now just needed some nursing and recovery time.

Unbidden, the face that had fascinated her since the fourth grade appeared in her mind and memories of him spread to her heart, bringing a melancholy pleasure and unrelenting pain. Though their friendship—and more—was long over, she would always cherish the memories of their childhood together, and their years as lovers in college.

But theirs had been a love that had resulted in the worst thing ever to happen to either of them.

She squeezed her eyes more tightly shut, as though she could squish the memories right out of her brain. It hadn't happened in nine years, so clearly there was no point in trying now. Still, she worked to think, instead, about her mother's idiosyncrasies, which made her laugh and sometimes drove her crazy, even though she loved her to bits.

From the time Rory had been barely more than a toddler, she vividly remembered her mother insisting that she call her Twinkle-Toes or Twinkie instead of Mom. Possibly because she adored wearing dance and fairy costumes, but mostly because actually acting like a mom had never been on her radar.

There were memories of the two of them doing all sorts of unorthodox things—like painting every lampshade in the house neon so they'd glow in "pretty colors"; like deciding that creating rock sculpture Voodoo talismans all around the house would keep them safe after Rory's father died. Rory had helped with all that to make her mom feel more comfortable even as she had inwardly rolled her eyes—as she had when her mother danced spontaneously whenever the mood struck, not caring if there were other people around or not.

So many of the things her mother did were adorable and funny. But sometimes embarrassing—especially once Rory had become a teen. She found herself managing to smile in anticipation of what might greet her today at the house she'd grown up in, knowing that spending time with her unique mother was the only thing that would make this trip bearable.

The moment the plane touched down at the Fairbanks Airport, Rory felt like a ten-pound weight had dropped onto her shoulders. Looking out at the snowcapped peaks of the Alaska Range, she felt the memories she'd tried to stuff down flood back. They forced her to think about what had happened the last two times she'd been home.

One thing had turned out to be the biggest mistake of her life, which had left her with a shredded heart she knew would never be repaired. The other had been her father's funeral, two years later. He had bravely suffered through diabetes, then kidney failure, for more years than she could remember. Neither one of those memories were things she wanted to revisit and remember, but being here again thickened her throat even as she promised herself she wouldn't fall apart.

The forty-five miles from Fairbanks passed way too fast, and soon she was driving into the city limits of Eudemonia. The moment she saw the familiar stores and homes, and the trees which were now mostly naked except for a few straggling golden yellow leaves still clinging to the branches, her chest squeezed even tighter.

Finally the tiny house she'd grown up in came into view, surrounded by birch, aspen and spruce trees that were bigger than she remembered. Cozy and charming, in a worn sort of way, the house stood atop the small hill she'd rolled and sledded down as a kid, her mother rolling and laughing along with her while her dad watched and applauded—the hill she'd run down nine years ago, stumbling and falling, somehow getting in her car, tears making it hard to see, grief making it hard to breathe, to leave for LA.

God, she *had* to get these feelings under control before she went in to see her mother.

She hit the brakes and sat there, waiting for the sickly feeling to pass. She gulped in a few breaths, admitted she was as ready as she'd ever be, then turned her rental car off the road to bump across the uneven grass.

She could *do* this. She had to. She had to find a way to get through the next week without becoming a weeping mess all over again.

A single bulb dangled over the crooked wooden front porch, and a giant stuffed rabbit wearing a green army helmet sat on an overturned bucket to greet visitors. Why a rabbit, Rory had no clue—since it was early October, not Easter—but, boy, she couldn't wait to find out. Though it was likely her mom didn't have any reason other than she liked the way it looked.

The whole place appeared even more dilapidated than it had when she'd last been here for her dad's funeral. She'd called regularly, but she knew it had been cowardly of her to avoid this place, and consequently her mother.

She felt bad about it—she did—except that being here made her feel even worse. Maybe someday she would be able to face what she'd done and deal with the pain.

Nine years hadn't accomplished that—which meant that "someday" was still a long way off. If it ever came.

She knew she was beyond blessed that her mom had lots of friends to spend time with. Close friends who always looked after one another. People who were a big part of the reason why her mother sounded like her happy self whenever they spoke.

But what her mom had gone through with her surgery wasn't normal, everyday stuff. Rory knew her mother was supposed to be doing all right, but she might still be in a lot of pain. How on earth would her mom have coped if Rory *hadn't* come home?

She had no idea. Which made her realize all over again that, despite everything, she felt glad to finally be here for her mom.

She planned to nurse her mom with lots of TLC. Then, with any luck, she'd be close to her normal self by the time her mom's sister, Rory's Aunt Patty, came to take over. Much as she dreaded spending time at home again, getting her mother healthy enough for Rory to feel okay to leave her had to be the goal.

She stepped up to the front door and paused to pick at the paint flaking from the side, making a mental note to call a painter to get it done next summer. She knew it was too cold to paint now, but getting it on the schedule would be better than nothing.

Her job as a resident pediatric orthopedic surgeon provided her with enough money to live on and pay for this kind of repair stuff. And now that she'd passed her boards she'd be making a lot more. Assuming she got the permanent job—which was another reason to get back to LA as quickly as possible for her interview, before someone else snagged it away from her.

Even though it was barely six thirty, the vibrant golden sun was already setting in Eudemonia, Alaska—long before it would be in LA. She gazed at the fading orb, loving the way fingers of light slipped through the branches and lit the yellow leaves and hills. Up on the mountains the brilliant reds of the moss and lichen in the tundra glowed beneath the setting sun, and Rory was surprised at the warm nostalgia that filled her chest. It was so completely different from the warm temperatures, the concrete roads, the masses of cars and buildings and people that made up LA.

Thinking of the warm temperatures made Rory shiver as the chilly air sneaked down inside her jacket, and she shook her head at herself. Her friends here would laugh at what a wimp she'd become, thinking it was cold now, in early October. They'd probably all still be wearing shorts and T-shirts and thinking it felt downright balmy—but, hey, when she'd left Southern California earlier that day it had been almost eighty degrees. *Anyone* would feel the contrast, right?

She turned the knob and the door squeaked open. No surprise that her mom hadn't locked it, since Rory didn't think it had ever been secured in her whole life. In fact, thinking about it, she wasn't sure it even *did* lock. And wouldn't her California friends be flabbergasted at *that*?

"Hello? Mom? Twinkle-Toes?"

The light in the small living room was so dim it was hard to see, and she peered at the worn chairs, not seeing any sign of her mother's small frame. Sounds of marching band music, of all things, came faintly from the back of the house, and Rory had started to move toward her mother's bedroom when she appeared in the hallway outside the living room, with a small, curly-haired brown dog trotting beside her. Rory hadn't met him yet.

"Aurora! I'm so happy you're here! Come give your mama a big hug."

She hurried toward her mom, partly because she looked a little unsteady, walking with the pink cane she held in her hand. "Mom. Twinkie."

She gently enfolded her in her arms, being careful not to squeeze, and her throat clogged with emotion at how good it felt to hold her. Until this moment she hadn't even realized how much she'd missed seeing her and being with her. The pain of being in Eudemonia was so intense, the pleasure of seeing her mom often just wasn't enough to counteract it.

No doubt about it, she was a coward. A weakling.

"You shouldn't be wandering around with no one here. You just got out of the hospital this afternoon. What if you fell?"

"I knew you were coming. I knew you'd be here to take care of me, marshmallow girl."

Marshmallow girl. It had become her nickname after they'd filled her hot chocolate cup to overflowing with them one Christmas. It had become a tradition, with the various pups they'd had over the years gobbling up the marshmallows that had scattered on the floor. Why that had stuck in her mother's mind she had no clue, but she'd always kind of liked it when she called her that, remembering all the silliness of her home life.

"Yeah. I'm here to take care of you."

She pressed her cheek to her mother's soft, warm one,

thinking of all her years growing up, when she'd played parent to her mom instead of the other way around.

"How are you feeling?"

"Like I had a knife stabbed in my tummy—that's how!" She looked up at Rory with a mix of a grimace and a grin on her face. "Can you believe I had a bad appendix? After all the special herbs I eat and drink to stay healthy!"

"Yeah. Who'd have thought it? Maybe your appendix has had too much fun all these years, just like you, and got plain worn out."

"I'm not even close to worn out." She grinned and playfully swatted Rory's arm. "So I'm just as happy to not have a boring appendix. Good riddance to it, if it couldn't keep up with the fun and appreciate all the special teas and foods I gave it, right?"

"Right. Good riddance, appendix!"

Rory had to chuckle as she led her mom to what she knew was her favorite chair. No point in getting into a discussion on the subject of herbal supplements, and which ones her mother might avoid, since she'd never been interested in her daughter's opinions in the past.

She reached down to scratch the dog's ears as he wagged his tail. "Is this Toby? You described him to me, but he's even cuter than I expected."

"He's the best little doggie. He keeps me company and protects me just like the talismans."

Noting that the dog hadn't even barked when she'd walked in, let alone come out to see who was there, Rory smiled inwardly. Her mother believing the dog protected her was more important than whether or not it actually did.

The fact that she'd only started worrying about

that after Rory's father had died had been a surprise, since her sweet dad had been an invalid for so long he'd hardly have been able to deal with an intruder. But in her mother's eyes he'd been a superhero. And she'd been right. The way he'd tried to be there for them even while bravely dealing with his illness had made him one tough, heroic man.

"I'm glad you found such a wonderful dog to be here with you." She tucked her mom into the chair and kissed her forehead. "Are you hungry? I'm going to find you a little something to eat. And later I want to take a look at your incision. But before that I need to see all your hospital dismissal papers and read the instructions. Where are they?"

"In the kitchen somewhere. Linda brought me home and put them on the table, I think."

"I'm sorry I wasn't here in time to get you from the hospital. They told me you were being released tomorrow, and then when I called from the airport they told me you'd already left. That really makes me mad, by the way. I wanted to be there for you."

"I know. I was hoping you'd see the hospital gown they had me in—it was a powdery blue, with these funny little cats on it that were *too* cute. One reminded me of our old Brutus..." Since nothing much ever irritated her mother for long, she gave with a smile and a shrug. "But *you're* here now and *I'm* here now. We'll have lots of big fun once I'm feeling better."

Fun. The name of her mother's game. It was going to be nearly impossible to feel like having fun while she was here, but she'd give it a try for her mom's sake.

"You're going to have to take it easy on the fun while you heal. They told me the rupture was an emergency and they had to use a full traditional incision instead of doing it laparoscopically, so it's going to be a while before the pain is gone."

The thought of how serious that might have been had Rory reaching for another, longer hug.

"I'm going to see if there's food in the kitchen. If not, I brought some stuff in my bag to tide us over until I can get groceries from the store tomorrow. Sit tight for a minute."

The kitchen light was an overly bright fluorescent strip in contrast to the low living room lights, and Rory made another mental note to get more lamps in the other room, so her mother didn't trip over something.

Two gritty, slippery steps into the kitchen brought her to a halt.

From the look of the coffee cans full of colored sand all over the table, her mother's newest creative project was sand art. Glass containers were filled or partially filled in landscape scenes, and Rory recognized one of them as being the Alaska Range they could see from the back of their house—those beautiful mountains she'd always stared at as a child, dreaming about climbing them someday and crossing over them to somewhere different and big and amazing.

She picked up the jar with the mountain scene and ran her finger across the glass, looking at the brown and green sand topped with fine grains of white. She'd done that, hadn't she? Crossed that mountain. Become the kind of doctor few women were.

She'd thought she'd be looking at those mountain ranges forever, together with Jake. She'd thought they'd make a home and a family in Eudemonia, that they would work as doctors here and in Fairbanks and live happily ever after.

Except their "happy" had died, leaving an "ever after" impossible. She'd run hard and fast away from here—because she hadn't been sure she would survive if she'd stayed. She'd made a new life for herself—going to medical school in LA instead of Anchorage, like she and Jake had planned.

But her life still felt hollow. Full to the brim with work to keep her mind busy and her heart detached from the rest of the world. That detachment had taken a lot of time and effort to achieve. It was exhausting.

She drew in a deep breath and glanced around the kitchen to see that there was as much sand on the floor and the table as there was in the cans. Crunching toward the refrigerator, she peered inside, deciding she'd better get the floor cleaned up as soon as she'd taken some food to the living room and read the discharge papers, so her mom wouldn't slip on all the tiny grains. The last thing her mother needed was to fall and rip open her stitches.

The refrigerator was bare of anything but milk. There was also a little cheese, so Rory sliced it to serve with some crackers she found in the cupboard. She shook sand off the bottom of the hospital papers Linda had put in the middle of the table and went back to the living room.

"Here's a snack for you. I'm going to read through this stuff, then get some more food from my bag."

"This will be plenty. I'm not very hungry."

"Just eat what you can and we'll go from there. I understand if you're not feeling like it, but you do need at least a little so you get your strength back."

Rory straightened from putting the plate on her mother's lap, and was about to sit in the only other chair that had a decent light when she heard the front door open and looked up.

Her heart stuttered, then slammed hard into her ribs. *Jacob Hunter.*

She didn't want to look at him for more than a moment, yet she found herself staring, riveted. He looked like he always had—and yet he didn't. A little older but, impossibly, even better. He was still tall and lean, with angled features that were still startlingly beautiful: dark eyes that could see right through a person, and lips that were almost too full and yet perfect for his face. The black silky hair she'd loved to run her hands through long ago, when it had spilled to his shoulders, had been cut short enough to be respectable for the town doctor, but still it brushed his collar, not fully tamed.

He held a bag in one hand and, yeah, just as she would have expected, despite the chill in the air he was wearing a slightly shabby T-shirt that showed his shoulders and biceps were even more muscular than seven years ago, at her father's funeral. No shorts, but the jeans he wore fit his physique perfectly, making him look more like an Alaskan cowboy than a medical professional.

Her heart beat its way up into her throat, making it hard to breathe. She'd thought she was prepared to see him—but not this soon. Not tonight. Not when she was barely ready to deal with being back in town at all.

"Hello, Aurora."

He and her mother were the only two people who called her that. Her mom did because she'd always thought it such a romantic name for a baby born under the Northern Lights. The *aurora borealis*. And Jacob had often called her that because he'd known it annoyed her, and teasing had always been his way of telling someone he cared about them.

Not that he cared about her anymore. Not after all that had happened between them. Not with all the time that had passed since they'd spoken.

"Hello, Jacob."

"I didn't know when you were getting in, so I thought I'd check on Twinkie."

Twinkie. It also struck Rory that he was the only person who called her mother that other than her. Until that moment she hadn't thought about the familiarity that came with names and nicknames. None of her other friends had ever called her mom Twinkie—why had *he* picked that up?

Probably because he'd been around the house and participating in an awful lot of the crazy over the years. Funny how he had the kind of steady, predictable, wonderful family almost anyone would appreciate, and yet he'd enjoyed being at her zany, very unpredictable and unorthodox house just as much as his own.

"That's nice of you, but you don't need to worry about her now that I'm...here." She'd almost said *home*, but had stopped herself, because this wasn't her home anymore. Never could be.

"Might as well take a look while I'm here." Jake scratched the dog's head and it looked up at him with the same delighted expression as her mother did. "How are you feeling? Have you taken the pain medicine they gave you?"

"Oh, yes. I'm following all the directions they gave me. But I'm still in a lot of pain, so it's not working too well."

"Sorry you're in pain. It's not always easy to control

the first couple days out of surgery. Let me take a listen to your heart and lungs."

He reached back to the stethoscope he had looped into the back pocket of his jeans, then pressed his long fingers to her wrist while looking at his watch. Afterward he even pulled a portable blood pressure monitor out of his bag to check that, too.

Meanwhile Rory just stood there, feeling strangely uncomfortable, having no idea what to say or do now that he was here. The awkwardness hanging between them wasn't surprising, even though she'd foolishly hoped that seeing him might leave them both feeling indifferent. That had clearly been a pipedream, considering their parting years ago hadn't exactly been full of rainbows and smiling understanding between the two of them.

Her legs felt a little wobbly, and she briefly considered sitting down, but that would have left her on an uneven footing with him—looking up even more than her five feet four inches required her to.

Jacob's gaze suddenly turned back to Rory, and she swallowed at the mix of emotions in his eyes—the same anger and hurt and confusion that she felt tangling around her own heart…that had seared her to the depths of her soul when she'd left nine years ago.

"Your mom said your Aunt Patty's coming to take care of her after you're gone. She still working at the army base in Anchorage?"

"Yeah. She lives with her son Owen, who's stationed there. She scheduled next week off, so I'll only be here for a short time."

Those dark eyes seemed to bore right into her, and the long pause after she'd answered left her fidgeting—

until he finally broke the silence with the question she didn't want asked.

"So, how's your life?"

"Good. Everything is great."

God, when had she become such a liar? If there was one person who had to know that wasn't true, it was Jacob. But there *were* good things about her life, right? Although her job was about the only thing that came to mind.

"I just passed my board exams, so I'm officially a doctor of pediatric orthopedic medicine. I was supposed to be interviewing today, for a permanent position at the hospital, but I had to reschedule it for next week."

Again, he didn't speak, and even as she squirmed under his serious gaze memories of the time they'd been apart got mixed up with all the years they'd been together. It was as if nothing had changed between them.

For a brief moment she had the shocking urge to go up on her tiptoes and give him a kiss hello on that luscious mouth. Which proved that her brain's muscle memory was stronger than her common sense when it came to him. But of course that wasn't surprising, was it? They'd known one another since they were kids in elementary school.

Except kissing those lips hadn't happened until college, so that might not be the best explanation she could have come up with. Besides, all that felt like a lifetime ago.

He didn't respond, instead handing her a business card, his expression unreadable. "I'll be going, since you're here to look after Twinkie. Here's my number if you need to reach me. She's supposed to have a follow-up appointment with her surgeon in a few days. I can take over after that."

That uncomfortable flutter in her chest just wouldn't go away, and she swallowed at the realization that she'd be seeing him way too much during this visit if she had to do as he suggested.

"Maybe you forgot I'm a doctor too," she said, trying to somehow infuse some light humor into the words, even as the air felt like a heavy shroud hanging over her. "And a surgeon. Very used to dealing with post-op issues. After she sees her own surgeon I can take care of any problems she might have."

"Just the same as always." Annoyance and disapproval were clear in the dark eyes that flicked across her. "You can do *everything* better than anyone else. You never *listen* to anyone else."

"That's not what I said. I just meant—"

"I know what you meant. But here's the thing: I have all the equipment to take her vitals and deal with any problems at my office, not to mention pain meds and antibiotic ointment for her incision and replacement bandages. So get over your ultra-independent self and bring her to my office after her appointment so I can take a look."

"Jake, it's just not necessary to—"

"Don't worry," he interrupted with a mocking smile on his face. "Since you have to be in control of everything, I won't shut you out of the process."

"I don't… I don't have to be in control of everything!"

She folded her arms across her chest, which was starting to burn a little. She'd made one horribly bad decision—admittedly a life-changing decision, but still…

That didn't make her controlling. It made her foolish. Regretful. Broken.

"What's that supposed to mean?"

He didn't bother to answer that, just picked up the bag he'd brought and moved toward the kitchen.

"I have some food. I figured you wouldn't have had a chance to go to the store. I got it when I was in Fairbanks earlier, since the selection at Green's Market can be slim pickings sometimes. In case you don't remember."

Rory stared after him, trying to figure out how to handle all this as he moved out of sight.

Then her mother spoke. "It's so sweet of that Jacob to bring us food, isn't it?" her mother said, with the adoring smile on her face she always had when Jake was around, clearly oblivious to the tension between the two of them. "He always was something special. I remember—"

"I'll see if he needs help." Rory didn't want to be close to Jake in the small kitchen, but she definitely didn't want to listen to her mother's glowing diatribe about how perfect and wonderful he was.

But the truth...? He really *was* nearly perfect.

Yes, he had that impatience thing that sometimes boiled over into irritation. And he'd always left his socks in the middle of the floor, apparently not considering them to be "real" clothes that had to be put in the laundry bag. And somehow, he'd never seen pot lids as counting toward actual dishes that should be washed. But otherwise...

Perfection in human form. He just was.

She was the one who was totally and horribly flawed.

Just before she got to the doorway, a loud curse and then a series of crashing sounds came from the kitchen, and suddenly she remembered.

The sand. *Crap!*

She sprinted the last few steps, and once she hit the kitchen the toes of her boots slid across the linoleum and nearly jammed into the top of Jake's head, where he lay flat on his back on the floor. Cans and boxes were strewn everywhere, and a split plastic jug glugged a small river of milk onto the ancient blue linoleum.

"Oh, my God, are you all right?"

She knelt down next to him, her hands on his shoulders, his chest, traveling down his arms to see if they felt intact.

His deep brown eyes, surrounded by thick lashes, looked up and met hers, and for a long, arrested moment time felt suspended. Her heart thumped hard in her chest and it took all her willpower not to lean over and kiss him, just as she'd wanted to do earlier. Just as she'd done for so many years.

Her heart squeezed with familiar pain and longing as she forced herself to lean back instead of forward. "What hurts?"

"You're the orthopedic surgeon. Take a guess."

Something about the expression in his eyes told her that maybe he wasn't talking about physical injuries. That maybe his mind was going back in time too, the same way hers was. To the pain they'd shared and yet experienced in totally different ways.

She choked back all those wonderful and awful feelings that insisted on flooding back. "I'm guessing your tailbone is bruised, and maybe an elbow or two, but otherwise you feel okay."

For a split second his hand lifted toward her, before his fingers curled into his palm and he dropped his arm. He sat up, then shoved to his feet.

"Yeah, a few bruises."

He glanced down at his clothes and brushed off some of the clinging sand, clearly avoiding looking at her, before he began picking up the groceries that had been flung all over the kitchen.

"Don't worry about the milk," she said, hurrying to grab a kitchen towel to mop it up, even though it looked like Toby's happy licking was going to take care of it for her. "Or anything else. I'll put it all away. Thanks for bringing it."

His eyes met hers again, grim now. Probably he could tell she was beyond anxious for him to leave— but wouldn't he want to get away from her just as much?

"No problem. Also, even though neither of us wants to hang around each other, we need to do what's best for your mother." He shoved a few things in the fridge, then set the rest on the counter. "Which means you bringing her in to see me in a few days. Just let me know when."

Unexpected tears clogged her throat as she watched his long legs take him from the kitchen in fast strides, despite the risk of slipping, and she angrily swallowed them down. It shouldn't make her want to cry that he didn't want to spend time with her. Why *would* he? If she were him she'd keep as far away as possible from the woman who'd wrecked their dreams. And hadn't figuring out ways to avoid him been at the top of her mind the minute she'd bought her plane ticket?

But the quiet tears slid down her cheeks anyway.

CHAPTER TWO

"I'M GOING TO up your dose another twenty-five milligrams, Wilma," Jake said as he wrote a prescription for his elderly patient. "Your blood pressure is better, but still a little high."

"Okay, Dr. Hunter. I'll take it every day if you think I should."

He paused and glanced up at her. "You told me you *had* been taking it every day."

She took the paper he handed her and made a sheepish face. "Maybe not *every* day."

"If it's hard for you to remember I can have Ellie get you a pill box that helps you keep track. Are you going to Fairbanks soon, so you can fill this? Or do you need one of us to get it for you?"

"I want to get supplies before the snow comes, so my son's taking me tomorrow."

"Good."

He helped the woman down from the examination table and gave her a few more instructions. After she'd left the small room he wrote a note to himself to talk with her son to make sure she both got and took her medicine, then started typing his exam notes into the computer.

Ellie, who'd been office manager of this place for as

long as he could remember, poked her graying head in the door. "Your mom's here with Mika."

"Already?" He glanced at his watch, wondering how it had gotten so late. "Have her come in here while I finish this up."

The gleeful shriek that had been part of his world for the past eight months had him smiling before he even looked up from the computer. "I see he's in a happy mood. Thanks for watching him again, Ma."

"He's such a good boy." His mother beamed down at the baby in her arms. "He was cranky before his nap, but he's been all smiles since."

"I just need to finish up these notes, and then I have one more patient to see. Can you take Mika to my office to play until I'm done? Shouldn't be long."

"You still have things for him in there? Your dad bought him a new toy in Fairbanks today, but it's at our house for when we're babysitting. I told him he was going to spoil the child to death, since he'll be getting all kinds of toys for his birthday. One-year-olds deserve a special party, don't you think?"

"I don't think he cares if he gets a party, but I *do* know he'll love the attention." He glanced up and smiled. "As for the spoiling—you were both good at that with all three of us, growing up, but I think we turned out okay."

"Yes, you sure did. Two doctors and a lawyer? Not bad at all."

"Yeah, except Timothy always said I'd be the doctor, Grace would be the lawyer and *he* wanted to be the Native American chief. I think he still kind of wishes that had happened, instead of planning to come work here next year when he's finished with his residency."

He finished the notes and stood. The serious look

his mother sent him was a surprise, considering their light conversation.

"What?"

"Have you invited Rory over for dinner yet?"

"No, and I'm not planning to—which I already told you."

Seeing her in the office when she brought in her mother was going to be difficult enough. The last thing he wanted was hours of small-talk with the woman he'd thought would be with him forever—the woman who'd crushed his heart into tiny pieces, then stomped on them for good measure.

"She's busy with her mother, and I'm busy with work and Mika."

"Then *I'll* invite her. I want to catch up with all she's been doing since she moved to LA."

"Go ahead and invite her, then. Just don't expect me to come, too."

"Jacob," she said in a disapproving voice. "It's been a long time. I know things were…bad for both of you. But can't you two just be friends now, since you went through the same heartache together? You were such good pals for such a long time."

Good pals. That had been true for what seemed like nearly his entire life—until they'd become lovers. And then had come the happy surprise…before the horrible shock and the heartbreak. The fact that his mother wanted him to be friends with Rory now told him she had no clue how bad it had really been.

He wished he didn't still feel the bitter resentment and hurt. But seeing her for even a few minutes last night had proved he still wasn't ready to move on from that.

Maybe he never would be.

The moment he'd walked in through her mother's front door a storm of emotion had swarmed up and strangled him. Far more than he'd expected, considering it had been seven years since he'd last seen her at her dad's funeral, and they'd barely spoken then.

But he hadn't forgotten the amazing deep green of her eyes—like moss on a hillside in the summer. The honey highlights in her silky brown hair. And when he'd slipped and fallen on that damned floor, and she'd leaned over him, he'd been stunned that she smelled exactly the same as she always had. She obviously still dabbed grapefruit oil on her skin—something her mother had encouraged her to use as a child, claiming it boosted the immune system and made people feel more cheerful.

Rory had always rolled her eyes at her mother's conviction about all the things herbal oils would do for a person, and he'd sometimes wondered why she used it when it she claimed she didn't believe in it. Obviously she liked the stuff, no matter what she said about it.

If he closed his eyes he swore he could still smell her. But he wasn't going to tell his mother about all those memories and the discomfort—damn it, the *anguish* he'd felt when Rory left. Or that it was careening around inside of him all over again.

Before he could come up with some kind of answer that would satisfy her, Ellie poked her head in the door again.

"Rory Anderson is on the line. She says she thinks her mom has a urinary tract infection. She's having trouble passing urine, and it's cloudy. She's wondering if she can get an antibiotic from you."

He hesitated, then opened his mouth to say he'd write it and Ellie could call it into the pharmacy in Fairbanks.

He forced himself to close it again. His policy was never to prescribe medicine—especially antibiotics—over the phone. He had to see the patient first, make sure it was really what they needed.

But maybe this time he could make an exception, since Rory was a doctor. He could leave a prescription at the front desk for Rory to pick up, and he wouldn't have to see her—except for the day after her mother went to her surgeon for a follow-up.

No. Much as he didn't want to see Rory, he couldn't let his feelings urge him to violate good medical practice. Rory dealt with bones in her job. Who knew when she'd last had a patient with a UTI? Not to mention that a lot of surgeons called in antibiotic specialists for post-op infections. Truth was, there was no way around it.

He grimaced. "Tell her to bring Wendy in right now. We'll fit her in before the day's over."

"I feel fine, Aurora. I mean, yes, it really hurts to go to the bathroom, but my stitches hurt, too. I don't see any reason we have to go see Jacob. Can't I just take more pain medicine?"

"A urinary tract infection isn't something to mess around with, Twinkie. Not when you were on a cath-eter post-op and are having fever and chills now. You don't want it to get worse and result in a kidney infec-tion. Plus, you'll be more comfortable when an antibi-otic gets rid of it."

"I just hate going to doctors."

"Who doesn't? Except *this* doctor is one of your fa-vorite people, so quit complaining. He already said he'll squeeze you in this evening."

Which had her feeling relieved that her mom would

get the meds she needed, but totally dreading having to see Jake again, even though her mother would love it.

"Okay. I guess it's true that seeing Jacob is always fun. But why can't *you* just get me an antibiotic, if that's what you think I need? Isn't that why you went to doctor school?"

"I went to doctor school for a little more than that." Trust her mom to make her laugh, even as Rory was a ball of nerves. "But I can't prescribe medicine here. I don't have a medical license or privileges in Alaska."

"Well, that makes no sense. You were *born* here, for heaven's sake! Can't you just show them your birth certificate?"

"It doesn't work that way. I'd have to apply and take a test." Which she wasn't going to do, even though there had been a time when she'd thought she'd work here forever. Now the goal was to get that position at the hospital in LA and make her move away from here permanent.

She stroked her mother's wavy blond hair that barely showed any silvery threads. It still hung nearly to her waist, as it always had, and Rory wondered if she could convince her to let her cut it, at least a little, so it would be easier to take care of.

Then again, it was such a part of who her mother was that it was probably worth the extra work, so she gently twisted it and secured it into a semi-tamed ponytail.

"Then just take the test."

"Maybe someday." Meaning *never*. "But until then the only way for you to get an antibiotic is to go to a doctor here, and Jacob is close by."

"Well, if that's what we have to do," her mother said, shaking her head in clear disbelief of the protocols involved in medical care. "When do we leave?"

"Right now." Her stomach squeezed, but she stiffened her shoulders and helped her mom get her coat on. The sooner they got there, the sooner it would be over with. "They're closing his office soon."

It was just a ten-minute drive from her mother's house to downtown Eudemonia—if you could call it downtown.

At the age of eight Rory had been amazed when she'd gone to Fairbanks for the first time, to do some clothes shopping. Before then her mother had sewn or knitted all of it—until her dad had decided they should stop home-schooling her, and send her to the public school instead.

She'd stood out like a sore thumb at that school for a while, until she'd learned how to fit in, and one of those ways had been wearing off-the-rack clothes. She'd met Jacob Hunter at that school, too—the boy who'd become her hero.

She'd had no idea that a real downtown had more than a post office, a few stores, a medical clinic and multiple bars. Bars being the most important things in a town, as far as many residents were concerned. But, hey, *something* had to help everyone get through the nearly twenty-four-hour darkness of winter and the bitter cold and isolation of those months, right?

No doubt the bars were still the places where Eude-monians and others from nearby towns got together to listen to local musicians, play cards, checkers or poker and socialize.

Memories of those days had her smiling for a split second—until she remembered she wasn't a part of this place anymore, and sure wouldn't be doing any of that while she was here.

A couple of cars were parked behind the clinic, and

as soon as she spotted a gleaming black pickup truck, with big, knobbly wheels ready to tackle the snow when it came, she knew it was Jake's. He'd always loved black cars and manly trucks, saying how he'd have one someday, when he was a doctor like his dad.

A vision of his first beaten-up car, which he'd bought in high school with the money his dad had paid him to keep the clinic clean and take care of the medical waste, popped into her head. He'd still been driving it when all hell had rained down on their heads, and she was glad it wasn't still around so she didn't have to see it and remember.

Not that she didn't remember it as if it were yesterday anyway.

"No need to hurry in, Twinkie," she said as she helped her mom from the car. "Take your time."

"I know I'm a pain, marshmallow girl. I'm walking slower than Grandma Lettie did when she was ninety-five. But my belly still hurts a lot, darn it."

She grinned up at Rory, and the tightness of her chest eased at her mother's upbeat attitude toward life. Wendy Anderson had always been an odd little thing, but she was special in so many ways. Rory knew she was blessed to have her as a mother, even though she had often been more like the parent and her mother more like the child.

"You could never be a pain. I love you." She kissed her mother's cheek, then opened the clinic door for her.

Ellie Sanders stood there, ready to take them back to the examination room, and Rory smiled at the woman who'd worked in the clinic for as long as she could remember. "Hi, Ellie. Thanks so much for fitting Mom in."

"No thanks necessary, Rory. Besides, it's thanks to

Dr. Hunter, too, not just me. I'm never in a hurry to leave all the excitement of this place and be all alone at home."

The twinkle in her eyes showed she didn't really feel lonely, and Rory nearly asked about her kids and grandkids but decided not to go there. She didn't want to reconnect too much to this town she'd be leaving again soon.

"He's waiting for you in Room two."

Rory's heart seemed to skip a beat with every step down the hallway until they finally reached the room. The door was partly open, and inside she could see Jake's mother standing there, talking to someone out of her line of vision.

Her heart gave another unpleasant kick. She didn't really want to make stiff and uncomfortable small talk. But then she started to get annoyed with herself. Was she going to hide away like a child the whole time she was in town?

She pushed the door fully open and there was Jacob. She blinked, and for a second her brain couldn't quite grasp what she was seeing. Then her heart shook hard, before diving straight into her stomach at the realization that he was holding a baby close in his arms…smiling and kissing its cheek.

Had he married and had a child? He might have. Why wouldn't he? Growing up, all he'd wanted was to take his dad's place as Eudemonia's doctor. To marry, have a family and put down even deeper roots than his partly Alaska Native family had generations ago.

She gulped, trying to get air. Maybe the baby was a patient. Except there was no one in the room except him, his mom and the infant. It wasn't likely he'd be taking care of a child without any parent around, cuddling it and kissing it and looking at it adoringly.

"Hello, Rory. I haven't seen you in forever," Beth Hunter said with a tentative smile. "I was worried I wouldn't get to see you while you were in town."

"Hi. I'm... I'm only here for a short time. Until Mom's sister comes to take over."

Jake glanced up from the baby and his smile faltered. The effort he put into shoring it up again was obvious as he moved his gaze to her mother.

"Twinkie, I'm glad you've come in. If you do have a UTI we definitely need to get it taken care of so it doesn't make you sick while your body is already working so hard to recover."

"I hate to bother you, but Aurora insisted."

Her mother walked closer and gave the baby a couple of gentle pokes in its tummy. It grinned.

"He's getting so *big*! My goodness, I can't believe it. Then again, I haven't seen him since the party your mom gave to celebrate his adoption. How old is he now?"

"He's almost a year, Wendy. Can you believe it?" Beth said. "We're having a birthday party for him next week—I'll be sure to send you an invitation, if you're feeling up to coming."

"Oh, I think I will be—with my Aurora here to help me get well and my sister Patty's coming soon. How are *you* doing, Beth?"

"Doing very well, thanks. My grandson keeps me hopping, that's for sure."

Rory watched everyone beaming at the child and it took her a herculean effort not to pass out, she felt so woozy.

Adopted? The baby was really *his*? Did the baby belong to a lover, too? Someone he was committed to? Had he wanted to adopt for that reason? Had he married the baby's mother and her mom just hadn't thought to tell her?

The baby reached up his little hand to grab a wad of Jake's hair and he turned, chuckling, to extricate it from the chubby fist. "Ouch! I don't tug on *your* hair, now, do I?"

The baby gurgled and laughed in response, and the sound, along with the sweet, loving smile on Jake's face as he looked down at the baby, made Rory feel physically sick.

This was what *they* should have had together. *She* should have had this baby and the life they'd always planned. Instead it had been stolen after one catastrophic decision, changing both their lives forever.

"Twinkie, why don't you take a seat on the exam table?" she somehow managed to croak. "I'll meet you out in the waiting room."

Blindly, she stumbled down the hall and out of the building, gasping in gulps of cold air. Her knees wobbled and she sat on the step, tucking her head between her knees to try to gather herself.

How embarrassing to fall apart this way. What had happened was long ago and far away, and the last thing she would ever want to be was an object of pity. To have Jake's mother, Jake himself, shaking their heads sadly because she hadn't been able to move on the way he obviously had. Because she hadn't even wanted to.

Selfish. She was being horribly selfish—just like the night she'd made that terrible decision. Going out on that rescue, being all self-righteous, telling herself and everyone else that she was doing it to save someone, when in truth it had been for the adrenaline rush of it. The feeling of self-satisfaction she'd craved. There had been a half-dozen other people who could have taken her place to rescue that man...

She *had* to put aside her feelings. The right thing to do was to try to feel happy for Jake that he had the kind of life he'd always wanted. That he was living in this town, working alongside his dad as a family physician, with the child he'd adopted. Maybe a woman he loved. He deserved that kind of happiness even if she didn't.

She heard the door open behind her and lifted her head. She stared across the parking lot at the ruby and gold sunset and tried to compose herself. A gentle hand landed on her shoulder. It was too small and light to be Jake's.

"Rory, I'm sorry if it was a shock to see Jacob's son. Obviously your mom didn't tell you."

Rory just shook her head, not trusting her voice.

Beth Hunter sat on the cold step beside her and propped the baby on her lap. He had on a little red jacket and knit hat, though Beth wasn't wearing any kind of coat. But then, she was a Native Alaskan through and through, and her children were just like her and their dad. This baby would grow up like all of them, special and wonderful, and Rory swallowed down the tears that suddenly threatened to choke her.

"Do you want to hear the story about Mika? That's what his mother named him—Mika. Do you want to know how it came about that Jake adopted him?"

Did she?

Turning her head so she couldn't see the baby's sweet face as she shook from the inside out, she nearly told Beth that she'd rather not hear it. But not knowing the story wouldn't change a thing, would it? She'd still feel this deep ache that he had this beautiful little child. That they didn't have one together. And if he was in love with someone else—that wouldn't matter, either.

"Sure."

"A single woman came to Eudemonia to take a job with the oil company nearby. She was pregnant, and either didn't know who the father was or didn't want to say. She came to Jake for prenatal care, and he delivered little Mika here at the clinic. When the baby was only about two months old, his mama came in feeling very feverish with a stiff neck. She was confused, and presented with photophobia."

A fear of light, along with the other symptoms Beth mentioned, likely would have meant one thing for the woman, and that one thing would have been very bad. Rory kept quiet, but forced herself to turn and look at Beth and the baby cuddled against her.

"Jake suspected it was bacterial meningitis, and immediately gave her a combination of IV antibiotics while he did a spinal tap to confirm the diagnosis. But she'd waited too long to come in, and while Jake and his dad did everything they could she died within hours. There was this sweet, tiny baby boy in the office, with Ellie watching him and his mother was gone... Jake—well, it was hard on him. He wondered if there was something more he should have done. And little Mika was all alone."

"Jake shouldn't have felt that way. He knows that kind of virulent bacterial infection has to be caught early or it's over. It's not his fault that she died," Rory said dully, knowing that everyone had said nearly the same thing to her, nine years ago.

Not her fault. But it had felt like her fault anyway, and how could she ever know for sure?

Beth nodded. "He knows that—but still… It was hard. He'd brought little Mika into the world and he felt a connection to him, you know? He was allowed to foster the baby until the adoption went through a couple months later. And now he's a member of the family and my first grandbaby."

"He's a lucky boy."

And Rory meant it. He was. The Hunter family were some of the best people she knew, and he'd be raised in the same awesome way Jake and his brother and sister had been raised. With love and guidance, a strong work ethic and a love for Alaska—especially Eudemonia.

Somehow the news that Jake wasn't married and wasn't in love with the baby's mother had her breathing slightly easier, even as she tried to figure out how to deal with him being a father. Then again, not being in love with Mika's mother didn't mean he wasn't in a serious relationship.

And why was she even wondering about that? It wasn't as though either one of them wanted to get involved with each other again.

"So," Beth said quietly. "How are you? Happy in Los Angeles?"

"I'm good. Fine. I love my job."

What else could she say? That she loved her job and spent all her time doing it so she wouldn't have to think about anything else?

"Tell me again what kind of doctor you are? Jake never said."

Of course he hadn't. Because he didn't want to think

about her and what had happened to make her change her plans and go to LA any more than she did.

"I'm a pediatric orthopedic surgeon. I take care of children's broken bones and congenital bone disorders. You might remember I broke my leg falling out of a tree when I was ten? That whole experience amazed me— when I saw the X-rays and how they put it back together. I knew then I wanted to be a bone surgeon."

She wouldn't share the fact that the only reason she'd even thought about becoming a doctor was because of the Hunter family, how Jake and his brother had always known that was what they wanted to be, just like their dad.

"Sounds like you're making a big difference in people's lives. You must be proud."

"Yes, it's a good job."

"And LA is light-years from here. I bet that was a big adjustment."

"Warm and sunny year-round? Yes, very different from here." She forced a smile. "Then again, there's nothing like the clear air, open skies and bright stars of Alaska. I admit there are times when I miss it."

"Well…" Beth hesitated, then seemed to change her mind on whatever she'd been about to say. "We'd love to have you over for dinner some night while you're here. Before you go back. Your mother is more than welcome, too."

"I doubt she'll be feeling up to it."

Beth probably knew it was Rory who wouldn't feel up to it, but she let it pass.

"I'll ask her, though. Thanks. And, Beth…?"

"Yes?"

Rory let herself reach out to stroke the baby's round

cheek, and its sweet softness made tears sting the backs of her eyes. "Congratulations on your grandbaby. He's just beautiful."

"Rory—"

The door opened and there was Ellie again, interrupting whatever Beth had been about to say. It was beyond a relief.

"Your mother is all set, Rory."

"Thanks."

She stood and reached down to help Beth to her feet as the woman propped the baby on her hip.

"Thanks for telling me about Mika and his mother. That...helps."

Beth squeezed her hand. "I'm always here if you ever want to talk."

No, she didn't want to talk. She wanted to hide in her mother's house, take care of her, then get out of Eudemonia and bury herself in work again. She wanted to commit to that job in LA, far away from here.

"Thanks, but I'm fine."

That lie stuck in her throat as she met her mother and Jacob walking down the hallway to the front entrance. He was so handsome, so familiar, so...distant. He'd schooled his expression into one of cool professionalism, obviously as intent on keeping an emotional distance from her as she was.

"Definitely a UTI, so it's good you brought her in. I have a couple of sample packets of antibiotic here," he said, handing them to her. "I'll have Ellie send a prescription to a drugstore in Fairbanks, too, because she'll need to be on them for at least five days."

"Thanks. We appreciate you seeing us tonight. Sorry we kept you from...Mika."

Their eyes met, and the pain she felt deep inside was reflected in his eyes as he reached to take the baby from his mother's arms.

"Not a problem. He'll have to get used to having his daddy get home late when there are patients to see. Right, buddy?"

Daddy. Buddy. Her throat tightened all over again, and she knew she needed to get out of there.

Just as she was about to turn to her mother the baby leaned forward, slapped his little hands against Jake's cheeks, and pressed his nose to his. God, it was like something out of a beautiful family movie, and the sweetly intimate picture nearly made the dam burst.

Somehow she gulped back the tears and grabbed her mother's arm to hustle her toward the front door. No way was she going to humiliate herself by crying right there in front of all of them. But if she didn't leave right that second, that was exactly what was going to happen.

She felt like every hour would be a matter of survival.

CHAPTER THREE

WITH THE CLINIC CLOSED, Sunday was the best day for Jake to catch up on life, and he strapped Mika into his car seat so they could head to Fairbanks. His parents had offered to have him and the baby drive with them to get supplies, but he'd rather not be stuck going to some of the stores to do the things his mother considered vital. Like picking out balloons and other stuff for the party she was planning for the boy.

"Your grandma is pretty excited about your birthday, Mika," said. "Does it hurt your feelings that I don't want to do any of the decorating she thinks is so important? All I want is to show up with you and eat cake—does that make me a bad dad?"

Mika grinned, babbled and kicked his feet, which Jake took as confirmation that the child didn't think he was a bad father at all. He leaned in to kiss the baby's cheek, and as he did so he suddenly remembered Rory's expression when she'd walked into the office and seen him doing exactly that.

It could only be described as *devastated*. Every drop of color had drained from her face, and he'd been about to hand the baby to his mother and reach for Rory because he'd been so worried she might faint. Then she'd turned and practically run from the room, and he'd let her go. He knew the woman inside out, and the last thing she ever wanted from anyone was sympathy.

Even when life had thrown such a cruel blow at them she'd refused to lean on anyone, had cut herself off from her parents and her friends.

And from him. Especially him.

He hadn't known what to do. He'd tried over and over to reach out to her. To hold her. To have them grieve together. To heal together, somehow move on with their lives together after this huge loss.

But what had she done?

She'd upped and left, crushing his dreams. She'd abandoned their plans, their future, the deep love they'd shared. She'd abandoned *him*, leaving him to bleed alone.

His jaw tightened with the memories. Yeah, she'd left without so much as a goodbye, and as far as he was concerned the shorter her stay here in Eudemonia, the better. He wanted to be the bigger person, to forgive and forget and move on. He thought he had. But from the first second he'd seen her in her mother's living room, he'd known he was wrong.

What he'd felt at that moment had forced him to face the fact that he'd never forgotten even one little thing about her: her spunky, take-no-prisoners attitude toward life, softened by her loving and giving nature, her independent-to-a-fault spitfire nature that got her into trouble sometimes, her heart-shaped pixie-like face that always changed expression with the wind. Sweet, amused, angry, contrite… You never knew for sure what you'd see there.

He still remembered the exact moment he'd met her, in the fourth grade at the school outside Fairbanks he'd gone to since kindergarten. Remembered the way her beautiful green eyes had fixed on his when he'd told the kid bullying the new girl with the weird clothes to buzz off.

She had looked at him with admiration and awe, as if he was Superman, and from that moment on he'd loved spending time with her. Fishing, bicycling, playing ball, riding snow machines. She'd always acted like he was the best person in the whole world to spend time with, and he'd felt exactly the same about her.

Then college had come—and living in the same dorm building had changed things. One night, with a few illegal beers under their belts, talking had turned into kissing, and the electricity had shocked them both. From that moment their relationship had changed, and what he'd seen when he looked into her eyes had been exactly what he'd felt for her. A love so deep and clear it had made him weak, just as it had also made him strong.

He closed his eyes. She'd been a part of him for so long. And then she'd been gone for nearly as long. All through medical school without her, then moving back here with no Rory around anymore, he'd been able to fool himself that she no longer was.

He'd been wrong.

He shoved down the memories and opened his eyes to kiss Mika's soft hair before closing the door, wishing he could kiss Rory, too, and hating himself for that. What they'd had had been special, but she'd destroyed it—and a part of him along with it. He'd better keep remembering that. She couldn't be trusted to be honest, to share what she was feeling, to stick around. No way could he let her sneak back inside his heart for even the few days she would be home.

Not *home*. Not for her—not anymore.

He dragged his thoughts back to the list of things he needed in Fairbanks and got in the driver's seat. The truck started with a roar. He stared up at the heavy gray sky, thinking he should get in more supplies than usual, with the possibility of snow on the way. October didn't usually have precipitation, but you never knew. And any Alaskan had to be well prepared for anything.

He'd barely gone five miles past the fourth and last traffic light in Eudemonia when his phone rang and he saw it was Ellie.

"What's up?"

"I got a frantic phone call from Pooky Green, saying his son got hurt riding his dirt bike. He's sure his arm's broken and wants to bring him to the clinic. I called your dad, but he said they're already in Fairbanks."

"Did you tell him we don't do broken bones? He needs to take him to the ER in Fairbanks."

"Well, actually, I...um..."

Something about her sheepish and apologetic tone had him wondering what was coming next. "What? Spit it out."

"I know Rory is a bone specialist, who works with kids, even. So I told Pooky to bring him into the clinic and see if *she* can look at him. His car isn't running too well, and he's worried about driving it all the way to Fairbanks before he works on it. So I figured why not see if she can do something first?"

"Damn it, Ellie." He didn't want to see Rory, and he sure as hell didn't want to work with her. "I wish you'd stop trying to take care of everyone in town. I'm going to Fairbanks, so I'll take the kid to the ER."

"Um... I already called Rory. She said she'd come to

the clinic to look at him, and see what she thinks. She's already on her way. But you don't need to come—I'll let her in and show her where everything is."

Jake swore under his breath, counted to ten, then unlocked his jaw. "No one's going to work at the clinic without either me or Dad around. I'll meet her there. But please don't do this again."

"Oh, I won't! Thanks, Jake! I know Pooky and Eli really appreciate it. You're the best."

Her elated tone had him shaking his head, realizing she considered this a huge victory and hadn't listened to a thing he'd said. "I'm going to talk to Dad about docking your pay for this."

Her peal of laughter in his ear before he hung up tugged a reluctant grin out of him. Yeah, there was nothing like working in a place where you'd known everyone your whole life.

But Rory had chosen to leave it all behind her.

He wasn't going to think about it. Not now, and not ever. It was long ago and didn't matter anymore. He'd gotten pretty good at almost forgetting all about her. He'd moved on with his life, successfully shoving away all the hurt and pain and disbelief that, in the middle of the worst time in both their lives, she'd left without a word. Now here she was again, bringing memories back.

He didn't want to get stirred up about her again. His life here was good, and he had little Mika now, to enrich his life and make him laugh. Yeah, maybe it would be nice to find a woman to share his life with someday, but when he did he'd be sure it was someone who'd stick it out through the tough times. Who'd be truly committed to staying in Eudemonia forever.

He swung his truck into the parking lot and recognized Rory's rental car from when it had been parked in front of her mom's house. It looked like Pooky was already there, too, and he fought down the burn in his gut at the fact that the woman who'd abandoned him had waltzed into his clinic like she had a right to be there.

He drew in a deep, calming breath. It probably wasn't fair of him to feel that way. She'd come because Ellie had asked her to, and she was obviously trying to help. If she could save Pooky and his kid a trip to the ER he should be happy about that.

With Mika in his arms, he went in and found the whole crew in the first exam room. Rory was taking the boy's pulse, looking down at her wrist. The bright overhead light brought out the highlights of her smooth soft hair that skimmed across her cheek as she studied her watch.

"Your pulse is a little fast, but it's probably because you're in pain," she said, sending a smile to Eli. "Doesn't look like any break has affected your arteries or circulation, but I'm going to examine your hand and wrist now, just to be sure. Does it feel numb or tingly?"

"No. Just my arm hurts super-bad."

She nodded. "From the position of your arm, I'm positive it's a dislocated elbow—and, yeah, that's *really* painful, I know. The good news is I can manipulate it back into position. But we'll get an X-ray to confirm that there's nothing broken before I do that."

Jake could see the kid's arm was misshapen, and twisted right at the elbow, and found he had to agree with her diagnosis. He handed Mika to Ellie, then stepped forward. Rory lifted her head, obviously surprised to see him—which seemed ridiculous, considering he and his father were the only two doctors who worked there.

"I'll get the X-ray taken care of," he said.

"Ellie said she'd get the machine. I know how to operate most all of them."

"Yeah, well, this is *my* family's clinic and it's *my* responsibility to make sure everybody here gets the care they need."

Her lips tightened before she turned back to examine Eli's hand and fingers, moving them up and down and asking the boy questions.

Jake felt slightly annoyed with himself that he'd spoken in such a harsh tone. It wasn't very professional and she didn't deserve it. But somehow he hadn't been able to help the way it came out. Being around her seemed to dredge up all the bad feelings and resentment he'd thought he'd put behind him.

"Thanks again for seeing him, Rory. I can't believe you're a bone doctor these days," Pooky said.

"Neither can my mother." Rory sent him one of her cute grins before her expression turned calm and professional again.

Jake watched Rory work, carefully touching and examining the boy's arm until she finally placed his hand gently on his lap. "Everything seems okay circulation-wise," Rory said. "Let's get that X-ray to confirm nothing's broken before I move your elbow back into place."

"Here's the machine," Ellie said, rolling the portable X-ray into the room with one hand, holding Mika on her hip with the other.

"I was just coming to get it," Jake said, frustrated that he was standing there doing nothing while everyone else was working in his clinic. "Why don't you take Mika to my office now?"

Ellie gave him a look that said he was being rude and, damn it, he knew he deserved it.

He focused on getting pictures of the boy's arm in several positions, with Rory silently assisting beside him. When they were finished her shoulder pressed into his side as they both studied the X-rays, and he edged slightly away to try to escape the warmth of her body.

"Yep—see there?" she said, pointing. "Thankfully nothing's broken. I can reduce the elbow back to its correct alignment, but you probably know it'll hurt like crazy." Her eyes looked up to meet his. "Do you have any twilight sleep or some other conscious sedation he can have while I do it?"

"We do. Hardly ever have a need for it, since we don't do this kind of thing here, but occasionally I have someone in a lot of pain or nearly hysterical, and we need to get them relaxed and out of it."

"Good."

They both showed Eli and his dad the X-rays, explaining what they were looking at and what Rory planned to do.

Considering Rory's take-charge nature, Jake was surprised at how she included him in the conversation—like they were a team instead of her taking over the whole thing. Which made him feel even more ashamed of his attitude about her being here today and taking care of the boy so he didn't have to take a trip to the city and wait hours to be seen in the ER.

To make up for it, he knew it was time to verbally give her credit.

"You're lucky Dr. Anderson is in town for a few days and can take care of you, Eli," he said. "Only a trained orthopedic surgeon should do an elbow reduction on anyone other than a toddler. Otherwise you'd have had to go to Fairbanks."

"But it's good that you have all the other stuff we need here," she said, and the smile in her eyes made him even gladder that he'd made the gesture to applaud her. "I bet you have the right kind of splint, but if you don't I brought a few different kinds of splints and casts, not knowing what we might need."

"You brought splints and casts in your luggage? I guess you don't believe in packing light."

"You never know when a medical emergency is going to arise. I like to be prepared—as you know."

Yeah, he *did* know. He'd often teased her about it, since she'd always made sure she had a more extensive emergency preparedness supply than most. Probably because for a long time her dad hadn't been well enough to take care of such things, and her mom had been very blasé about it, despite living in a place where you needed to be ready for all kinds of weather and storms.

As she had through much of her life, Rory was the one who had taken care of running the house and all that needed to be done. She'd done it without comment or complaint, which was one of the things he'd always admired about her.

Their eyes met again in a long connection that told him they were both remembering all kinds of things her comment had brought to mind.

Such as the time they'd gotten lost together on a hiking trip near Denali and spent the night in a pup tent he'd thought was ridiculous for her to bring along for a day trip. But she'd insisted—just in case. When it had got too dark to find their way until the next morning, that tent had made their night a lot more comfortable than it would have been without.

Memories of being spooned together with her in that small cocoon, her firm rear and soft body pressed against his, made his breath feel short and his heart heavy.

He quickly turned to get the anesthetic that would help the boy to be semi-asleep, so he wouldn't feel the pain of the reduction.

Jake placed an IV in Eli's arm and administered the medication. He gave it the few minutes it needed to kick in, made sure the boy was in twilight sleep, then nodded at Rory. "Good to go. You need help?"

She was still such a small thing, and he couldn't imagine the strength she needed to manipulate bones and do the kinds of surgeries she did. Obviously, though, she wouldn't have passed the five years of residency training it took to be a pediatric orthopedic surgeon if she didn't have the physical ability.

"I'm good. This particular manipulation is more technique than raw strength. Hip surgeries are the toughest, in terms of muscle power, but I manage."

She sent him a half smile, then moved her attention to Pooky. "I'm going to pull down hard on his wrist to fully release the bone from the socket, then lever it back into place. It looks kind of awful, so you might not want to watch."

"I'll be okay," Pooky said. "I've done and seen all kinds of stuff in my years of hunting."

Jake decided he'd better keep an eye on Pooky anyway. Being a hunter who butchered animals didn't have a lot to do with watching your young son's arm being manipulated in a way that looked completely unnatural.

"Ready? Here we go," she said.

He watched Rory pull hard on the boy's wrist, then slowly and gently maneuver it back into the socket in what was clearly a very expert maneuver.

"Looks like…that's it," she said, leaning back with a satisfied nod. "In place and good to go—but let's take one more X-ray to confirm."

Jake moved toward the machine, glancing up at Pooky as he did so. Sure enough, the man looked ashen, and was listing to one side on his chair. Jake switched direction, striding over to grab him before he fell out of the chair and they had another broken bone or a cracked head on their hands.

"Whoa, there. Steady, now."

In seconds Rory was right there with him, obviously seeing Pooky move at about the same time he had. She went to Pooky's right arm, with Jake to his left, tugging him upright, and then they both pressed their hands to his back to tuck his head between his knees.

"Take some deep breaths and keep your head down for a few minutes," Jake said.

"I'm…sorry. Felt a little lightheaded. Can't believe it."

"Trust me when I say it's totally normal. When it comes to your own kid, especially, it's upsetting to see a limb all out of whack like that."

Rory's green gaze met his over the man's head, and for the first time since she'd been back they shared a real smile. It felt better than it should, but the way his chest lifted in response to that smile of hers told him he couldn't deny that he still cared for her. That even after all this time, and all that had happened, the closeness he'd felt with her still wrapped around his heart like a twisted, deeply rooted vine. So deeply rooted he knew he might never be free of it completely.

"You go ahead and get the X-ray," she said. "I'll stand here and make sure he's okay."

Glad that the film showed the elbow right back where it belonged, Jake got busy getting the splint they needed while Rory talked gently and quietly to Pooky. Not all surgeons had good bedside manners, but she did. Not that it came as a surprise. She'd always been one of the most caring and empathetic people he knew.

"It'll feel sore and bruised for quite a while, Pooky, so don't be surprised by that. Over the next few hours I want you to pay attention to how his circulation seems. If his hand or his arm starts to discolor or feel tingly, call me or Jake right away—okay?"

Together, they worked to put an L-shaped splint on the boy's arm, managing to get it fully in place and in a sling before the anesthetic wore off and he slowly became alert.

"Not quite good as new, but you'll be there soon," Rory told the boy, with another one of her warm smiles. "You'll need to keep it in the sling for two or three weeks except when you're resting. Keep your arm elevated as much as you can, ice it when the splint is off and come back to see me in two days. We'll see how it looks then."

A questioning frown dipped between her eyes and she looked up at Jake.

"Is it okay with you if he meets me here? It's not entirely necessary—I could go on a house call to see him instead."

"No, definitely see him here. How about 10:00 a.m. Thursday?"

His selfish feelings about her working here had been

childish and stupid. She was obviously a good bone doctor who knew what she was doing, and taking care of patients in and near Eudemonia to the best of their ability was the whole reason the clinic was here.

"And you don't even need to bring your own supply of splints—if he needs a new one we have plenty. In several colors."

"Except I brought the perfect ones for Alaska—camouflage, if you can believe they make them. I guess they're for hunters who want to hide in the trees, even with a broken arm."

Another shared smile, this one bigger and more intimate, and he turned away from the power of it. Tried to move his thoughts from that moss-green gaze and her sweet lips by talking with Pooky and Eli. He was hyper-aware of how close she was, and how that damned grapefruit scent kept sneaking into his nose, bringing with it memories better left forgotten.

Both answered a few more questions, and Rory handed Pooky a card with her phone number on it before they left.

With the patient and his father gone, Jake couldn't decide exactly what to do. Probably send Rory back to her mother's house, then he and Ellie could get the place cleaned up with Mika in his playpen for a short time. Except, ridiculously, he found he didn't want to ask her to leave quite yet, in a total reverse of how he'd felt an hour ago.

"It was nice of you to come take care of Eli. Saved them a long trip and an even longer day."

"I was happy to. I'm sure there are plenty of times you have to play doctor here after hours."

"Yeah. But still, it was nice. So, thanks."

"No thanks necessary. So…"

Her voice faded away, as if she didn't know what else to say, and he sure didn't, either. An uncomfortable silence hung between them, until they both spoke at once.

"Listen, I'm sorry I was…unpleasant when I first came in. It's just that—"

"I know this is hard for both of us, but—"

They both stopped and chuckled awkwardly.

Jake figured he'd better spit out his apology so they could get this discomfort over with. "Like I said, I'm sorry. I didn't know how it would feel, seeing you again, and it's been harder than I might have expected. I know it's been a long time, but I'm going to be honest. After everything that happened, being around you churns up too much of the past, you know? I just don't want to hang around you and try to be friends again. It doesn't feel like somewhere we should try to go. But I do want to be civil and respectful while you're here."

"All right." She gave him a slow nod. "I agree that friendship isn't a goal we can have. So, civil and respectful it is."

He reached out to shake on it, enfolding her hand in his, and the feel of it there had him staring at her for several long heartbeats. He wondered how the memory of the way her hand felt in his could be so strong, as if it was yesterday and not years ago that he'd held it every chance he could.

He pulled it loose and dropped his hand to his side. "Deal. You probably want to go on to your mom's now, in case she's needing you. If you need me for anything, you know how to reach me. I'll be here when Pooky and Eli come back for their appointment with you."

Her eyes stared into his and he thought for a second

she had more to say, until she turned, grabbed her coat from the wall hook and left without another word.

A dozen emotions clogged his chest as he watched her go. He didn't like feeling any of them. Didn't like the upheaval currently tipping his world uncomfortably sideways. Yeah, the quicker Rory's aunt came to take care of her mother, the faster his life would go back to normal again.

And it couldn't come too soon.

CHAPTER FOUR

"I'M SO GLAD my surgeon thinks everything's going as it should, aren't you?" Wendy asked as they got into Rory's car, parked outside the hospital and the doctors' offices in Fairbanks. "I mean, I really didn't think so, since it still hurts so much. But he must be right that I'm healing."

"See? I said you were doing well post-op."

Though why she bothered commenting she had no clue, since it was clear her mother didn't believe she knew much of anything when it came to medicine. And she was well aware that it wasn't just Twinkie who couldn't think of her as a surgeon and a doctor who knew what she was talking about. Plenty of her friends in LA lamented the same thing—that their families always thought of them just as a son or daughter or a sibling, and had a hard time truly believing in their professional skills.

Then again, they'd also noted that there were a few friends and relatives who called all the time to talk about their aches and pains, or cornered them at every gathering to show them something on their body that they'd prefer to look at in an office setting instead of at a party.

Since Rory kept pretty much to herself outside the

hospital, she didn't have that kind of thing happen to her. Another reason isolating herself in LA wasn't a bad thing, right?

Her mom's lack of confidence in her knowledge didn't matter. Rory felt blessed to be here, keeping tabs on her recovery and reassuring her until it was time for her to go back to LA—even if her mother respected her surgeon's and Jacob Hunter's opinions a lot more.

"I just don't understand why it still hurts so much, though."

"Your body was sliced open and one of your organs was taken out just a few days ago, Twinkie. Your body needs time to heal, so try to be patient."

Rory wouldn't tell her that she thought the stitching wasn't the *best* job she'd ever seen, and hoped her mother wouldn't care much about what the scar looked like after it was healed.

"Trust me, you're going to feel up to dancing again in no time."

"I hope so! I just wish you'd be here all winter, so we could have our holiday party and hang homemade biscuits and seed sculptures on the trees for the critters. So we could sing our Christmas songs and dance together with some friends."

Rory's throat closed at the sweet smile on her mother's face and the look in her eyes. Never would she criticize Rory for not living in Eudemonia, no matter how much she wanted her there. In fact she couldn't remember a time when her mother had gotten on at her about much of anything, having always believed in live and let live.

But kids needed guidance—though she supposed it had been her mother's attitude, combined with having to help take care of her dad, that had made Rory the strong, go-getting person she was.

Too much go-getting, sometimes—which had proved to be a very bad thing.

For all her faults and quirks, Rory loved her mom. She realized all over again how much she missed spending time with her.

An idea struck her, and while it wasn't even close to the first time, maybe right now she had some real leverage behind her to convince her mom to come to LA with her. She'd wanted to make that happen ever since her dad had died. And now she couldn't deny that the thought of getting away from Eudemonia and Jacob Hunter as soon as possible made her want it even more.

"You know, even though you're recovering well, it's still going to take a while for you to be good as new. How about coming back to Los Angeles with me? Now that you've seen your doctor we could leave pretty much right away. Tell Aunt Patty she doesn't have to worry about taking time off work to help you. I can take care of you until you're feeling like yourself again. It's warm there, and we'd have a great time doing all kinds of fun things."

"I don't know, marshmallow girl..." A frown dipped between her mother's brows before she turned away to look out the side window. "This is where I belong. I grew up here. My friends are all here. All my memories are here. You as a little girl...me and your dad."

"I'm not asking you to move there, Twinkie." Though if it were up to her that would be the perfect scenario. "Just to have an extended vacation. With me. Until you feel better. How bad could it be?"

Her mom finally turned back to look at her. "I just don't think it's for me. I'd miss my house. I'd miss everyone, everything that's here. Though I *do* miss you so much."

Familiar guilt chewed at Rory's gut, since she knew all too well that she should come back to Eudemonia more. Now, with the years of training behind her, she'd have a little more vacation time. But the deep ache from all the reminders of her past mistakes made her hate being here. Not to mention the horrible discomfort of seeing Jake again, which was even worse now that he had his own little one. His clear statement that he didn't want to try to be friends anymore.

Thinking about all that made her feel like she was suffocating from the pain of it all—which told her loud and clear that she still couldn't handle it.

"Will you at least *think* about coming back with me? Trying it for maybe a month?"

"All right. I'll think about it."

Rory couldn't recall her mother ever agreeing to do even that, so that was a small step forward, right? Now she needed to ponder on what might convince her mom to move past just thinking about it to doing it, because she wanted to be near her so much, but staying in Eudemonia just wasn't an option.

She glanced at her watch, realizing that since her mom's appointment had run long she didn't have much time before she was supposed to be at Eli's house to check on his arm.

When Ellie had called her, confirming their Thursday appointment in the office, her chest had tightened with that suffocating feeling again and she'd offered to go see Eli at his home a day earlier before she'd thought twice about it. Maybe Jake would be mad about her not including him, but that was too bad. She'd see the child, pass her opinion on to Ellie and Jake could follow up if he wanted to.

"I need to check on the boy I saw in the clinic the other day—do you know Pooky's son, Eli? I told him I'd swing by the house to make it easy on him. You want to come along and talk with Pooky? Or would you rather go home first?"

"I think I'll go on home. If that's okay? Walking around more than usual and then the doctor poking and prodding me has tired me out."

"Of course that's okay. Listening to your body and when it's telling you to rest is an important part of getting stronger."

Ten minutes later she had her mom tucked into her chair with an ancient knit throw over her knees and the small dog happily curled on top of it. With a snack on the table by her side and the television on, she should be good until Rory got back.

"I shouldn't be gone long. See you in just a bit, okay?"

"Don't worry about me. Toby and I will probably take a nap."

Her mother's eyelids were already drooping, and Rory smiled as she leaned down to kiss her forehead. "Get some rest."

She crept out through the front door and managed to find Pooky's house about twenty minutes later, despite her GPS getting totally confused. The outskirts of Eudemonia hadn't changed much in the years she'd been gone, and the simple directions and landmarks he'd given her made it pretty easy to remember her way around.

As she approached the hill where the worst decision of her life had begun, her throat thickened with unwanted memories.

"What do you mean, I shouldn't come along? Part of what I do, what we both do, is go on rescue missions, Jake. There's no physiological reason for me not to get on that snow machine and help, and you know it. It'll be fine. We'll be fine. I promise."

She worked to haul in a few deep breaths. Somehow she had to shove down the horrible emotions clogging her chest—because what was the point in reliving the past? Thinking about it, crying about it, reliving it over and over, couldn't change a thing. It hadn't before, and it sure wouldn't now.

In a hurry to put that hill behind her, she pressed the accelerator nearly to the floor. The danger in navigating these curves forced her to focus on the road instead of on all the other things she didn't want to think about.

A wooden board appeared next to a gravel drive, an address written on it in thick black ink, and she nosed the car up the slope, glad to finally be there. She drew a few deep, calming breaths before knocking on the door. In mere seconds it swung open, and a slightly worried-looking Pooky stood in front of her.

"Thanks for coming, Rory. Really appreciate it. Especially since my truck's still not working right and I've got it up on jacks to try and fix it."

"Happy to."

Maybe Jake wouldn't be so annoyed if he knew about Pooky's car problems and how he couldn't have made it to the clinic anyway. As soon as the thought came, she asked herself why she cared if Jake was annoyed or not.

"How's Eli doing?"

"Been hurting a lot, to be honest. Doesn't like me taking the splint off to ice the arm, but I've been doing it anyway."

"That's good. Keeping the swelling down as much as possible will help it heal. It'll also help with his mobility when it's time to start using it again."

"He's back here, feeling a little grumpy," Pooky said with a small smile as he led her to a small living room. "He's not happy having to sit around until it's better."

"Can't blame him. Sitting around is a drag—especially for a kid."

The boy's glum expression showed his dad hadn't been exaggerating about how he was feeling.

"Hi, Eli. How's the pain?"

"Hurts. But not as bad as when I first did it—that was the worst."

"You were really tough and brave, though. A dislocated elbow is no joke, and you did so well through the whole reduction. Let me take a look."

She crouched down, concentrating on getting the splint off without jarring his arm. The knock on the door didn't get through to her brain until Pooky moved to answer it.

"That's probably Jake."

Her heart gave a quick thud before she lifted her head to stare at him. "Jake?"

"Yeah. I told him you were coming here today, instead of keeping to the first plan we had to meet at the clinic tomorrow, and he said he wanted to be here, too."

She bit back a groan. *Why* couldn't she get away from the man for more than a day?

She heard the murmur of the two men talking, then all too soon Jake was standing right next to her. It wasn't hard to avoid eye contact, since she was concentrating on Eli's arm and asking him questions, but that didn't help her hyperawareness of his closeness, his broad form, the scent she realized she'd never forgotten even after all this time.

"Looks good," she said to both Pooky and Eli, studiously ignoring Jake. She reached to pat the child's shoulder and gave him a reassuring smile. "I know it probably doesn't feel that way to you. Bruising isn't pretty, I know, but your elbow is definitely in the right position. Just keep icing it and elevating it and be patient."

"We need to get another X-ray at the clinic in a few days, when your car's up and running," Jake said. "I wish Dr. Anderson had told me she'd decided to take a look at his arm here today. I would have picked him up and taken him to the clinic myself."

Even if he hadn't called her *Dr. Anderson* she'd have known he was beyond irritated, as the vibration of anger in his voice was more than clear. Without knowing she was going to, she stole a look at him. Yep, those beautiful lips of his were pressed tightly together and the eyes that met hers weren't even close to warm. Instead, they glittered with an edge of anger she'd seen on only rare occasions, and she knew that a blowup just might follow.

It didn't matter, she told herself, even as her heart beat a little faster. He could be upset and disapproving all he wanted, because her coming here today for a follow-up with the boy had made it easier for Eli and Pooky. And for Jake, too, because she knew he felt as uncomfortable around her as she did him. Except here he was anyway.

"Probably in a couple weeks you should find an orthopedic surgeon in Fairbanks, to take one more look before you take the splint off for good," she said.

"*You're* not going to be here then?" Pooky asked in obvious surprise.

"No. I'm leaving in just a few days."

"Which is why it was important for me to be here today—even though you obviously didn't think so," Jake said. "Because *I'm* not going anywhere."

Her fluttering heart kicked hard. His words obviously referred to a lot more than just this moment. They were a statement about nine years ago when, devastated and consumed with guilt, she'd fled this town, refusing to look back.

"So." Somehow she forced herself to sound relaxed and professional as she stood to her full height and managed a smile. "Call me if you have any concerns over the next couple days, and get a referral from Jacob to whatever orthopedic doc he recommends. If I don't see you before I go, best of luck, Eli. I'll see myself out, so Jake can talk with you a little more."

She reached for Pooky's hand, noticing the way he glanced at her and Jake, clearly sensing the strange vibe going on between them. Then she patted Eli's shoulder one more time, slid on her coat and hurried toward the door.

It was ridiculous to feel she needed to escape conversation with Jake, but for some inexplicable reason she did. Finally in her car, she was nearly free and clear when she heard Pooky yelling her name.

She turned to see him running out through the door with a huge shopping bag in his arms, and wondered what in the world was in there.

"Rory! Wait!" He came up next to her car door, a little out of breath.

She wound down the window, and had opened her mouth to ask what he needed when he started talking again.

"All of a sudden I realized I need to pay you something."

"No, you don't. No need at all—I promise. I'm not working. I'm just here to see my mom. I was happy to help."

"I want to. Please." He held out the bag, and the way it listed toward the car told her it weighed a ton. "I'm sorry I don't have cash to give you, but I want you to have this."

"Seriously, Pooky, you don't—"

"I went hunting a week ago and bagged a caribou. It's already butchered. Fresh and good, I promise."

She opened her mouth to protest some more, but by now Jake had come up behind him. The expression on his face reminded her of how things went around here, with everyone helping others and sharing what they had when they could. If she didn't accept Pooky's payment it would probably be upsetting to the man, so it was the only polite thing to do.

"Thank you. It's really unnecessary, but I appreciate it. I haven't had caribou in a long time. Mom will love it."

"Great! Makes me feel good to think I can help your mom get well."

His wide, pleased smile as he opened the back door of the car and set the bag on the seat made her glad she'd accepted the meat, even as she wondered how long it would take her mother to eat it all by herself. It would probably be in the freezer for the next couple years.

"Well, thanks again—and best of luck to you and Eli. Take care."

"Come back and see us soon, Rory. It's been way too long."

She didn't answer because, yeah, it *had* been too long, but seeing Jake standing there with his arms folded across his chest, looking at her with slightly narrowed eyes, didn't exactly make her want to book a flight back next month.

Pooky headed into the house and Jake wrapped his hands over her car door and leaned forward. It probably wouldn't be nice to wind the window up, even though she wanted to, so she sat there trying to look relaxed.

"We need to talk," he said.

"About…?"

"About us."

Her heart lurched. "Us?"

"Yeah. Us. We've agreed we can't be friends anymore, that we'd go for civil and respectful. But what happened today was neither of those."

"I don't know what you mean. When Ellie called me about the appointment I figured it would work better for me to come here to see him, and then you could follow up as you wish. It doesn't seem to me that it was uncivil or disrespectful to have us see him separately. So what's the problem?"

"The problem is that *I'm* the kid's primary doc, and *you'll* be waltzing out of here any minute, without a goodbye to a single soul, just like before."

His voice was filled with that vibration of anger again, and he leaned through the window, practically nose-to-nose with her.

"You can't disappear for years and then, when you show up for a few days, try to take over the place before you take off again. I don't want you seeing anymore patients while you're here. It's not good care for them when I get left out of the loop then have to play catch-up, trying to figure out what you might have said or done when I wasn't around. You understand?"

"Who elected *you* King of Eudemonia?" She planted

her palm against his chest and gave it a shove, but he didn't budge. "I was doing Pooky a favor, since his car isn't running right now."

"Which I'll bet you didn't even *know* when you talked to Ellie, because I sure didn't."

She never could put anything past Jacob Hunter.

She sucked in a breath, which unfortunately dragged his scent into her lungs, and she leaned back the few inches she could to get a tiny bit of distance. "I didn't want to see you again, okay? I admit it. I admitted it before. Hopefully there won't be any reason for us to have to talk at all before I leave. But, fine. I see your point about you needing to know about me examining Eli and my recommendations."

"So it won't happen again?"

"No. I'm leaving soon anyway, so I won't be here to make your life miserable anymore."

"Miserable? You don't know the half of it, Rory. And you know what? I've changed my mind. Before you leave, we *do* need to talk about all you did back then."

His temper had spiked further; his eyes were snapping with it as he closed the inches between them. Mixed in with that temper was something else, and shock skidded through her veins when she saw it.

Desire.

Her heart pounding against her ribs, she watched him spin away, clasp the back of his head for ten long seconds, then turn around again.

He leaned in close once more, his hands balled into fists. "Miserable? Yeah. Confused, furious and a whole lot of other things that made me wish I could hate you. Do you have any idea how—?"

Her cell phone shrilled in interruption, and she'd

never been so glad to hear it in her life. No way did she want to have this kind of upsetting conversation with Jake, and she dug into her purse with shaking hands.

"Hello?"

"Rory? It's Linda. I'm at your mom's house, with some cookies I baked, but the door's locked. When I knocked I could hear her calling from inside, but she's not coming to the door. I'm really worried that something's wrong. Are you close by?"

Her heart felt like it had stopped in her chest. "About twenty minutes away. I'll be there as fast as I can." She tossed her phone on the seat and started the car.

"What's wrong?" asked Jake.

"Linda's at Mom's but she can't get in. Says she can hear Twinkie's voice, but apparently she can't get to the door for some reason. God, *why* did I decide I had to lock the door when she never does?" She gulped back the panic rising in her throat. "I gotta go."

"I'll be right behind you."

"No need. I—"

She stopped herself. There was nobody better in an emergency than Jacob Hunter, and she realized that she wanted him there with her, no matter what had been boiling between them seconds ago.

"That would be good. Thanks."

Shoving her car into Reverse, she swung it down the driveway and saw Jake jumping into his truck. Once she hit the paved road she jammed down the accelerator, trying to fight the fear gripping her.

If Linda could hear Twinkie calling out, that was a good thing, right? Maybe it wasn't something terribly bad. Maybe she'd fallen and couldn't get up because she wasn't very strong yet. That seemed unlikely, but still…

She pushed harder on the gas, and this time driving by the dreaded hill didn't cause even one second of bad thoughts and emotions. All those were concentrated on her sweet mother, and the fear that had her heart beating double-time.

CHAPTER FIVE

JAKE WAS RIGHT behind Rory's car as she tore up the grassy slope toward her mother's house, and he was beyond glad to finally be there. Not only because Wendy might need help, but because Rory had driven like a maniac on the steep curves of the road—to the point when he'd feared she'd lose control and crash.

He didn't want to think about how it would feel to see that happen…to see her get hurt. He pulled up behind her car as she practically leaped out, running up to the uneven front porch, where Linda stood clutching her hands together and looking anxious.

"Can you still hear her?"

"Yes. I yelled to her that you were on your way with the key, but I don't know if she could understand what I was saying. She must be somewhere in the back of the house, because all I could hear was the sound of her voice, but not the words. I walked around back, calling, but still couldn't understand her."

"It was *stupid* of me to lock the door," Rory said. "A habit from living in LA, I guess."

Jake could see her hand shaking as she fumbled to get the key in the door, and gently took it from her to get it unlocked. "You want me to go in first, since we don't know what's going on?"

Her worried gaze met his for a split second before he pushed open the door. "I... Can we go together?"

"Sure." He reached for her hand, because she looked like she needed the support.

There was no sign of Wendy in the main room when they ran inside, with Linda following.

"Mom? Twinkie? Where are you?"

"In the bathroom. Thank God you're here. I'm... Oh, it's a mess."

Mess? Jake steeled himself for what they might find. Maybe she meant a bathroom mess—which might embarrass her, but would be a hell of a lot better than her being hurt.

Since they couldn't both get through the narrow bathroom doorway at the same time, Rory let go of his hand as she went into the small space. With her in front of him he couldn't see her mother well, but what he could see made his pulse quicken.

The good news was that her mother was obviously lucid, even as she lay on her back. The bad news was that blood covered the floor, and Jake could only imagine how Rory was feeling on seeing it.

"Mom!" Rory dropped to her knees and reached for her mother's hands, which were splayed across her stomach. "What happened? Where are you hurt?"

"I woke up and had to go potty pretty bad. So I got up fast and I hurried too much, I think. I felt dizzy while I was on the potty. When I got up again I think I stumbled over Toby and fell. Right on my stomach...across the side of the bathtub. Oh, it hurts so bad! I'm not sure, but I think my stitches have split open. Can you tell if any of my organs fell out?"

Her eyes were wide and scared, and Jake realized he'd rarely seen her look anything but happy and relaxed. Those two times had been when Rory had been in the snow machine accident that had destroyed their future together, and the week they'd buried her husband.

"That's not likely, Twinkie, so try not to worry. We'll...we'll take a look."

To Jake's surprise Rory turned and reached for him, looking panicky.

"Can you help? I feel... I think it would be good if you helped me find out what's going on."

The fact that she was letting herself lean on him during a crisis did something funny to his chest. If she'd let herself lean on him nine years ago maybe things would have turned out a lot different. Maybe she'd never have left Eudemonia at all.

Not that it mattered anymore. Too many bridges had been burned to go back to the way things used to be.

"Let's take a look."

He ran his hand up and down Rory's back, then kneeled next to her and caught his breath. He could see now that Wendy was fully dressed, wearing tie-dyed pants with a loose waistband that she or someone else had cut to make even looser. The blood staining them down to her thighs was bright red, and the volume of it showed him why Rory had reached out to him. Because it was scary as hell.

He carefully tugged the pants down to expose the long, vertical incision from her surgery, and sure enough it was split open a good four inches. It was still bleeding a lot, and he heard Rory gasp. Thank the Lord Linda had come when she had, because even fifteen more minutes of this kind of blood-loss might have been catastrophic.

"Oh, my God, I can't believe it's wound dehiscence! Who *did* this surgery?"

"It isn't necessarily suture error," he reminded her. "But we do need to find out why it opened up like this."

"She's lost a lot of blood," Rory said in a tight whisper, though her mother could doubtless still hear her. "We need to get this closed as fast as possible."

He nodded, and reached to grab a hand towel from the sink, quickly folded it, then placed it on the open wound to slow the bleeding, flattening his palm on top of it to apply pressure.

"You sure did a whammy on yourself, Twinkie. But we're gonna get you closed back up, and then we'll get you to Fairbanks."

"Fairbanks? Wh...why?"

"You already know you've lost blood. We need to get some tests done that I can't do at the clinic, and there's a chance you could need a transfusion. They might want to keep you overnight for observation. But don't worry. It's gonna be okay."

He glanced at Rory. She had both hands pressed to her mouth as their eyes met, and he wrapped his free arm around her shoulders.

"Hang in there. I can do this—or we can do it together if you're up to it."

"I... I'll do it. I can do these kinds of sutures and close a wound in my sleep."

"It's harder when it's your own mom—and you're shaking like a leaf."

She was. Without thinking, he tugged her closer and kissed her forehead. Now wasn't the time to worry about keeping his distance from her. Not when she needed him like this.

"You have sutures and supplies? If you don't, I have a big first-aid box in the truck."

"I have everything. I'll go get it now."

"Of *course* you do. Always prepared, Aurora." He sent her a smile and resisted the urge to drop another quick kiss to her forehead. "Get something to elevate her feet, too, so she doesn't go into shock."

She nodded, lurched to her feet and disappeared.

Which apparently gave Linda her first clear view of Wendy and the bathroom floor, and the strange low moan that Linda let out had him cursing under his breath. All they needed was her passing out and needing help, with Twinkie already in such bad shape.

"Linda, sit down. Right now—out in the hall. Put your head between your knees and you'll feel better."

Without responding, she did as he asked, and Jake focused on compressing the wound to stop the bleeding.

The pounding of feet told him Rory was on her way back.

"Check on Linda!" he called. "She wasn't feeling well and I told her to sit down."

The murmur of voices told him Linda was doing better, thank heavens, and in just a moment Rory came into the small room.

"You get scrubbed up first, then take over with compression while I do," Jake said. "We won't get anywhere near sterile, but that can't be helped."

"Okay." She shoved an old blanket and some towels under Wendy's feet. "How you feeling, Twinkie?"

"A little funny. Kind of weak and woozy."

"Hang in there. We'll be able to get this done pretty fast, then head for the hospital, okay?"

She pulled out the items that were inside sterilized baggies, ripped them open so they'd be easy to access after she was scrubbed and set everything on the tray she'd brought. She placed it on the floor, next to her mom, then stepped to the sink.

"I have antimicrobial soap and gloves, so after I scrub you can put the gloves on me," she said, while lathering her hands and forearms.

"Of *course* you do."

"What? You don't carry soap in *your* first aid kit?"

"Yeah, but the possibility of me having to stitch up an injury on an ice fisherman or a hunter in the woods is a lot more likely than you needing it in Los Angeles."

"Well, you already know how I feel about being prepared."

The half smile she sent him was strained as she stuck out her hands. But he couldn't help but be impressed that the scared woman who'd been shaking just minutes ago had been replaced by the efficient surgeon standing in front of him.

"Glove me."

"Are you this bossy in the OR in LA?" he asked as he worked to get the gloves on her hands while trying to follow the correct protocol.

"Not bossy—just efficient." She kneeled to press her forearms against the towel on Wendy's belly, keeping her disinfected hands clear. "When you're done scrubbing, glove up and we'll get started."

"Yes, ma'am."

"You two are so funny together," Wendy said, her

voice noticeably weak. "Always ribbing and teasing…
even when you were kids."

Rory didn't respond, obviously choosing to ignore
Wendy's comment about the two of them and how they'd
used to be long ago. He glanced at her face in profile as
she lifted the towel, and the familiar way she pursed her
lips, narrowing her eyes in concentration, took him back
in time to all the things they'd done and studied together.

Along with her mother's words, it made him think
about how much he'd missed her—missed her beautiful smile, missed touching her soft hair. Missed the way
he'd catch her looking at him sometimes, like he meant
everything to her.

He suddenly wondered if he'd miss her all over again
after she was gone.

The feelings for her that had tried to resurface from
the second he'd seen her again told him he would, damn
it. But there was no way it could be even one iota as
much as the way he'd yearned for her for a long, long
time, even as he'd felt abandoned and betrayed.

"Ready, Twinkie?" Rory asked. "I'm putting analge-
sic cream around the edges of the wound, so you won't
feel it when I'm putting in the stitches. I'm going to hold
it together with my fingers and keep compressing for a
few minutes to slow the bleeding, then I'll get started."

"I can't believe you can do all this, marshmallow girl.
I'm so proud of you."

Jake saw her eyes widen in surprise and she turned
to look at him for a second, emotion flitting across
her face. Rory's mom and dad had always been happy
living simple lives here in Eudemonia, and he knew
they'd never understood or even cared much about her

goal to become a doctor. He also knew it had bothered her sometimes.

"Thanks, Mom. That's… It means a lot to me to hear you say that."

Jake hoped the tears she blinked back as he handed her the needle and sutures wouldn't interfere with her ability to get the wound closed. "You want me to do it?"

"No. I'm good. Really."

And she was. Her technique was flawless—not that he was surprised. The Aurora Anderson he'd known since fourth grade had always excelled at everything she attempted.

"I'm feeling fine now," Linda called from the hall. "Sorry about that…so silly of me. But I wasn't prepared for… Well, you know. What can I do?"

"We're okay right now, but maybe you can find some clean, older towels we can wash her up with when we're done? Ones she wouldn't mind throwing away?" Jake said.

"I know just where she keeps them. Be right back."

He and Rory worked silently together, except for answering the few questions Wendy asked. Very few, because it was obvious the ordeal had left her feeling weak and tired—which was hardly a surprise.

As Rory finished the last few stitches, Jake dug into her bag and found antibiotic cream. "I figured you'd have this in here," he said. "You want to put it on the closed wound while I get the bandages ready?"

"Yes. Good."

After everything was done, and Wendy was bandaged up, Jake glanced at his watch. "Twenty minutes from start to finish. Think you'd get a world record for that?"

"It was just stitches—not surgery." But she sent him

a wide, relieved smile before she snapped off her gloves and reached for her mother's bloody hands. "We're going to get you cleaned up and in fresh clothes, Twinkie, then head for Fairbanks."

"Oh, I don't think we need to go there, do we? I'm fine now."

"Just need to check a few things," Jake said.

"Will you come, too?" Wendy asked with a hopeful expression.

"Are you kidding? Would I let my favorite patient go to the hospital without me? No way."

"I have clean clothes here, Rory," Linda said as she appeared in the doorway. "I'll help you get her washed up and dressed, then I'll take care of the bathroom mess after you leave for the hospital. I'll take Toby home with me, too, so you don't have to worry about him if you have to stay in Fairbanks overnight."

"I really appreciate you looking after him. But I hate to ask you to clean the place up, Linda. You—"

"Not another word. You're not asking—I'm offering. It's the least I can do for my best friend and her amazing daughter."

Amazing. That she was—suturing her own mother with remarkably calm efficiency, her surgical skills making her work far superior to any stitching job *he* would have done.

"I'll wait in the living room," Jake said. "I'll carry her to the car when she's ready, so give me a holler."

"Good. Thank you."

Once Wendy was settled in Rory's car, he moved toward his truck, but paused when Rory placed a hand on his arm. "You don't need to come to Fairbanks. Seriously, we'll be fine."

"I told Wendy I would."

"Jake..." She lifted her hand from him and wrapped her arms around herself. "I can't begin to thank you for all you did today. That was...so scary. And you being here to help was huge in so many ways. But I think it's better if we keep the time we're together to a minimum, like we talked about before. All that at Pooky's was... Well, it's clear how you feel about me. And there's nothing to be gained by dredging up the past, you know? Being around each other isn't going to help with that."

He knew she was right. His anger and frustration with her—which was really about what had happened nine years ago and not today—had nearly boiled over at Pooky's, and he still wasn't sure what exactly he might have said if they hadn't been interrupted. What part of his heart he might have let her see. It wasn't a place either of them wanted to go.

"All right. Send me a text and let me know what they say and if they're keeping her at the hospital overnight."

"Will do. And... Well, thanks again."

She turned, and within moments all he could see were the taillights of her car.

CHAPTER SIX

FEELING A LITTLE rough around the edges after spending the night in her mother's hospital room, Rory sat next to the hospital bed and gulped some coffee. It was a huge relief to see the color back in Twinkie's face after the blood transfusion she'd received yesterday, and her usual sweet smile was back, too.

"Since you're stuck here until this afternoon, I'm going to go ahead and get some winter shopping done while we're in town. Will you be okay until I get back? It won't take me too long."

"Of course, Aurora. I'm happy resting in this comfy bed, and the nurses are all so nice. The medicine they gave me really helps with the pain."

"I'm glad."

"Did you look at the supplies I have left from last year? I think there's a lot…"

"I took an inventory of your bottled water and batteries, and your dry and canned goods. I checked your portable camping lamps and flashlights, to make sure they're working if the power goes out, and one needs a new bulb. It's not bad, but you definitely need more stuff."

"Okay. Whatever you think."

Her mother's utter confidence in her—well, except for the doctoring thing, which just might have changed yesterday—tugged at her heart, and she leaned over and kissed her mother's cheek, emotion filling her chest because she could; because her mom was still here, when yesterday might have been catastrophic if she'd been alone for too long.

And didn't that reality force her to rethink her plans a little? Was it really okay for her to pass her mother's care on to Aunt Patty when this had just happened? Maybe now she'd be feeling about the same as she had the first day she'd been released after surgery. Or maybe she'd be weaker and need more care for longer than expected. And if that was the case Rory would have to reconsider her plans.

If that had to happen, seeing Jake more would be inevitable. But she couldn't put her own feelings, the guilt and pain that kept getting stirred up when she was around him, above her mother's health and recovery.

"Get some rest. I'll be back as quickly as possible."

It was just a short drive from the hospital to the big grocery and supply store where they got all the things they needed that they couldn't get at Green's Market in Eudemonia.

She swung the car into the parking lot, grabbed her purse and list, and headed into the store. In no time she had the cart half full, and realized that a second trip before she went home would probably need to happen. Or a third, if she ended up staying longer.

Rounding a corner, she had to pull up short when she nearly banged into a cart coming the other way.

"Sorry—"

Before the word was barely out of her mouth she saw

that the person pushing the cart was tall and gorgeous, with black hair skimming his collar. A baby wearing a knit hat sat in the front of the cart, clutching a sippy cup in both hands, and she could see Beth Hunter behind them, farther down the aisle.

"I see you're no better a driver than you used to be. Always in a hurry," Jake said, his eyes showing a hint of the humor she remembered so well, although at the same time he wore a frown, as though he were genuinely irritated.

Her heart clutched in a way that had become uncomfortably familiar these past few days.

"Yeah, well, the visibility in this store isn't the greatest, what with all the end-caps and cardboard displays they have everywhere."

"True. Except even in a grocery store there are rights of way, and tearing around a corner into the wrong lane is a clear violation."

"Are you going to give me a ticket? Oh, wait—you're a doctor, not a cop."

"A doctor who's on the volunteer police and fire rescue squad in Eudemonia. Maybe I can extend my privileges to here in Fairbanks."

"I'll be long gone before you can make *that* happen."

"True." The humor that had expanded into a half smile flattened into cool indifference. "Stocking up for your mom before you leave?"

"She's not being released until this afternoon, so I figured while we were here it made sense. Though I think I'll have to make a second trip before I go back to LA. I don't want her stranded without enough water and food and essentials if a huge storm comes through."

"How's she feeling?"

"Surprisingly, she seems pretty good. But of course that's while she's lying in a hospital bed, getting pain meds. Being home and moving around might be a different story. I... I want to thank you again for being there for both of us. Doing it all alone would have been rough."

"You do realize your thank-you is more of an insult, don't you? As if you wouldn't have done the same for me, or anyone. As if we weren't always there for each other when we needed to be. Until you left."

His words and the intensity in his eyes made her chest squeeze hard. "I...yes, I know. Sorry, it's just that—"

"Hello, Aurora," Beth said, coming to stand next to Jake. "How's your mom? What a scary thing!"

"Yeah, it was scary. Thank heavens Linda called me and we were able to get there fast."

"And that you and Jacob are both doctors who knew how to take care of her right there. Sounds like trying to get her to Fairbanks while she was bleeding like that might have been bad."

"Yeah. It was a huge help that Jake was there with me." He deserved that credit, no matter what he'd said to her seconds ago. Though it was true. They had always been there for each other. He'd always been there for her. Until she hadn't been able to accept that unwavering support from him anymore.

"Does this mean you're going to bring your mom to my office so I can check on her in a couple days? Or stubbornly refuse to, like before?" Jake asked.

"I've come to appreciate your point about having all the equipment for checking her vitals and drawing blood to send to the lab," she said, trying to sound professional and unemotional. "And her surgeon wants to have her follow-up doc be someone he can reach, or who can reach him, if she has some complication up the road. Which makes sense, obviously."

"Glad you agree."

He inclined his head, and she could just see him battling wanting to say something more, but resisting.

"Call the office and get it scheduled with Ellie for before you leave. Or after, if you want, and your aunt can bring her instead."

"No, I'll bring her. One less thing to bother Aunt Patty with."

"Are you leaving soon, Rory? Or staying longer now?" Beth asked.

"I'm not sure. It depends on how Mom's doing after she's been home a few days. I don't want to overburden Aunt Patty if she needs more help getting around, bathed and dressed than she did before."

"What do you think about coming to Mika's first birthday party? Bring your mom, too," she said. "You could see Jake's beautiful house and some of the family again. I don't think Tim's going to be able to make it, and Jake's dad will be at a conference in Anchorage, but Grace will be there. And friends you haven't seen for a long time."

Probably old friends, who knew all about what had happened. Who probably thought it was long ago and far away and that neither she nor Jake thought about it anymore. Except she did, and it was obvious that he did, too.

"When is it?" Hopefully after she was gone, so she'd have a good excuse not to go. Not to see the small but beautiful family being formed around Jake and his son.

"Sunday."

"I'll see how it goes. Twinkie might not be well enough." Her stomach balled into a knot at the thought of spending the afternoon in the midst of all that family happiness, celebrating beautiful Mika turning one year old. Then she realized that maybe Beth might help convince her mother to leave Eudemonia for a while.

"Although if she's feeling well enough to attend, maybe you could encourage Twinkie to come back to LA with me. She's reluctant, but I think it's the perfect solution. I can make sure she's healing fine, and getting stronger, and she wouldn't be all alone here as winter comes. She could get outside to walk and exercise, since it's warm year-round."

"That's a very good idea, and I'd be happy to do that," Beth said. "Though your mother's pretty stubborn, despite being the sweetest person I know."

"Runs in the family," Jake said under his breath.

"Anyway, I hope you can make it to the party. Speaking of which—I have some more things I need to get for it. I'll meet you at the car, Jake. Okay?"

"Sure."

As his grandmother walked away the baby practically turned himself into a pretzel in order to face Rory, his brown eyes studying her. She found herself unable to look away from his sweet face, noticing how thick his dark lashes were. Very like his daddy's, despite their not being biologically related.

He sent her a sudden wide smile that showed four white teeth—two on top and two on the bottom. The tightness in her belly loosened, to be replaced by a warm glow around her heart. How adorable he was. She wanted to reach out and touch his soft cheek, the way she had when Beth had held him on her lap in front of the clinic that first night she'd met him.

"He's so precious," she murmured, giving in to the

urge to run her hand down his small back. "Like a little angel."

"Not always an angel," Jake said. "Sometimes he—"

The baby's arm flailed backward, and then in a quick release he flung his plastic cup right at her, hitting her in the sternum. Startled, she let out a cry, somehow managing to grab it and clutch it to her chest before it fell to the floor.

"Mika! No throwing things," Jake said in a firm voice. He looked up at Rory and shook his head. "Sorry. Just proving he's not an angel, I guess. Are you okay?"

"Fine. Though it's surprising that a plastic cup thrown by a little hand can actually hurt some."

She handed Mika his cup and he threw it back, clearly enjoying this game, and his gurgling laugh had Rory smiling, too, even as her heart pinched.

"I recall that your games of choice were football, basketball and soccer," she said, deciding it was safer to hand the cup to Jake than the baby. "But you might have to add baseball to that list—he's got quite an arm."

"He does. But I'm hoping that's going to pass, since flinging projectiles to get attention sometimes results in bruises and broken things. I had no idea how much a house had to be babyproofed."

"Yeah."

She swallowed down the ache that had stuck in her throat. The ache that was there because she'd lost her chance to experience all the things that came with having a baby, and because her desire to even try again to make it happen had been permanently flattened.

"Where do you live these days? I didn't think to ask."

"I have a house up the east hill. You remember Dave and George from back in high school? They do construction now, and they did most of the building, with me helping when I could. Which gave me a whole new appreciation for the skill involved in that."

A vision of Jake hammering and sawing, possibly shirtless and wearing a tool belt on his lean hips, made her feel a little short of breath.

"Do you think they'd prep and paint Mom's house? I think it's probably too late in the season now, but I'd like to get it on the schedule for next summer. I could pay a deposit, if they want."

"I'm sure they would. They usually have to go to Fairbanks or other towns to get jobs, so they're always happy to have work in Eudemonia when they can. I'll get you their number."

"Thanks." She looked down at the baby again, who was reaching up to Jake and starting to complain a little, obviously fidgeting to get out of there. "Well, I'll let you go. See you in the office when I bring Mom in, I guess."

She swung her cart around and past his, anxious to get going. Relieved to finally be done and through the checkout line, she rolled the cart to her rental car and loading up the trunk.

She was startled when a hand wrapped around her arm.

With a gasp and a near shriek, she slapped her palm to her thudding heart and whirled to see who'd grabbed her.

Jake.

"What the heck?" she demanded. "You scared me."

"Sorry. I didn't mean to scare you. But the things I want to say to you keep rolling around and around in my head. I have to get them off my chest, and I might not have another chance."

They stared at one another, and there it was again.

That familiar longing, sadness and confusion that kept filling her heart every time she was around the man.

"You wanting to take your mom to LA makes sense right now, while she recovers, I admit it," he said, his voice taking on a hard note. "But you know what? I understand why she wants to stay here, in her hometown, where she's lived her whole life. And I just have to say it. I thought *you'd* always want to stay here, too—no matter what."

"I *had* to leave," she choked out. "You know that."

"I *don't* know that. Why, when I begged you to stay? You left anyway, without even saying goodbye."

So there it was. She'd hoped maybe he'd forgotten that she'd decided to leave without telling him. Or that he didn't care anymore. That the pain she'd seen on his face since she'd come back was all about their baby and not her. Except if she was honest with herself she'd known since she first moment she'd seen him at her mother's house the night she'd arrived that he still felt upset about all of it.

God, she needed to get out of Eudemonia—before she ended up all messed up again.

"I couldn't stay another day. I couldn't face what I'd done. I couldn't live with it staring at me every day I was in this town. The whispers when I left a store. The sympathetic or disapproving looks wherever I went. Surely you can understand that?"

"No. I didn't understand it then and I still don't. You had *me* here to help you through all that. We'd have gone through it together." His hands balled into fists. "I loved you. I loved our baby...the future we'd planned. We should have grieved together, healed together. But instead all you could think about was yourself."

"I... I was thinking of him. Of you, too."

"No, you weren't. You left me high and dry. You abandoned me when I was hurting from losing our baby, then broke my heart a second time when you left. You smashed it into tiny pieces when you never came back. And you never even tried to get in touch with me."

Her heart shook hard, then fell into her stomach as she stared at the raw judgment in his eyes, at the anger and hurt. "I... I didn't mean to abandon you."

"No? Well, that's sure as hell what you did. I never knew you could be that self-centered. But you were."

"How can you not understand at *all*?" Anger welled up in her chest, matching his. "How dare you judge me that way? I lost our baby because of a stupid decision. How do you think that made me feel? You can't understand the pain I felt."

"You think I don't understand that pain? I *lived* it, Rory. I lived it twice because of your selfishness."

"Selfishness? It seems to me *you're* the self-centered one, thinking only about how *you* felt. I was—"

The rumble of a truck parking two spaces over had Jake pressing his lips together and tugging her to the other side of the car, his other hand pulling the cart holding Mika, still sipping away on his cup.

Rory gulped, her heart pounding. She didn't want to talk about this. Not now, not ever. But even as part of her wanted to run the other way, jump into the car and take off, she knew she had to endure this conversation.

She'd already run the other way long ago, hadn't she? She hadn't even realized he believed she'd been thinking only of herself when she had.

It was past time for them to have this conversation—

horrible or not. To clear the air and put all this behind them once and for all.

She saw Jake glance around to make sure they were more or less alone before he spoke again, his voice tight.

"You were what? Heartbroken? Grieving? Join the club. Yet you didn't care enough to stick it out with me. For us to deal with it together. I lost you both at once. And I have a hard time forgiving you for that."

A lump formed in her throat, so big she couldn't speak. When she'd finally swallowed it down, she managed to croak out just a tiny bit of what she wanted to say.

"I have a hard time forgiving myself for any of it. If I let myself think about it the guilt drags me under. I had to leave to survive. Don't you understand that?"

Before she even knew it was going to happen tears spilled from her eyes and she swiped hard at her cheeks. She hadn't fallen apart in a long time. The last thing she wanted was to break down right in the middle of this stupid parking lot. In front of Jake and this beautiful child he was building a new life with.

"Rory... Don't."

Strong hands closed around her shoulders and pulled her closer to his warm, firm chest. Emotion welled up all over again. It was just like Jake to reach for her, to try to comfort her at the very same time as he'd expressed how angry and upset he'd been with her. How angry and upset he still was.

The sweetness and strength of character that had always been a part of who he was weakened her even more. She knew if she didn't get out of there she might fall apart completely. She put her hands against his chest and could feel the steady beat of his heart. She forced herself to push him away, even though it felt so good to touch him again, to feel his warmth against her palms.

"I'm done talking about this," she said, working to pull herself together. "You've said what you wanted to say and I hear you loud and clear. It sounds like you practically hate me, in fact, so the sooner I get to LA the happier we'll both be."

"Damn it, Rory!" Anger flared in his eyes, showed in the jut of his chin all over again. "Why do you—?"

His sentence unfinished, he cursed and dropped his mouth to hers in a hard kiss that lasted just a split second before a shriek and something whacking into Jake's jaw set them apart.

They stared at one another for long seconds before Jake took a step back and reached to retrieve the plastic cup now rolling on the asphalt of the parking lot.

Dragging in a gulp of air, Rory watched him give the cup to Mika and turn without another word to stride toward his truck, apparently feeling exactly as she did. That there was nothing more to say.

She lifted trembling fingers to her lips, wondering why he'd kissed her. Except she knew. Yes, he'd been angry and frustrated with her. But just before that… He'd always hated to see her cry.

Shaking, she managed to get inside the car and she closed her eyes, remembering what she'd forgotten for so long. How he'd stayed up for who knew how long the night they'd lost their tiny boy, building the box they would bury his small body in. How he'd carved the name they'd chosen—Adam—into a candle, along with the date he'd been stillborn. How Jake had held her close as they'd watched the candle burn in memory of the tiny premature infant, both of them in floods of tears.

The next day she'd been released from the hospital. He'd taken her to her parents' house so she could rest, and she'd stayed in her room until the funeral. After they'd buried their baby boy in the cemetery she'd told Jake she needed to get a little more rest. Back in her old bedroom, she'd packed up her things, left a note to her mom and dad, and another to Jake. Told them she needed time alone to think, and got on a plane to LA.

And she'd never come back.

Everyone had told her the accident wasn't her fault. That it probably *wasn't* why she'd gone into labor so early. That it had nothing to do with why the baby had been stillborn.

She'd been so sure it was a perfectly reasonable decision to go on the snowmobile to search and rescue that day. Now it seemed beyond stupid. But no one knew for sure why her baby had died in utero at seven months along, and doctors had reassured her that probably something had been wrong before she'd even gone out that night.

She'd wanted to believe it. She'd tried so hard to convince herself it wasn't her fault. But in the end she'd had to get out of Eudemonia to try to heal. To move on somehow when her grief, guilt and despair told her that if she'd been smarter, less stubborn, if she'd listened to Jake, who had told her to stay home that night, that they'd have their son, Adam, in their lives today.

The day she'd left, and all the days after, she'd never considered that it had been a selfish decision—probably because she hadn't been thinking straight. She was stunned that Jake saw it that way, and she realized he was probably right.

It *had* been selfish of her to go out on that snowmobile, even convinced she was doing it for the right reasons. It had been selfish of her to leave Jake when times had gotten tough, thinking only of herself when she'd taken off for California.

Was she continuing that trend? Leaving her mom alone so she could get the permanent job in LA? Was selfish the kind of person she wanted to be?

No. But she didn't think she could come back to Eudemonia, to be reminded of her fatal mistake every single day.

This trip home had become an even worse mess than she'd expected, and she'd expected it to be pretty bad. So how, exactly, was she going to fix it? The solution, again, was to somehow convince her mother that Southern California was the perfect place for her to get strong again, so they could leave soon.

Much as she dreaded going to Mika's birthday party, taking her mother there so Beth could help convince her to go to LA for the winter was her best shot at making that happen.

CHAPTER SEVEN

WHY THE HELL had his mother asked Rory to come to Mika's birthday party? He hoped she wouldn't come. Hell, he hoped Wendy would be feeling well enough for her sister to take over and that Rory would be gone by then.

He put a sleeping Mika into his crib, tucked the blanket under his chin and kissed his plump little cheek, smiling even as his heart squeezed with all the feelings he'd buried long ago, which had insisted on floating back to the surface since Rory had come back to town.

At the beginning, he'd planned not to say a word about it to her. About all they'd lost and what she'd done. He'd been sure it was long behind him—until this week. And he couldn't even put the blame on her for stirring all their history up again.

He was the one who'd brought up the past—first at Pooky's, then right there in the store parking lot, like a fool, for some reason unable to control the need to get it off his chest. Then he'd made her cry. God, he hated to see her cry, and even as she'd infuriated him he'd kissed her without thinking, wanting to somehow stop the tears that weren't even flowing anymore.

And then…?

Despite getting beaned by Mika's cup, and the kiss

lasting only a nanosecond, he'd wanted more. He'd wanted to pull her warm curves close against his body, to feel how she'd always molded perfectly against him; to mindlessly kiss her for real until neither of them could breathe, right in front of Mika and whoever else might be watching.

Just that tiny taste of her lips had sent bittersweet memories surging through his heart and his body, making him remember how much he'd loved her, how close they'd been, how she'd once been his—making him remember how sure he'd been that she'd be his lover and his soulmate, his life partner forever.

But all that was ancient history, and now that he'd told her how he'd felt when she'd left he had no intention of revisiting it again. Rory had made a new life for herself, and he'd made the life he'd always wanted here in Eudemonia, even though she'd abandoned it. Now, with Mika bringing new joy to his life, he was one step closer to the full dream. His plan of having the lifelong love of a woman and children of their own right here where he'd been born and raised.

Rory was no longer that woman—and the less contact he had with her while she was here, the better for both of them. But fate seemed to keep throwing them together anyway.

He put away the food and supplies he'd bought, and couldn't help but think about Rory doing the same thing at her mother's house—lugging multiple jugs of water and all kinds of things into the cellar. Wendy Anderson was pretty independent, but through all the years Rory's dad had been sick it had been Rory who'd kept the place running, even coming home from college every month to make sure her parents had everything they needed.

After her dad had died, her mother had accepted that there were things she needed help with. Letting some of the teens and the men in town chop firewood and do heavy lifting around her house made it easy for her to live there alone—a good thing, since by then Rory had been long gone.

That kind of community was just one of the reasons to live in Eudemonia. Everyone knew everyone else, and while that was sometimes a bad thing, mostly it was good. The folks in town took care of each other. Anchorage had been plenty big enough when Jake had gone to college and medical school there. He couldn't imagine living in a place like Los Angeles, where you probably didn't even know your next-door neighbor.

Could that be part of why Rory had chosen it? Had she wanted to be anonymous? Able to disappear into a crowd? She'd said people looking at her, talking about her after she'd lost the baby, had been among the reasons she'd felt she had to leave. He'd never thought about that, but she'd always been so strong he was surprised she'd let that bother her.

It didn't matter anymore. She had her life and he had his, and there was nothing else to say. No more conversations about their past and how he'd felt, because it wouldn't accomplish anything other than to upset them both.

"Hi, Jake," Ellie said as he walked into the clinic. "I see you brought your king-size coffee cup with you this morning. Bad night? Did Mika keep you up?"

"No, he slept great." He sure wasn't going to tell her it had been reliving his argument with Rory a couple days ago that had kept him tossing and turning these past two nights. "You have the patient list for the day?"

"Here. Not too many, so hopefully we'll have some emergencies to keep us busy."

"I wonder what the locals would think about their clinic assistant gleefully hoping for illness and injuries to keep her from being bored?"

Ellie laughed and handed him the list before she sat down behind the front desk. Jake scanned the paper, surprised to see Wendy Anderson's name listed. Probably Rory had scheduled it quickly, so they wouldn't see one another again too many times before she left, and the way his heart bumped told him it was a very good thing to get it over with. Maybe, with any luck, that meant she wouldn't be coming to Mika's party after all.

He'd seen three patients before he moved toward the exam room where Wendy and Rory waited. His heart gave another weird kick, which annoyed the hell out of him. Why did he keep feeling this way when he kept reminding himself how stupid and pointless it was to get all riled up about her?

The moment he opened the door his attention moved involuntarily to the woman sitting in the chair next to the exam table instead of his patient, the way it should. Like before, the overhead light skimmed over her shining hair, and her green eyes lifted to meet his for a split second before she cast them down, then toward her mother.

Her uncomfortable expression told him she was remembering the anger, frustration and resentment that had spilled out at the parking lot. Maybe she was also remembering the electricity that had zinged from the briefest touch of his lips to hers, the way it was coming to *his* mind as he looked at her beautiful mouth.

Damn it.

He moved his attention to Wendy and forced a smile. "How are you feeling?"

"A little better, I think. Aurora keeps telling me that when your body's been cut open it's normal for it to hurt until it heals. And since it split open again something awful I'm having to heal all over again. I'm trying not to complain and to remember that it's slowly getting better."

"She's getting around better than I expected she would," Rory said. "I've been looking at the old sutures, and the new ones we did, and they look good. But of course you should see what you think."

"The type-A surgeon is offering to step back and let the general practitioner give his opinion? Now there's a shock." He couldn't help but raise his eyebrows in utter surprise. "You're evolving."

"And apparently you're not—still wanting to annoy me at any opportunity."

Her small smile took any sting out of the words, and the tightness in his chest loosened as he smiled back. "Never claimed to be. But, since you're setting such a good example, I'll give evolving a try."

A moment of silence followed, and Jake was filled with a confusing mix of feelings. He was glad they could share light banter like this, even while he was still feeling they hadn't truly finished their heavy conversation from a couple days ago. Except he'd decided there was no point, hadn't he?

He turned to Wendy. "It's good to remind yourself that you're getting better all the time. But you know what? It's okay to complain, too. I remember Rory used to complain about all kinds of things—like the kids who teased her at school, or that the bike she had that was pink when she wanted a bike a boy would ride."

"I'd forgotten that," Rory murmured.

Another small smile tugging at her lips made him feel glad he'd said something to take their minds off their last conversation and all the bad stuff from the past, way back to the fun times when they were kids.

"I spray-painted it blue and black and hand-painted a few swords on it. I didn't realize until years later how awful it looked."

"My Aurora usually did want to run with the boys, didn't she? Always a spitfire, my little marshmallow girl."

"Yeah, she was. I had to keep her from punching some of those boys in the nose when they teased her. Which was mostly self-preservation on my part. I figured if she got into a real fight I'd have to jump in and beat them up, which wasn't something I was particularly keen to do."

Her gaze lifted to his again as a wry smile twisted her lips. "I was a trial to you, wasn't I?"

Not for most of their relationship. Just at the end.

"Not a trial. An amazing mix of tough little girl and sweetness and adventure and generosity, all wrapped up in a beautiful package. You were like nobody else in that whole school. You were special."

The minute the words were out of his mouth he felt a little foolish. Going down memory lane wasn't advisable—particularly when those memories involved the way he'd felt about her back then, and so many of the years that followed.

"Well, thank you. And a belated thank you, too, to the boy who stood up for me in fourth grade, when I was the fish out of water in a public school setting. You were my hero from that moment on."

Their eyes met again and he felt a strange expansion in his chest, as though her words *meant* something, even though she'd told him something similar many times before. Maybe this was the kind of closure they needed. Compliments to one another...an acknowledgment of what they'd meant to one another before life had got in the way and they'd moved on. It would put a positive ending to the chapter that had had such an abrupt, upsetting and unsatisfactory conclusion nine years ago.

He forced himself to go into doctor mode, asking Wendy a few more questions, taking her vital signs, drawing blood, and looking at her incision. When he was finished he gave her directions on what should happen next.

"Want me to write this down for when Rory is gone? Any word on when your sister is coming to take over?"

"I'm not sure. Aurora...?"

"Aunt Patty's taking this Friday off, so I'm planning to—"

A muffled ringing sound came from the purse on the floor next to the exam bed. Wendy tried to reached down for it, and Rory picked it up and gave it to her.

"Here. But you should let it go, Twinkie," Rory said. "We can't keep Jake waiting while you yak. You can see who it is after we're done here and call back."

"It might be Linda, wanting to know what time to come over with supplies to make the gourd birdfeeders. We're going to give them to everyone before winter."

"It's okay—go ahead and answer, then we'll finish up," Jake said, since the elderly woman looked a little distressed about not answering.

With a disapproving frown, Rory fished the phone from her mother's purse—then frowned even more when she looked at the screen. "It's Aunt Patty."

"Helloooo, sis!" Wendy said, taking the phone and smiling broadly. Her smile faded as she listened, morphing into a worried frown deeper than Rory's. "That's terrible! Oh, dear, of course I understand. Don't worry at all. Aurora will be here for a few more days—and I'm doing pretty well, considering. I'm sure Linda and some of the others will check on me and bring food until I'm feeling up to fixing it myself. It's fine. Please give him a huge hug and kiss from me—and Aurora, too. Tell him we're hoping he gets well soon."

"Wait! Let me talk to her." Rory reached to grab the phone, but her mother hung up before she could get it.

"Well, that's just *terrible* news!" Wendy said. "Owen was injured during a training mission at the base. Broke his arm, and his ribs, too. He's in the base hospital, but they're going to release him tomorrow. She's going to have him come to her house to get better and she'll take care of him there."

"So she's not coming here?" Rory said in a grim voice.

"No, but that's okay. I'm sure Owen needs help a lot more than I do. I'll be fine, Aurora. Don't you worry. I'm moving around okay, don't you think? You said so. And you need to get back to LA for that job interview. I know it's important to you."

"Yes, it is…"

Jake saw her chest heave in a big sigh and their eyes met, hers telegraphing the same thing he was thinking. Her mom shouldn't be left alone just yet, and the amount of time Rory would be here had probably gotten a week longer.

"But I can't leave you alone, Twinkie. I was thinking I should stay a little longer anyway, to be honest. I'll call the hospital and hope it won't be a problem to postpone the interview again. Unless you're willing to come to LA with me? Are you still considering it?"

"I don't know. I mean, I *guess* I'm thinking about it. But there are things here I need to do. The gourds and the Halloween decorations. Our Bunco tournament next month."

Another long, audible sigh left Rory's lips in response to her mother's statement, and Jake felt like sighing along with her.

"Are there other people interviewing for the position?" he asked.

"Yeah." Her face twisted in a grimace. "I don't know exactly how many, but quite a few people who trained at other hospitals are trying to get it, since it's a large orthopedic practice. I'd hoped that training there would give me a big advantage, but..."

Her voice faded away. Then the Rory he knew straightened her shoulders and put that determined look he'd seen so many times on her pretty face. This was the woman who'd climbed trees, operated heavy equipment in various search and rescue operations, and trained to be the kind of doctor few women in the country became.

"Anyway, it is what it is. I'll figure out how to beat everyone else. Maybe being the last one to interview will be an advantage, somehow? Will stop them deciding on someone else before I have a chance."

Yeah, that was indomitable Rory in a nutshell. There was only one time he'd seen her utterly defeated. And now that she'd be here longer he was glad they'd finished talking about it. Maybe they could be near one another without dreading it, or even have a conversation that didn't stir bad memories. Maybe they would be reminded of why they'd been friends for so long before it had all gone wrong.

CHAPTER EIGHT

"OH, COME ON—don't look like that," her mother scolded as she slowly tottered toward the front door of Jake's house. "It's a birthday party. Parties are *fun*! You always loved Jake's family, and they love you. And then there's Mika! Is there a cuter baby on earth than him?"

Rory closed her eyes against the sudden and unforgettable memory of holding her tiny, lifeless baby boy. He hadn't had time to grow to be a pretty, plump, full-term baby. Hadn't lived to grow to be an adorable one-year-old. But for her he would always be the most beautiful baby in the world.

She tried to concentrate on the tree line higher up the hill behind the house, shoving down the image and the memory.

"Mika is very cute—no doubt about it. But, like I said before, it would be better for me to just leave you here and come pick you up later. Can't you understand that it's hard for me to spend time with Jake?"

"No, I can't. You two were together for a long time, and I believe with all my heart that you'll be happier if you bury the hatchet and become friends again. I've lived long enough to know that you can't carry bad feelings around in your heart forever without it affecting your whole body. Poor digestion…your liver…high blood pressure and heart problems. Why, Sam Abbott got diabetes just from worrying too much about money and his business."

Rory bit her tongue. Resigned to her fate for the afternoon, she carried the shopping bag of wrapped gifts she'd gotten on her trek to Fairbanks and helped her mother up the stone steps as a few fat snowflakes began to float from the cloudy sky onto their heads.

They crossed a wide wooden porch that bore zero resemblance to her mother's small, creaky and listing front stoop. It gleamed with what looked like a new coat of polyurethane, and four comfortable-looking rocking chairs with plush pillows sat on either side of the front door. She wondered if Jake left them out all winter or took them to a shed somewhere, and then decided that the less she knew about how Jake lived in his new home with his new baby, the better.

She knocked on double doors painted a deep forest green, and Beth Hunter opened them with a smile. "Rory! Wendy. So glad you could make it. I can't believe you knocked on the door, though. You're like family, after all."

Family. It had felt that way, once, hadn't it?

They stepped across an oblong rug woven in the traditional Alaska Native style that graced so many homes in Eudemonia and elsewhere, and into a room with a vaulted ceiling made of pine logs. The space was nearly as big as her mother's entire house, but even with the high ceiling it somehow felt cozy. Possibly because a crackling fire blazed in the large stone fireplace and large, overstuffed sofas and chairs sat on either side of it.

But the biggest reason it felt cozy was because it was

full of people. Jake's immediate family, plus cousins and lots of neighbors, sat and stood everywhere, talking and smiling. Balloons bobbed gently around the room, and a table holding platters of all kinds of food sat beneath one of the large windows, perfect for letting in what light was available during gray days and dark winters.

Rory stood there, absorbing the feel of the place. Warmth. Happiness and pleasure. A place you could count on as being a respite—a place you wanted to be, no matter how tough the outside world had become.

Much like Jake himself.

Her gaze roamed the beautiful room until it landed on the man who owned this house, who'd said he'd helped design and build it. He stood in the center, big and handsome, with a relaxed smile on his face. Mika was curled into Jake's muscled arm, one small fist hanging on to the collar of his daddy's yellow polo shirt.

A mix of emotions fluttered in Rory's heart. Sadness, envy and, yes, a warm and real happiness for Jake. He deserved to have everything he wanted in life and it looked like he was nearly there, with his home in Eudemonia, his clinic practice, his beautiful son. At some point he'd be sure to marry, and the hollowness that filled Rory's chest at that thought told her it was a very good thing she'd decided to stay in Los Angeles for good, so she didn't have to see who he chose to be his bride.

"Jake! Look who's here!" Beth called.

He lifted his gaze and she could see his smile falter before he shored it up again. Maybe someday everything that had happened between them, and his anger toward her because of it, would be so far away as not to matter anymore. She hoped so. For her sake, and for his, she hoped with all her heart that there'd come a time when being around each other didn't bring to the surface feelings and memories they both wanted to forget.

He walked toward her with that easy gait of his, and with one hand reached for her mother's coat. "Thanks for coming, Wendy... Rory. My mother tells me a first birthday party is all-important, so I'm glad you're here to help celebrate."

"Oh, they're just so cute as little ones. No need for any other entertainment when there's a toddler around, is there?" her mother said, beaming. "Is he walking yet?"

"A couple teetering steps, then back down. I keep holding my breath, thinking he's going to bang himself hard somewhere when he falls, but he's like a rubber ball. Just rolls with it."

"I'll take Mika so you can get Rory and Wendy something to drink," Beth said, reaching for the child. "Help yourselves to food, then he can open his presents before we have cake. I don't want to rush things along too much, but the forecast is for a storm moving in. Look, it's starting to snow already. We need to give our out-of-town friends plenty of time to drive home before it comes down harder."

"There's barely any right now, Mom. And I doubt the storm's going to bring much snow this time of year," Jake said, handing over the smiling baby. "But I agree that you should grab some of the Sloppy Joes my dad made, Wendy. They're the best. He's in Anchorage for a conference, and not happy he couldn't be here, so he made them for everyone else to enjoy."

"I'll be sure to have some, then. I didn't even know your dad likes to cook."

"Only very selective things, Wendy, believe me," Beth said, chuckling. "Come on over here and sit down."

Rory watched her mother move away to chat with Linda and some other folks, then looked up at Jake. "Your house is beautiful. You must be proud of it. So it's probably wrong of me to tell you I don't want to be here."

"Because my son's turning one and ours would have turned nine this past spring?" he asked in a quiet voice, shocking her. He knew exactly what she'd been thinking.

"Yes," she whispered. "That and other things."

"What other things?"

She wouldn't tell him that she couldn't get that kiss off her mind. It barely even counted as a kiss, really, since he'd been frustrated and angry with her when it had happened and it had lasted all of one second. Shockingly, though, that briefest touch had reminded her of all the kisses they'd shared. And, if she was honest, she'd like another one—or more. But that would be the worst idea ever. What was the point of kisses that would make her feel even more lonely after she was gone?

"Nothing. Never mind. I'm going to get some food for Twinkie."

She could practically feel him watching her as she moved away, and she hoped he wouldn't notice that someone had gotten her mom a plate of food which she was already enjoying as she talked with her friends. Probably she should eat something, too. But her stomach felt a little queasy.

She'd just decided a carbonated soda might do the trick when Beth stepped in front of her, looking a little harried.

"Rory, can you take Mika for a minute? One of the kids spilled red punch on the throw rug in the kitchen. I want to get some water on it before it stains, and I see Jake just went outside to get another load of firewood."

Before she could answer the child was thrust into her arms. She reacted instinctively, reaching out and then pressing his small, warm body close against her. For a second she hesitated, and then, with a sigh, let her cheek rest against his temple. His wonderful scent—all powder and milk and sweet baby—filled her nose, and she closed her eyes and breathed him in.

She'd expected that holding him like this would make her feel emotional. And she did. But they weren't the kinds of emotions that hurt. Yes, her throat closed a little, but what she felt was mostly a strange calm. A quiet joy. The same deep feeling of happiness for Jake that had filled her earlier.

What an amazing blessing a healthy child was. This little boy who'd so tragically lost his mother was beyond fortunate to have become a part of the Hunter family— and they were beyond fortunate to have him.

"Your daddy is a special person—you know that, don't you, Mika?" she whispered, moving her cheek to his soft hair. "You're a lucky boy to get to spend your life with him. *So* lucky."

He must be feeling tired from all the company and activity, because he laid his head against her shoulder, poked his thumb into his little rosebud mouth and closed his eyes. She looked down at the fan of dark lashes against his round cheeks, breathed in the smell of him again and let her heart ache and warm at the same time.

She gave herself up to enjoying the moment as long as she could. As long as it lasted.

"Sleepy, little guy?" she murmured as she swayed back and forth. "I'll hold you while you get some rest. You've got big stuff going on today, with your birthday cake and all those presents waiting for you to open them. I got you some books for your daddy to read to you, and a little drum so you can drive him crazy. I hope you like them."

"Did you say a drum?"

The low, deep voice in her ear had her lifting her head, then turning her face to see Jake's, just inches from hers. He smelled of the outdoors, and ever so slightly of musky woodsmoke, and of *him*.

"Um…yeah. I looked for a horn, or a tambourine, but I had to settle for a drum. It's only plastic, though, so not super-loud. Darn it."

"I don't know what I ever did to you to deserve that kind of punishment."

"Nothing. You know that." She faced him, and the humor of their conversation fell away as that familiar hollow feeling made her stomach hurt. "I'm the one who deserves the bad stuff. But don't worry—I live with it every day."

"Rory—"

The sleepy baby lifted his head, blinked, looked up into Rory's face and started whimpering. Relieved that she didn't have to listen to whatever empty platitudes Jake had been about to offer, or hear him lambast her like he had before, she handed the child to him and quickly moved away to sit near her mother.

Cake was being served, and everyone was laughing at the way Mika used both fists to pick his piece up from the highchair tray and stuff it into his mouth, enthusiastically licking at his messy lips and fingers.

Grinning, Jake took a video of the moment, and Rory couldn't help but think about Jake and Mika watching it together and laughing when the boy was older, about the bond the two of them were already forging.

After Mika had eaten as much as possible, and gotten bored with smearing icing around his tray, Jake and his mother cleaned the child up, sat him on the floor and let him rip the paper off his gifts. It was clear that some of the presents weren't quite as interesting to him as the paper, and everyone enjoyed the fun of watching him.

Glad she'd been able to melt toward the back of the room, Rory managed to chuckle along with everyone else, even as she kept glancing at her watch, wondering how long they'd have to stay.

It was beyond hard to watch Jake with Mika and see what an absolutely great father he was—to see the light in his eyes when he looked at the baby, to see an indulgent smile of such love on his face. It squeezed her heart so hard she thought it might bleed.

Yes, she'd seen Jake and Mika together since she'd come back, but not quite like this. Playing and teasing and laughing. Jake picking him up to hug him and kiss him. The baby wrapping his small arms around his dad's neck and hanging on tight.

This was how Jake would have been with Adam. How Adam would have been with Jake. How they'd have all been together, as a family. Staring at Jake now, at his handsome face and beautiful smile, she realized for the first time since she'd come back, really admitted it to herself, that she'd never stopped loving her best friend.

She was about to turn to her mother and suggest they go, so she didn't have to think about all that anymore, when Jake handed the baby the gift she'd brought and sent her a grin.

"I think I already know what's in here, Dr. Anderson. And it scares me."

"Maybe he'll like the paper more than the present."

"Probably no such luck."

Jake helped Mika open the gift, picked up one of the rubbery plastic drumsticks and tapped the drum a few times. Mika's eyes lit, and he immediately grabbed both sticks and starting pounding on it.

Everyone in the room howled.

Beth covered her ears and said, "Rory Anderson! Did *you* give him that?"

"Um…guilty as charged. Sorry. I couldn't decide what to get him, and I thought it would be fun."

"That's a clear fib," Jake said. "You thought it would torment me."

"Maybe."

Their eyes met, and they shared a small smile that banished some of the melancholy she'd been feeling the past half hour. Mika moved on to whacking the sticks as hard as he could on the hardwood floor, then stood to stagger a few steps to the rustic wooden coffee table, wildly swinging the sticks against the side of it.

"Um…maybe I should have thought this through a little more," Rory said, feeling sheepish about possible furniture destruction.

"Maybe you should have," Jake said, but the brown eyes meeting hers still smiled. "Well, he probably can't do a lot of damage with those sticks. And I already told you I've baby-proofed the house pretty well."

Rory let her gaze travel over the planes of his face, memorizing them all over again since this might well be the last time she saw him. Her mother was more functional every day, and even her extended stay wouldn't keep her here more than another week. Getting back to LA as soon as her mom was able to fully take care of herself had to be her priority. Much as she was enjoying talking with Jake and being near him, she knew it would just make it all the harder to leave.

She made herself turn to see how her mom was doing. "You feeling tired, Twinkie? Ready to go home?"

"I guess I am a little tired. Oh, but it's been a fun day, hasn't it? I'm so glad we came."

"It's been good." Which was something she hadn't expected was possible when they'd been getting ready to come today. Maybe, as she'd thought before, this closure on a more positive note between her and Jake would be a good thing for both of them. "I'll go get your coat."

As she walked toward the front closet she could see Jake watching her, and then Beth stopped her progress.

"I have some food on the kitchen counter for you to take home with you. It'll be good for a few meals, and then you can freeze some of the Sloppy Joe meat for Wendy to eat after you're gone."

"Thank you. Everything was so good, and it's always nice for her to have stuff ready to eat that she can just thaw."

"Also…" Beth lowered her voice. "Do you still want me to talk to your mom about going to LA with you for the next few months? I'd be happy to, since I think it's a very good idea."

"That would be great." More than great, as then they'd be able to leave soon, solving all kinds of problems. "Could you talk to her while I go to the kitchen? I'll hang around in there for a bit, so she doesn't feel like we're ganging up on her and thinks that it's your idea. Then we'll go, because I think she's getting tired."

"I'll talk with her right now."

Rory found her way to the kitchen, curious to see how Jake had designed it. It had an open feel, like the living room, with a large center island with stools, light-colored cabinets, more hardwood flooring and big windows. It was the perfect size and the perfect design for Alaska, with its long winter nights and long summer days.

Several containers sat on the counter with her mother's name on them and she thought about how nice Beth was, always thinking of others. How she always had been. Jake was like that, too. It struck Rory that maybe she wasn't as much like that as she wanted to be, and just as she was pondering that Jake came into the kitchen to stand behind her.

"Find them?"

"Yes." Her throat closed at his nearness as she remembered her revelation a short time ago. That she'd loved him practically her whole life and always would. "I appreciate all your mom does for everyone."

"She does a lot for me, that's for sure. She takes care of Mika quite a bit, and she planned this party."

"That's…good. I'm sure everyone with a baby, especially someone single, needs lots of help."

Which made her think about him not being single in the future, and how awful that would make her feel. But how could she think like that? She wanted him to be happy, didn't she?

She'd opened her mouth to say goodbye and hightail it out of there when his hands rested on her shoulders and he turned her around to face him.

"I saw how sad you looked when Mika was opening his presents. I wanted to tell you I was thinking about Adam, too."

"You were?" She stared up into his brown eyes and saw he meant it. "I… That surprises me. You looked so happy, having fun with Mika."

"I *was* happy having fun with him. He's changed my life, and I'm beyond thankful for that." He caught her face in his hands. "But that doesn't mean I'm not still sad for the son we lost. It doesn't mean I don't understand how you feel."

"Thank you," she whispered, and her hands lifted to his chest, slid to the sides of his neck, even before she'd known she was going to touch him.

Everything she'd felt during the party—all those thoughts about him and how they'd been when they were together, how she'd loved him and couldn't stop thinking about kissing him—seemed to short-circuit her mind and stop her heart.

"Jake, I..."

"I know. Me, too."

The eyes staring into hers held something different now. Something hot and alive. And she knew she wasn't alone in remembering the way they'd loved one another once. The way it had felt when they'd kissed and made love, which had always been so much more than just sex.

Fixated on his beautiful lips, her heart thudding hard against her ribs, she quivered as she watched his mouth lower to hers.

The kiss was sweet and slow and wonderful. A gentle rub of his lips against hers as his arms slipped around her, holding her close against his warm, firm chest. Memories of all the yesterdays when he'd held her this way, of the hundreds of kisses they'd shared, melted her heart and stole her breath.

Her hands moved to his hair, tunneling into the thick softness as the kiss deepened, no longer sweet and soft. His body trapped hers against the counter as the kiss escalated into a passionate tangle of tongues that weakened her knees and had her desperate for more.

This was what she wanted. She couldn't lie to herself about that. From the first second she'd seen him again she'd wanted to kiss him. Hold him. Have him hold her. Sensations she hadn't experienced in nine long years overwhelmed her, and she found herself arching into him, feeling his hardness, wanting so much more.

He pulled back, his eyes glittering, his jaw tense. "Rory?"

She tried to speak, but found she couldn't think of a single thing to say or do other than tug his head down to kiss him again. His hands roamed her body and sent shivers down her spine as his mouth devoured hers with a single-mindedness that felt so intense, she was dizzy from it.

"Jacob! Where are you?"

The sound of his mother's voice had them stumbling apart. Rory could see his chest heaving as he tried to catch his breath, which was hardly a surprise since she felt like she couldn't breathe at all.

"Uh…" He shoved his hand through his hair and cleared his throat, then took a quick step away from Rory and worked to adjust the front of his pants. "I'm in the kitchen."

Rory could only imagine what her expression might be like. Jake looked stunned and flushed and she felt that way but times ten. She was about to turn to the sink, to splash cold water on her face, when Beth appeared at the kitchen doorway and hurried toward them.

Something about her expression told Rory that this wasn't about the party, or their guests, or either one of them. It was clear that something was definitely wrong.

CHAPTER NINE

"WHAT IS IT, MOM?"

Rory was impressed that Jake had managed to get his voice under control so fast, answering his mother in a tone that said he, too, could tell she was worried about something.

"Jameson Woodrow just called. Natalia's gone into labor a couple weeks early and he said he's afraid there's something wrong. The midwife they've been seeing is away in Anchorage, probably at the same conference as your dad. He was going to ask your father to open the clinic, but she's in so much pain he can't get her up to move her to the car. I told her your dad's in Anchorage, too, but that you're here. I think you should go up there and see what's going on. Is there someone here who can go with you? If she needs to be moved to the clinic, or even if she has the baby, you might need help with that."

Instantly Rory could see his professional doctor mode take over. "There are a few people here who would come with me. I'll ask. I assume you can stay here and watch Mika? You might as well plan to spend the night here, just in case it takes a long time."

"I brought an overnight bag, thinking the weather might get bad."

"Perfect. Thanks."

They moved back to where everyone was gathered and Rory watched Jake scan the room, presumably looking for a helper. Even though she dreaded the thought of spending more awkward hours with him, she knew what needed to happen and placed her hand on his forearm.

"I'll go with you. I haven't delivered a baby in a long time, but I'm sure I can help."

He looked down at her for a long moment, his expression inscrutable. She knew what he was thinking, because she was, too. Being together after that scorching and ill-advised kiss wasn't the best idea. But this was an emergency, and having two doctors made a lot more sense than him finding a random friend to assist him.

Finally, he nodded. "All right. But what about your mom?"

"I'll see if Linda can drive her home. Stay with her, too, if she can."

"I'll call Jameson to tell him we'll leave soon, then I'll pull together some supplies."

Linda was more than happy to take her mother home and spend the night. "It's looking like we'll get more snow than we thought," Linda said as she peered out the window at the light flakes steadily falling to the ground. "So I'd just as soon stay put once we're at your house. It'll be fun having a slumber party, don't you think, Wendy?"

"A slumber party! I *love* that idea! I probably can't dance around yet, but we can work on those paper pumpkins and ghost strings for Halloween. Rory got me all the supplies we need."

Wendy's eyes shone with pleasure, and Rory had to face what she'd been trying to ignore. Her mom truly loved living here. She loved her friends and her life here. Much as she wanted her mother to come live with her for the winter in Los Angeles, and was convinced she'd enjoy the warmth of Southern California, she couldn't deny the truth. Moving her to LA for the winter would be more for *her* benefit than for Twinkie's.

"That's perfect, Linda," Rory said. "In case we're gone a long time there's leftover stew and noodles in the fridge, to heat up for dinner, or the things Beth is being kind enough to send from the party. Plus Twinkie and I made cookies the other day, so there's plenty to eat. You'll need to help her get into her jammies, though, because she's still having trouble getting undressed by herself."

"I'm happy to do that. Goodness knows I've had plenty to eat here already, but I'm sure we'll want a late-night snack."

Glad to have all that settled, Rory hugged Linda and her mom, and went to grab her coat. There was no sign of Jake yet, and she hovered around the door, nervous and worried about spending this time with him, but at the same time feeling wired about the trek and perhaps helping this woman deliver her baby.

Now that Jake was about to leave a number of guests stood, obviously wanting to say their goodbyes. Beth was holding Mika and talking with them, but she came over when she spotted Rory by the door.

"Thanks for doing this, Rory. I know Jake appreciates it, too."

"Taking care of people, whether it's this kind of situation or something in my own specialty, is why doctors go into medicine. I'm happy to do it."

"I hope Natalia's okay, and that the baby is, too."

Beth's anxious expression made Rory's stomach drop. For some reason when she thought of labor and birth, even a difficult one, she thought of a happy outcome, with a beautiful newborn.

How was it possible that it hadn't even occurred to her that it might be a terrible situation, like her own had been nine years ago?

That tonight a baby might be born, but not healthy. Maybe not even alive.

God, she'd shoved all that down so deeply. How was she going to handle it if this turned out to be the kind of life-altering heartache her own pregnancy and labor had turned into?

She sucked in a steadying breath. She was a doctor. She had to be brave and tough—be there for this woman and her unborn child and stop thinking of herself. It would be okay. She'd get through it no matter what happened. She could do it. *Would* do it.

"I hope so, too, Beth. I'll do the best I can to help the momma and Jake bring a healthy baby into the world."

Beth's brown eyes were filled with worry for Natalia Woodrow, and with a kind of deep sympathy she knew was about her and the baby she and Jake had lost.

"I know you will."

Jake appeared by her side with several bags stuffed to overflowing. "Ready?"

"Ready. What have you got in there?"

"Transport monitor. Exterior monitor to track the baby's vitals. Pain meds. Surgical equipment. Hopefully everything we'll need, no matter what the situation is."

"You keep all that *here*?" she asked, astonished that he'd have medical supplies beyond the simplest things at his own house.

"You've been gone too long. When storms come through, or the power goes out, or we need to go on search and rescue or whatever situation, we've got to be ready. Getting to the clinic might not be an option."

Search and rescue. Another thing she'd apparently shoved down so as not to think about it too hard after what had happened.

"Of course," she muttered. "So, let's go."

Her heart squeezing all over again, she watched the sweet hug and kiss Jake gave the baby, then another to his mom, before he led the way to his truck, stashing the equipment on the second set of bench seats behind the front set.

She climbed up into the truck and in moments they'd driven the half mile or so of gravel road that led from his house to the main paved road, where they picked up speed. She tried to ignore the fluttering in her heart from being so close to him after what had happened between them, even as she was thankful this wasn't the small car he'd had so long ago, when she would have been mere inches from his big body.

Tension—sexual and otherwise—seemed to vibrate between them, and she didn't think she was the only one feeling it.

"Where do they live? How far is it?"

"Pretty far—which worries me. About thirty-five miles away, in a little town that sprang up near one of the new oil fields that wasn't open when you lived here. Remember the dry cabins up on the ridge? Where lots of hunters go? It's about ten miles from there."

"What's the road like?" She wasn't worried about the road, but avoiding a heavy silence between them by making small talk might calm her nerves.

"Not bad, really. The oil company put a lot of money into it, so it's fairly smooth all the way into the town. I think the Woodrows live off a gravel road, but in the truck it won't be a problem even if it snows more."

She glanced around at the snowflakes, clinging to the car and starting to cover the landscape. "I didn't really look at the forecast, but it seems early for any kind of real snow."

"Yeah, I can't imagine we'll get much. But I guess you never know."

His face was in profile as he watched the road, and the years fell away as she remembered all the times they'd driven together in a car. Sometimes it had been in his small sedan, other times in her own compact little SUV, which she'd bought once they were in college in Anchorage with the money she'd made waiting tables there.

Confusing and contradictory thoughts swirled through her mind as the miles passed. Thoughts of that kiss, and wanting more of them, warred with her self-protective mode that had been telling her from the day she arrived that she needed to get away from him and Eudemonia and the memories as quickly as possible.

But at this moment that attitude was selfish—like he'd said she'd been before, right? Tonight it was a good thing she was here to help this woman with whatever problem she was having. Surely the distraction of that would put everything out of her mind but work?

But then there'd be the torture of driving back with him.

Except, in a strange way, this didn't feel like torture. It felt oddly nice to be sitting close to him in this truck, despite the slightly disturbing tension zinging around the cab. And suddenly, after wanting nothing more than to get back to California as soon as possible, the thought of going back into her hidey-hole and her normal life in LA felt strangely distant.

Which clearly proved that being back home was making her crazy.

Jake seemed to want to fill the silence, too—but not with conversation about what had happened between them in his kitchen. Which she was glad about, since she didn't want to go there, either.

He asked questions about her potential future job in LA, and told her about the general medical practice in Fairbanks, where he and his father took turns working since the clinic in Eudemonia didn't need both of them full-time.

The conversation helped her relax and forget her strange confusion. And when they finally pulled up in front of the Woodrows' house, flooded with outdoor lights presumably to help them find it, her heart had returned to a normal rhythm.

"Why don't you go knock and tell them we're here?" he said, half of his face lit up, the other in shadow as he leaned into the back seat of the truck. "I'll bring the stuff in."

She turned away from the striking angles of the face she'd seen in her dreams for so long and moved toward the front door. She'd barely lifted her arm to knock when it cracked open and an obviously agitated man peered out.

"I'm Dr. Anderson, and Dr. Jacob Hunter is with me."

"Thank God."

He swung the door wide, then turned and moved into the house, leaving Rory to assume he wanted her to follow. She glanced over her shoulder to see Jake's tall, broad form moving out of the shadows toward the house, and decided to go on in.

"Back here. She's in a lot of pain. I don't know what to do."

Moving through a pretty modern foyer into a good-sized living room, Rory was surprised to see the poor woman lying right there on the carpeted floor, writhing and moaning. Her heart beat harder. She hated to see the obvious distress the poor woman was in. Hopefully it was normal labor pain, but if her husband hadn't been able to get her into the car even between contractions there was a good chance it was more than that.

She knelt down and grasped the woman's wrist to take her pulse. It was high, but that wasn't a surprise, considering how much pain she must be in.

"I'm Aurora Anderson, a doctor from LA, and Dr. Hunter is here with me." She sensed Jake coming up behind her. "Tell us what's going on."

"She said she thought she was in labor, so we called the midwife and were upset to find out she's in Anchorage. She gave us some instructions on the signs to look for—timing how far apart the contractions were and stuff—and said we should go to Fairbanks to the hospital there when they were twenty minutes apart, to give us plenty of time to drive there."

"But she didn't feel able to do that?" Jake asked, also crouching down beside the moaning woman.

"It seemed okay for a while, but then the contractions starting coming closer and I got worried and said we should go. And then she was like this." Worry etched the man's face. "She'd been sitting and walking around, but then she was in so much pain she just lay down on the floor, and she's been like this ever since. The midwife said last week that the baby was breech, but she expected it would turn. But now it's coming early. Is that the problem? I'm scared. Do you think something's wrong?"

"Let's find out."

Rory watched Jake take the woman's pulse, and didn't think it necessary to tell him her own findings.

"Where does it hurt?"

"Oh, God…" The woman shrieked and moaned simultaneously. She clutched her hands to her swollen abdomen, rolling from side to side. "It…it hurts so much. Is…is the baby…?"

"Hang in there."

Jake's lips tightened and his gaze met Rory's for a moment. She knew it was possible the woman was just having normal labor contractions and had a low tolerance for pain, but somehow this seemed like more than that. Obviously Jake thought so, too.

"Let me feel your belly, okay?"

Rory reached for the woman's hands, gently squeezing, both to try to comfort her and to keep them away from her belly so Jake could give her an external examination.

He glanced up at Rory again. "I think she's in the second stage of labor. I need to do an internal exam. The baby might still be breech, which would account for her extreme pain."

Rory nodded, but didn't say what she was thinking, and knew Jake was thinking, too. A breech baby was going to be a lot more difficult to deliver, unless they could turn it, and a C-section would likely be necessary if they couldn't. These were far from ideal conditions for that, and they'd have to get her to the hospital in Fairbanks to recover, but if that was what had to happen, they'd make it happen.

"Natalia, I want to do an internal exam, to see how much you're dilated. I'm willing to bet you're close to delivering, but let's find out."

He turned to Jameson.

"We're going to need some towels and hot water. Can you light that wood-burning stove and put a kettle on it? Or heat some water in the kitchen? And bring a sheet to put on the floor beneath her. But first a glass of water so she can take some pain medication. I assume you want that, Natalia?"

"Ye-e-s…" she gasped. "Hurts…bad."

"I'm on it, honey," Jameson said as he ran from the room.

In moments he was back with a water glass, then he hurried off again.

"Rory? How about you try to help her sit up enough to take the narcotic while I get it?"

She nodded as Jake rifled through one of the bags. "We know your pain is bad, Natalia, but the narcotic should help," she said. "You're going to have to sit up to swallow. Can you do that?"

The woman gave a jerky nod, even as she cried out again, and Rory struggled to help her to a sitting position. The effort was only partially successful, as she slumped sideways against Rory, but it was enough for her to be able to drink without choking.

"Here."

Jake held the glass to Natalia's lips, tipping it up as he held the pills in his other hand. He poked them onto her tongue and Rory stroked her throat, because she knew that sometimes that helped a person in tremendous pain swallow when it was hard for them to focus on anything but how much they hurt.

Water dribbled down her chin, and she choked a little, but finally she got them down.

It struck Rory how odd it was to be working with Jake this way again. As though they knew what the other needed without having to speak. Was it from all the years they'd been so close that they'd practically been able to read one another's minds?

Jameson ran in with a pile of sheets and towels. Rory spread a sheet on the floor, then the two men helped move Natalia on top of it.

"I need to give you the internal exam," Jake said. "We're going to get your clothes off, and then you're going to feel me touch you so I can check dilation. Okay?"

His calm and gentle voice was so different from his everyday speech. Different from the way he'd spoken to Rory since she'd been back. Except that wasn't entirely true. Tonight, when he'd told her he understood what she'd been feeling at Mika's party, his voice had held that same, caring warmth.

There was no doubt the man was good at reassuring patients, even in stressful situations. But even long ago he'd been good at that, hadn't he? If she let herself, she could still remember his sweetness and concern for *her*, even in the darkest times. Even when he had been hurting, too. And she knew it was past time to finally tell him that.

The two of them worked to remove Natalia's pants—which wasn't easy, considering she was on her side on the floor again, rocking. Rory hated to see her in so much pain, and she had a bad feeling the worst was yet to come.

Even though she was pretty sure the last thing the woman was thinking about was her modesty, Rory placed a towel over her as Jake reached to examine her. After a long moment his gaze lifted to meet Rory's again, before moving back to Natalia, and she could tell it wasn't good news.

"Baby's ready to come. It's still breech, but not engaged in the pelvis yet, so that's good. It's possible to deliver it that way, but not ideal. So we're going to try to turn it. Are you ready?"

"Oh, God. No!"

"I'm here, honey. I'm here for you. It's going to be okay," Jameson said, holding her hand.

The anxiety on the man's face took her back to all those years ago, when she'd been delivering Adam. How Jake had been there, holding her, kissing her head, trying to soothe her even as his own heart had been breaking. She realized now, feeling a little ashamed, that his suffering was something she hadn't thought about enough.

"We need to get the external monitor on her, so we can check the baby's heartbeat and make sure it's normal before we try this."

The baby's heartbeat. Briefly, Rory squeezed her eyes shut, not wanting to remember when they'd done that for hers. *Theirs.* When it had shown there was no heartbeat at all. Was Jake remembering, too? Or had he delivered enough babies over the last nine years that it didn't feel so personal anymore?

She swallowed hard and focused fiercely on Natalia.

Not the time for memories to keep resurfacing, good or bad.

"How do we do this?" she asked in a near whisper. "I kind of remember from med school, but not really."

"Wait a minute. Let's get this done first."

His brows lowered in concentration as he attached the monitor. Rory held her breath as they waited for the reading, and slumped in relief to see the strong, steady beat of the baby's heart.

"Baby's okay," she said. Her voice was a little thin but she couldn't help it. "Heartbeat's *good*, Natalia."

The woman nodded, huffing breaths in and out, and Jake sent her the kind of smile that would reassure anyone.

"All right. I'm going to give you an injection of a drug that will help your womb relax, making it a little easier for us to turn the baby. What I'm going to do," he continued as he drew the medicine into a syringe and injected it, "is put my hands on your belly. One by the baby's bottom and one on its head, and see if I can turn it. Are you ready?"

"Won't it be hurt? Won't it hurt the baby?"

"No. Baby is protected by all the fluid and tissue around it. And we'll keep a close eye on the baby's heartbeat to make sure it isn't distressed. If it is, I'll stop. Rory, I want you to keep an eye on the monitor."

"Got it."

She watched Jake do as he'd said he would, his big hands pushing and twisting on Natalia's belly. Her throat tight, Rory glanced at Natalia, wondering what she was thinking. Wouldn't it be disturbing for *any* woman to see the mound of the baby in her belly being shoved and turned? But Natalia didn't shriek or moan at his efforts, at least no more than she had before, so the narcotic and the relaxer he'd given her must be working.

"Heart rate looks good," Rory said, staring at the monitor.

"Okay. I think we're getting there. Baby's definitely moving. Hold on a little longer, Natalia." He continued his manipulation as the minutes ticked by. "How's the heart rate now?"

"Still fine."

"Good. Almost...*there*."

He leaned back, and the broad grin on his face had Rory sucking in the first breath she'd taken for a while. She watched Jake pull new surgical gloves from his bag and snap them on.

"It's head-down now. And I have a feeling your little one is ready to rock and roll now that it's not stuck. Give me some good pushes, Natalia."

She pushed, and to Rory's shock the baby actually crowned. "Oh, my gosh—you were right! There it is!"

It was probably not the most professional thing to blurt, but birthing babies wasn't something she'd done much of, and the last time had been years ago.

"See it crowning, Jameson? Your baby is coming!"

"I can't believe it. You're doing so great, honey." He clutched Natalia's hand. "*So* good. I love you. I love you so much."

Jake spoke encouragingly to Natalia as she pushed, his fingers working to free the baby's head, and then with one more big effort the infant's tiny pink body came into the world, held in Jake's strong hands.

"You have a beautiful baby girl! Congratulations,"

Jake said, that big smile back on his face. "Can you grab the bulb suction, Rory? And a towel?"

"Yes. Of course."

It was hard for her to speak through the thickness in her throat. Tears stung the backs of her eyes as she grabbed what they needed. She handed the bulb to Jake, so he could clear the baby's nose and mouth while she took a towel to begin wiping the tiny feet and hands. The little pink belly and wet brown hair.

What a miracle. What a beautiful thing to witness, to be a part of in even the smallest way.

Of course she'd seen babies born when she was in medical school, but back then her own experience had been too fresh, too raw, for her to be able to enjoy and appreciate seeing the birth of a healthy baby when her own had died, knowing it might have been *her* fault.

She swallowed back the tears and smiled at this sweet new life. Maybe this was exactly what she'd needed to truly heal. Maybe she'd needed to come back home for a little while, back to where the worst day of her life had happened, to see Jake one last time, to talk about it now that there were years between that awful day and now—and to see this beautiful baby born and be able to feel true happiness for the new parents instead of grief and melancholy.

Rory laid a clean towel across the new mother's chest and Jake wrapped the baby in another towel before giving the infant to her mother.

"There she is. Was it worth all that pain now that she's here?"

"Yes. Oh, yes. She's so beautiful. I can't believe it…"

Natalia beamed as she looked up at her husband. He

leaned over to give her a kiss so sweet it made Rory's eyes sting all over again.

"Do you have a name picked out for her?" Jake asked.

"I don't know. Do we?" She smiled weakly at Jameson. "We had two girl names and two boy names, figuring we'd decide what it looked like when it came."

"I think she's definitely a Shae. Don't you?" said Jameson.

"Shae…" Natalia whispered, softly stroking the baby's cheek. "Yes, it's perfect. *She's* perfect."

"I like that." Jake touched the baby's temple. "Little Shae has had a bit of a rough time of it, just like her mama, so we need to make sure she's good and warm. After you've held her for a few minutes Rory's going to get her cleaned up and swaddled while I take care of you. Jameson, is the fire hot and the water warm? Do you have baby clothes and baby blankets that Rory can put her in?"

"Fire's lit and the water's close to hot. Um…where are the baby's clothes, honey?"

"In the dresser your mom gave us. Get a snap undershirt and one of those warm little onesie things with feet. And there are baby blankets in there, too."

"Sounds nerve-racking, but I'll do my best to find what you're talking about." With a wide grin, looking totally different than he had an hour ago, Jameson dropped another lingering kiss to his wife's mouth, moved to throw some more logs on the fire, then headed down the hallway.

"Is it okay if I look for a bowl in the kitchen? I need to put the warm water in it so I can get baby Shae cleaned up," Rory asked Natalia.

"Whatever you need." She stared raptly at her newborn, not bothering to look up at Rory—and who could blame her?

As clearly as if it were yesterday, Rory remembered feeling exactly the same way as she'd held her own newborn in her arms. Staring at tiny Adam's small, angelic face. Kissing his still-warm cheeks.

Beautiful and perfect, even in death.

Her heart constricting, she reached for the baby and Jake lifted his gaze to hers. She drew a deep breath, not sure what she saw in the brown depths of his eyes. Concern? Contrition? If that was the case, surely he couldn't feel bad about her being here, worrying about her reliving their baby's birth. This new family had needed her, and she was more than glad to have had the privilege to help.

The emotions twisting through her made her wonder what her expression was like, and yet at the same time it felt impossible to school it into something only joyous and happy. Something not shadowed by the regrets and pain and guilt of the past.

"I'll get her cleaned up while Dr. Hunter takes care of you. Don't worry, I'll be very careful with your new miracle."

She tried to smile at Natalia, hoping the new mother wouldn't notice how strange her voice was, how nervous and uncomfortable she felt. At the same time she wanted nothing more than to hold this baby and bathe her, get her ready for the big, new world she'd just joined.

With the baby pressed close against her breast, she looked down into the small, wide eyes looking up at her, seeming to study her. "Your mommy and daddy are *so* lucky," she whispered. "Welcome to your life, little Shae."

Jake's arm reached out to touch hers as she moved toward the warmth of the fire, his dark gaze pinning hers. "You okay?" he asked, his voice so low Natalia probably wouldn't hear.

Her eyes met his, but she couldn't speak. Even after this beautiful experience she had hoped would help her heal, she wasn't sure she'd *ever* be okay. But she was going to try to be. She was.

And maybe this time she'd let Jake help her through it, when she just hadn't been able to before.

CHAPTER TEN

"LIKE I SAID, if you're feeling like you want me to come see you and the baby tomorrow, I'm happy to do that," Jake said.

"Thank you," said Jameson, pumping his hand for the tenth time. "I hope she'll be comfortable, and that I'll be taking good care of both of them. But I'll call if something seems wrong."

"I'm sure your midwife will want to come check on both of them, so I suggest you give her a call in the morning to let her know the baby's here. But don't hesitate to call me, if you feel you need me."

If the snow kept coming it wouldn't be an easy trek in the morning, but he couldn't leave them stranded up here if Natalia wasn't feeling well or they were worried about the baby. He definitely wouldn't be bringing Rory, though. From her strained and bleak expression, it was clear that helping deliver this baby had been beyond hard for her.

He thrashed himself for letting her come at all. Yeah, she'd been a huge help, and if he hadn't been able to turn the baby he would have had to call on her surgical skills to do an emergency C-section. But her reaction to the baby's birth, the way she'd looked holding the newborn in her arms, had just about destroyed him.

He'd delivered a lot of babies since they'd lost theirs nine years ago. So many that the birth of a healthy child, or even one with problems, didn't feel personal anymore—didn't bring back the sad and horrible memories of that day, and the days after when Rory wouldn't lean on him. When she'd decided to just up and leave, smashing his heart to bits, along with everything he'd thought he'd have with her.

He'd been hurt. Devastated. And, yes, angry. Understanding why she'd taken off had felt impossible, and he'd been left to grieve alone, with bitterness gnawing at his gut over her actions. Her attitude.

But seeing the pain etched on her face tonight, the deep longing as she'd stared down into the baby's small face, had softened the shell he'd closed around his heart, vowing never to let her back in for even a minute. Maybe it was time to try to forgive. Not forget—because there was no way he'd let himself get close to her again—but perhaps move on from his resentment? Try to understand at least a little why she'd left? He could work on that.

He turned to the woman who'd broken his heart and realized it felt achy all over again. "You ready?"

He watched her look back at Natalia and the baby, now resting comfortably on the sofa instead of on the hard floor, and give them a smile. Someone who didn't know her might think it was a regular smile, but *he* knew it was full of all kinds of emotion. The emotions he could see swimming in her green eyes as she turned them back to him.

"Ready."

He led the way out—and stopped short for a second, not believing the winter world in front of them.

"What the…?"

"Oh, no! How could there be this much snow? And it's coming down so hard!" She stared up at him. "Are we going to be able to get back?"

"Good question." He waded through the thick white fluff and stowed the equipment in the back seat again. "The roads won't be plowed until we get closer to Eudemonia, but my truck can handle deep snow pretty well. I think we'll be okay."

"Should we just stay here?"

"I'd rather not. Unless you want to?"

He didn't particularly want to bunk down there—for a couple reasons. One was interrupting the new little family having quiet time on their own. And the bigger reason was he didn't think it would be good for Rory to have to spend that many hours around the baby—seeing her again in the morning, maybe even helping care for her.

He couldn't bear the anguish in her eyes. He wanted to get her back to town so she could find her equilibrium again, since this experience had obviously cut her off at the knees.

"No. If you think we'll be fine then I'd prefer to go."

He saw her pumping her thighs up high, nearly to her waist, as she trudged through the snow, and realized that, while he'd grabbed boots at his house before they'd come up here, she was wearing flat, slip-on leather shoes.

"Jeez, Rory! You can't walk through a foot of snow in those. Why didn't you say something?"

"Why would I? I doubt if you have boots in my size hanging out in your truck."

He strode around the car and she squeaked when he

swung her up into his arms. "No, but I do have a different solution."

She scowled, and at the same time a breathy laugh slipped across his face.

"Put me down. I'm perfectly fine."

"Yeah?" The feel of her body in his arms, held close against him, felt beyond good—the way it had when he'd been unable to stop the need to kiss her in the kitchen. "The California city girl who's been wearing a heavy winter coat even in early October has no problem walking practically barefoot in cold snow?"

"It's a good thing I am wearing a coat, too, since you're not dressed nearly warmly enough for this kind of weather and I'm perfectly comfy."

Looking down into her eyes, he saw they still held a tinge of sadness, but they were filled with a smile, too. It was the kind of smile that reminded him of the Rory he'd known and loved before it had all got away from them. Unbidden, memories burned through his brain to join the feelings, the tenderness for her that welled in his chest, and he nearly dropped a kiss to her mouth again.

That would be a bad idea, so he drew a deep breath and looked away from that beautiful green gaze, trying to focus on getting to the truck.

He juggled her in his arms and opened the truck door, then placed her in the seat. "I'm glad you're comfy. And I won't say that coats are for sissies, since I admit it's handy to have one when we're in the middle of a snowstorm."

He lifted his finger to swipe thick snowflakes from her lashes and somehow, without his meaning it to, his finger drifted down her cheek and across her lips. All the laughter left her face and her lips parted as she looked up at him. He could tell she was feeling it, too. All the heat that had been there for so long between them, that had flared into fire in the kitchen, now swirled inside the truck and left him breathless.

Damn. He straightened, then shut her door to go around to the driver's seat. He stomped the snow off his boots before sliding into the dark interior next to her. No way was he going to start things up again with Rory. Too much bad stuff had happened between them, and the last thing either of them needed was to stir it up all over again—especially when she'd be leaving again in a matter of days.

"Put on your seat belt. Things might get a little rough."

"How can you even *see*? It's a blizzard out there."

"Definitely not the best conditions for driving, but once we get about twenty miles closer to town the hilly roads give way to the main road, which is pretty flat."

"I assume you have enough gas to keep us warm if we get stranded?"

"I'm not even going to answer that ridiculous question." He shot her a grin, not wanting her to be worried. "You were always a survivor girl when you lived here, having your parents' house stocked up and prepared for Armageddon. I learned from you—so, yeah, I not only have extra gas, I've got water and food. We could stay up here for days if we had to."

She didn't answer. He turned to see her eyes looking at him across the bench seat and his heart quickened. He hadn't been thinking about what he'd said, really, but suddenly images of the two of them stuck inside this truck, holding one another close and making love to stay warm, were suddenly all he could think about.

He was glad that getting the truck out on the road took all his concentration and his mind off sex with Rory. And keeping the vehicle on the road when he could barely see became a bigger challenge with every passing mile.

After traveling for only about twenty minutes, in the worst conditions he'd ever driven in, he knew there needed to be a change of plan.

"Rory?"

"Yeah?"

"It's bad out here."

"Yeah…"

"I know there's a dry cabin nearby, where a lot of hunters go. I'm pretty sure it's off a road I think we'll be coming to soon. What do you say we bunk there for the night and see how it looks in the morning?"

A long silence was followed by a deep sigh. "I don't think we have a choice. If we keep going there's a good chance we'll end up in a ditch. I'd rather be in a cabin, where we can build a fire, than stuck in the truck in a snowstorm."

"Then that's our plan. Don't worry. We'll be fine, I promise."

"Being fine isn't what I'm worried about," she said, in a soft voice that had him thinking bad thoughts all over again.

"I know."

His hands tightened on the wheel because, yeah, being fine *wasn't* the issue. Being close together for the whole night alone definitely was.

"Help me keep an eye out for the road. It's off to the right, and there's a sign marking it, but it's going to be hard to see until we're practically on it."

They drove in silence, but he could have sworn the car hummed with something. There was an electricity between them, a new awareness now, with their plight of being in close quarters together. Thoughts of making love with her had his heart beating harder and his body stirring. But he wasn't going to go there. *No way.* Neither one of them needed the tangled-up emotions that would follow a night of ill-thought-out intimacy.

Unbidden, memories of all the great sex between them shortened his breath. With her, it had always been more special than with anyone—both physical and emotional. A deep, multi-layered connection that he'd never experienced before or since. But what would being with her in that way again accomplish? All it would do would be to stir up the feelings clearly still between them, and his heart was sure to feel bruised and battered all over again—maybe hers, too.

No, they'd get set up in the cabin, have something to eat, then sleep. Somehow, though, he had a bad feeling that knowing her body was close and warm might make sleeping more than difficult. Even worse, he couldn't deny that some masochistic part of him was excited about it. Anticipating being alone with her for the first time in a long, long time even as he told himself to cool it. He hadn't wanted to admit to himself that he still missed her being part of his life, but the way he felt at that moment proved he did.

"There!" Rory exclaimed into the silence. "Is that the sign for the road?"

Jake peered through the thick flakes, finally seeing the sign, covered with snow and barely visible. "You have cat's eyes. I think I would have passed right by it."

"You're having to concentrate on driving in this mess. I had the advantage of focusing on one thing."

True. He'd been focusing on driving, finding the sign and her nearness—whether he'd wanted to be or not. "Yeah, well, thanks to you we might be able to bunk down in front of a warm fire very soon."

"You think there'll be wood in the cabin? Or are we going to have to scrounge for some underneath the snow?"

As he slowly made the turn onto the road he sensed her looking at him and dared a quick glance across the seat. Her lips were tipped up at the corners, and his own mouth curved in response.

"I'd think most hunters restock the wood, but probably there are some who don't. If we have to dig under the snow, though, I'll get you some thick socks to put on over your shoes."

Her soft chuckle drifted into his chest and widened his smile. "As if. You've always had an 'I'm the man, and I'll do the heavy lifting' mindset. No way would you let me gather firewood outside while you're the one wearing heavy boots."

"Maybe I've changed."

"No," she said softly. "You haven't changed—at least not in any way that I can see. Mika's lucky to have a man like you adopt him."

"*I'm* the lucky one."

The unspoken hung between them. The fact that neither of them had been lucky when tiny Adam had died inside Rory's womb, shattering their dream of having a family together. Neither of them had found someone to share their lives with. Except he had Mika now, and his son was the best reason of all to keep his relationship with Rory friendly but distant.

She'd already proved she was a flight risk, hadn't she? There one minute and gone the next. The last thing Mika needed was to get close to someone and then have them promptly exit his life.

The road came to an abrupt halt, with a hilly dead end right in front of them, and through the heavy snow the silhouette of a dark cabin appeared as a shadow.

"We made it." He heaved in a breath that was full of relief, trepidation and anticipation as to how this evening was going to shake out. "Sit tight and I'll carry you in."

Rory looked at his dark profile through the blackness of the truck's cab. When he'd picked her up and held her close to his hard body it had felt disconcertingly wonderful—just like when he'd kissed her earlier. How were they going to find a little distance in this small cabin? She didn't know, but somehow that needed to be the plan for the night.

"Honestly, Jake, I can walk—"

"Stop being your usual stubborn self." A disgusted sound left his lips. "The last thing you need is to start out with frozen feet when we're going inside a freezing cold cabin. So just wait 'til I come around."

She picked her purse up from the floor, watched his shadowy figure cross in front of the truck and considered it really bad news that her heart was already beating an odd little timpani rhythm in her chest and he hadn't even touched her. They weren't yet close together in that cabin, and she knew it was going to be both terrible and wonderful at the same time.

The door opened and his wide torso filled the cab

as he leaned in, his eyes glittering in the darkness as they met hers.

"Hang tight in here, promise? It's pitch-black, so I'm going to grab supplies from the back of the truck so we'll have light." He pointed his finger at her until it touched the tip of her nose. "Don't move."

She might be a little stubborn—as he'd always told her—but she wasn't stupid. Much as she didn't want him to carry her in—or kind of *did* want that, if she was honest with herself—she knew getting her feet and the bottoms of her pants wet wouldn't be too smart when they didn't even know if there was firewood in the cabin.

Feeling worthless, not helping him carry stuff inside, she fidgeted until she saw the beam from a flashlight dancing through the snowflakes, illuminating a wooden front door.

Jake's dark form shoved it open. She couldn't see what he had in his arms, but she could tell it was a pretty significant pile and she had to smile. He teased her about always being prepared, yet it looked like he had enough stuff to stay here a week.

Short minutes later her door was swinging open again and strong arms were reaching for her. "There's not a lot of firewood, but there's some. With what I brought we'll be able to get a good fire going until I collect more."

"You had firewood in the back of the truck? Why didn't you tell me?"

With her purse strap slung over her shoulder, she snaked her arms around his neck, figuring it would help if she supported some of her weight as he trudged through the snow. The temptation to press her lips against his cold cheek was almost too much, and she forced herself to turn her face toward the cabin and away from his tempting jaw.

"I didn't want you to think you wouldn't still have to wear thick socks over your shoes to help me gather it up out here."

This buoyant feeling welling in her chest was absurd. They were stranded in a snowstorm, in a cabin with an outhouse and no running water, and she was there with a man she didn't want to be around. Except obviously, deep inside, she did. Their banter together was like old times, happy times, and she hadn't realized until this moment how much she'd missed feeling lighthearted and happy with Jacob Hunter.

"Uh-huh. And how much stuff do you keep in your truck bed anyway? To think you always accused *me* of being hyper-prepared for disasters. Looks like you're every bit as bad."

He shouldered open the door, quickly shoved it closed against the cold wind and set her on her feet. The flashlight sat on a rickety table, aimed right at his hips and the front of his pants, and she jerked her attention away from wrong thoughts.

"Like I said, I learned from you," he said.

"Where's the wood? I'll get started on the fire—I have some papers in my purse I don't need that I can use to help get it started. What else do you have?"

He pounded his gloved hands together, then reached into a box, pulling out a battery-operated lamp and clicking it on.

"See, I'd have a bigger lamp with a bigger bulb. That thing hardly throws any light at all."

"Do we *need* a lot of light?"

One dark eyebrow was raised slowly at her, and her

pulse kicked at the gleam in his eyes that said he was thinking exactly what she was thinking, even though they shouldn't be. Because she'd just looked around enough to notice that there was only one bed in the cabin, and if they were going to stay warm they were going to have to get in there together.

She swallowed hard. "No. Because we'll have the firelight, too. Looks like the stack of wood here will last maybe a couple hours, so that's not too bad."

Quickly, she moved away from him toward the wood-burning stove and flipped open the door, shoving inside a few pieces of paper and a new notebook that she hadn't used yet.

"Here's the kindling and the bag of wood I brought. I'm going outside to see what I can scrounge up, since I'm already dressed."

The words *already dressed* made her think of getting *undressed*, but of course he just meant he had on his jacket and hat and boots. Her face warmed at the place her brain kept going—which she supposed she should be happy about, since it was so cold she could see her breath in this place.

Time to get the fire built, you idiot.

The wood was nice and dry, and in no time welcome flames crackled and spat, filling the space with warmth and light. She stared at the fire, breathed in the smell of it, and felt her heart warm along with everything else. How long had it been since she'd built a fire? Sat in front of one? Must have been when she'd still been in college—long before she'd moved to LA.

She sat on her rear and poked her feet toward the fire, since they felt half-frozen in the flimsy shoes which she realized now she shouldn't even have brought to Eudemonia. She looked up as the door opened and found she couldn't take her eyes off him.

Yes, he was older. They both were. But the way he looked now, with a knit hat covering his beautiful black hair, his nose and cheeks pink from the cold, his arms filled with snowy sticks, took her back in time to all those years, from boyhood to manhood, that she'd loved him with every ounce of her soul.

"You... Looks like you had some luck," she managed to say. "How did you unearth it? I supposed you carry a shovel in your truck, too?"

"Is that a *real* question?" He stomped the snow off his feet just outside the door, then kneeled next to her to dump the wood onto the floor next to the dry logs. "Looks like you had luck, too. Good fire. You haven't lost your touch."

No doubt he hadn't, either—but the touch she was thinking about had nothing to do with the fire.

"So, now what?" she asked, and then wished she hadn't. Because the way he was looking at her told her he was thinking exactly what she was. Which was to get the fire blazing as hot as possible, cuddle in that bed naked and relive the past.

"Guess we should eat—though all I have to offer is camping food that'll keep forever. Mom had a great spread for Mika's party, but that was hours ago. You hungry?"

She was *not* going to answer that honestly. Because what she was hungry for was what she'd run away from. What she could never have again.

"A little. What's on the menu?"

"Canned beans. And, yes, I have a can opener." He

flashed his devastating grin. "Canned corned beef. Beef jerky. Beef stroganoff."

That brought her out of her rapt attention to the way the firelight flickered across the beautiful planes of his face, his unbelievably sexy mouth. "Clearly beef is your pantry staple. But beef stroganoff? Like, freeze-dried? *Yuck.*"

"Yeah. Pretty awful, but it's better than starving."

"Maybe I'll wait 'til I'm starving."

"Suit yourself."

He pulled off his boots, placed them next to the door, and came to sit cross-legged next to her in front of the fire. He pulled a few cans out of the bag he'd carried in, and several bottles of water, handing her one.

"I recommend against drinking too much, or we'll have to shovel a path to the outhouse."

"Sounds like the perfect way to cap off my stay at home. Haven't been in a frozen outhouse in a long time."

"So there you have it. The highlight of your trip back."

His brown eyes were filled with something she couldn't quite read, and they stared at one another without speaking until he looked away to pull a package of jerky from his bag.

"This one is venison," he said, handing her a piece. "A guy who works for the oil company started a side business, buying meat from some of the hunters around here. It's pretty good."

She took a bite and chewed at the dried stuff. "I've got to admit that's delicious. Or maybe I'm hungrier than I thought." She watched him open the beans and eat a spoonful right out of the can, then scoop another bite onto the spoon and hold it to her mouth.

"What happened to warming it up on the fire first?"

"What happened to the girl who used to love cold beans?"

His eyes were dark and alive, lit with humor and a heat that matched exactly what she was feeling as she stared at the way he slowly licked the sauce from his lips. It made her feel so breathless she opened her mouth without thinking, and he poked the spoon into her mouth, then followed it with a brief press of his lips to hers.

He pulled back an inch, and she managed to swallow the beans before he came in for another. The way his mouth moved on hers, soft and unhurried and tasting of sweet beans and hot sex, made her heart beat in slow, heavy thuds. Barely able to breathe, she cupped his warm, stubbly face in her hands and let the feelings wash over her, let herself absorb it and feel all the things she shouldn't be feeling.

Their mouths separated and she looked into his eyes, now deeply serious.

"I shouldn't kiss you. I know that," he said, his breath feathering across her moist lips. "When you first came to take care of your mom I wanted to keep my distance. When that didn't work out I promised myself I'd work on being your friend, putting the bad stuff behind us. Putting aside my anger with you and remembering why we'd liked each other from the time we were kids. But sitting here with you now, I can't do that, either. Stupid or not, I want to be with you one last time."

"Me, too," she whispered. "I didn't know it. I didn't want to see you, either. I know you hate me. But I want to be with you, too, just once. Once more."

"Rory." His hands tightened on her shoulders. "I

never hated you. I loved you more than I've ever loved anyone. Was I furious with you? Beyond disappointed? Hurt bad? Yeah, I was all those things. But I never hated you—even when I wanted to."

He kissed her again, and she clutched at him as he lowered her to the hard wooden floor, devouring her mouth until she felt dizzy from it. Flames leaped inside her, hotter than any fire, and she slipped her hands inside his shirt, loving the softness of his skin, the way it shivered at her touch.

Memories of all the kisses they'd shared tangled with the incredible deliciousness of this one. He tasted the same. He tasted like Jacob Hunter—the man she'd loved her whole life. Rory's heart shook and fell, and she wrapped her arms around his warm back and gave in to the sensations she'd missed so much.

Then he sat up abruptly, leaving her confused. She pushed onto her elbows, her heart sinking as he stood and walked away from her across the room. Had he decided this was such a bad idea that he was able to stop? She knew it was beyond a bad idea, but she'd never have been able to stop, to walk away, when all she wanted at that moment was to kiss him and get naked with him and make love with him for the rest of the night.

"You...you changed your mind?"

"Hell, no," he growled as he grabbed the bedframe and started dragging it toward her. "But this floor's too hard to make love with you the way I want to, and it's too damn cold to get naked this far away from the fire. So the bed and all the blankets are coming to the fire."

Relief had her laughing, then getting up to help. "I always said you were a genius."

"Not a genius—just a man who wants to get both of

us stripped as fast as possible and under the covers without freezing in the process."

The fire in the stove was the perfect height for the mattress. She and Jake tucked a sheet over it before he threw a few more logs in the stove. Then he reached to undo the big buttons on her coat and slide it off her shoulders. Without moving his gaze from hers, he pulled her sweater up over her head, and the rush of cold air from the back of the cabin skimmed her skin, even as the fire warmed her.

He must have seen her shiver, because he pulled her close and kissed her, at the same time tugging down her pants. With a gentle push he sat her on the bed and pulled off her shoes and socks, breaking their kiss again to wrap his hands around her foot.

"Your feet are like ice! Why didn't you *say* something?"

"Once you started kissing me I didn't notice."

"I can relate…" His eyes gleamed. "And I know just the thing to warm you up."

Like he had when he'd carried her to the truck, he scooped her into his arms and practically dumped her into the middle of the bed. He grabbed the blankets and an old comforter he'd brought and tossed them on top of her.

She watched him do a quick striptease, throwing his clothes far enough from the fire that they wouldn't scorch, until he was standing in front of her breathtakingly naked.

For a long moment she let herself admire the masculine beauty that was Jacob Hunter: the way the firelight flickered on his skin, highlighting the dips and angles and defined muscle, the jut of his erection, the body she'd explored so thoroughly that she'd known every inch of it—every tiny scar, every imperfection.

She lifted her gaze to meet his and her breath caught in her throat at the way he was looking at her. The way he had all those years ago, when their lives had been wrapped together completely. And somehow, here tonight, it felt as if the entire world had shrunk down to just the two of them, emotionally and physically close in this tiny cabin covered with snow.

"There's a problem here," she said. "You're still out there freezing, and I'm under the covers waiting for you."

"Fixing that right now," he said, and he crawled on all fours across the mattress and dropped a kiss to her mouth before joining her under the heavy blankets. He slid off her bra, then his hands roamed her body, making her shiver in a totally different way than she had been moments before.

He kissed her again, deepening it, and all worries that this was a bad idea, that they shouldn't be doing it, fell away and she kissed him back, desperate to feel that connection with him once more.

His arms brought her body tight against his, and the way his skin slid against hers felt so delicious she gasped into his mouth. She stroked her hands up the hard planes of his chest and over his shoulders, remembering every little bump, every crevice, as though it was yesterday they'd been together and not years ago.

He lifted his mouth from hers and stared down at her. "I want to see you. Just for a minute. I want to see your body in the firelight. I promise I'll warm you up."

He tugged the blanket down to expose her breasts, his fingers slowly tracking its downward slide. Across her collarbone, over her breasts, caressing her nipples.

She arched up in a silent invitation. His lips tipped at the corners, then he lowered his mouth to suck and lick, and she clutched the back of his head, moaning from the pleasure of it.

God, she'd missed this. Missed feeling this way—missed holding him and touching him and kissing him. She waited for the guilt to wash over her, the awful regret for her actions that terrible day, but it didn't come. All she felt was a deep need to be with him, to enjoy this one time they had together before they went back to their separate lives.

"Frozen yet?" he asked as his mouth and tongue slid leisurely across her skin, his hands following. "I love looking at you. Your body is more beautiful than I remembered. But if you're cold I'll cover you up."

"Cold? Are you kidding? I feel like I'm burning up."

He chuckled against her skin as his hands moved lower to touch between her legs, making her gasp. "Burning up is exactly how I'm feeling, too."

The touching, the way his tongue licked her breasts and her stomach and her hipbones, made her quiver and gasp, and she reached for him, wrapping her hand around his erection to make him feel good, too.

But in moments he pulled himself loose. "God, Rory. I need to be inside you now."

"That sounds good to me."

"Damn it."

He got up from the bed and she felt suddenly cold, had to reach for the covers. "What the heck…? What are you doing?"

He rifled in his jeans pocket and held up a condom. "You're not the only one who's always prepared."

Breathlessly, she laughed as he put it on, but her

amusement quickly died in her throat as he slipped between the sheets and covered her body with his. Warm and hard and oh, so wonderful, he grasped her hips and slowly filled her, and it felt like all the times before, but somehow even better. She wrapped her arms around his back and kissed him, everything gone from her mind except the amazing way he made her feel.

They moved together in a devastating rhythm, faster and harder, their kiss broken as he stared down at her, his eyes glittering with the passion she remembered so well.

"Rory…"

Her name fell from his lips in a way that told her he felt the same deep connection that had filled every broken piece in her heart. As their bodies convulsed together in physical pleasure the past was forgotten, and for this short moment, at least, she felt almost whole for the first time in nine years.

CHAPTER ELEVEN

"YOU COLD?" JAKE held Rory's sweet body close to his beneath the covers, her head pillowed on his shoulder.

His heart was all jumbled up at how good it felt to have her in his arms again, even as he reminded himself that she'd be gone again all too soon. And that even if by some miracle she might want to stay, he couldn't trust her not to up and bolt just like last time. He couldn't ever trust her with his heart again.

"Only the top of my head. Your body is like a furnace," she murmured.

"I can get my hat for you."

"No. Stay in here with me."

He looked down at her. At the way her hair swept over his skin. At her beautiful lips, which somehow tasted even better than he remembered. At her pert little nose and heart-shaped face.

Part of him wanted to just lie there peacefully with her, warm and snug together in front of the fire. But another part of him—the part that had never fully gotten an answer on why she'd left the way she had—still wanted an answer to that question.

Maybe it made no sense to care about that after all this time, but he couldn't help it. He'd wondered for the past nine years, and he needed to know why she hadn't let herself lean on anyone—least of all him—when times had got tough.

Yeah, he wanted the answer more than he wanted the peace, he supposed, and there would never be another time like this to ask. Cozy and intimate and all alone, with no interruptions and nowhere to hide.

"Why did you leave, Rory?"

She was silent for a long time, and he thought maybe he wasn't going to get an answer after all when she finally spoke. "You know why. We already talked about this."

"We lost our baby. It was hard and it hurt, but it didn't have to mean the end of our relationship. Of all our plans. You told me you hated hearing the whispers, seeing people talking about the accident. About the way the snow machine flipped with you on it. But was that a good enough reason to leave me without even a goodbye?"

"I didn't say goodbye because I knew you must hate me," she whispered. "God knows, I hated myself."

"I never hated you. How could you think that? I was upset with you, yeah. Even before we lost the baby, I admit I was mad. You ignored me when I told you to stay home. You insisted on going on the snow machine with the rescue crew when you were seven months pregnant and that was stupid. I *get* that you'd done plenty of search and rescues, but that situation was different. And you wouldn't listen."

"I know. And I'll regret that decision for the rest of my life. Which is why I left."

"Regretting, I understand. But running away from everything? Our plans to go to med school in Anchorage together? Dumping me and leaving me high and dry?"

"If I hadn't gone out on the snow machine our baby might not have died inside me. I have to live with that. I couldn't live with everyone else knowing what I'd done. Blaming me like I blamed myself."

"How many times did I say no one blamed you? How many doctors and nurses told you that Adam being still-born probably had nothing to do with that night?"

"But no one knew for sure."

Warm wetness touched his chest. The fact that she was crying tempered the frustration rolling around in his chest and he pulled her closer against him.

"No one ever knows for sure why a baby is stillborn. Still, you turned away from me, you wouldn't lean on me. Wouldn't grieve with me. Help me understand why."

She tipped her head up to look at him, her teary eyes wide as they met his. "I... I'm not sure I even *know* why, other than the guilt I felt. And I'm sorry," she whispered, lifting her hand to cup his jaw. "I wasn't able to think straight. But see...? You were *lucky* to be rid of me. I'm not the kind of woman you'd want in your life forever."

Lucky to be rid of her? That was the last way he would ever view what had happened back then. Being with her now, holding her like this, made him face the truth. He'd never stopped loving her—even when he'd tried to convince himself he had.

"You're wrong. You were the only woman I wanted in my life." And now that he'd seen her again, he knew she still was. "Even now, there's nothing I wouldn't do for you. Except trust you. I learned the hard way I can't ever let myself trust you again."

"I understand."

When her eyes filled with tears again a part of him felt bad about what he'd said, but it was simply the truth.

And maybe more than saying it to *her*, he was reminding himself not to fall in love with her all over again. Not to put himself in a position where she could crush his soul a second time.

"You have a good life here, with your family and little Mika," she said, sniffing. "I get that maybe I was wrong to run away. But that's behind us now. I'll be leaving soon, so you won't have to look at me and feel angry anymore."

"When I look at you now I think you know that angry isn't how I feel." He couldn't regret sharing that truth with her, because he wanted her to know that, no matter what, he'd always care about her. "And, since you're leaving soon, this might be our last chance to be alone together. How do you feel about making the best of it while we can?"

A real smile, like the ones he'd used to love to see all night, touched her lips. "There might be a lot of things I'll never feel good about. But kissing you isn't one of them."

She rose up over him, the firelight flickering over her glorious nakedness, and he looked up at her beautiful face before she kissed him. Heat hummed between them and he held her close, giving himself up to the moment while he could.

No matter that he knew he'd miss her again, far too much, when she left.

"I can't get it loose to fix it, Twinkie," Rory said, lying on her back as she stared up at the stupid pipe connection under the kitchen sink that wouldn't stop dripping. She gave the wrench another mighty twist on the pipe, but it didn't budge. "It's like the elbow is frozen to the other piece. We'll just have to keep this bucket under here until a plumber can come."

"Jacob's always happy to fix stuff around here when he can."

Rory scooted out from under the sink and sat up so fast she nearly cracked her head on the top of the cabinet frame. "What? Don't call Jake. It's not fair to bother him with stuff like this. He's busy at work, and with the baby."

And his busyness wasn't the only reason she didn't want him here. Their night together had been the best thing to happen to her in a long, long time, and she'd keep the memory close to her heart when she went back to LA. But they'd both agreed that spending any more time together while she was still here would just shake up old feelings that were better left alone.

"I already called him. He said he'd come over when he could," Twinkie said as she walked into the kitchen with an armload of stuff and a big smile. "Leave that and come paint with me. We haven't done finger paints since you were a little girl. Won't that be fun?"

"Finger paints?" She stared at her mom. Was she kidding? "Uh… I think I'd rather use a brush. You do have some, don't you?"

"Yes, but don't be a traditionalist. Humans have used their fingers for eating and artwork and all kinds of things forever. I feel like being primal today."

A snorting laugh left Rory's nose at that—until the word brought that night with Jake roaring into her brain again. *Primal* was exactly how it had felt. Making love almost with desperation, like they couldn't get enough of one another. If she closed her eyes she could still picture his spectacular nakedness in the firelight, and she got a little short of breath just thinking about it.

Maybe spreading paint around with her fingers would be a good outlet for the sexual energy surging into her head and body after all.

She took some paper from her mother and unrolled it onto the table as her mother lined up the paint pots next to it.

"I think I'm in the mood to make fairies," Wendy said as she sat down, so excited that she was waving her hands around. "I might even add some glitter—which I have here if you want some. What are *you* in the mood to make?"

Rory couldn't say what she was in the mood to make, as more visions of Jake burned her brain. "I think I'll just go with something abstract."

"I always liked your abstracts. Very creative."

They chatted and painted, and Rory had to admit there was something therapeutic about swirling paint with her fingers. It made her think about how enjoyable it would be to swirl some on Jake's body and then…

Stop it, she scolded herself for the tenth time. *It was one night and one night only, remember?*

She tried to switch her attention to her mother's painting, and it struck her that she was recovering remarkably well—able to get around quite easily on her own, now. She'd even mostly dressed herself this morning, other than Rory putting on her socks and shoes, since it still hurt a little for her to bend over. It was clear her mom would be fine without her, so long as she had Linda and her other friends to check on her each day.

"You seem to be feeling almost yourself now, Twinkie. Maybe all those herbs really do have healing qualities," she said, and then took a breath to talk about heading back to California. For some inexplicable reason she wasn't sure she was ready to go, even if Twinkie was well enough to be on her own. "How do you feel about me getting my job interview rescheduled for pretty soon?"

"Do you have to go?" Her mother's eyes were suddenly sad as she looked up from her art.

"My job is there. Or will be." She leaned across the table. "Please come with me. Just for the winter. Please?"

"Aurora, I just don't know. But I'm thinking about it. We'll see if one of my fairies here gives me a sign about what to do."

"You're going to let a fairy that you made yourself help you decide?" Rory had to smile. And then she wondered what kind of paint she could swirl on her mom's picture that would tell her to come live with Rory for a few months, because the thought of leaving her made her chest ache.

"I hear you, poking fun. But it's like tea leaves or coffee grounds. Patterns come together to tell a story. To see the future."

"I wish—"

"Anybody home?"

Her heart dipped, then jumped. How could Jake be coming in the middle of the afternoon like this? She'd expected he'd be hours, probably showing up just before dinnertime.

He appeared in the kitchen doorway with Mika in his arms. Her heart pitched again as she stared at the man who'd had his hands and mouth all over her body just days ago. Filtered sunlight from the kitchen window lit his features, and he looked beyond handsome in a flannel shirt and jeans that had her attention going straight to his body. Those memories got stirred up all over again, and she yanked her gaze back to the bundle in his arms.

Looking at Mika's adorable little face had her relaxing, and the quickened beat of her heart settled into a warm calm. "What are you doing here?"

"Plumbing, I believe."

"Why aren't you at the clinic?"

"Dad's back, and I have the day off."

"Well, it's nice of you to help us on your day off. We're finger painting, believe it or not," she said, wiggling her painty fingers. "How about joining us?"

Jake grinned as he put Mika down on the floor. The child toddled a few steps before going back to his knees and crawling remarkably fast until he pulled himself back to a standing position at the table.

"Looks like he might have some interest in that."

"I'll get some paper for him," Wendy said, standing to move toward the art closet in the living room. "Smaller pieces that'll be just the right size. I bet he'll like all the colors."

Still clutching the table leg, the child grinned up at Rory and the warmth in her chest grew. She looked at Jake, and the way he was watching the child with love and pride made her heart both pinch and expand.

"He's walking even more than he was at his birthday party, isn't he?"

"He can walk—he just gets impatient with the slow pace and switches to crawling because it's faster."

"You sure he belongs in Eudemonia and not LA? A slow pace is practically the law here."

Jake's smile faded, and she wasn't sure why. Could it

be because he wasn't ready for her to go back? Or maybe he knew she wasn't sure she was ready, either.

"No, he's an Alaskan through and through. Maybe he can paint while I look at the pipe. Is it this one here?"

"Yes, but the pipes are stuck together tight. Did you bring some spray oil to loosen it? I couldn't find any, believe it or not. Clearly dropping the ball in my usual preparedness."

He shook his head, and as he headed toward the sink paused beside her chair. His fingertips brushed her neck, making her shiver.

"You saying you think *I'm* a weakling? I'm insulted."

"If you think that's what I'm saying, then since I couldn't do it, I guess you mean I'm a weakling."

"No. It's just that men are physically stronger than women. It's a fact."

"Something I heard endlessly when I was studying orthopedic surgery as a reason why I should choose something else."

Amused brown eyes met hers, and she thought of all the times he'd teased her about so many things. About how even when it had annoyed her she'd loved it at the same time, because it was the way he'd shown her how much he cared about her.

A sudden vision of his big, muscular body, naked and warm and beautiful, made her breath catch. No doubt about it—Jacob Hunter was one physically strong specimen of a man. Emotionally strong, too.

Her chest got a little tight, and she knew she needed to do something to loosen it. She reached up with a paint-covered finger and marked the left side of his jaw with a swirly green X. "Want me to show you how strong I am?"

"What? Is this X marks the spot? You gonna pop me?"

"Brace yourself. Are you ready?" What she really wanted to do was kiss the X and then move on to his mouth, but she waved her fist at him before tapping his chin with it.

He grasped her wrist and lowered his face close to hers. "You've heard about playing with fire and getting burned? You want to go up in flames?"

Oh, yeah, she *did* want to go up in flames, if the burn was from Jake.

When he lowered his mouth to hers, she parted her lips, and when she touched her tongue to his she heard him draw in a breath just before the kiss got deeper and wetter. Without thinking, she lifted her hands to his cheeks as she tipped her head, wanting more of the deliciously tempting taste of him.

"You think he'd like colored paper better, or plain white?"

At the sound of her mother's voice they pulled apart, and the heat in the brown eyes inches from hers had her quivering from head to toe. And then she laughed as she looked at the paint all over the poor man's face.

"Why, you two are really getting into the spirit of this, aren't you?" her mother said, beaming. "I never thought to paint myself or you. What a wonderful idea, Aurora!"

"Rory's always been full of good ideas," Jake said, his voice rough. He straightened and turned toward the sink. "But I'd better get these pipes fixed if I don't want to be driving around with paint all over my face."

"Before you do, can you put Mika on my lap?" asked Rory. "I don't want to get paint on his clothes."

"I have a feeling he's going to have paint all over his clothes anyway."

Jake sat the small boy on her lap and she breathed in the baby scent of him, letting herself rub her cheek against his soft hair. She picked up one of the paint pots and had to laugh at the way his pudgy fingers happily dipped inside before rubbing the paint all around the paper.

"Look at him having fun!" her mother exclaimed. "He's like one of the family already."

Her belly tightened at her mother's words. Rory held out a second color to Mika, kissed his round cheek and wished with all her heart that she had a beautiful child like this. But he belonged to Jake, and Jake would never belong to her again. She'd made sure of that, hadn't she?

They played with the paint together and his joy, the delighted baby noises he made, were so adorable she found herself wishing the moment would go on for hours. But his attention on swirling the paint didn't last very long, and in a short time he was wriggling to get off her lap.

Shoving down her disappointment, she tried to secure him with her elbows so he wouldn't fall. "Jake, can you get Mika? My hands are all gooey."

"Yep. Done here anyway."

She watched his long body scooch out from under the sink and unfold into a standing position. Two long strides and he was lifting the boy from her lap, and she couldn't help but feel a little bereft.

"All fixed, thanks to my superior strength. You can wash up now, if you want."

"Thank you for getting us water again. I think I'm done with finger paints for the day." Unless Mika decided he wanted to play with the paints a little longer after all. "But maybe you should wash your face first. You look a little scary."

"Geez, I forgot." He laughed. "Thanks for not letting me walk around town like this."

"Wouldn't want people to think the town doctor had lost his marbles."

"Except there've been a couple times recently when I think maybe I have."

Their eyes met and she found it hard to turn away from that intense brown gaze. Yeah, maybe they'd both lost their marbles, getting involved again even for such a short time. But she'd always been crazy when it came to Jacob Hunter. Probably nothing would ever change that.

As she washed her hands she realized the pleasure of holding the baby and playing with him wasn't over just for today—it would be over permanently very soon. That reality made her feel melancholy enough that she figured she should book her flight home as soon as possible. Staying away from Jake hadn't come close to happening, and while she was glad they'd had this time to clear the air a little and make peace with the past, it was time to get back to her life.

Her life filled with work and not much else.

"You know what I haven't had in front of my house for a long, long time?" her mother said as she washed her hands, too. "A snowman! It's warmed up some today—perfect for snowman building. How about you two take Mika outside for his first snowman?"

"I think he'd like that," Jake said. "Rory?"

She turned, and the entreaty in his eyes made her chest expand all over again. The clear desire she saw there was to spend another hour with her, the same way she wanted to with him, despite them agreeing not to. It was too late to protect her heart from caring about him again, and taking new memories back to LA—memories of her time with both Jake and Mika—seemed like the best idea in the world.

"Not much possibility of making a snowman in Los Angeles. So, yes, I'd love to make a snowman with the two of you. Let's go."

CHAPTER TWELVE

ROLLING THE BALLS of snow to make a snowman was more exciting to Mika than Jake would have thought, and for some reason the baby laughed out loud when Jake stacked the smallest one on top of the other two.

"There's the snowman's head, Mika. Now we need a face."

"Stones for the eyes," Rory said, poking them into the snowball. "More for the mouth. And here's a carrot for the snowman's nose. Can you put it right where its nose should be?"

She handed him the carrot and Mika stabbed it into the side of the snowman's head. It made Jake laugh, but Rory actually doubled over with mirth, tears in her eyes that this time he could tell were happy ones.

The joy he could see on her face, which was glowing with the pleasure of the day, made him wonder about what her life in Los Angeles might be like. She'd always worked hard, from the minute she'd arrived as the odd one out at the public school after being homeschooled for the first eight years of her life. But he wouldn't be surprised if she'd buried herself in work in order to forget about everything else. It was easy to do when you were studying medicine, and probably even easier if you were a woman competing for an orthopedic residency, and then a job, in a field filled mostly with men.

Rory's cheeks were pink from the cold and the exertion of rolling snow and stacking it, and Mika's were, too. Probably time to head back home, though he couldn't help wanting to spend as much time as he could with Rory before she left. Watching her now, though, enjoying the sparkle in her green eyes, loving the sound of her laugh, brought back that uncomfortable feeling he'd had before. The feeling that he could fall hard for her again, and God knew he didn't want his heart to hurt the way it had the last time she'd left.

"All that painting and snowman making means Mika missed his nap," he said. "I should get him home."

The mirth and joy faded from her face before she nodded. "Of course. It's been...so much fun. Oh, Lord, now I sound like my mother. But it has been. Thank you."

"For what? The plumbing repair?"

"For forgiving me enough to hang out with me. For letting me spend time with your son."

"Rory... I thought we'd talked this through." He hated the idea of her going to LA still dragging along the burdens she'd carried with her the last time, and he pulled her close so she could look into his eyes. "I've forgiven you. The past is the past."

"I... Thank you. It means a lot to me to hear you say that."

He dropped a quick kiss to her forehead and then let her go, resisting the urge to kiss her for real. Everything that had needed to happen between them—a new understanding and forgiveness—had been accomplished. Time for both their lives to go back to normal.

"When are you heading back to LA?"

"I'm going to call tomorrow to schedule my interview, then book a flight, so probably in just a day or two."

"Well, I probably won't see you before you go, then. Good luck with getting the job."

"Wait—we have one more thing to do." She pulled off her hat and handed it to Mika before picking him up in her arms. "Let's put this on the snowman's head so he stays nice and warm, okay?"

Jake watched her lift up his son, so he could try to put the hat on the top snowball, and the picture of the two of them made his heart physically hurt. She looked so vulnerable, and a mix of joy and deep sadness flitted across her beautiful features. She was obviously loving the time with Mika that they'd never gotten to have with Adam.

It was good she was leaving in just a day or two. His emotions—and hers, too, he thought—were getting tangled up together again, and that was the last thing either of them needed. Probably he should have resisted kissing her and making love with her, but he couldn't deny that being with her that way again had been incredible. The best he'd felt in a long, long time.

But sex between them, however good, was fleeting and dangerous. Even when he didn't plan to, he found himself kissing and touching her anyway. What could he do now, though? Say goodbye this minute, before things got any stickier between them? Before something else happened that would make it harder for both of them when she was gone.

He stepped over to take Mika from her arms, but the baby fussed and resisted. He'd thrown Rory's hat on the ground and pulled off his own, determined to flatten it onto the snowman's head. Finally, he wriggled so much she had to put him on his feet.

"I guess the snowman *does* look better in your hat, Mika," she said.

She turned to Jake, and the look of longing in her eyes made his heart beat harder at the same time as he took a backward step. Self-preservation was kicking in, big-time, and he feared if he didn't get away from Rory right now his heart would get pummeled in a way he never wanted to experience again.

Mika might not be happy about it, but he moved to take the boy's hat off the snowman anyway.

"How about dinner tonight?" she asked as their eyes met. "I'll bring stuff from here...cook dinner for the two of you."

"Rory, I don't think—"

"Just dinner. That's all. Then I'll be leaving for good."

Dinner, and then after Mika was in bed hot sex between the two of them, which would make it harder for both of them when she left? God knows, he wanted it again more than anything...

Except that wasn't quite true. He wanted it more than anything except another aching heart.

Somehow he made himself reach around to pull her arms from him, and his chest constricted at the confusion and hurt in her eyes as he did so.

"I'd like that, but I can't. I have plans I can't break. Sorry. Best of luck in LA, okay?"

He grabbed Mika and strode to his car, afraid that if he slowed down he'd cave. He'd turn back and reach for her and kiss her breathless and invite her to his house. And where would that leave them? One step closer to falling in love again, and he just didn't want to go there.

Yeah, his gut told him, spending the evening with her

would be a very bad idea, and he got Mika into his car seat as quickly as possible.

Then he made a mistake. He let himself look back at Rory, to see her with her arms wrapped around her body and her beautiful face looking as wistful and forlorn as he'd ever seen it. And he could swear he felt her eyes on him even as he hit the gas and drove down her mother's snowy hill to the road.

Rory finished cleaning the dishes that had been waiting for the sink pipes to be fixed, staring out the window at the snowy scene that earlier had delighted her.

Now it just made her feel sad. Empty. Embarrassed.

And utterly confused.

In the kitchen earlier, Jake had teased and touched her. Flirted with her. Even surprised her with a delicious kiss that had curled her toes and made her forget that her mother was close by in the other room. Then he had seemed to be having the same wonderful time she'd been having with Mika. Snowman building and laughing at the baby when, awed by the cold white flakes, he had started stuffing them in his mouth.

Jake had tossed a few snowballs at her that had scored direct hits and had had both of them chuckling and remembering all those years they'd played and rolled in the snow together, from the time they were kids and all the way through college.

But then the thought of never seeing him again, or at least not for a long time, had made her chest hurt and her throat close. She'd impulsively asked to have dinner with him and Mika. Be with them one last time. Enjoy more of Jake's heart-stopping kisses and maybe make love the way only they could.

How that felt was something she'd nearly forgotten, and she wanted one more close moment with him to cherish. Wanted to take those memories back to LA with her, to keep her company during all the lonely days.

And what had happened?

He'd basically told her to take a hike and head on back to LA, then practically left skid marks on her mother's snowy yard as he'd driven away.

She tossed down the dishtowel and shook her head. The only explanation was that after the flirting and fun he'd gotten cold feet about seeing her anymore, knowing she was about to leave. Which she just didn't understand—because they'd already kissed and made love and talked things through, hadn't they?

"Aurora?"

She turned to see her mother walking toward her, remarkably steadier with her pink cane than she'd been the day Rory had first arrived, despite the scare of her sutures opening.

"Can I get something for you, Twinkie?"

"No, I want to talk to you."

She came close and wrapped her arms around her, much the way Rory had wrapped her arms around Jake not long ago.

"I've been thinking a lot. I just can't come to California with you. To live with you. But I will come for Christmas. If that's okay?"

Rory folded her slim body close, looked down into her mother's eyes, and suddenly found it hard to speak. Her quirky little mother, like no one else in the whole world, was willing to visit her at Christmas, even though it was one of her favorite times of year here. She didn't particularly like LA, and she missed her friends and her home when she came, but she loved and wanted to be with Rory enough to visit anyway.

It struck her like a sledgehammer between the eyes that Jake had been right. Escaping to California, leaving her parents and Jake behind, had been selfish. She hadn't seen it that way, but it was the painful truth.

The sledgehammer hit a second time. How she felt right now—missing her mother and Jake and the place where she'd grown up before she'd even left town—told her that all the emotions, all the reasons she'd left didn't exist anymore.

Living in LA wouldn't bring Adam back. It wouldn't let her spend time with her mother, either, and after being with her these past two weeks she knew she didn't want the long miles between them anymore. And it wouldn't let her and Jake explore the fire, the love, that had started burning between them again, and she knew right then that she wanted that more than she'd ever wanted anything in her life. Wanted to see if the two of them could continue to talk and work through their past. To be together and to love one another on their way to a new future. To create a family of three, with Mika.

Would Jake want that, too? Did he feel the same way about her that she did him? God, she didn't know—which terrified her. But what she did know was that she had to find out.

"I love that idea, Twinkie." She swallowed hard before she tried to talk again. "But you know what? I might not even get that job. And if I don't I might even come back here to live. I... I might try to date Jake again. What would you think about that?"

Since she had no idea how Jake would react to her telling him she wanted to stay in Eudemonia and be with him, she couldn't make any promises to her mom. If he rejected her it would crush her heart too much for her to stay here full-time. But the days of her not seeing her mother for months on end were over—even if that meant steeling herself to endure seeing Jake with someone else.

"Oh, my goodness, Aurora, I can't think of anything I'd like better than for you to move back home and to be with Jacob again. That would be a dream come true."

For her, too. Her new dream.

"I'm not promising. I have to see how it goes."

She had to see what the man who held her heart and future in his hands had to say when she told him she still loved him. As scary as that felt, she'd do it.

Hadn't she always gone for what she wanted?

And she wanted Jacob Hunter back.

They clutched one another and Rory kissed Twinkie's cheek, then let her go. "I have something I need to do. Will you be okay for a while? I'll make a plate for you to warm up, in case I'm not back for dinner."

And if things went the way she hoped, she definitely wouldn't be.

"I'm just fine, marshmallow girl. I'm going to rest for a bit anyway."

With her mom settled in her favorite chair, Rory felt her stomach churn with nervous energy. How was she going to approach this? Just knock on the door and have him wonder why she'd come chasing after him when he'd told her he had plans?

That thought made her heart stop. What if he really did have plans? What if he had a date?

She wrung her cold hands and paced the kitchen. Maybe she should wait until tomorrow, just in case... But as soon as the thought came she knew that now she'd had this earth-shattering revelation she'd never sleep tonight if she didn't go over there and get this done.

The snowman caught her eye. "That's it! The perfect excuse," she murmured to herself.

Mika's hat was still perched on the snowman's head. She'd take it over to the house, say she'd thought he might need it. Yeah, it was probably a weak and transparent excuse, but it was better than nothing, right?

She shoved on her coat and boots, ran out to grab the hat and jumped in her car as butterflies flapped in her belly.

Getting to Jake's house and getting this over with as quickly as possible was the plan. She could only hope the evening would turn out the way she wanted. If it didn't she knew it would end up being the second-worst day of her life.

CHAPTER THIRTEEN

JAKE SAT BACK and took a swig of beer, thinking about all that had happened between him and Rory and wishing she hadn't come back at all. He'd thought that other than wanting answers from her about why she'd left without a word, any feelings for her were long gone.

But here he was, sitting here and wanting her beside him. Wanting to kiss her again, to get her naked again, to laugh and joke with her again. It was stupid when she lived thousands of miles away and had already proved she wouldn't hesitate to abandon him if life got tough.

Having her back in town was messing with his mind—no doubt about that. And the truth was he wasn't sure it wouldn't still be messed up long after she'd gone again.

Mika crawled across to the sofa and pulled himself to his feet, trying to get a toy that he couldn't quite reach from the cushion. He started to wail way more than usual for something like that, and Jake wished they'd foregone the snowman making and come home for his nap. Both because his baby would now be happier and because he might not have these uncomfortable feelings rolling around in his chest.

He picked the child up and poked a pacifier into his

mouth, gently rocking him back and forth. Then the doorbell chimed. He frowned, wondering who could be at his door. He hoped it wasn't a medical emergency, because he felt pretty worn out and he had a feeling that it was due more to emotional stress than lack of sleep.

When he opened the door his heart kicked in surprise. Rory stood there, wearing her puffy down coat and holding Mika's hat.

"Hi," she said, sounding a little breathless. "You... we forgot about Mika's hat. I thought he might need it."

She held it out and he took it, trying to decide if he should just thank her, say goodbye and shut the door, or if that would be too rude.

"Thanks to Mom and her knitting he has more hats than one baby could ever need. But I appreciate it."

"Can I...can I come in?"

He wanted to say no, but even as he was thinking that was the best response for both of them he found himself swinging the door open wider.

"Sure. Your California blood is probably too thin for this weather."

"I think my blood is thickening a little, and I'm finally remembering what it's like here in October. I wasn't even tempted to put on long underwear today."

Lord. He was not...*not*...going to ask her what kind of underwear she did have on. Even though suddenly he desperately wanted to know.

Time to cut to the chase—and if he had to be abrupt, like he'd been earlier, to protect himself, then so be it. "What can I do for you? Mika's pretty cranky from all the outdoor activity and missing his nap. I need to get him down for the night."

"You can go ahead and do that. I'll just...you know... wait down here in a chair."

"Rory. What's this about?"

"I realized there's something I need to say to you. Something I need to ask you. If you'll just give me five minutes of your time, I'd appreciate it."

He drew a deep breath, wondering what she could want to talk about. Hadn't they covered all the bases in their prior conversations? Still, he'd needed to talk to *her* when she'd first shown up, to get some things off his chest even when she hadn't wanted to go there. He owed her the same courtesy, whatever this was about.

"All right. Take a seat and I'll be back shortly."

The baby was nodding off as he carried him upstairs, and barely stirred when Jake slipped on his footie pajamas and held up some picture books.

"What do you want to read?"

Mika's response was to droop his head against Jake's shoulder and close his eyes, and he knew a book wasn't happening tonight. Which was just as well, since Rory was waiting downstairs. He hoped whatever she wanted to talk about wouldn't end in something uncomfortable or unpleasant. But he had a bad feeling that was exactly what it was going to do.

Gently laying Mika in his crib, he tucked in his blanket and kissed his soft cheek. "Sweet dreams."

The words had him thinking of his own dreams. They had altered some when Rory had left, but the fundamentals of what he wanted were the same: to live and work and grow old in Eudemonia, and raise a family here with the woman he loved. He knew that wasn't asking too much.

But Rory wasn't that woman, and he found himself dreading whatever she'd come here to say to him tonight.

Rory watched Jake come down the stairs and her heart jerked hard in her chest. Now that she was here, all her carefully rehearsed words seemed to dry up and choke her. But it was too late to run, and she had to tell him how she felt.

He came to within a couple yards of her, which made her feel even more nervous. Gone was the Jake who'd been angry, talking with her in that store parking lot, crowding her and grasping her arms as he spoke. Gone was the Jake who'd kissed her in his kitchen and made love with her in the cabin. Gone was the Jake who'd teased her at her mother's house, who'd touched her and kissed her.

No, this was the Jake who'd told her earlier that he had plans, then walked away. His expression was cool and unreadable and she stood up—because she couldn't keep sitting in that chair for another second, trying to act like this was some normal, relaxed conversation between the two of them.

Too much of her future happiness was riding on this.

"Jake?"

"Yes?"

"I…um…"

He took a few steps closer and a sigh left his chest. "What is it, Rory? What is it you need to talk with me about? I'm listening."

She stared into the familiar face she'd loved for so long and gulped, before blurting out the first thing she needed an answer to. "How would you feel about me living here again? Permanently? In Eudemonia?"

He went still and stared at her. "What do you mean?"

"I've been thinking a lot." She nervously licked her lips but forged on because his reaction, his words, were so important she could barely breathe. "I miss my mother, and the older she gets the more she's going to need me. I...I didn't admit to myself that I missed this town until I came back. And I definitely didn't admit to myself how much I missed *you*, until this time we've spent together forced me to see it. But I did, Jake. I missed you so much. Every day of these past nine years I've missed the man I fell in love with in the fourth grade."

He didn't respond, and her knees began to shake.

"I love you," she whispered, laying her heart on the line. "I've realized I never stopped loving you. And already I love little Mika. The more time I spend here, the more distant LA feels. The more I ask myself if I really want that job, want to live alone like I have for nine years. I've wondered if it would make me happier to come back here to work instead. To be with you and Mika instead. And now I know the answer. *You're* my happiness, Jake. You and Mika."

He stared for a long moment, shock etched on his face. When he still didn't speak, she forged on with the biggest question of all.

"I love you. And I'm ready to lean on you, now, in a way I wouldn't let myself before. For us to lean on each other, like you talked about." She drew a shaky breath and finally asked the question. "So I want to know... Do you still love me, too?"

He stood still as a stone for ten long seconds before he spun around, his back to her, his hands locked behind his head. Her heart beat so hard against her ribs she thought they might break, because while she hadn't known what to expect, his reaction—this silence—couldn't possibly be good.

Finally he turned, and she clutched her throat at the sight of his grim expression. This was *not* the look of a man about to declare that he loved her in return, and she started to shake from the inside out.

"I will always care about you," he said, obviously choosing his words carefully.

Oh, God. The brush-off. The *I like you as a friend* speech. His kisses, his touch, the sex—none of it had been about love. Obviously for him they'd been about the past and lust and long-lost memories. Not even close to what she'd been feeling.

"But I can't risk loving you again, Rory. You have to understand that. I can't trust you to stay, because I know how bad it felt when you betrayed that trust before. And I have Mika now. My son is a huge part of my world, and I can't risk having you become a big part of my life again—a big part of *his* life—knowing all that could blow up in our faces. Do you understand?"

"I wouldn't leave again. I've grown. Learned. Put the past behind me. Surely you see that?"

He slowly shook his head, and as he did so she could practically feel her heart breaking into a million tiny pieces.

"I'm sorry, Rory. I just can't. It was too hard the first time. It's better for both of us not to go there again."

She wanted to argue. Wanted to convince him she meant every word. Wanted to hang on to him, beg and plead with him to love her and be with her.

Somehow she managed to cling to the thin, frayed

edges of what pride she had left, and stayed silent. She nodded, turned and walked out the door.

Somehow she made it home, with tears coursing down her cheeks and dripping onto her coat.

Home. No, it wasn't home. Eudemonia wouldn't ever be her home again.

Jake had thought that once Rory had left for LA, life would smooth out and become normal again. That her being back was what had tipped his world sideways and messed with his equilibrium. The past showing up in the form of Aurora Anderson had left him frustrated and confused, his feelings for her something he just couldn't figure out.

But she'd been gone for almost a month and everything still felt off-kilter. Her shocking declaration of love and her insistence that she wanted to move back here, try to find again what they'd lost, had knocked him utterly sideways.

He'd made the right decision, telling her it couldn't work. That he couldn't risk it. There was no way he could be sure she wouldn't take off a second time, crushing him all over again—and maybe Mika, too.

But that conviction—his certainty about that—hadn't kept her from his dreams. Every night in his sleep he was thinking of her, laughing with her, making love with her. Tasting her mouth, feeling her soft skin against his. Then he'd wake with a smile, and the feeling that he was holding her sweet body in his arms, except when he'd look they were empty.

He shook his head, irritated with himself. It hadn't been that long since she'd been gone. Lord knew it had taken years for him to get over her before. He just needed a little more time to forget her—which would be a whole lot easier than letting her back into his life only to have her take off again, leaving him even more devastated than last time.

He moved from the exam room to ask Ellie about his next patient—then stopped dead when he saw that both his mother and Wendy Anderson were standing in the clinic foyer, staring at him with very strange expressions on their faces.

Something about the way they were looking at him made him oddly uncomfortable, and he frowned. "Is something wrong?"

"Yes. Can we talk to you privately?" his mother said.

His mother and Wendy wanted to talk to him privately? What the hell could *this* be about?

"Uh…sure. Come to my office."

The two women sat in the chairs in front of his desk and for some reason he went to sit behind it, instead of in a chair next to them. He felt the need for an inanimate object to be between him and the stern disapproval he could clearly see on their faces.

"What's going on?"

"Wendy recently heard from Rory that she was offered the job she wanted in LA," his mother said.

He had no idea why his stomach pitched and tightened at that news, because it was hardly a surprise. "That's what she'd worked for—what she wanted—so good for her."

"Wendy has also learned that it's actually *not* what she wanted. That she'd decided to move back home, work here or in Fairbanks, and try to have the kind of relationship with you that you had before. Except you told her you had no interest in that."

Well, hell. The fact that Rory had told her mother surprised him, but it didn't change anything. Didn't change that her thinking she wanted to move back might last all of a nanosecond. Didn't change that she could crush him to pieces all over again. "I will always care about Rory. But I'm sure you can both understand why I didn't think that was a good idea."

"Why not?" his mother demanded. "She's had a long time to grapple with the past. With the decisions she made. You've had time, too. And I know you still love her."

He leaned back in his chair and looked up at the ceiling, trying not to let them see what he was feeling. What he'd felt since the second Rory had come back.

Did he still love her? The way his heart still ached and his stomach churned proved that was a no-brainer. If there was one thing he'd learned for certain during those few weeks she'd come back was that he'd always loved her. That he'd never stopped loving her.

Never would.

But that had nothing to do with reality. With trusting her to be there for him and for Mika no matter what.

Missing her might pass. His heart being broken a second time never would.

He decided not to go into that whole conversation and cut straight to the point. "Why are you two here?"

"Jacob." Wendy leaned forward, and the sweet smile she always had on her face had flattened into an expression of such seriousness he couldn't quite believe it was her. "My Aurora loves you—has always loved you. I know this. When the bad things happened it messed everything up, which broke her heart and your heart and my heart. And Beth's, and your dad's, and my Walter's heart, too. So many broken hearts… But now she wants to fix things. Don't *you* want to fix things? Don't you want both your hearts…all of our hearts…to be whole again?"

"It's too late." Apparently, not sharing his feelings wasn't an option, and he drew a deep breath before he forced himself to go on. "When I thought about her coming back home, making a life here, it also made me think about how bad it would feel for her to leave again, and I knew I couldn't go through that one more time. It was…" He had to stop and swallow down the surprising emotion that thickened his throat. "I just don't want to do it. She could be here for a few months, or a few years, then change her mind. What would that do to me and Mika?"

"Jake." His mother's voice was soft now, caring. "I know how bad it was for you. I also know how bad it was for her. But don't you think it says something that even after all these years she still loves you and you still love her?"

"Love isn't everything. Her leaving nine years ago proved that, didn't it? I loved her more than anything, and she supposedly loved me. But she left anyway. Surely you know that trust is just as important as love. Maybe more important."

"Jake. You know as well as anyone that there are no guarantees in life. People get sick, people die, people hurt one another." His mother pressed her hand to the top of his. "If you live your life looking for a guarantee that nothing will ever happen to hurt you, if you won't let yourself be vulnerable to that hurt, you'll end up missing out on the best things in life. Don't you see that Rory coming to you and letting herself be vulnerable that way proves she's learned that hard lesson? You need to trust that she has."

He rubbed his hand over his face. It sounded so logical, so easy to do—just trust her again, let himself be vulnerable to the kind of pain that had twisted him in knots for years. But the way the knots had tightened all over again told him it sure as hell wasn't something he could risk.

"If she comes back to Eudemonia and then leaves again the place I belong...the place I've made my life... will never feel the same. I'd finally gotten past thinking of her during everything I did here. Missing her everywhere I went. Missing her every damn day. I don't want to be messed up like that again. I don't want *Mika* messed up like that."

There. He'd laid his bashed and bloodied heart on the table for both women to see. Surely they understood what he was talking about? They loved this place as much as he did, and had painful memories of their own. No guarantees—he understood that. But to *ask* for that pain by letting Rory back into his heart and his life...?

"Well, I have a solution that will give you a chance to be with Rory again, see how it would be for the two of you, without the risk to your life in Eudemonia that you're so worried about," Wendy said.

"What?"

"You and Mika move to LA. Simple. You take on one of those temporary doctor jobs, live with Aurora and see what happens. If in six months or a year you still don't trust her, believe in her, love her enough, you come back home and your life here will be waiting for you. Just like you'd never left. And Mika will still be little enough that he'll soon settle right back in to his life here, with you and everyone who loves him."

He stared at her, absolutely incredulous. "Twinkie. You love Eudemonia as much as anyone I know. You hardly even wanted to visit Rory in LA—you didn't even want to go for the winter. You of all people should understand why that's a terrible suggestion. All I've ever wanted was to live and work *here*."

She stood and leaned across the desk in a distinctly un-Wendy-like move that surprised him all over again.

"I loved my Walter. If he hadn't been by my side all those years my life would never have been as happy, even after he got sick. Did I always love Eudemonia, too? Yes. But if my husband—the only man I ever loved— had wanted to move somewhere else, and wanted me to go with him, I would have. Because a place is just a place. But the person you love is everything."

Wendy's words seemed to echo in his chest, demanding that he listen. He absorbed them, let himself really feel what she was saying, finally realizing she was one hundred percent right. He still loved Rory, had never stopped loving her, and since she'd been gone he'd missed her all over again anyway—just like before.

Could going to LA be the perfect solution to his fears and doubts? Give him the possibility of finding the kind of life with Rory he'd always wanted, always thought they'd have? If it didn't work out, the bad memories would be in LA, not here. Being in Eudemonia without her wouldn't feel as bad as if she came back for a while, then left. And it wasn't as though he wasn't missing her here anyway.

But, God, he couldn't deny that the thought of putting

his heart and body and soul in her hands again scared him to death.

His gaze moved to his mother, who sat there nodding in firm agreement.

"You've got nothing to lose, Jake, except a little time. But what might you have to gain? I don't think I have to tell you that being with Rory the way you used to be just might be the key to real happiness for you. Happiness to last the rest of your life. Living with less risk might be safer. But also sadder and more lonely. Isn't the kind of love and happiness you used to have with Rory worth a little risk?"

He stared at both women, his chest expanding with emotion. Adrenaline surged through his veins, because they were both right. What he and Rory had before Adam died, before it all got away from them, was worth the risk to his heart.

It was worth everything.

CHAPTER FOURTEEN

BEYOND GLAD TO have finally finished packing the last of her things, Rory kneeled to tape shut a box of books. Was she nervous about the decision she'd made? That was an understatement. But she was done hiding. Done running. She had hidden and run for so long she hadn't even realized she was still doing it until she'd gone back home.

Until she'd fallen in love with Jake all over again.

Not exactly accurate. That love had always been there. She'd just refused to let herself feel it anymore, and staying away from him had let her stuff it so far down it had lain dormant until being with him again had brought it all to the surface.

Maybe he'd never trust her...maybe he'd never let her be in his life again the way she wanted. Maybe the love he'd had for her was gone in a way hers never would be. But hiding in LA wasn't going to help her have the life she wanted.

It had taken nine long years of hiding, but she finally felt like herself again. The woman who went for what she wanted.

Jake would shake his head if he heard her say that, but once in a while her stubbornness just might be her best asset. Because she'd decided she wasn't taking Jake's rejection lying down. Until she'd done everything she possibly could to convince him she loved him, that they belonged together and that she'd never, ever leave him and Mika and Eudemonia, she wouldn't accept that it was over for good.

The doorbell rang and she figured it was the moving guys, ready to get all her things on the truck to take to Alaska. She squared her shoulders. This was it. The first step toward her new life. A better life. A life where she could see her mom whenever she wanted. A life in the town she loved.

A life with Jake and Mika, if all went as she planned.

And if it didn't she'd accept that pain. Because even trying to have a life with the two of them would be worth every second of the heartache that would follow Jake's rejection of her love, if that's how it turned out.

She wiped her sweaty hands down her jeans and went to answer the door.

When she opened it her mouth fell open and her heart dove straight to her stomach.

"Jake. What...? Why...? How...?"

"Lots of questions there, Rory." He gave her a crooked smile, but she could see the tension in his eyes. "Can I come in?"

She swung open the door, unable to find her voice. They stood in the small foyer of her apartment—the place she was leaving behind for good—and stared at one another for long seconds before Jake finally spoke.

"It's been a month since you showed up at my door to tell me you love me." He reached for her hands, tightened his fingers on hers. "Every day and every night of that month I've thought of you. Missed you. Wished things could be different between us. But I was too scared to let myself be with you again. Too cowardly to risk my heart again."

"I know," she whispered, hardly believing that he was here, that he was talking about what had happened the last time she'd seen him. That he'd missed her and thought of her. "I understand. I was cowardly, too."

"I planned to stay being that coward, wrapping myself in a self-protective blanket of mistrust, convinced it was what I wanted and needed to do. Until two women named Beth and Wendy came to my office."

He drew her closer, and her heart pounded so hard in her ears she feared she wouldn't be able to hear what was coming next. "And what did those two women say to you?"

"They pointed out that hiding away in Eudemonia, refusing to see what could be between us again, was no way to find my future happiness. I'd convinced myself I was plenty happy until you came back. But that was when I knew there was a big piece of happiness missing from my life, and that piece is you."

"Oh, Jake." She swallowed down the emotion filling her chest and stepped toward him. "All I want is a chance. A chance to prove to you how much I love you and that I'll never, ever leave you again. That's all I want."

"Me, too."

He cupped her face in his hands and her heart shook hard at the sweetness, the love she saw so clearly in his eyes.

"Which is why I'm moving to LA to be with you. Me and Mika. I'm going to take a job here, and we'll see where being together again takes us. We'll be away from the bad and the good memories of Eudemonia that might cloud things up and confuse the issue. It'll just be you and me, finding out what's still between us. A new beginning. What do you say?"

She sniffed back the tears that threatened and flung her arms around him. "I'd say I love that idea almost as much as I love you. Except there's one thing—I didn't take the job. I packed all my stuff and it's going to be trucked to Eudemonia today."

"What?" He stared down at her. "You didn't take the job? You're planning to move back to Eudemonia?"

"Yep. When I came back here I wallowed in misery because you didn't trust me and didn't want to be with me—didn't want to love me, and let me love you and Mika. But then I realized I'd wallowed for nine long years and I was done with it. I decided to be the stubborn Aurora Anderson you teased me for being over more years than I can remember. I decided to come back to Eudemonia and pound on that heart of yours until you let me inside again. I love you too much to quit now. And if you never love me back, I will know that at least I tried."

He pulled her close and buried his face in her hair. They stood for long minutes, just soaking one another in, until he finally lifted his head.

"I do love you, Rory Anderson. I love your stubbornness and preparedness and adorableness. I love your adventurous spirit and toughness and sweetness. I love everything about you. Even when you hurt me I loved you. And what I've accepted this past month, let myself appreciate and be happy about, is that I will always love you, no matter what."

His mouth lowered to hers in the most beautiful kiss

of her life, which slowly moved from tender to hot until they finally broke apart.

She looked up into the brown eyes she loved so much and tightened her hold on him. "If you want to move to LA I'll stay. But what I really want is to move back to the place I belong. The place we both belong. With you."

"Other than hearing that you still love me, those words are the best thing I've ever heard in my life."

He kissed her again, and when they came up for air his smile was so dazzling her heart squeezed tight with the overwhelming love she'd felt for him forever.

"Come on. Eudemonia and Mika are waiting for us to come home."

EPILOGUE

Three years later...

WENDY ANDERSON'S SMALL house was filled to overflowing for her annual Christmas party. She and Rory and the others had spent weeks making biscuits and seed sculptures for the animals, and everyone had enjoyed hanging the treats on the trees outside.

"Time for our own goodies now!" Twinkie called to everyone, clapping her hands and grinning. "Come on inside."

Chatter and laughter moved from outside to inside as the guests took off their coats and hats and headed to the kitchen to grab food from the table.

Rory looked at Mika's adorable face, pink from the cold, and reached for his hat—because otherwise it would probably end up on the floor for Toby to chew on.

"You hungry?" she asked the four-year-old.

"Starving!"

"I have something just for you," Twinkie said. "Come with me to the kitchen."

Jake came in the front door, carrying Audrey, their

Christmas baby. Their miracle baby, who'd be celebrating her first birthday in one week.

"We need to get some food in this child because she keeps trying to eat the animals' biscuits," Jake said. "I know it won't hurt her, but—*yuck*!"

"Yuck!" Audrey repeated as she beamed and waved her hat around.

Rory wrapped her arms around her husband and their baby and laughed. "Don't let Twinkle-Toes hear you say her biscuits are 'yuck,' Audrey," she teased, kissing her daughter's soft round cheek. "She's said she has a special treat for your brother, so I'm betting she has something for you, too. Come on."

Jake reached for Rory's hand and the three of them squeezed their way through the crowd and into the kitchen. Rory stopped next to Mika and laughed at what her mother had given their son.

"You think there are enough marshmallows in that hot chocolate, Mika?" Jake asked. "Did you leave any for me?"

"No. They're all in here."

Mika pointed at his cup, which was overflowing with a teetering mound of small marshmallows. The top ones were tumbling onto the counter and the floor, where Toby was munching them down.

"Our little marshmallow boy," Twinkie said, an indulgent smile on her face. "I have another whole bag so don't worry. There's plenty for Audrey. And for you too, Aurora."

"Good thing. I'd hate to be left out of the marshmallow fun."

She looked up at Jake and their eyes met over their baby's head. Her heart gave that familiar squeeze that happened every time she saw her husband. Her children. The beautiful family she'd been blessed with. The family she and Jake had come so close to never having together.

She picked up a few marshmallows, poked one into Audrey's mouth and another into Jake's, then lifted onto her toes to press her lips to her handsome husband's.

"Now you taste sweet, like a marshmallow."

"And you taste sweet like Aurora Hunter."

He lowered his mouth to hers again and her heart expanded with an overwhelming joy at how incredibly lucky they all were.

He moved his mouth to her ear. "You about ready to go home? Because I am. These two are going to be tired from all the excitement, which means…"

"Which means you'll want to go to bed early, too?" Rory asked in faux innocence.

"Funny how you've been reading my mind for about twenty-five years now." He grinned. "Not sure I can read yours, though. What are you thinking?"

"That I'm the luckiest woman in the world to have the world's most wonderful husband. And the *other* thing I'm thinking is for me to know and for you to find out."

He laughed. "You know I love a challenge, Dr. Hunter. Is it that you're thinking about how much I love you?"

"And how much I love *you*. And something else."

His eyes gleamed and he tugged her close to whisper in her ear. "Then hurry up and eat your marshmallows, so we can go home and I can get started on finding out what that something else is."

* * * * *

MILLS & BOON

Coming next month

REUNITED WITH
HER BROODING SURGEON
Emily Forbes

The gorgeous man with amazing bone structure stepped forwards and Grace's heart skipped a beat and her mouth dropped open.

Marcus Washington.

She could not believe it.

It had to be him. Even though he no longer resembled the twelve-year-old boy she once knew, it *had* to be him. There couldn't be two of him.

She hadn't thought about him for years but if she had she never would have imagined he would become a doctor. She knew that sounded harsh and judgemental but what she remembered of Marcus did not fit with her image of someone who had clearly ended up in a position of responsibility and service to others.

But what did she really know of him? She had only been seven years old. What had she known of anything?

Her father was a doctor and, at the age of seven, everything she knew or thought was influenced by what and who she saw around her. Particularly by her own family. And Marcus's family had been about as different from hers as a seven-year-old could have imagined. But she knew enough now to understand that it wasn't about where you came from or what opportunities you were

handed in life, but about what you did with those opportunities, those chances. It was about the choices you
made. The drive and the desire to be the best that you
could be.

She would never have pictured Marcus as a doctor
but now, here he was, standing in front of her looking
polished, professional and perfect. It had to be him.

She knew a lot could change in twenty years and by
the look of him, a lot had.

She was still staring at him, trying to make sense of
what was happening when he looked in her direction
and caught her eye. Grace blushed and, cursing her fair
skin, the bane of a redhead, she looked away as his gaze
continued on over her. She finally remembered to close
her mouth.

Had he recognised her?

It didn't appear so, but then, why would he? She was
nothing like the seven-year-old he had last seen.

Continue reading
**REUNITED WITH
HER BROODING SURGEON**
Emily Forbes

Available next month
www.millsandboon.co.uk

COMING SOON!

We really hope you enjoyed reading this book. If you're looking for more romance, be sure to head to the shops when new books are available on

Thursday
4th October

LET'S TALK
Romance

For exclusive extracts, competitions
and special offers, find us online:

f facebook.com/millsandboon

🅞 @millsandboonuk

🐦 @millsandboon

Or get in touch on 0844 844 1351*

For all the latest titles coming soon, visit
millsandboon.co.uk/nextmonth

*cost 7p per minute plus your phone company's price per minute access charge